SHADOW
MOUNTAIN

BOOKS BY TESS COLLINS

FICTION

The Appalachian Trilogy:
The Law of Revenge
The Law of the Dead
The Law of Betrayal

The Midnight Valley Quartet:
Notown
The Hunter of Hertha

Shadow Mountain Saga:
Shadow Mountain

Other Fiction:
Helen of Troy

NON-FICTION

How Theater Managers Manage

Casebound: 978-1-937356-46-0
Trade: 978-1-937356-47-7
ebook: 978-1-937356-48-4

Library of Congress Control Number: 2016910195

Publisher's Cataloging-in- Publication Data
Collins, Theresa.
Shadow mountain / Tess Collins.
p. cm.
ISBN: 978-1-937356-46-0 (hardback)
ISBN: 978-1-937356-47-7 (trade)
ISBN: 978-1-937356-48-4 (ebook)
1. Sacred space—Fiction. 2. Witchcraft —Fiction. 3. Appalachian Region—Fiction. 4. Misogyny—Fiction. 5. Environmental degradation—Fiction. 6. Magic realism (Literature). 7. Historical fiction. I. Title.
PS3603.O4559 S53 2016
813—dc22

2016910195

Published by BearCat Press: BearCatPress.com
BearCat Press logo by Golden Sage Creative
Book design by the Frogtown Bookmaker:
Frogtownbookmaker.com

SHADOW MOUNTAIN

Shadow Mountain Saga
Book One

Tess Collins

San Francisco

For teachers never to be forgotten

Gladys DeMarcus
James Baker Hall
Harry M. Caudill

And teachers whose voices remain ever in my soul

Gurney Norman
Ed McClanahan
Ramona Lumpkin
James N. Frey

Prologue

Cumberland Mountains, late 1870s

THROUGH A VALLEY named Midnight and across a ridge called Creation is a mountain known as Shadow. Shadow Mountain.

The first Europeans to traverse this land in the 1700s told tales of its ghostly fog. The Cherokee claimed the mist to be the breath of their Dragon Spirit and left gifts of tobacco and corn when journeying the mountain's paths. From time to time, white settlers saw apparitions but transfigured them into their own belief of what was holy: Jesus meditating on Gethsemane, Mary holding the blessed infant, John the Baptist pouring water from a cup, but unlike Indians, the newcomers paid no homage.

Toward the mountaintop is Hekate's Crossroads where the skeleton of a Pawnee Indian hung until bone by bone it fell to dust. Three states, Tennessee, Kentucky, and Virginia, meet here, as do three paths: one leading to Cumberland Gap, one to Sand Cave, and the other leading to a budding coal town yet unnamed. Found at the peak are three massive black stones packed together in a crude pyramid. No man could have brought them to the pinnacle of Shadow Mountain and that's why the rocks are called Arn's Volcano. No one believed Arn Marlon was a man. They believed he was the devil.

Arn lived among a people known as the Melungeons, solitary folk, often called dark-blooded. Some were dark-skinned and dreamy-eyed with Indian cheek bones or African coloring while others were pale and moved among white people as if they belonged with them. If their heritage was ever discovered, the whiteness of the skin would not be reason enough to ignore their dark blood. Arn's hair was a mass of black curls, his skin fair and eyes a slate blue, making his true ancestry unclear.

The only being more feared than Arn was the Wampus, a beast deadly as a panther and big as a bear that, if seen, would freeze the blood of the unlucky soul. No one could clearly describe the Wampus, but its work was known when bodies were found so viciously ripped it was impossible to tell if the remains were human or animal.

In these early days Arn Marlon and the Wampus often tangled. And if the Wampus plagued folks, Arn made it his mission to rid them of its attacks.

As a young man Arn was called out from his people and named the *Watcher*. This chosen one, known by deeds great and significant, lived on Shadow Mountain—a sacred place where settlers claimed to see ghosts, and witches ruled the crossroads. The Watcher waited for the Dragon Spirit to return and proclaim the new age. And while the hero served, his or her presence offered protection to deserving mountaineers.

Sitting atop his volcano, scanning the stars, Arn looked like a wolf howling at the moon. As he grew older and no other Watcher came forth, Arn grew powerful. He was said to bring the wind to his aid and call lightning down from the sky. In time what the Watchers waited for was forgotten. True believers passed on, and Arn, wandering the mountain, frightened those who saw him. They began to think that what Arn waited for was evil, and therefore, Arn, too, was evil.

As time passed, another kind of man came to populate the Cumberlands. He saw only the land's riches. He had no time for holy visions or for evil, and anyone who placed either in his way usually ended up dead. This kind of man smiled and cajoled the mountain folks, but he would be as dangerous to them as the feared Wampus.

King Kingsley was such a man. King bravely diverted a Shadow Mountain creek into his valley. After Arn tore down the dam for the third time, King swore he'd have his hide, but capturing Arn became a fool's errand for King's band of enforcers.

Armed with two pistols strapped to his waist, a shotgun on one side of his saddle and a Winchester rifle on the other, King hunted Arn every day for a week. He climbed the narrowest ledges, crossed dense Tyme forests, thicker ones of tulip, oak, and birch, fields of ferns as tall as his waist, but failed to track down his adversary. Every plant on Shadow Mountain seemed to aid Arn, especially the Tyme trees, said to be the strongest tree living. Arn hid behind them, in them, among their dense leaves, and the Tyme trees accommodated him as if they were personal allies. When a pack of wild dogs trapped King on a narrow crag, he escaped by jumping ten feet into the branches of a giant pine. He lost his rifle and broke his arm. But even then, King was unwilling to believe that Arn was more than a man.

A year later, King was given his chance when his young son, Henry, stepped into Arn's path. King's golden palomino so enchanted Henry that he saddled the horse for a ride. To hide from his father, Henry jumped the horse onto the hidden and rarely used paths of Shadow Mountain.

It may have been the cinnamon smell of the Tyme trees, or the cold water of Tyme Creek, or the desire for freedom that infects animals on Shadow Mountain, that caused the palomino to rear and throw the boy. Defiantly, the horse galloped to the ledge overlooking King's timbering operation. He pawed the rocks and neighed, twisting his strong neck as if to taunt King.

King and a dozen men gave chase. Two lost their horses in Tyme Creek and another crashed into the low-growing branches of a Tyme tree, fell backwards and broke his neck. King thought he'd lost the animal when he heard a slow, steady whistle from a sweet clover field. He moved gingerly among the giant Tyme trees and watched Arn Marlon stand on one leg, arms stretched to the side, whistling to the palomino.

The horse shuddered, a clump of clover hanging from his mouth as he shifted toward Arn. The men started forward, but King stopped them, recognizing a chance he might never have again. Arn Marlon was a tall man, and stretching his body like a spider's across a web must have required all his concentration, for he seemed unaware of King's men. The palomino came to Arn, eating from his hand then nuzzling his neck.

King spread his people in a circle, and with Arn preoccupied with the horse, they moved and were upon him. This was the closest many men had been to the secretive Arn Marlon, and they couldn't help but stare. They believed him to be of Melungeon blood, but his blue eyes were a curiosity and his black, curly hair, grown long in the back, was fine and not like that of a African or an Indian. His smooth, white skin lacked the coarseness of a man who could grow a beard. He did not match the eerie tales told round the fire. To battle their wariness, they accused Arn of stealing King's horse, then sat him on the palomino and looped a rope around his neck.

Arn sat silent as men laughed and spat at him. When King Kingsley told them to cut the Melungeon down because they'd scared him enough, Arn dug his heels into the horse. The palomino charged, escaping up a hilly crag, leaving Arn hanging by the neck.

The steady whippoorwill trill was the only sound as the hard-faced enforcers stared open-mouthed at Arn Marlon's hanging body. Those who later described it said his long legs kicked once and then his body hung still as a sleeping bat. Yet his eyes, still half open as his head lay limply on his shoulder, shone crystal blue even in death.

King ordered his men to search for the horse and left the suspended body as a reminder to those who might try and steal from him. No man could admit that they'd actually seen Arn hang himself—in spite, it seemed.

Young Henry hid in his father's barn, crying and shaking, afraid to think about what would happen to him for losing the palomino. The harsh moonshine stench grabbed him as King and his men rode into the barn. One let out a whoop, and King laughed hard through puffs of cigar smoke.

Henry peered at them from the hayloft as his father bragged about hanging Arn Marlon for stealing his palomino because all those dark-blooded souls were thieves, liars, and cowards. A board under Henry's feet squeaked and his father looked up at him. Henry's knees began to shake. A bruise on his leg pulsed painfully. He tried to speak but sound froze in his throat. The horses swayed and banged against their stalls as another horse trotted toward the barn. Henry's face burned with shame under his father's stare and he panted quick, shallow breaths as he caught the horse's nervousness.

The opposite barn door swung wide in a long, slow whine. Moonlight flooded the entrance, making the glow from the barn's lone lantern pale by comparison. A bat swooped from the rafters and a wild dog howled. Henry wet his pants as the palomino trotted into the barn with Arn Marlon on its back and very much alive. Men stepped aside as if witnessing the risen Lazarus. King pointed his rifle at Arn.

"Daddy, no!" Henry jumped from the loft and grabbed the muzzle of his father's firearm. "I took the horse. It spooked, and I fell. Couldn't catch it. I lost the palomino. Mr. Marlon didn't steal it! I lost the horse!" Henry sobbed and wheezed, his face scarlet as tears flooded his cheeks. His trembling hands betrayed his fear, and he wished he could hide them from Arn's sight. This tall man's eyes burned a scar across his heart that he would long remember.

Arn dismounted, swinging his gangly legs over the horse's bare back. His long-limbed body towered over the boy. Arn glared at King, then studied Henry. His blue eyes flashed like the lightning he was said to call from the sky.

"I'll remember you, boy," Arn said and slipped from the barn, disappearing over the hillside before any man dare speak.

Henry did not hear what the men or his father said. He could only hear Arn Marlon's voice burning in his mind. *I'll remember you, boy*. Henry didn't know how to take Arn's words, but he did know he would never forget them.

Part 1

∞ July 1894 ∞

Ѱ 1 Ѱ

"I AIN'T AFRAID. I ain't afraid. Ain't afraid of the Wampus. Ain't afraid of Valentine Tolliver. Ain't afraid of witches. Ain't afraid of Bloody Bones. I ain't afraid of nothing." Ten-year old Lafette Marlon repeated these words over and over as he stacked creek rock in his secret hiding place. His sanctuary, inside a century-old Tyme tree, hollowed in the center with a hole at the base just big enough for him to crawl through, was one of a dozen trees at his disposal. Tyme trees made the best hiding places because they were the strongest wood in the mountains. Their silvery-green, diamond-shaped leaves were so shiny they reflected with water's clarity.

This particular tree was Lafette's favorite because it hung over Tyme Creek, and also, his father's name was carved on the inside bark. He often ran his fingers over the ragged letters *ARN MARLON*. The wood, blackened with age, still smelled of cinnamon.

Lafette barely remembered his father, but knowing that Arn had been in this tree bonded him to a muse he respected. From inside the tree Lafette reached down into the creek and pulled out a palm-sized stone. He slid his arm through a squirrel hole and was delighted to find he could throw rocks easily and not get hit himself. He could hardly wait until his next fight with Valentine Tolliver. He'd rock him good.

He fingered the letters of his father's name and of another name carved just above it, *Elisha Thunderheart*. Must've been Daddy's friend, he always figured. How else would he have gotten inside this tree? Lafette hoped to meet him someday, and maybe Mr. Thunderheart could tell him where his father had gone. To foster that wish, he called this tree the Elisha Tree.

The trickling water lapped over the stones as constant as the chirping blue jays in the limbs outside. Beneath him brown crawdads lazily sunned themselves on the creek bottom. A shadow spread over them and they scattered. Birds ceased chirping and Lafette froze. That he hadn't heard anything approach made him imagine the Wampus. Only a beast bigger than a bear, as mean as a panther, and as crafty as a rattler could move without being heard.

The Wampus was the only creature in the mountains that could tear a Tyme tree in half, so Lafette figured he'd better make a run for it. He peered through the squirrel hole but saw nothing.

Cautiously, he threw a stone to see if whatever was outside moved. The stone landed with a thud. Then, something scraped against the tree.

Lafette held his breath, hoping it wouldn't hear him.

I ain't afraid, he said to himself, even though his stomach flip-flopped. Lafette knew he needed to distract the Wampus so he reached for another rock to throw in the opposite direction. His biggest rock was set against the base of the tree, just within reach. He slipped his arm through the squirrel hole and felt for it. His hand was on what he thought was the smooth black rock when it moved. Lafette held tight.

A man yelled in surprise. Lafette, equally startled, lost his footing and fell bottom first into the creek.

♆ 2 ♆

WHEN HENRY KINGSLEY regained his balance, he turned to see water splashing every direction.

"Help, I'm drowning!" cried a frightened boy.

"Stop struggling," Henry yelled. "Not but four foot deep!" He leaned out over the creek and got a face full of water for his trouble. The floundering child relaxed at the sound of his voice and a tuft of blond hair poked out from underneath the Tyme tree. The boy ducked under the roots and popped up in front of him, a lanky frame with tanned skin and golden brown eyes that made his hair appear white as cotton. Henry recognized Lafette Marlon, son of Delta Wade, the woman Henry was here to see. Lafette was Arn Marlon's illegitimate son, and without realizing it, Henry heard the words, *I'll remember you, boy.*

"Why'd you trip me?" Henry asked, holding his hand out for Lafette, who ignored the offer and slogged out of the creek, shaking his arms like a dog shrugging off water. "Your momma know you hide out in trees?"

"Ain't none of my Momma's business any more than it's any of yourn." Lafette looked down at his wet clothes, his bottom lip pouting. He stared at the measuring tape Henry held. "What's that?" he asked.

"Nothing a little boy like you need be making his concern." Henry stepped back as Lafette peeled off his shirt and wrung it out. "Most these Tyme trees are ten to twelve feet in circumference," Henry said. "Got any bigger?"

"On Kate Huston's side of the mountain, but you go over there and she'll turn you into a frog."

"I take from the way you say that you've been over there."

"Yep, I have."

"Then why aren't you a frog?"

" 'Cause she has to catch my fast ass first."

Henry chuckled and tweaked Lafette's ear. "Here, a minnow's in your ear."

Lafette rubbed his ear and Henry threw a small stone into the creek. As it landed in the water, Lafette looked at the waves spiraling out in circles and the minnows darting about in the creek, then assessed Henry suspiciously. Henry decided to look sternly at Lafette and make him believe he was angry.

"You made me turn my ankle," Henry lied. "Reckon you're gonna have to help me up to Delta's so I can rest a spell."

"Be right glad to help you off the mountain," Lafette said. "You don't want to see Momma today."

"Why's that?"

"It's woman's day," Lafette said matter-of-factly, "that's why I'm out here so far from home. I don't like women."

"You're pulling my leg, son." Henry shook his finger. "Hear tales all around about your storytelling. Don't you try me 'cause I'm liable to throw you in the creek."

"Suit yourself," Lafette said, patting his shoulder for Henry to lean on.

Henry stared at the thin shoulder, amused that Lafette believed him so easily. It was hard to reckon that this round-faced, talkative boy was Arn Marlon's son. His cheeks were full like Arn's, making him look bigger than he actually was, but his eyes and nose were Delta's, giving him a friendlier appearance than either parent.

"Momma can wrap a sore ankle better than anybody."

Henry leaned as much weight on Lafette as he figured the boy could manage. They walked along the Tennessee road looking over treetops at tiny, unnamed towns in Midnight Valley's basin. They stopped to watch hawks swoop over distant ridges.

Near the mountaintop, Henry steadied his nerves. After all, Delta had lived with Arn Marlon, whom he'd gotten hanged years ago when he was about Lafette's age. *Arn's not been seen in five years,* he thought, trying to reassure himself. *If'n he's not dead, he sure don't have the gumption to face Delta after all this time.*

Honeysuckle vines and purple violets covered both sides of the road and the sweet smell reminded Henry of his deceased wife. Delta had sent violets to Rebecca's funeral but had not attended. Arn Marlon probably wouldn't let her, he told himself. Probably hid Delta away so she never realized she still had friends.

Henry nervously smoothed his hair. *Arn's ghost,* he repeated to himself. *Delta lives with a dead man's ghost.* There'd always been stories that Arn had paid five silver pieces to Delta's father and that was how she'd come to live there. *A dead man,* his mind repeated again.

"Reckon I'll make it okay from here," Henry said, easing away his weight, truly impressed at the youngster's stamina and noticing that he had the same smile as Delta.

"Rooster feather's on the door," Lafette said. "Means Momma's with somebody. Sit yonder on the porch, and I'll fetch some cool water."

Henry waited until Lafette rounded the corner then stepped surely toward the triangular-roofed house cushioned like a barn owl at the base of Arn's Volcano. The house, bigger than most in the mountains, had a square front with two windows on either side of a center door. A pole porch with steps leading up one side stood several feet above the ground and was centered into a creek rock base cemented with mud and built in Cherokee fashion. From the porch rafters a swing gently swayed though there was no wind. Most the facade was black locust, grayed with age, but the window frames and stoop were Tyme wood that still possessed the honey-gold color of a newly cut tree.

The sun warmed Henry's back and sweat dripped from his scalp onto his neck. The black rock of Arn's Volcano shone like coal. Its immensity made Henry feel like an insect next to it. Henry grabbed a porch pole and started to swing himself up when he heard a familiar voice. Not able to place the inflection, he leaned down and slipped under the porch, walking in a crouched position until he was underneath the room where Delta and her visitor were talking.

"Delta, I can't lose this baby. I lost three already. I can't lose this'n."

"You promise me you won't let Amos hit on you no more," Delta said. "It's the reason you lost them other babies, Nancy."

Henry recognized his cook's voice and an irritated surge rose through his chest. He had his disagreements with Nancy's husband, Amos, but liked less Nancy's telling Delta about private matters that went on in the Kingsley household, matters that were best left between a man and his wife. Henry hurried forward when he saw Lafette's feet at the back of the house turning toward the front. He stepped from under the porch just as Lafette came round, carefully balancing a tin dipper brimming with water.

"Reckon this'll cool you down." Lafette eased the dipper into Henry's hands.

As Henry drank the cold mountain water, the cabin door opened in a long whine. Delta stepped out just as a breeze caught her long, blond hair and floated it around her. Nancy followed, taking small, mouse-like steps. His cook's face registered fear and he reinforced his disapproval by staring at her for several seconds before speaking.

"Amos know you're up here, Nance?" Henry clanked the silver-colored dipper onto one of the flat creek rocks leading to the porch steps.

Nancy's voice squeaked at a high pitch. "Lord, mercy, Mr. Henry. I, I..." One hand fluttered in front of her face and the other clutched a tiny bottle of green liquid.

"Me and Nancy's cousins thrice removed on my Momma's side," Delta interjected, her voice cool as the water he'd just swallowed. "Now and again we women folk like to visit. More'n I can say about you being here."

She stood above him, meeting his gaze like a perched screech owl. In that moment, Henry felt the heat of her. He grabbed the porch banister and pulled himself up. He stood a head taller than both women, but while Nancy cast her gaze toward the ground, Delta cocked her head to one side and looked directly into his eyes. Despite the glare of sun behind him, she never looked away.

"Come visit your ole cousin again," Delta told Nancy while peering steadily at Henry. Nancy crept away, her hands twisting around the bottle of green liquid, and her graying hair escaping the bun at the nape of her neck. "Got something against kin seeing each other?" Delta asked.

"Not me," he teased, noticing the fine, chiseled line of her lips.

She stepped back from him and sat on a pine stump that had been cut into a chair. "Dog days'll be on us soon and Nancy needs to be careful of upset. Wouldn't want nobody riling her." At the same time, she swept her waist-length hair to one side of her head and fanned her neck with a free hand. Lafette leaped onto the porch and straddled the banister. He stared at Henry's ankle.

"My ankle." Henry began, trying to remember which one he'd limped on. "Turned my ankle down the hill and your boy said I could rest a spell."

"Give it here," Delta said, holding out her hand and bending down on one knee. "Come on, give me your foot."

Henry waited as Lafette jumped from the porch banister and landed cross-legged at his mother's side. Clumsily, Henry raised one leg, nearly losing his balance when she impatiently grabbed hold and tugged off his boot. Lafette grinned and Henry realized the boy was getting immense pleasure from seeing him in the awkward position.

"Mr. Kingsley's been measuring our Tyme trees, Momma," Lafette said.

" 'Fate, hitch up Ole Sal," Delta said. "You're gonna ride Henry down the mountain."

Lafette swooped off the porch, spreading his arms wide like eagle wings and hooting a grinding noise in his throat as he skipped toward the barn. He and a gray puppy scattered a flock of chickens pecking in the dirt.

Henry was glad the boy left so that he could discuss the Tyme trees with Delta. She massaged his foot, concentrating hard around the ankle. He worried that Delta realized there was no swelling. "Ain't bad," he said.

"Maybe not, but can never tell what might happen."

"Ouuuch!" Henry yelled when a bone popped in one of his toes. He held to the banister, wishing he hadn't told a lie just to see her. "Feels better now." She held his foot firm. "Never see you at the trading post anymore, Delta," he said, figuring to make use of his time.

"My boy does my trading these days." She kneaded the sole of his foot and pushed his toes backward.

Henry strained as the stretch pulled his calf. "Must be hard for you here alone."

"Arn'll be back any day now," she snapped, as did another bone.

"Some say he's dead, Delta."

"Folks say lots of things."

"You need to think of your future and Lafette's."

"Next time you turn your ankle, don't do it on Shadow Mountain. 'Fate hadn't been there, you might've fell off a sharp ridge."

"Been five years since Arn disappeared—"

"You gonna tell Amos that Nancy was here?"

Henry smiled, looking into her soft, brown eyes fading into green. He'd noticed the striking color the first time when they were children. She'd been drawing a picture of the mountains on a chalkboard and he'd told her it was ugly. She'd cried and the green in her irises turned as dark as jade. "Not rightly decided," Henry said, teasing her about Nancy. "Not a good thing for a woman to discuss her husband with others."

"Which is why I won't discuss Arn with you." Delta smacked his ankle.

The finger pressure grew stronger. Henry realized he'd angered her. "I came here," he said, figuring he'd better change the subject, "to inquire about buying some timber from you."

"Some nice white oak near the Virginia border," she said.

"Tyme trees."

"Tyme tree aren't for sale."

"Now, Delta, don't be silly." He reached out to pinch her cheek, but her hard look discouraged him.

"Tyme trees are not for sale," she repeated more firmly.

Lafette came out of the barn and led a mule to the porch so Henry could lower himself onto the animal's back. Delta untied a white sash from her waist and wound it around Henry's foot and ankle before sliding on the boot.

"As my Daddy always says, 'Not a thing on God's earth you can't buy'." Henry chuckled, hoping she'd smile too. "Like Nancy there, Amos makes her see the town doctor, but every chance she gets she runs up here to buy your potions." Henry noticed her eyebrows scrunch toward each other so he assumed she was thinking seriously about selling him the Tyme trees. "I understand wanting to hold out for a good price. Think on it a spell. Bet you could come up with a cost for fifty or so Tyme trees. Hardly make a dent in those groves."

Once on Ole Sal's back, Henry smiled to himself, feeling like he was doing Delta a personal favor in buying a few of her trees. He knew she could use the money and by putting the price into her hands, he'd let her control the process. He silently congratulated himself.

"Lafette," Delta said before Henry could speak. "Take a good look at this man's face." She brought her hand up under

Henry's chin. "This is the son of the blade who tried to kill your father and if you've ever the chance you should return the favor."

Henry flinched at a stabbing spasm in his ankle shooting up his leg. He twisted backwards on Ole Sal to explain but Delta turned briskly and slammed the door behind her. Lafette led Ole Sal forward. "Wait a minute, son, I gotta talk to her."

Lafette kept walking. "Nope, don't want to talk to her when she's like that. Should've listened to me. I tried to tell you it was woman's day."

"Let me down!" Henry hollered at Lafette.

Lafette ignored him. "That's why I stay far away from home on woman's day."

Henry tried dismounting, but his leg seized up, cramping through the calf and into his toes. By the time they were down the mountain, his ankle had swollen into the boot.

⩔ 3 ⩔

DELTA VENTED HER rage at Henry Kingsley's arrogance by swatting the cat and emptying her teacup on a nesting hen outside the window. If Arn was here, she thought, men wouldn't be half so bold with me. Then she paused, smirking to herself at how swollen Henry's ankle must be by now. "Teach him," she said aloud, thinking about the perfectly healthy ankle she'd found when she pulled off his boot. Should've pressed a little harder on those nerves, she mused, and caused him to limp for a week. Then she threw back her head and laughed heartily.

She dampened a cloth from the water pail and wiped the day's warm stickiness from her arms and chest. A fly landed on the bucket edge, and she shooed it, splashing water where it had landed. Dog days, she thought. Got to remind Lafette to stay out of the creek for the next two months.

She re-wet the cloth, cleaned the pine counter then tightly tugged a curtain across the shelf to protect her strawberry leaves from insects. She'd used them last year on Lafette's infected leg sores and she chilled, recalling the half dozen infants from surrounding towns who'd died of dog days sickness. Even two mothers had succumbed to the scorch of lingering fevers.

Delta caught the soft padding of footsteps near the back door. No one ever approached the rear except those few who knew the mountain's secret paths. She peered outside and saw the long silver hair of Kate Huston plaited into a single braid down her back. Kate motioned with her hand for Delta to come out but never turned toward her. The old woman stood, eyes averted upward at Arn's Volcano. Delta went no farther than the doorway, annoyed by Kate's commanding manner that hadn't changed since the days Delta had learned herbal lore from her. "Staring at that volcano ain't gonna bring Arn back," Delta said.

Kate circled toward her, her eyes so light a gray they were almost as silver as her hair, and her skin, pale as white corn, never seemed to absorb sunrays. "Been my way of thinking for a while now." Kate dropped a burlap sack, revealing twisted ginseng roots. "Ain't nothing gonna bring Arn back."

"Don't talk of what you don't know." Delta's cheeks burned and she clutched her hands behind her back, trying her best to say as little to her former teacher as she could.

"Arn's and my blood's the same," Kate said, tapping her finger against her heart. "With him gone, probably dead, it's me that ought to stand as Watcher."

"Arn'll be back in his own time." Delta's lips quivered slightly when she spoke.

"By right..." Kate stopped speaking as a blue jay lit on Delta's shoulder. She reached out for it, her hand nearly a claw, but the bird flew toward the top of Arn's Volcano. "T'were a blue bird that led Arn away. I kill every one I see."

"I stand watch in Arn's place." Delta stepped forward, blocking Kate. Had it not been for a passel of wasps circling Kate's boots, she would have tramped barefooted into the yard and knocked her backwards. "Enough of you showing up every July claiming Shadow Mountain. It's Arn's, and Arn was mine. I stand in his place, do the things he did, and someday, his son will follow me." A wasp flew at Delta's face and she swatted it, looking fiercely at Kate, believing she'd caused it to attack.

"How can Lafette be a Watcher? You've not even told him he's part Melungeon."

"You don't know that he is. You don't know that Arn was. Arn was a woodcolt. Everybody knows he only lived with Elisha Thunderheart."

"I feel Arn's blood, Delta. I've always felt Arn's blood." She stroked herself seductively from breast to waist, her throaty voice coarse as old rope. "You're white. Me, Arn, and Lafette, we're of the dark blood."

"Keep a distance from Lafette, or I'll come after you."

Kate laughed, threw back her head and slapped her thighs. In an instant, she'd transformed back into a dirty old mountain woman.

Delta had to make a stand now or Kate would plague them until winter snow made the paths too difficult to climb. "Mountain's mine now. Best get acclimated to it."

Kate touched the black rock of Arn's Volcano. "To most folks, this mountain is dirt, roots, trees, creeks, rock. T'was that corner yonder where Pappy Thunderheart and me found Arn. Was like the earth itself gave birth to him. I weren't no more than ten." Her fingers spread as if she spoke to the stone. "Changed his diapers, taught him to talk, to walk, to know the pith of the land. Learned him to fight the Wampus and hunt quiet as a hare." She paused, lowering her eyes up and down Delta's body. Kate sniffed the air as if the scent brought back a memory of when she lived in this house. "When Elisha Thunderheart gave Arn his training, I knew my boy was a true Watcher, 'cause he had more of me in him then if I'd been his own momma." She pointed a long, delicate finger at Delta. "You don't belong here! Watchers prove they're worthy. Show me you can raise the power like I can raise the power. Show me the power Arn showed me!"

"Arn taught me," Delta tried explaining.

Kate, still pointing her finger at Delta, continued, "Elisha Thunderheart schooled me as well as he taught Arn and he honored my presence here."

"You're a fool, Kate. Arn let you live in that shack down the hill 'cause he felt sorry for you. You had nowhere else to go. He felt sorry for you." Kate dropped her hand. Her eyes were flaring torches, and Delta knew to proceed with care. "Arn's the one who wants me to stand for him. When he returns, he'll make you regret what you've said."

"You raise the power, and then, I'll believe you." Kate looked up into the sky and then to Delta, a hateful sneer on her face.

A gray storm cloud shaped like a dragon drifted behind her. Lightning struck the Volcano peak. A second later came the thunder, so loud that Delta folded her arms across her chest so she wouldn't tremble. Around the black rocks shimmered a fiery blue electricity. Delta shaded her eyes for fear she'd be consumed in it. Kate stood in the vortex, regarding Delta as she would a disobedient child.

"Leave here," Delta managed to say, regretting her voice was slight and childlike. The glow faded but the stillness remained.

Kate cackled, "Scared you, did I?"

"Summer storm," she whispered, waving her arm as if she'd seen nothing unusual. "If'n you did it, then strike me down where I stand." Delta widened her stance, hands on her hips. She repeated to herself, *Arn wants me here. He'll protect me.*

Kate picked up the burlap sack and slung it over her shoulder. "First you mock me, then you challenge me." She bit her bottom lip. "It would be so easy." Her eyes narrowed. She whistled. A gray dog sitting in some tall jimson weeds heeled then followed Kate through a corn patch and into a copse of Tyme trees.

Relief surged through Delta's muscles as she watched Kate leave. When she was sure her former teacher hadn't dallied to spy on her, she lightly placed her fingertips on the volcano, wanting to dig into the blackness. Kate had awakened the delicate, humming power that the rocks gushed at Arn's command.

Delta could hardly stand it that Kate had called lightning. She'd watched Arn awaken the rocks many times, but try as she may, the stones were dead to her touch. Arn called forth the power, sending it into the mountain ranges like a fog to do his bidding and then disappear with the morning sun. Why would it not come forth when she called?

She hurried into the house, closing the door so hard that a Mason jar of crushed rhubarb leaves fell from a shelf and shattered. Looking through all the herbs she had, and all the ones Arn had told her never to touch, she knew one must work. She had to learn to raise the power. She had to learn Arn's secrets.

♆ 4 ♆

HENRY USED THE wall to steady himself as he limped into his home. The marble staircase leading to the second level looked as difficult to climb as a mountain. He paused at the banister when his father's voice and those of Pete McGinnis and Jonathan Quinn argued from the library. A knot tightened in his stomach as McGinnis complained about the heat in a whining tone.

Henry wished his father had never agreed to build the Quinntown Coal Camp for the Quinn family. Bad enough listening to Jonny-boy brag of the British Empire's glories, but McGinnis could find nothing admirable about the mountains in comparison to his home state of New Jersey.

The oak banister, polished to a high sheen, reflected Henry's blurred likeness as twisted and gaunt. He rubbed a hand along the wood, wishing that he'd left Delta on better terms. His ankle pulsed painfully. Balanced on tiptoes, he started upstairs. On the third step, the banister squeaked. Henry's shoulders tensed. His father had the hearing of a stalking cougar.

"Well?" King asked, swinging open both library doors and twirling his hand urgently for Henry to enter.

Henry thought his father looked as comfortable as a cornered rooster. "Tyme trees are still there," Henry said, "and they're as big as you remember, Daddy." Henry lowered himself into a sitting position while trying to protect his ankle.

"See!" King said to Pete and Jonathan, who followed from the library. Both men buried their hands deep in the pockets of their black suits. "Told you I was the only contractor who knew where to get Tyme wood."

"So you did." Jonathan Quinn's English accent gave his voice more strength than his pallid complexion indicated. "I suppose constructing Quinntown with Tyme lumber justifies these exorbitant prices you intend to charge me." He opened his coat on a sweat-stained silk lining and pulled out a paper stuck in an inside pocket. Holding a round eyeglass to his right eye, he perused scrawled numbers.

"We built Essex Fork Coal Mines with Tyme timber," King said. "No easy job finding it these days, but I'll tell you, the beams in those mines will last 'til Kingdom Come." He nodded his head to emphasize his point.

"We only need them to last to the next coal boom," said Pete McGinnis. "Any fool knows to hold off mining now. We just want to be ready."

Henry squeezed his hands together, feeling embarrassed even though his father had let the insult go unnoticed. "Lot of mines 'round here went belly up," Henry pointed out. "Why not buy one of them?"

"A Quinn never purchases secondhand," Jonathan said, in as icy a voice as Henry had ever heard. As the thin Englishman thrust the letter at Pete, he checked the time on a gold pocket watch embedded with diamonds.

"One problem with all this," Henry said, dreading to approach the subject. "Delta Wade won't sell her Tyme trees."

"What!" McGinnis slapped the letter against his hand.

"She'll sell you some white oak or maybe some cedar but not the Tyme trees."

"May I inquire why?" Jonathan asked. He stroked his chin, and his pencil thin mouth pursed out, giving it a hint of width.

"How much you offer her?" King asked.

"If you promised more than we've agreed to, we'll not pay the difference." Pete shook the letter of agreement in King's face.

"Never got 'round to talking price." Henry's stomach churned.

"You *never got 'round* to negotiating cost," Jonathan mocked Henry's accent through gritted teeth. He paced the hallway, toeing the Oriental carpet. He picked up a miniature ballerina figurine and passed it from hand to hand while staring intently at the floor. The heirloom had belonged to Henry's mother and he struggled against telling Quinn to put the statuette down.

"What'cha thinking, Mr. Quinn?" McGinnis asked, shifting nervously from foot to foot.

Henry knew Jonathan Quinn was looking at him as if he were a fool. "Tyme tree is the strongest wood that ever was. They were so in demand that timberers cut 'em down and didn't replant any." Henry's neck sweated as Quinn's pallid face reddened. "Other than Shadow Mountain, there's just a few scrawny ones left. Rabbits and squirrels live around 'em so they can eat the leaves and nuts come winter."

"Stop babbling!" Quinn slammed a hand so hard on a burl table that the minute hand on an antique table clock dropped off. "I will speak as plainly as the Queen's English will allow. I want Tyme lumber. I will have Tyme lumber."

"Get as mad as you want," Henry's eyes weighed on his mother's figurine in Quinn's left hand, "but if Delta Wade don't want to sell, she won't." Henry stared hard as he could at the ballerina. Quinn haphazardly snapped it down on the wrong side of the table.

Pete lit a cigar and sucked in deeply, as if inhaling smoke more in frustration than pleasure. He cleared his throat and tapped the cigar on a brass spittoon. "Reckon if it's Tyme trees you want, King Kingsley'll have to find some Tyme trees." Pete shifted his weight toward Jonathan Quinn and cocked an eyebrow at King. "Well? Can you handle it, Kingsley, or do we go elsewhere?"

Henry realized he'd just witnessed an important part of Jonathan Quinn's gumption. That King wanted the job was in every line of his face, but Henry couldn't guess if his father would bend under pressure from the strong-armed McGinnis. King picked up the ballerina. Henry watched his father run a finger around the white porcelain skirt and stare into the brown-eyed, red-lipped face of the ballerina as if she were alive. For a moment, Henry sensed the room filling with the gentle presence of his deceased mother. He felt stronger as his father moved the ballerina figurine to its correct setting.

"You heard my boy say Tyme tree is timbered out," King said in a low and gentle voice, " 'Cept for what's on Shadow Mountain. If I can't deliver it, then nobody can. If that means I don't do business with you then I'll build outhouses 'fore I sit here and admit somebody can do a better job building a coal camp than me." King crossed his arms, the muscles in his throat pulsed like a heartbeat.

Pete dropped his cigar onto the floor and crushed it underneath his boot. Jonathan Quinn began to laugh. His womanish laughter was the first hint of humor Henry had seen in Quinn. The Englishman looked to be in his mid-twenties, but he strutted with a royal demeanor. "And here we all stand," he said, opening his hands up toward the ceiling. He looked at King, then Henry. "We have one other contractor to speak with, Mr. Kingsley. Rethink your position and I'll have McGinnis stop by early next week to see if you've secured the Tyme trees." He moved to the door, then turned, motioning for the befuddled Pete to follow him.

The door hung halfway open and chandelier crystals tinkled in the breeze. King stared for several seconds before Henry reached out and touched his father's arm, bringing him back to himself.

"What do you make of that?" King said, closing the front door with his foot.

"Think Mr. Jonathan Quinn plays his cards with an ace up a sleeve."

"Not necessarily his own." King scooped up the discarded cigar Pete had crushed.

"Daddy, Delta won't sell."

"He gave us another chance, Son. We have to get those trees."

"He knows nobody else can get the trees either." Henry rubbed his temples. "What other choice does he have?"

"He also knows that I'm King Kingsley. I get my way around these mountains just like he gets his way in England. That's why we got a second chance."

"Delta Wade's as solitary as a cat." Henry put weight on his left foot and a sharp pain shot up his leg. He quickly sat to avoid the embarrassment of explaining what had happened to his ankle. "Can't tell what she might do."

"Everybody sells for the right price."

"And the bigger Tyme trees are on Kate Huston's side of the mountain. What if she starts up with us?" Henry asked, remembering back to Lafette's childish warning of being turned into a frog. "Ain't scared of her, but she could cause trouble."

"I'll show you how it's done." King stared out the window after Jonathan Quinn and Pete McGinnis. "That man's never had anybody stand up to him the way I just did." He pointed to Quinn climbing into a black carriage. "That's the reason he gave us another chance. Get some lunch while I saddle the horses."

"Folks say Kate's a witch, and Delta, well, she's liable to shoot anybody that comes 'round asking to buy trees again, especially a Kingsley."

"Son, ain't a witch or a bitch I can't handle." Rubbing his hands like an excited child, King marched out, letting the door swing so hard it hit the wall and bounced back.

"Fine mess you got yourself," Henry said to himself, easing off his boot. The swelling had lessened but his sole tingled and the ankle was circled with a red bruise. He chuckled at the thought of Delta Wade and her small hands massaging his foot. Now there's power, Henry thought, comparing her mentally with Jonathan Quinn. Reckon I'll not underestimate her again.

Henry wiggled his toes, feeling returned to his foot. She didn't bewitch me after all, he scolded himself for having thought it. Probably just cut off the circulation with that scarf. His calf muscle began to cramp. "Damn!"

Even with his swollen foot, Henry hummed with excitement of seeing Delta again. Still lovely as she'd been as a girl, she had a way of talking to him that made him feel like he wanted to please her. She'd never been like her family. Sorry no-accounts who spent their days sleeping and nights thievin'.

Maybe it was good Arn had bought her out of that life. He felt glad that the Tyme trees would give him an excuse to see her twice in one day.

If his father was able to convince her to sell, the least he would do was tag along, make sure she got a fair price. They were just trees. Maybe I'm wrong, maybe she'll sell after the right kind of courting, he thought. He folded her white scarf and pushed it into his pocket.

"Amos!" Henry yelled toward the kitchen. Amos came running, followed by Nancy with her nervous hand-wringing. "Get me some ice water. Gotta ride to Shadow Mountain again and my foot ain't gonna last me."

"I'll have Nancy do it right away, sir."

"No, I want you to do it. Carrying ice is too heavy for Nancy, too heavy for any woman," Henry said, thinking about what he'd overheard Nancy say to Delta. "About time the men around this place started doing men's work and acting like gentlemen."

"Yes, sir," Amos said, casting his eyes to the ground.

Nancy exhaled a relieved breath, her hands resting on her full stomach. Henry smiled, wondering, even hoping, that she might mention his taking up for her to Delta.

5

LAFETTE SWORE HE'D never be afraid of witches. Folks in the mountains called Kate Huston a witch, but he didn't mind 'cause she always had a honey cake or a bit of gunpowder for him. She was also beautiful. Lafette could stare at her icy ashen eyes and silvery hair all day long and never tire of looking at her. Sitting on her front porch, Kate cleaned a Mason jar with a yellow rag torn from a dress she no longer wore. He swore to himself again that witches had to be the best thing about living on Shadow Mountain.

"Sure I can't help you none?" Lafette ran a hand down the oak pole holding up her porch and savored the smell of stewed rabbit drifting from her cabin.

Kate stopped polishing the jar, reached out and stroked his head. "Possum, you help me best with your secrecy."

"Momma won't ever find out that I run errands for you." Lafette grinned at the tingling sensation of her touch.

A crow landed on a Tyme branch, and as Kate spoke, her glance always returned to the bird. Lafette grabbed a stone to throw at the creature, but Kate motioned him to stop.

"My ancestors," she said, "are said to've rode on the wings of a black crow to these highlands." She waved her hand to indicate the line of the Cumberland Mountains crooked against the horizon.

"Aunt Kate," as Lafette called her, "folks can't do that."

"Now, how would a little possum like you know what a people can or can't do?"

"Ain't so little. I'm near eleven now."

"Reckon I'm wrong. You're a man as clear as your daddy. Arn Marlon was a powerful man. You recall him, don't you?"

Lafette pondered a moment before responding. Sometimes he thought he remembered his father, but the hazy outline lingering in his memory faded as quickly as it appeared. "Can't rightly say I do," he said.

"Your daddy was descended from the smartest cougar in these parts. It lived at the peak of Creation Ridge and ain't a hunter in these mountains could track it."

"I don't believe in such stuff." Lafette stood and peered into a steep ravine bordering Kate's cabin. "I don't even believe in the Wampus." He watched to see what she would do, but the old woman seemed not to hear him. "I said, I don't believe in magic."

"I could track that cougar, of course. That's how I come to know your daddy." Kate held the Mason jar out for Lafette to take. The hide of a black bear was underneath her rocking chair, and she leaned down and stroked between the bear's ears as if it were a pet. "Turned myself into a hare and sniffed that cougar out, then turned myself into a she-wolf, and me and that cat, we become friends.

"You and momma made up this stuff about daddy believing in magic." Lafette tossed the Mason jar in the air, catching it on his fingertips. Kate didn't react. He tossed it again, waiting to see if she scolded him. "Bet Daddy thought magic was silly."

"That's an answer you'll know in time," she said, "and one I'll never be sure of."

Lafette was unsure what she meant by that, and he always got a strange, uncomfortable feeling when she talked about his future, as if she knew more about it than he did. "After this trip, I get a hawk chick, don't I?" Lafette asked, figuring to avoid the subject of his destiny. He pointed at a majestic hawk perched on the porch banister. Shiny, yellowish-brown feathers looked tipped with gold. The bird's nest was in a nearby Tyme tree, and Lafette could hear the chirping chicks. The hawk would come to Kate when she whistled to it, and of late, she'd been teaching him how to call to birds. Lafette could hardly wait to have his very own hawk.

"We agreed on four errands." She held up four fingers. "Four to get one of Cerridwen's pups," she said, indicating her dog, "and four to get one of Thera's chicks."

"But that last trip to White Rocks took all day long and I near fell off the side when a cougar got after me."

"A cougar?" Kate said, giving a hint of a smile and rolling her eyes to one side. "If I recall, when you got back, all out of breath and with a ripped shirt, you said the Wampus had chased you."

"I said cougar! I said cougar if I said anything!" Lafette's words choked in his throat and tears edged up in his eyes. "Want me to run your errands or not?"

She slowly let out a long, soft breath. "I guess maybe I heard wrong. Must've been cougar that you said. I recall that day me and your momma had a disagreement, and it probably rattled me." She nodded as if remembering but Lafette was keenly aware how closely she watched him.

"Must be a reason Momma don't take to you being that you and Daddy was such good neighbors."

"Lafette, that's a matter 'twixt me and your ma. Now, do you understand what to do?" she asked, pointing to the Mason jar.

"Yes, Ma'am." Lafette nestled the jar in the crook of his arm.

"When you get to the far end of Midnight Valley, look for Tabu," she said, sighting the black crow. "He'll lead you up the hollow to my sister's place."

Lafette figured he could follow directions to Polly Huston's cabin without a crow's help, but he nodded to Kate nonetheless, and set out toward Sand Cave.

∞

Midday, Lafette came to the two hundred foot opening of a clam-shaped cave with its many-colored sands. Mountain laurel cascaded around him, and honeysuckle sweetened the air. He scaled a stone staircase spiraling down to the mouth of the colossal cavern. Each time he visited he felt like Jonah about to be swallowed by a whale. Sand Cave's opening towered higher than a hemlock, and the white sand spilled out in an ivory wave.

Lafette sat in the center of the cave, just as Kate had instructed, with the Mason jar between his legs. He cupped a handful of white sand, poured it into the jar, then dug a few inches and found blazing yellow grains. He sifted the yellow on top of the white, then burrowed deeper until he came to red sand. The pure color, scarlet as the last of sunset, lay separated on top the yellow, as did the blue, purple, brown and finally black sand. Just as Kate had told him, the black sand filled the jar, and he tightly sealed the top and walked carefully so as not to stir the colors together.

Before he left, he drank from a pond at the cave's edge, fed by a fluttering waterfall. Two water spiders darted across the pool and Lafette wondered if this might be a good place to go frogging. He rested the container on the charred stump of an oak tree burned by lightning. As he rose, a black crow tapped its beak on the jar top. "Shooooo!" Lafette cried out and the bird flew to a redbud tree. He picked up a palm-sized stone and aimed. The crow squawked and disappeared into the higher branches.

"Lucky I don't got a gun, you ole codger!" he yelled up into the tree limbs.

Once over Creation Ridge, Midnight Valley stretched like a lazy cat as far as Lafette could see. Cumberland Gap's soft V-shape cushioned a smattering of cabins like small stones surrounded by a pine forest. Several horses and a few wagons pulled up to Gap Trading Post, and he hitched a ride on a peddler's cart through Middlesboro, stopping only to cool his feet in Stony Fork Creek.

When he was sure no one was watching him, Lafette sneaked onto an L & N train and rode comfortably until he jumped off at a row of juniper trees marking the entrance to a hollow called End-of-the-Road. He'd been here only once before but had never gone as far as Polly's Huston's cabin. Hundred-foot-tall poplar trees grew with their branches locked together so that the sun did not touch the earth, and even though this was a July afternoon it might as well have been dusk at End-of-the-Road.

Lafette passed a gray clapboard cabin and watched two dark-haired children play hide-and-seek. He figured them to be

Polly's kin since only Hustons lived at End-of-the-Road. Lafette was curious about their coppery skin and watched a woman hang wet clothes on the stripped branches of two birch trees. She, too, was dark-skinned, with hair black as pitch. Kate sure don't favor her kin, he thought.

Lafette continued up the hollow, gripping the jar as if it were a precious jewel, proud he'd traveled all this way and kept the sand from mixing together. To amuse himself, he hopped back and forth across a creek. Then the water split off into two streams, something he'd not expected. Each branch led into thick fern groves. What'll I do now? he wondered, sitting on the creek bank and cradling the Mason jar.

A red bird swooped past him, bounced into a dogwood tree and landed on the ground. Chattering and flapping its wings, it spun in a circle. It's lost, Lafette thought, realizing the bird couldn't see the sky. The cardinal beat its ruby-colored feathers against the muddy, chestnut earth. It had broken a wing. Shrill chirps were its agonized screams of fear, and Lafette couldn't stand hearing its pain. Quickly, he strode over to the small red bird, still fluttering. Its chest pulsed with as much fear as effort, and as hard as he could, he stomped on the fowl's head.

A hushed humming quivered in the air. Relieved not to hear the bird's writhing screams, Lafette could not lift his boot. Then came the coarse, aggravating caw of a crow. He looked up. The black bird stared at him with one eye, then flew up the right fork of the creek. Lafette shook off the incident, picked up his jar of sand and followed.

Just as Kate had said, and much to Lafette's displeasure, the crow led him to a lopsided cabin that looked like it might slide into the creek. A pole porch matched the one on his home, and two hounds lay sleeping underneath. He approached silently as he could, hoping the dogs wouldn't charge him. His foot crunch an anthill, and the two animals set upon him and nipped at his feet. They weren't dogs. They were foxes, a squat gray one that wove between his legs trying to trip him and a large red that bounced around in front of him blocking the way. He twisted sideways to protect the pattern of the many-colored sands. With both hands, he steadily lifted the jar to the porch.

Something whizzed passed his fingers, and he pulled back. Lafette shrieked, clutching the jar to his chest. A nest of copperhead snakes lay on the porch. Dozens more coiled near a rock wall, and a few draped like ribbons on the porch steps. How could he have not noticed them? He held the jar high above his head as the two foxes jumped on him.

"Down boy, down boy," he said to the foxes as if they were hounds. One yodeled a steady stream of chirpy barks. Lafette stepped sideways to avoid a reddish-brown snake sliding through the grass toward the creek. Its diamond-shaped head was slightly raised, and its tongue shot out of its mouth. Lafette shivered all over. He hated copperheads.

"Hush up out there!" came a strong, raspy voice from the cabin. The foxes heeled obediently, positioning themselves between Lafette and the cabin. Out stepped a tiny, misshapen woman, Polly Huston. "Well, if it's not a guardian of the gate."

Lafette's breath caught in his throat. She glided among the copperheads as if they were no more than cats sunning themselves, and once down the steps, she reached about his height. Her arms were so long that her fingers were nearly even with her knees. Dark like the people he'd seen earlier, she clearly had features favoring Kate. Polly's skin was more weathered as if accustomed to working under a harsh sun, but the same almond-shaped eyes and high forehead kept Lafette fixed on her face.

"You come from my sister?" she asked, staring at the jar of sand. Her voice was gruff as a man's and her eyelids drooped, half closed.

Lafette lost his voice. He held out the jar to her, not daring to step any closer to the snakes. Taking it, Polly stared at the pattern of sand then placed the jar on the ground between her feet. She pulled a silver coin from a pocket, tore the hem of her dress and wrapped the coin before giving it to him. Lafette figured she must be praising him for coming such a long way without mixing the colors and couldn't help smiling.

"Tell my sister that the fate of the mountain is in the hands of Judas, and Judas answers only to God." Behind her, snakes gathered at the porch edge. Two serpents dropped onto a fox that seemed not to mind. "Don't like Polly's little friends?" she teased as he stepped backwards again. "Wanna come in, my little guardian?" She pointed to the cabin.

Lafette twisted his head to indicate no. His knees shook, and a strange dreaminess came over him. He was looking up at Polly, even though a moment ago they'd been the same height. She cackled a slow, barely audible voice. Suddenly, she thrust the jar of sand in front of his face and shook it vigorously. The multicolored grains turned white before his eyes. Lafette shoulders tightened into his neck. He pushed the jar away from him. Polly hissed a strange laugh sounding like a screech owl. Lafette spun, running fast away from End-of-the-Road.

∞

Once in sunlight, Lafette's fear seemed silly. He shook off the odd sister and made good time by cutting across Fork Ridge. As he approached Kate's cabin, she swung open the door and motioned for him to hurry.

"What did she say?" she asked urgently.

Looking at Kate was strange to Lafette. He kept seeing her twin sister's face, distorted by the sinister laughter.

"What did she say?" Kate asked again, more impatient.

"She talked about Judas, said the fate of the mountain was in the hands of Judas, and Judas answers only to God." Lafette described the lopsided house and the copperheads. Surely, she must not know her sister lives with snakes, he thought, but Kate faced away from him, absorbed by her sister's message. "She called me a guardian, a guardian of the gate. What's that mean, Aunt Kate?"

"My foolish sister doesn't get to make that decision," Kate said, turning toward him and studying his face in a way she never had before. "That all?"

Lafette held out the wrapped silver coin. Kate snatched it, letting the material drop and held the coin up toward the sun. Both hands clenched to fists, and from deep in her throat, a voice growled until the sound became a holler of fury. Lafette retreated, too afraid to speak. Kate drew back her arm, and threw the coin far as she could.

"Why'd you throw money away?"

"Because silver is not gold."

Lafette's shoes felt planted in the earth. Beside him, the golden hawk spread its wings and swooped above his head. Kate whipped around. Her eyes blood red. No trace of the pale irises. Terror shot through him. He twisted, tripping on his own feet and didn't dare look back for fear Kate would turn into one of those hateful creatures she always described roaming the mountains in the bleak of night. He ran until he reached the Elisha Tree and hid inside. After a couple of hours, he crawled out, still unsure what to make of the things he'd seen this day.

♆ 6 ♆

NOT FAR FROM Kate Huston's cabin, Henry and his father let the horses drink from a babbling brook. The creek's source cascaded down a rocky cliff and splashed onto gleaming black rocks before pooling below path level. King stood grandly on the hillside, one leg propped higher than the other. He sniffed loudly, his lips curling into a grin as he judged the trees.

"Money to be made on this mountain," King said. "Damn shame it's in three states."

"What do you mean, Daddy?"

"I can buy my way through the Tennessee and Kentucky government, but it's damn hard to pay off a Virginia politician. Too much Tom Jefferson in 'em."

"Sounds like you want the whole mountain."

"Son, there'll come a day when I'll own this mountain. Gonna put up a big lodge like the Four Seasons in Harrogate, Tennessee. It'll be a place where kings, queens, and presidents come to rest their bones a spell."

"Way up here? Kinda impractical," Henry said. He detested the Harrogate lodge. Didn't care for the people who stayed there especially. They might be rich, but seemed to him they held an ornery disrespect for mountain folk.

"Nothin' impossible for a man with brains, money, and a vision," King said. "And when I'm dead, it'll all belong to you and your children." One eyebrow arched when he said *children*. The static between them silenced a jumble of birds chirping in the overhead trees, leaving the creek gurgling unnaturally loudly. King slapped his son's back and turned to scale the rocks beside the waterfall. "Meet you at the top. Spied a shiny silver piece in the rocks. Gonna prove something to you."

Henry observed from below as King held to a Tyme tree and stretched out over a rocky crag. A blade of sunlight reached through the dense branches as if its sole intention were to shine on this slim silver piece. The coin balanced precariously on the ledge, and as King reached for it, Henry was sure that his father would tumble over into the creek.

"Daddy, probably not worth the effort." Henry held his breath and wished his father would forget about the coin.

"Ahhhh!" King groaned just as he grasped the silver. "See, money comes to me, always has, always will." He flipped it in the air and whistled. "Learn a lesson from this, boy." He slipped the coin into his pocket and crawled up the man-sized brown boulders that lined the cliff. "Bet it's worth fifty dollars!"

Late afternoon brought a chilly breeze off the creek water and Henry shivered as he led the horses back to the path. His ankle tingled and caused him to limp. He shook it to loosen the blood flow to his foot, then tightened the harnesses and fed carrots to the horses. The chores gave him a few more moments away from his father's lecturing. Henry wanted to stay focused. If he allowed himself to get frustrated now, he'd be giving his father a chance to take advantage of Delta. The way King browbeat people, he might end up with the whole mountain in his possession. Keep a clear head, he repeated to himself, as he massaged his ankle through the boot leather.

Up the mountain, King inspected the Tyme trunks and used a string to measure their circumference, smiling widely each time he discovered an extra large one. Henry wondered if his father would give him any credit for finding the giant trees.

King kicked a pile of dead leaves and marched ahead. “Once I get this wood, it’ll shut up that surly Pete McGinnis.”

“Kate Huston lives yonder,” Henry said, pointing to a flattened path leading into a castle of rocks. “Reckon we ought talk with her.”

“Naw! That old Melungeon woman don’t own this land. Arn Marlon did, best I can figure. Least his is the best claim, being a man and all.” King pulled out the silver piece and flipped it in the air. “Probably his silver I got here. Might use it to sweet talk his woman.”

“Might have better luck with Kate,” Henry said, irritated by the reference to Delta being Arn’s woman and remembering her threat of a few hours before. “Why don’t you chat her up while I speak to Delta? Let’s pay ’em both to be on the right side of this.”

His father ignored him, mounted his horse, and galloped up the mountain path toward Cat’s Crossroads. Henry lagged behind, looking at a twisted ground fern. His father didn’t care what he thought. He might as well be a farmhand. Nobody told King Kingsley how to do anything. Henry blew a long, deep breath. It didn’t make him feel any better, but as he inhaled, the spicy fragrance of the Tyme tree reminded him of Delta, and an excited tremor filled in his chest.

The only other time he felt like this was the night he'd told Rebecca Baker to marry him. She'd slapped him and said he'd spoken improperly. But the way Rebecca smiled as she marched away, he knew she would marry him. Delta had that same way about her, turning away from him and calling out to him at the same time.

A branch of Tyme leaves rattled softly, breaking his daydream. A gray squirrel scurried up a tree with a twig of violet between its jaws. Rebecca's favorite flower. He took that as a good sign and reminded himself to take some violets to his wife's grave. Henry swung himself onto his horse and followed his father.

∞

Cat's Crossroads blossomed in a maze of blackberry bushes, rhododendron and waist-high green ferns. Wisteria growing along the tree branches hung in clusters over the three roads, giving rise to a candy-sweet fragrance. King slowed his horse for Henry to catch up. "Cat's Crossroads," he said. "When I was a kid, it was Katie's Crossroads, 'fore then Hekate's Crossroads. Unlucky place to get caught at night." Spurring his horse, he bounded up the hillside to Delta's cabin.

Henry trotted after him, wishing he could arrive at Delta's house first. He dreaded the impression his father might make. Henry promised himself to do what he could to secure the best price for her. If only she'd stay calm enough to hear them out.

Delta squatted on a wooden stool in her front yard, out of the shade of Arn's Volcano, with two tin buckets beside her and a gray beagle puppy sunning itself on her other side. The puppy leaped to attention when they approached, yodeling at their approach. As he and King rode up, Delta finished scaling a smallmouth bass.

"Them's a pretty sight." King pointed to a greenish-brown fish in her hand.

Delta ripped the fish's belly with a knife. She spread it open watching them—suspiciously, Henry thought. The blood smell unnerved him and he exhaled deeply to calm himself.

"Me and daddy got good news for you," Henry said. His ankle ached and he figured he was in for a bad time.

Delta studied him steadily while tearing out the bass' guts. She tossed them toward the puppy, who chomped down heartily. Henry swallowed, realizing this was not going to be as easy as he'd hoped.

"Got more Tyme trees up here than a pack of puppies." King stepped in front of Henry. "I've a need for Tyme trees. Prepared to offer you twenty-five cents a tree."

Delta tore out the bass's spine and threw it to the ground, then dropped the headless fish into a bucket of clean water before starting on the next one.

King leaned forward, towering above her but his imposing presence didn't have the desired effect. Henry admired the way she held her own. So far, so good, he thought, wiping a clump of fish scales off his boot.

"Can see you're attached to them pretty trees, but I'm a fair man," King said.

"Let's allow Delta to think on it," Henry said, hoping she realized he was looking out for her. He winked at her.

"Fifty cents a tree," King said. "Double. Don't tell me that don't interest you."

Delta's knife bit hard into the bass' neck until the head severed. "A'soon see Shadow Mountain change into a frog pond than you with a single Tyme tree."

King laughed, slapping one hand against his thigh. Her knuckles turned white as her grip on the knife tightened. Henry realized she meant to be stubborn. "We should return when Delta's not working, Daddy," he said, the fish smell beginning to nauseate him

"Ain't so busy." Delta scraped the bass steadily and scales flew upward, causing King to duck.

"Can see that you're a woman who holds a grudge." King rubbed his hands together and leaned in close to speak softly as if she were a dear friend. "Now Delta, all that be'twix me and Arn was settled years ago. Why, it happened when you were a young'un. No need of you holdin' it against me."

"Not selling my trees," Delta said. "That's all there is to it."

"I'll pay you a hundred dollars." King held up one finger to emphasize the amount then pulled the found money out of his pocket. "A genuine silver piece." He flipped the silver coin in his air.

Her eyes followed the spin of the silver and narrowed as she ripped the guts from the second fish. "No. Now that's the end of it."

"You might not have a choice, little Missy." King shook his finger the way he did before losing his temper. "Ought to at least learn from the example I made of Arn."

"Sic, sic!" Delta said to the puppy.

Before Henry knew what was happening, the beagle charged King. Delta shot up, brandishing the knife in front of her chest. The beagle leaped, sinking its teeth into King's trousers.

"Get off me!" He struck the dog, but it held fast, growling and tugging until the cloth ripped, causing King to fall backwards. His legs flew up in the air and his arms waved wildly as he hit the ground.

"Here, Blue." Delta heeled the dog to her side. The puppy trotted back, gripping a brown swatch in its teeth.

Henry helped his father, but King shoved him away, struggling up on one knee. He clenched his fist and spat through gritted teeth. "Delta Wade!" he yelled. "Just you wait, woman!" King pushed himself up and swiped his horse's reins. His pants ripped again as he straddled his horse then slapped the reins and galloped away.

"Next time I'll turn you into the skunk you are!" Delta hollered after him.

"Daddy never had much manners when it come to dealing with ladies," Henry said, not bothering to hide his amusement.

Delta stuck the knife into the ground and tugged the material from Blue's mouth. She handed it to Henry, and both chuckled, unable to stop.

"If I was any younger, he'd beat my butt for staying up here with you." Henry snickered between words.

"If I was him, I would too." Delta laughed so hard she had to hold on to her side. She motioned for Henry to follow her to the west side of Arn's Volcano where the sun warmed the rock face.

They leaned against Arn's Volcano until their mirth subsided. The sky faded into a smoky blue color scorched with blood-red streaks. Fog crept in below them, turning the mountaintop into an island above the clouds. A breeze blew in a faint honeysuckle fragrance. Delta's profile favored a cameo from one of his wife's lockets. He reached out and touched her cheek and she smiled but did not speak. Her blond hair against the black rock of Arn's Volcano fell in as complex and beautiful a pattern as a spider web woven among spiky marsh grass. Something about her, for which he couldn't find words, held him to her.

"Remember when we were kids, how we collected Tyme leaves and dandelions?" Henry asked, as he reached out and brushed away a small ant crawling on her shoulder.

"It was fall, and I made you bring me all the red leaves."

" 'Cause you wanted to have red hair and tried pasting them on your head." Henry touched a strand of her hair that was caught by a twig shooting out from a crevice in the black rock. "Not thought of those times for quite a spell."

"Young'uns do silly things," Delta said, slowly freeing the hair strand. "I love these trees, Henry."

Her gaze made him feel warm inside. "Much as you loved Arn?"

Delta looked toward the sunset but Henry touched one finger to her chin and turned her face toward him. He moved his fingers softly over her lips then leaned down and kissed her.

"AAAAAA, Momma! I'm home and I'm hungry as a bear!" Lafette hollered out.

Henry and Delta jerked apart as Lafette ran up the hill and turned a cartwheel in front of them. Henry's face burned with embarrassment, though he was fairly certain Lafette had not seen them kiss.

"Howdy, Mr. Kingsley, how's your ankle?" Lafette asked.

"Be... Be... Better." He cleared his throat. "Was returning your momma's sash," he said, struggling to pull the long, white scarf from his pocket. It unrolled in his hand and the tip touched a drop of fish blood on the top of his shoe. The red blood spread up the white cloth like the blaze of color on the horizon. Henry started to apologize but Delta waved him away.

"Staying for ba... ba... bass?" Lafette bent over the bucket of cleaned fish. He planted his hands just above the knees and poked his tongue out of the side of his mouth. "Mmmm mmm," he said.

Every movement shifted clumsy. The horse smell from his pants seemed everywhere and he stepped backwards, hoping Delta didn't notice. She turned away unable to look at him. She seemed dazed, and he, too, felt like he stepped into a vortex of swirling wind.

"Goin' be dark soon. Best be on my way. You'ins take care now." Henry whistled and his horse trotted to him. As he rode away, he could hear Lafette's incessant chatter about a bass dinner, but he did not hear Delta answer.

☫ 7 ☫

EVENING BLEW IN warm and Delta fried the bass outside over a campfire. She burned herself twice on the cast iron skillet.

Lafette scrutinized her quietly, looking down at the ground and then back at her for several seconds. He bit his lower lip and rolled his eyes mischievously. "Momma, are you in dreamland?" he asked, referring to her magic trances.

She laughed and mussed his forelock. "No, honey, just thinking on your daddy, and how brave he was to go off and fight the Wampus."

"Still hunting him, I reckon."

"I reckon." She stared up at the Volcano, grateful Lafette had not asked about the kiss. Henry Kingsley's affection disturbed her even more than King Kingsley's threat. She'd felt the heat of need when his lips touched hers, a want she'd been spared since her final night with Arn, nearly five years ago. She choked back the emotion of missing Arn and wished with all her heart that Henry had surveyed a different mountain this morning.

She cut up crab apples, sprinkled them with sugar and they climbed to the Volcano top to eat them. Katydids and crickets chirped in unison, and from time to time, a dog howled from the direction of Cat's Crossroads. Blue returned the howl. Orion sparkled brightly, and Lafette traced the constellation outline with a finger. He watched Delta cautiously and she suspected his curiosity was getting the better of him. She stroked his hair and scratched the back of his neck. "Go ahead, ask," she said.

"Why did King Kingsley's horse nearly run me down this afternoon?"

"King wants to buy our Tyme trees," Delta answered matter-of-factly.

"Could sure use the money, Momma. We could buy more sugar and white flour and even real coffee so you wouldn't have to make it with meal."

"Your daddy always said when Tyme trees were gone, the magic would sleep." She'd snapped more than she'd meant to and put an arm around his shoulders.

"What if we only sold a few, Ma?" Lafette asked insistently. " 'Cept the Elisha Tree. It's my tree."

"You believe in the magic, don't you?" She could see only the pinkish outline of his face in the dim light given off by the campfire below. Delta waited several seconds, watching Lafette gaze at stars and twist his palms nervously on the rock between his legs. "Here," she said, removing a thin silver ring off her left hand. "What's wrong is you don't remember your daddy." She pushed the ring into his palm. "Keep this as a memory token of him. He gave me this one and he wore one just like it."

Lafette fitted it on his index finger but avoided looking into Delta's eyes by throwing an apple slice to Blue, who gobbled it up. "You could draw a picture of him, Momma. You draw so good."

"Someday, your daddy'll come back and teach you all you need to know." She watched him fingering the ring. "Arn said I'd give birth to the next Watcher. You, son."

Lafette twisted the band on his finger, frowning uncomfortably. Delta squeezed his hand. "Remember the song about your daddy?"

He nodded.

"I'll sing the question and you sing the answer."

Is that yer dog on the railroad track?
That hound belongs to me.
Do you trust a dog running with the pack?
He's a hound of quality.
Do you lock 'im up in the middle of the night?
The devil's got the key.
Who does the devil look like?
He looks just like me.

"But you never tell me what it means, Ma." He twisted her sleeve, teasing her in a high-pitched voice. "Ain't enough to say I have to figure it out myself."

"Then, I won't say it." She tapped the top of his head. "Time you got to bed if you're going froggin' in the morning."

"Don't see why I can't go froggin' at night like ever'body else in the whole, wide world." Lafette slid down the side of the volcano, jumping the last few rocks until he hit the ground, then looked up toward her. "Momma, Henry Kingsley has a comely smile." Before she could respond, he skipped away.

Delta leaned her head sideways onto her shoulder and rubbed the side of her neck. Stars shone like cave crystals against an ebony sky. Kate would be looking at the same stars, and Delta blew out a hard breath that direction as if to blow her away. King Kingsley and his threats also stirred her ire. If only Arn were here, she thought.

"Arn, Arn, Arn." Whispering, she spoke his name into her hands until the fire burned low. On the ground she kicked dirt on the campfire, waiting for it to die out. Burnt wood colored the fragrance of mint growing nearby and the dying embers made her sad.

Yes, Henry Kingsley did have a comely smile. But Arn insisted on more from her than mere romantic love. He was the Watcher, and she had borne his son to stand in his place. Until Arn returned, if he returned, it was up to her to prepare Lafette for his destiny. She would need every ounce of magic the mountain would afford her.

A footstep crunched in the woods. She stood still as a stalking cat. No sound.

"Blue?" she called out, but the puppy did not appear. She hadn't heard clearly enough to recognize if the movement was animal or human. Bears, panthers, even the Wampus hadn't troubled them all year. Kate or even King could be lurking about. Flames licked at the campfire. The eerie orange glow reflected on the Tyme leaves, making them look ablaze. Delta's eyes adjusted to the darkness. Her heart pounded. She could sense a presence near to her.

An owl hooted. Just as she turned, a slender Tyme branch hit her squarely in the chest. She jumped backward and called out in surprise. Clutching the stick, she ran into the house, jamming her body tightly against the door, and with her free arm, pulled her heaviest chair to block it. She held the twig to a lantern Lafette had left burning and shivered at the mutilation of the diamond-shaped Tyme leaves, viciously torn.

As she turned the branch over, her fingers crossed scarred wood. The name *LAFETTE* was carved into the broken branch. Delta didn't know who to suspect—Kate or King. She could hear Lafette's soft snoring from his room. She paused at his door and he turned in his sleep. Blue lay cradled in the curve of his legs. Whoever had threatened her child had made a costly mistake. Of that Delta was sure.

♆ 8 ♆

TOLLIVER LAND
KEEP OFF OR FACE THE OWNER

THE CRUDE SIGN, painted in bright red letters on rotting fence wood, hung directly over Lafette's head. Over his favorite frog pond as well. Damp circles marked his trousers at the knees as he crawled underneath the fence through weeds as tall as his head. The yellowed marsh grass, frosted with morning dew, sprouted from mounds of doughy mud. Green and yellow algae coated the water's edge and his fingers sank into soft, wet sand.

He mashed a clump of grass and wiped it with a burlap sack to make it dry enough to lie on. Sliding on his stomach, he propped up on his chest and stretched out his legs. Then, silently, he waited. A woodpecker hammered a birch tree. A cow mooed. A grasshopper whipped past his nose. Bullfrogs croaked like old women hollering gossip to each other from across the road. Lafette smiled.

His burlap sack twitched from movement of the dozen or so frogs he'd caught early that morning. He peeked over the marsh grass one last time. An overcast sky melted into a gray fog wafting over the pond. Past the swamp, the land sloped into cleared farmland where cattle grazed. Lafette saw no one. He ventured onto the Tolliver property. If his former best friend, Valentine Tolliver, saw him... Fight for sure.

Last time he'd frogged in this pond, Valentine demanded half the frogs since the pond was partly on Tolliver land. Lafette's anger pumped through him as he recalled Valentine rubbing his face in slimy green algae before stealing his frogs. One of these days, he'd leave Valentine with less teeth then he'd started with. Lafette wished his mother would let him frog at night, then he wouldn't have to hide from Valentine.

Lafette wiggled his hand into the weeds and tapped the ground with one finger. The croaks stopped. He held still, sensing the direction one might jump. A fist-size bullfrog leaped over his head. Lafette spun backwards and caught a hind leg. Lafette held it by the backbones to see its full size. The frog gyrated its legs. "Healthy-sized feller." He dropped it into his burlap sack, satisfied with the catch, then wiped his hand on his pants and squatted down into the grass.

Water spiders shot across the lime-colored algae in criss-cross patterns. Good sign of big frogs, he thought, counting the insects. The pond's grassy smell made him sneeze as another deep croak rasped out. He held his breath, delaying a second sneeze and staring into the weeds, daydreaming of what he'd do with the frogs. He'd save half for his mother to fry. Others he'd barter for maple syrup and soda pop unless Delta insisted he get something sensible like white flour or salt. Might be enough left for sugar-rock candy.

His mouth watered thinking of sucking on candy. Next to him, the pond splashed, sprinkling his forehead. He spun around and was hit in the jaw by a rock. Salty tasting blood filled his mouth. His gums stung as he pressed a hand across his lips. Another rock struck his shoulder, knocking him off balance. His leg slid into the green, slimy water. He grabbed a handful of weeds and pulled himself onto land. Three more rocks landed to the right of him, but he could no more see who was throwing them than a fish could see who had hooked it.

Lafette scrambled out of the line of fire. Rocks steadily pelted the dirt around him. He lay tightly against the ground, hoping that the tall weeds hid him. His burlap sack popped up from the frog's springing motion and Lafette got an idea. He twisted the sack opening loosely and waited for the next rock. Soon as he saw the brown stone glide through the air, Lafette tossed the frog sack high as he could.

As the bag opened, frogs flew through the air like sailing leaves. Lafette whipped up to see who attacked him. On top the hill, Valentine Tolliver crouched behind a tulip tree. His mouth hung open and his head cranked upward watching the flying frogs.

Valentine, creek rocks piled beside him, held a stone in his hand poised for throwing. Fury surged through Lafette like grass fire and he ran the narrow strip around the pond. A rock barrage pelted the ground. Lafette dodged, forging his way uphill toward the other boy.

One rock struck Lafette on the shin and he ducked behind a maple tree. Close enough to hear Valentine grunt each time he hurled a rock, Lafette curled around the opposite side of the tree as another stone grazed him just above the ear. With all his might, he ran and head-butted Valentine in the stomach.

The boys tumbled downhill, locked in each other's arms, kicking, scratching, and biting. They landed on a grassy patch, cussing each other for all they were worth.

"Damn you!" Lafette swung at the air. "Ain't on your property."

"Are too!" Valentine shouted, pulling Lafette's hair with one hand and protecting his stomach with the other. "Gonna beat the tar out of you."

Lafette whacked him on head and ran up an embankment. Valentine grunted, chasing Lafette to the next ridge. Breathless, they confronted each other on a mossy knoll.

"Dunderhead!"

"Cedarhead!"

"I'll sock you!" Lafette cocked his arm. A neighing horse distracted Lafette, and Valentine's punch dropped him to his knees. Lafette rolled sideways, expecting Valentine to be on top of him. Instead, his enemy stared past him, down a rocky embankment to a dusty, worn horse path. A galloping horse slowed to a trot.

"Make a sound, I'll belt you one good." Valentine shook a fist.

Lafette rolled onto his stomach and watched a gray horse stop beside a shack. An older man, covered with road dust, dismounted. The horse was packed with a pick and shovel and several empty canvas bags. The man shook his legs out, then cupped his hands around his mouth and whistled like a whip-poorwill. He stayed close to his horse, looping the leather reins through his fingers.

Lafette wondered what Valentine's interest was in this man. He decided then and there that if Valentine had in mind tricking this gent, he'd warn the feller right off.

Before Lafette could come up with a plan, a voice called from behind the shack, "Over here." Polk Owens, an elf-like moonshiner, stepped cautiously toward the man, looking him up and down. "Take off yer hat so I can see yer eyes," Polk said.

"Gonna buy moonshine from Polk," Lafette whispered to Valentine. All the same, Lafette was unable to look away as the man dropped his hat upon Polk's order.

"Shut your mouth," Valentine squealed. "Been studying Polk for a week now, and it ain't moonshine he's a'sellin'." Valentine pointed to a flattened ledge, hidden by the interlocking branches of two pine trees. The boys slipped over the hill and waddled like ducks, inching their way to the shelf. They lay flat with only their heads hanging over the two men.

"Hear somethin'?" Polk asked and sniffed the air.

Polk looked toward their hiding place, and Lafette pulled Valentine back to keep from being seen. Both boys held their breath.

"Nary a thing," answered the stranger.

Only the thickness of the pine trees hid them from Polk's keen eyesight. Lafette had once seen the wiry Polk throw his ax with such strength and aim that he split a Tyme log from the distance of twenty paces.

"If'n some friends are hiding out yonder, thinking you're gonna ambush ole Polk, just you remember, I got me more kin in these hills than a hare." Polk stared intently at the man while scratching his fingers through a chest-level growth of black beard.

The man shook his head to indicate he was alone. Polk's cold voice made Lafette afraid for the man. Polk stretched out his narrow hand and Lafette saw yellow dandelions on the ground between Polk's fingers. The stranger dug into his pocket and pulled out crisp, green bills.

"Law-be!" Lafette tried to stretch for a closer look. "Look at that."

"Bejesuz! Shut up!" Valentine whispered

"Ain't seen cash in a month of Sundays," Lafette said.

"Knew something odd was going on. Everybody that comes for moonshine barters for it, but lately, only strangers are coming and paying cash for a piece of paper."

"Who'd be that foolish?" Lafette's curiosity now burned hot as Valentine's. He held to a pine branch, trying for a better view. Mud caked his pants, weighing him down. His jaw and arm pulsed painfully. Valentine motioned him toward the path down the hill.

"Aiming to find out what they're doing." Valentine clenched his fist and punched his open hand.

For a moment, Lafette suspected this might be a trick to pull him into trouble with Polk. "You a fool? Polk Owens'll shoot you soon as look at your sorry hind-end."

The boys peered over the ledge at the two men again. Lafette too wondered what Polk might be doing. Short and scrawny with a face hard and crinkled as cave rock, Polk stroked an ax handle looped through his pants, keeping his eyes roving in case someone might be out in the woods watching him.

"Whatever he's got, it's making him rich," Valentine said. "A sorry coot like him can get rich, then I can too." Valentine pointed through the pine branches.

Polk pulled a folded paper from his jacket then handed it to the man. Lafette wished he could hear the man's mumbles as he mounted his horse, clutching the paper tightly to his chest. After the stranger rode away, Polk chuckled and kicked a pinecone.

Lafette and Valentine scooted to the right, keeping Polk in sight. He skipped to his shack and lifted a melon-sized gray rock off a waist-high shed built just below a window. He reached inside and pulled out a folded paper like the one he'd given the stranger. Polk tapped the paper to his lips for a kiss, then placed it inside his coat.

"We can steal a bunch of those papers and sell 'em just as easy." Valentine's eyes opened wide with excitement.

Lafette rubbed his neck, watching Polk Owens, who made a game of tossing his hand ax up in the air and catching it before it hit the ground. Other than being afraid of the mountainman, he didn't feel right about stealing, and if Delta found out, she'd tan his hide. But if they could get cash for that paper, they'd sell twice as many in town as Polk could way out here. The old moonshiner wouldn't go into the towns because too likely of running into kinfolk of people he'd killed. Lafette could buy his momma a dress or maybe one of those fancy, knitted shawls he always saw her admiring, and he could buy all the sugar-rock candy he could eat.

"Then sit here like a cedarhead!" Valentine grunted. "I'm gonna get rich!"

"Not without me, you're not!" Lafette followed him down the hill, behind Polk's cabin. Polk whistled to the ax thrust against a log, and after a while, he sang:

"New Orleans Woman, won't ya come out tonight.
Won't ya come out tonight, won't ya come out tonight.
New Orleans Woman, won't ya come out tonight,
And dance by the light of the moon."

"I'll lift," Valentine whispered. "You grab as many as you can carry."

The boys tiptoed alongside the cabin, listening to the steady chop of Polk's ax on the opposite side. Valentine circled his arms around the large stone and gritted his teeth as he lifted. It scraped against the wood and tottered on the shed's edge.

Lafette anchored his back against Valentine, wobbling to and fro, trying to steady the rock. Polk stopped chopping. A fiery heat raced through Lafette and it was all he could do to keep from running.

He twisted around so he could see Valentine, whose bottom lip trembled and his upper curved in a grimace resembling a frog's mouth. Lafette's own quake emerged when he noticed a tuft of black hair nailed to the wall above Valentine's head. Beside it, another scalp of short gray hair, and beyond that a whole line of gray, withered skins with varying hair lengths. Lafette had heard the story of Polk's grandfather's Indian scalps, but this was the first time he'd ever seen them. He hoped it'd be the last time as his hand smoothed the back of his own head.

Lafette eyed the mountain for an escape route. Valentine unwound one arm from the rock long enough to punch Lafette's shoulder. Both boys inhaled in unison. Polk began chopping again, more slowly this time, and whistling rather than singing. Valentine lifted the rock three inches, just enough for Lafette to squeeze an arm into a small crack. He grabbed a fistful of papers only to have them slide from his grip. Valentine's cheeks puffed out into round circles filled with air.

Lafette stared at the Indian scalps, absorbing the eerie power of men whose heads grew that hair. He reached deeper into the shed until his finger caught hold of a string binding a paper bundle. The heavy rock weighted on the lid of the shed mashed against Lafette's arm. He drew the packet toward himself and Valentine stifled a grunt. Lafette jerked his arm free just as Valentine dropped the rock.

"See why you volunteered to lift the rock," Lafette growled, mad enough to punch Valentine. He shoved the bundle into the front of his pants.

"It's him!" Valentine yelled, pointing a shaky finger at Polk who barreled around the cabin. Valentine sped toward the mountains leaving Lafette to face the descendent of an Indian scalper.

"Aiiiiieeee!" Lafette screamed. His leg muscles hardened like rock and his chest expanded like a balloon ready to burst.

"Daggone it!" Polk hollered, seeing papers sticking from Lafette's pants. "Wait 'til I get my hands on you, young'un!" His mouth hung open, huge and wide like a cave. Most of his side teeth were missing, and for a brief moment, Lafette had the feeling of being swallowed. The moonshiner swung his ax up over his head and whirled it around so fast it became a silverish blur.

Lafette broke his trance and galloped after Valentine. The dusty mountain uphill path crumbled under his boots and Lafette slid. His left foot landed on Polk's head. Lafette grabbed onto ivy vines trailing down the mountain and propelled upwards. Polk stomped behind him, cussing as ivy vines snapped under his weight.

Lafette looked up. Valentine motioned him to the top.

"Give me my maps!" Polk shouted.

His gravely voice spurred Lafette the last few feet like a fox running from dogs. They ran along the ridge top through oak trees the size of monuments and poplar trees so tall they seemed like strings dropping from the sky. Both boys were too scared to look back, but every shadow, every noise, even a bird flitting through a tree, could have been Polk, and the boys ran a little faster.

As the mountain sloped into a gentle valley, Valentine pointed to a ridge across from them. Lafette nodded to indicate he understood that Cumberland Gap was on the other side and Polk probably wouldn't venture that far to find them.

They slowed to a trot. Valentine held his side and looked as if he might be sick. A shallow creek cut through the crease of the valley and both boys fell on their stomachs and sucked in water. Lafette sat up first and leaned against a fallen cedar tree. He pulled the bundle of papers from the top of his pants and straightened them in a pile before him.

"I earned more of these then you did," Lafette said.

Valentine rolled over onto his back and stared blankly at the sky. "What do you mean, you earned more?"

"I'm the one who almost had his scalp hung on Polk's wall." Lafette pushed up his shirtsleeves. "I'm the one who lost all my frogs on account of you, and I'll go straight to your daddy and tell him that you put them baby chicks in Teacher's boots that caused us to get kicked out of school."

"Was only fourth grade we got kicked out of." Valentine rolled his eyes.

"Momma got real upset."

"Never could figure why Teacher thought you put them chicks in his boots. He kicked me out cause I laughed at him, not 'cause he thought I had anything to do with it."

"He kicked me out 'cause of who my daddy is."

"Sure was funny when he squished them chicks."

The silence that followed was one the boys had shared many times. They'd fall into their silence on days when Valentine's father had worked him in the fields from sun up to sun down, or at times when Lafette was forced into defending the character of his own father, usually against adults whose cowardice and ignorance gave them pleasure in taunting children. *A fine quiet*, Valentine had once called it. After every fight, they fell into their silence and listened to squirrels chatter to one another, the gurgle of creek water or the sound of their own breathing as they sat on a high mountain peak, staring out at nothing in particular.

"Let's see what we got." Lafette opened a paper. He recognized Shadow Mountain but it was drawn as if someone had guessed about the northern slope where Kate Huston lived. Cumberland Mountain was sketched on the wrong side and Midnight Valley situated too far away. But a stranger might never figure it out, Lafette thought. And a dunderhead like Valentine would never see the mountain in a bunch of lines.

"Swift's Silver Mine Map." Valentine slowly sounded out the words as well as his fourth grade education allowed.

"Reckon these might bring a good price in town," Lafette said. "We'd have to go somewhere where they'd believe in Swift's Silver."

"I believe in Swift's Silver," Valentine said, strumming his thumb against his sleeve for good luck. "Story is a surveyor named John Swift found the mother lode of silver pirate coins. Hid 'em so well that nobody would every find 'em. Luck would have it, he went blind. Couldn't find his own fortune. John Swift's silver, everybody knows about it."

"Momma told me it was made up." Lafette scrunched his face to mock Valentine.

"Daddy thinks Old Man Kingsley owns the land where Swift found his silver."

Lafette looked at the map again and wondered if he should tell Valentine that it was a diagram of Shadow Mountain. "Where on his land?" Lafette asked.

"Don't rightly know, but Daddy's gonna buy land from the Kingsleys."

"All the more reason for us to sell these maps to somebody we can fool into believing it."

"We ought to follow it ourselves." Valentine's eyes sparkled at the prospect of treasure.

"Mountain people won't pay money on a fool's quest like this and I won't waste the time." Lafette tossed the map to the ground to indicate his disbelief in the legend. "Think Polk'll come after us?"

"Naw, he don't take to town folk and they'd never believe him over us anyhow."

"You sure?"

"Yeah, I'm sure. I'm a Tolliver, and you're a... a dern good salesman. You're in charge of selling the first map."

Lafette folded the paper and rebound the maps together with the string. A bluebird pecked in the dirt a few yards away. "Momma always says a blue jay is good luck," Lafette said, pointing at the bird. "Reckon we can't help but get rich."

Valentine beat his fists against his chest and howled like a wolf. "Richer than everybody in the world!" He jumped on a cedar log and marched along it until he missed a step and fell into a clover patch. "I'm so happy I could die!"

"Sorry is what you'll be when I get my hands on two little heathens!" Polk Owens stood twenty feet away. He spat tobacco juice about half that distance, then aimed and threw his ax. It lodged into the wood beside Lafette's head.

"Run for it!" Lafette yelled.

The boys splashed across the creek and into the woods. Polk whooped and hollered as he pursued them. He laughed a high-pitched nasal honk, almost as if chasing them was more fun than catching them.

They slid down an embankment to a seldom used road leading to Cumberland Gap. Lafette pointed at a rickety, wooden bridge strung across Cave Creek. "Hide there." They scrambled under the bridge, holding their hands over their mouths to slow their huffing breath.

"Look." Valentine pointed at a set of three cracked slats in the bridge's crosswalk. He reached up and pushed against the wood. A shower of rotting wood slivers dusted the boys. Valentine grinned crookedly.

"It'd never work," Lafette said, "He'll kill us if he catches us."

Valentine held his hands to his side, drawing in air gulps. "Can't run no more."

Lafette helped Valentine push the broken wooden slats so they looked solid as the rest of the bridge. Polk hollered uphill from them.

Valentine cupped his hands around his mouth and yelled, "Over here, cedarhead!" He motioned for Lafette to help him hold up the bridge slats.

Lafette moaned. Why had he let himself be talked into this? Polk stepped onto the bridge. The wooden slats creaked. Lafette squeezed his eyes closed. Any minute Polk's ax might slice into his skull. He opened one eye and stared into the water at tiny, brown minnows scurrying about.

Polk took another step closer. "Hee, hee, hee, gonna hang me some boys by their heels. Hee, hee, hee, gonna skin ye like squirrels. Fatten ye up, and feed ye to the hogs."

Dirt and wood-shedding sprayed Lafette from above. Polk stopped directly over him. Lafette held his breath. Sweat dripped down his forehead and tickled his nose. One more step. Please take one more step, Lafette prayed harder than he ever had.

"Now!" Valentine yelled.

Lafette released the slats just as Polk stepped onto them. Polk fell through and landed face down in the creek. He floated for several seconds, sat up and groaned. One hand rubbed a bump on his head, then he fell forward, knocked out as if he'd drunk too much of his own moonshine.

The boys waited until they were sure he was not playing opossum, then dragged Polk from the creek. They left him on shore with a map open across his face and the initials L.M. and V.T. painted with mud on each of his cheeks.

♆ 9 ♆

DELTA FORCED HERSELF to walk to Kate's cabin instead of raging in like a storm. She tightened her grip on the Tyme branch thrown at her the night before. Each time her fingers touched Lafette's carved name a chill slid up her spine. She vented that fear into anger, aiming it like an arrow directly at Kate.

The mountain's north side smelled like the old woman, a mixture of sour grass and burnt wood. Delta spat to clear the scent from her head. A rocky slope plunged into a series of gullies. She lost her footing, and to keep balanced, clung to Tyme roots whose trees grew far up the ridge. Sandy grit blew into her eyes, slowing her journey.

Though the flaky soil appeared incapable of supporting much life, Tyme trees grew twice the size of any on her part of the mountain; massive spider webs stretched between trees like bridges, gray lizards darted under rocks, and flora sprang from places as unusual as snake holes. Delta hated admitting this side of the mountain frightened her. Yet she was drawn to it in spite of her fear. Its isolation held an attraction as much as its odd combination of barrenness and life.

Soon a flat shingled roof appeared. Delta traveled a deeply worn path that wound down the hill into the backyard. She remembered the summer she'd spent cutting back wild rose vines and the thorns that stuck her bare feet. The extra time it took to climb a narrow ledge allowed her to collect her thoughts. Don't let her think she troubles me, Delta told herself. Act like she doesn't matter at all.

Wind blew white dandelion tufts into her face. She rubbed her nose as a wave of queasiness churned in her stomach. The mountain quivered with obstacles. Almost seemed the plants might reach up and bind her where she stood. So far, she had seen a fox den, lizards, a raccoon, and opossum. Any of those could be Kate's familiars.

A red ant train chained up a tree and a dozen dragonflies circled under a Tyme grove. She eyed the insects suspiciously and touched a safekeeping charm in her pocket. A golden hawk swooped overhead and landed in a tree beside the house. Delta watched it carefully, knowing the feeling of being a baby rabbit. The bird shot up into the sky like an arrow and she couldn't see where it landed. A squirrel poked its head from a fallen log and Delta hissed toward it. Must'nt let anything interfere with my thoughts, she said to herself.

The cabin balanced on a ledge overlooking a rocky gulf. Its gray hewn logs were ragged at the ends. Some from the porch had fallen and not been replaced. A Tyme tree, barely high as the porch back when she'd lived here, now overhung it, shading most the front yard. She swallowed the slightest bit of nausea as she approached, feeling the vibration of Kate's protection spells.

Delta squeezed her charm and stepped onto the porch. Every breath shivered as they rose in her chest. She couldn't help comparing her fear now to the first time she'd come here as a teenager. "You've grown up now," she whispered. "No need to fear Kate." The hawk, perched on a chicken coop, twisted its head sideways and blinked its eye at her. Beyond the coop, an outhouse and a smokehouse sat on opposite sides of the yard. Salted meat in the smokehouse smelled bloody.

Delta put a palm against the door. She started to call out, but her mouth dried up as quickly as she swallowed. The door scraped against the floorboards as she pushed it open. The woodsy smell of yew and cloves blew past. First herbs she taught me to use, Delta thought, unable to resist memories of learning herb lore and midwifery from Kate so many years ago.

A corn shuck mattress filled the east corner. A gray stone fireplace formed the south wall and a blackened cauldron hung over an unlit fire. Beside it, herbs, bones, and potions filled shelf after shelf. No jar seemed out of place. All as she remembered. Long, leathery tobacco strands hung from the ceiling and the acidic odor vied with the fragrance of herbs. Flies circled over a water bucket in the back corner. An oak table pushed up under a window served as the kitchen.

Kate sat in a cane chair, her back toward Delta. Her loose hair lay in silver waves down her back, hands moving in circles just above the table. Delta stared over Kate's shoulder. Her former mentor had yet to detect her presence. Every few seconds, she rearranged feathers and Tyme leaves against a red cloth. Delta recognized it to be the same kind of safekeeping charm she'd made for herself. Kate's shoulders rose up and drooped with deep breaths.

Delta tossed the Tyme branch on the table, scattering the feathers and Tyme leaves. Kate jumped, knocking the chair backwards. Her glazed eyes blinked several times before she realized who stood with her. She stared at the branch, picked it up, rolled it between her palms and studied it. Her lined forehead intensified dark circles under her eyes.

Delta hadn't expected restrained behavior. Kate always fought with her, ever since Delta had ceased being her student and had gone to live with Arn. This Kate looked older, more like an old granny than the tough woman Delta knew her to be.

"You did this?" Delta pointed at the branch, struggling to maintain an even voice.

Kate turned the branch in her hands, saw the carved name and wrinkled her face as if the sight pained her. "Delta," she said softly, "let me have the mountain."

Delta ripped the branch from Kate's hand and shook it at her. "You're lucky I even tolerate you on this mountain."

"I know you only tolerate me."

Kate's humility surprised Delta. Kate moved like a bear waking from hibernation. This skilled teacher Delta had studied with, picked up the overturned chair, replacing it in its exact spot.

"Everything in its place," Delta said. "Mine's on the mountain, waiting for Arn."

"You don't know what's happened." Kate lowered herself into the chair, crossed her arms, each hand grasping the opposite shoulder and rocked to and fro.

As sad as Kate looked, Delta was still suspicious. This woman plagued her and Arn like a mother hen for too many years. "For once," Delta said, "Think of what Arn would expect. He'd never approve of how you've acted these past years."

"Arn never loved you." Kate spoke without passion as if already drained of emotion the words might evoke. "He only needed you."

Delta's temper flared like coal fire. She picked up the branch and as she'd planned, began breaking it into tiny pieces. Kate didn't seem to notice or care as Delta dropped the pieces on the floor. *Returning your bad spell to you*, Delta repeated in her mind. *Returning your bad spell to you in pieces.*

"My sister sent me a bad luck coin and prophesied a Judas rising. She's Fox Clan so you know she knows."

"Only bad luck around here is you." Delta dropped the last piece of the twig, delighted that Kate hadn't realized the spell was broken in pieces. She'd done what she came to do, returned the bad spell to Kate. She turned to leave.

Kate shot up from the table and took hold of Delta's arm, jerking her around. "Open your ears, woman! Open your eyes! You'll know it too! Practice what I taught you!"

Kate's fingers pressed into Delta's flesh. It had been thirteen years since the two women had touched and the sensation stirred memories of what was once friendship. Kate's eyes watered, the white bloodshot with red streaks. Delta pulled back, inadvertently stepping on the dog's tail. The hound's high-pitched yelp caused the women to grab hold of each other. The awkward closeness repelled them a second later.

Delta reached down to soothe the dog and noticed Lafette's puppy was the same shade of gray. No, she thought. I warned him a dozen times to stay away Kate. "Your kind of magic is for children and old women. I've enough duties tending to things Arn said needed done. I guard the volcano and the Tyme trees."

"Don't you know what a bad luck coin means?"

Delta thought back to the time when she was a very small child. Alonzo Grandley had refused to sell corn meal to Melungeons, Indians, and black people. The watcher then had been a man named Elisha Thunderheart who protected deserving mountaineers like a cougar defending territory, and he'd buried a bad luck coin beneath the Grandley Mill. Delta could still see the orange flames carving into the night sky. The Grandleys lost all they owned and afterwards had moved west. The youngest daughter returned when Delta was a young woman and told the story of how half the family had drowned in a Missouri flood while others had been cut down by a blistering fever. The few Grandleys left in the world were scattered like leaves in the wind. Only Delta, Arn, and Kate had known that the bad luck coin still lay buried in the ashes. Each had been too afraid to retrieve it. Arn had told her to let Elisha's bad luck spell always haunt that place. Since then, no one had moved into the area, for reasons they could only cite as a *bad feelin'*.

"How could we fight a bad luck coin?" Delta said. "*If* you really got one." Kate's being sly, she thought. To trust Kate, even if there is a Judas, would mean aligning with her. What would be worse, having to deal with a Judas or Kate?

"For my own sister to send me bad luck means no escape from what's destined." Kate rose, untying her apron. She studied shelves of herbs and roots. Golden seal and chicory hung from the ceiling and ginseng she'd picked the day before was laid out on white cloth. Kate opened her arms toward her store of plants, flowers, and herbs that'd taken a lifetime to collect. "It'll take all I know to save this mountain."

"Tricks." Delta crossed her arms. "Just like a broken branch meant to scare me."

"I can change this bad luck before it's put in motion." Kate's voice had a pleading quality that made Delta nervous. "I must re-birth my link with the power of Arn's Volcano. I can't do it lessen I alone rule the mountain. I must be at the volcano night and day." She stood in front of Delta like a schoolmarm, holding her by both arms. "We'll both lose, if I don't do this. If you don't trust me, then leave Lafette with me, but only I can be at the mountaintop. Two women dilute the power."

Delta jerked free and started to the door. The gray dog barked as if to protect Kate. She shook her finger at Kate. "I know you too well. You'll smother Lafette the way you did Arn, break him the way you did that branch."

"A man without his heritage is like a fish in a stream," Kate said. "Always coming back to the same place but never knowing why."

"Don't you even think it!"

"Lafette should be told he's of Melungeon blood."

"You of all people know how Melungeons are treated. You know how Arn was treated. Probably a handful of people left alive who might suspect Arn was Melungeon, and when they're dead, no one will know. My son needn't find out. If you cared for Arn as you say, you'll respect his wishes."

"What do you know of Arn's wishes, silly girl? Should've sent you away the first time Arn laid eyes on you."

"Every man grows up to leave his mother and you could never let Arn go. That's why I'll never let you know his son."

Kate's face colored a cherry red and she bit her bottom lip, then glared at Delta. "This mountain is mine as Arn was once mine."

"You lost him by your own nature, Kate."

"Arn didn't even know how to become Watcher. I told him how. I told him and he betrayed me to become Watcher. Acted to Elisha like it'd come to him in a vision and Pappy took it to be the deed that proclaimed him the new Watcher."

"That's a lie."

"And you betrayed me, too. I took you in when your people barely fed you."

"The devil take you."

"Don't you even know where Arn got his silver? Don't you know he and Pappy Thunderheart had a falling out 'cause of it?"

Deltas whirled around to escape and slammed open the door, causing a patter of acorns from a nearby tree. The gray dog bared its teeth and growled. She threw the safekeeping charm and the dog yelped and sneezed. "You're a jealous old woman, Kate. I'll not lose the memory of Arn to you, anymore than I'll lose my son or my mountain."

Kate barreled out onto the porch after her, shaking a fist. "I've asked you as a sister, and you've refused, so the mountain will be mine by week's end or it'll be lost. You've your little tricks," she said, indicating the sneezing dog, "but you're no match for me. Lafette already thinks of me as more a mother than he does you."

Delta whipped around, staring at Kate in disbelief. Kate's hand covered her lips as if she'd spoken before realizing it. Delta narrowed her eyes. "My boy comes here?"

"You drive him away, Delta. You'll lose him to me as surely as I lost Arn to you. But I will have my mountain back. I will not lose that to anybody."

∞

Delta dashed up the path. Kate's tirade followed her until the voice blended with the wind. In her mind she argued with Kate. Could her words be true? Could Kate have told Arn how to become Watcher? Could he have betrayed Kate and fooled Pappy Thunderheart into placing him as Watcher? Kate would not have fought Arn because she loved him as a son, that was, until Arn took Delta to live with him. By that time, Elisha Thunderheart was dead, and Kate could appeal to no one. Could this be true? Was Arn no more than a confidence man?

Delta collapsed at Cat's Crossroads. The late afternoon sun burned, and her dress was soaked with sweat. Kate lies are meaningless, she thought, unbuttoning her dress at the throat. What matters is what's true today. Today, I own Shadow Mountain and it'll be mine for life and my boy's after that. Delta trembled as an unexpected, cold wind blew. She looked at the sun but no cloud had obscured it.

She squeezed her hands into tight fists. Deep in thought and trying to sense Kate's presence, she sniffed various directions. "What will you do?" she repeated softly to the road and the trees, to the flowers and rocks all along the road. The words repeated inside her mind over and over: *The only way to limit her power is to get her off the mountain.*

A trotting horse broke her concentration but not her link to the land. The horse appeared in a gray cloud, hooves drumming the ground. The horse reared and a rider nearly fell. Delta thought it was Kate's apparition sent to scare her.

The horse turned swiftly. "YOU WILL LEAVE THIS MOUNTAIN!" she hollered into the animal's face, imagining a clear picture of Kate. The horse reared again and galloped off, its rider unable to gain control. "You might make a cold breeze appear as a horse wanting to run me down, but I'll throw your tricks back on you every time. You've no chance, Kate! No chance while I'm alive and breathing!"

♆ 10 ♆

HENRY BATTLED HIS runaway horse, Zeus, tugging on the reins until he thought his arms would rip from the sockets. Shadow Mountain's terrain could unexpectedly drop like a cliff, or protruding Tyme roots could catch a hoof. Zeus galloped as if fleeing a fire. Henry could do nothing but cling to the panicking horse, keeping his weight centered to help Zeus' balance in the treacherous terrain, but the animal jumped a fallen log, slamming his shoulder into a tree branch. Henry gave a cry, as much of exasperation as pain. He'd trained Zeus himself, even won first place in an equestrian event at the Claiborne County Fair. What had got into the horse?

Near the bottom of Shadow Mountain, precisely next to Lafette's Elisha Tree, Zeus halted. Henry kept going, tumbling over the horse's neck. He landed on his back, the breath knocked out of him. Through half-opened eyes he stared up into Zeus's face. The stallion snorted. Saliva dripped onto Henry's chest. "What in blazes is wrong with you?" he snapped at the animal. Zeus stood quietly, his heaving sides and musky odor the only evidence of the wild ride down the mountain.

Henry worked each limb of his body to check for injury. His ankle cracked as he revolved his foot in a circle. "Took you up there to show you off, fool," he said to Zeus. "Was gonna offer her a ride. She's never been on a trained horse like you." He tapped the horse's nose. "Now we're going up there and apologize if I have to break your back to do it." Zeus slipped over to the creek and drank, ignoring Henry as he dusted off his pants.

Despite Henry's stern talk, the horse would not step a hoof up the mountain. He kicked Zeus's sides repeatedly, but the prize-winning stallion reared and bucked rather than go any farther up Shadow Mountain. Henry stared at Arn's Volcano and thought about Delta sitting up there, probably thinking she'd scared him away for good. He wanted to prove to her that he was above his father's petty arguments, that he could be her friend. He longed to see her, if only for a few moments. The want gnawed like hunger in his belly.

"Wonder what she thinks of me now, letting her scare me off like that?" He glared at Zeus. "Letting her scare you." Henry got off and tried leading the horse, but Zeus backed up, rearing again. "Stubborner than a mule! Enter you in a mule show next time! See how you like that!" Zeus snorted.

Finally, Henry mounted and started for home, shaking his head in disbelief. If he was amazed at any of these events, it was at Delta's power over his horse. "Delta Wade, Delta Wade, Delta Wade," he repeated. She had to be the most mysterious creature he'd ever encountered, and at the same time, he snickered, realizing that a woman had actually scared his splendid stallion so badly he acted like a scared mouse. Henry had spent years training horses, but he'd never seen anything like it. As child he'd loved horses more than anything else on earth. Merging his will with a horse's became his study and his art. Now, Delta had made a mockery of his years of work. No woman had ever made him feel so inadequate. It intrigued him more than he could even admit.

∞

All the way home, Zeus performed whatever task Henry commanded. The horse trotted, cantered, stepped sideways, and galloped as if it hadn't a care in the world. "No carrots for you," Henry whispered in the animal's ear as he threw the reins to a stable boy.

Henry dusted his pants again and tapped the toe of each boot against the front porch steps. He'd soak in a tub of hot water and try again tomorrow with a different horse. "Nancy," he yelled as he entered the hallway. "Bath. Now!"

Amos called out from the library, "Henry, your daddy's in the dining room."

Not up to a quarrel about the trees, Henry limped to the staircase. "Later."

"It's important, Henry." Amos looked up from his bookwork on the weekly accounts. "Getting high in your ways, Henry." Amos rose and sauntered to the door, taking in Henry's filthy clothes. "Sometimes we old school chums got to tell each other."

"Never been your friend." Henry leaned on the hall table, smearing the shine, and picked up a dusting cloth wipe down the top of his boots. "Don't forget who's the Kingsley and who's the butler."

"Ain't forgot. All the same, I'll still remind you if you get to acting like a prize cock in the hen house." Amos smiled in his set way when he prodded Henry and pointed at the dining room door.

Slapping dust off his pants, Henry stepped hard toward the room to display his annoyance. “Prize cock,” he muttered under his breath, turned toward Amos and threw the dusting cloth at him. Amos caught the towel and grinned sarcastically before returning to his bookkeeping.

The dining room door opened quietly. The drawn curtains darkened the room except for a yellowish glow of candlelight. “Daddy?”

“Surprise!” His father, Diane Pratt, and her daughter, Penny, were gathered at the dining room table. A pink birthday cake on a crystal platter centered the table. An embarrassed rush filled Henry as the three crowded about him. Penny reached around his neck and tried kissing him. Her beaked nose pressed into his chin, and reluctantly, he leaned down. Henry shuddered involuntarily as he watched the bony girl’s blurred reflection kiss him in the oak table’s shine.

“Congratulations,” his father beamed. “About time we had celebrations in this house again.” His father, dressed in a gray suit, smelled of cologne and chewing tobacco.

Diane Pratt held out a tiny hand as if expecting it to be kissed. Henry shook it. She was still handsome with her black hair piled atop her head, perhaps more so than her daughter, but Henry always noticed her greedy eyes and remembered the five husbands she’d already buried. She still wore her last wedding ring, a two-carat diamond that Henry suspected was only glass. She constantly twirled a hair ringlet so anyone looking at her would see the ring.

“Henry, you’re like a son to me,” Diane said, one eye on the crystal lamps adorning each corner table. “Penny and me couldn't miss your thirtieth birthday." She held Penny by her narrow shoulders and thrust her toward him.

"Daddy, not got words for how this makes me feel." Henry flashed stern eyes at his father and swore to himself that he'd get Amos for taunting him away from the bath. Penny pulled him to the table. The pink icing cake had blue letters spelling his name and the words: FOR A BRIGHT FUTURE.

"Don't you fuss at your pa," Penny said, "It was all my idea." She smiled widely, revealing a roan center tooth and an overbite that made her resemble his horse.

"You shouldn't have." Henry twisted his arm from Penny's grip.

Nancy brought in plates and a milk pitcher. Penny cut the cake, talking nonstop as she passed each piece. "I thought what a good excuse to get Henry Kingsley to our church social. If I bring him a birthday cake, he can't refuse."

"Don't go to church," Henry said.

"High time you did!" King patted Diane's arm and nodded as she leaned in and smiled at him.

"You don't go to church either." Henry stared hard at his father.

"I can do something about that." Diane beamed at King and pinched his cheek. "Even the Governor will be there. We're speaking to him about opening the Four Seasons Hotel again. If we can raise the money, we'll inspire a belief in our community and make a place where people like us can congregate."

"Pete McGinnis come by for the Quinntown bid?" Henry interrupted, hoping to change the subject and perhaps bore the women into leaving. If he had to listen to Diane and Penny's put-on accent much longer, he'd explode.

"He did and I'm sure as shootin' that we'll win it."

"Sorry it didn't work out on the Tyme trees but they'll be happy with white oak, even if we do only half as good a job as we did on the Inez Coal Camp."

"We'll do an even better job." King's lips curved up on one side. "Because we're gonna do it with Tyme tree."

The cake Henry swallowed stuck in his throat and he coughed. Penny rubbed his back and left her hand dangling on his shoulder.

"What do you mean?" Henry asked, swallowing hard.

"Gonna file a lawsuit," King announced.

"How exciting." Diane clapped her thin hands.

Henry noticed how both women looked like birds. Skinny, long-legged herons.

"Yep." King wolfed down a large bite of cake. "Ain't widely known, but Arn Marlon was Melungeon. Melungeons is descendent from slaves and they can't own land under Tennessee's miscegenation law. A Melungeon got their land taken away in Kingsport about a year ago for the same reason."

"Miscegenation is about marriage, Daddy, not land ownership. I know about the Kingsport case and that's not what the court ruled."

"We'll make it happen that way in our county." He nodded at Diane who smiled demurely every time King spoke.

Henry doubted that either woman understood his father's rambling. Diane steadily stroked King's arm and Penny pined at Henry with wide cow eyes. "You can't do that to Delta," Henry frowned at his father. "You know well as I do that some Melungeons, including Arn Marlon, are as white as you and me."

"Not like Delta Wade's anything to you, Henry." Penny touched a finger to his ear and caressed his jaw.

"Henry, you talk like you care for the girl." Diane fanned her neck with a bony hand. "She's a Wade and we all know about them."

Henry stood, sending his plate crashing to floor. "Rather kiss a horse than let a scrawny heron tell me who I can and can't care for."

"Those Wades were trash. That's not my opinion, that's fact." Diane talked to King and ignored Henry.

King kicked Henry's chair under the table but Henry was in no mood to take nonsense from a heron. "Might please you to know, I'm marrying Delta Wade. So watch how you speak about my future wife, Mrs. Pratt or whatever your name is now."

"Marrying?" King said, coming to his feet.

Henry realized what he'd said. Diane dabbed her forehead with a hanky, eyes intense, trying to figure her next move. Penny's eyes brimmed with tears.

"You'll marry a Wade over my grave!" King said.

"I can't believe this is happening to me again!" Penny fell into her mother's arms and bawled loudly on her shoulder.

Henry couldn't think. Nancy groveled around his legs, picking up broken plate and spilt cake. Penny sobbed uncontrollably. King's puffed-out cheeks turned red as a rooster's comb. Stunned, Henry realized he'd announced his marriage.

"You're an ill-mannered young man." Diane held her daughter and cocked her head stiffly. "Some day you'll learn that true quality is more than a romp in the hay." Diane shifted toward the door and touched King's arm. "I'm truly sorry for you, King."

"And I'm sorry for myself." King patted Diane's shoulder closing the dining room door behind them. His father whirled toward him, both hands anchored on his hips. "Insulting 'em weren't called for, Will Henry."

"Can't you see she's a grave-digging old heron?" Henry pointed out the window. Diane flung a whip over her shoulder and struck the horse pulling their carriage. "How can you compare them to Momma or Rebecca?"

"Son, when Rebecca died, it broke my heart as surely as it did yours. But that was two years ago and you've lived in grief long enough. High time you married. But not to a Wade."

"If and when I marry, it'll be my choice, Daddy." Henry crossed his arms. "Delta's a fine woman. I'll not have you talk against her."

"So fine she sicced a dog on your father." King slammed a hand against the dining room table, causing the crystal cake platter trembled. "Listen to me!"

Henry knew that had he been five years younger, he'd have felt his father's hand across his face. He drew strength from his mother's and Rebecca's pictures. The mahogany table created a burst of color under the photos' greenish tints. The silver frames faced each other, but the faces in the black and white photographs looked different directions as if protecting both sides of the house. Rebecca looked curiously at the camera; his mother stared into the distance. The sadness he'd felt standing over their graves returned to him. He picked up his mother's picture, wishing she were here. It had been his mother, and then Rebecca, who had given him the strength to stand up to King, and now, Delta inspired the same spirit in him. "You've bullied me all my life and I've given in, but I'll not be whipped on this one. Drop that lawsuit!"

"You'd turn against me for a Wade?" His father's stern eyes focused into his.

Behind King, a ray of sunlight fell on Rebecca's photo. There was a side to Rebecca that was like Delta, Henry thought, in the way she stood her ground when she believed he was wrong. At that moment, Henry would have given his life to be in Rebecca's arms, but his father, persistent as a wasp, circled in front of him. "I'm not against you, Daddy, but I'll not see Delta hurt." Henry swung open the dining room door and bolted up the staircase two steps at a time, not waiting for his father to answer. "If Delta don't want her Tyme trees cut, we won't cut them."

☫ 11 ☫

DELTA SPRINKLED TOBACCO around Arn's Volcano and stuck yellow hawk feathers in the cracks. She focused on dressing the rock exactly as Arn had during his rituals. On the opposite side, a smooth rock basin opened to the horizon. She removed a stone, allowing water to fill the bowl. Delta dusted cobwebs, removed stray leaves and cleaned with the tail of her dress. From this spot, Arn had awakened a volcanic power in the form of a giant, vaporous dragon. Tonight, she would attempt to do the same.

She bathed in the creek, crushed dried dogbane on her skin and rubbed verbena oil on her forehead, chest, belly, and feet. Scents to purify and protect her. Covered in a deerskin cape, she waited for sunset, then opened her arms to the vast expanse of sky as if to embrace the scarlet horizon. Delta moved around the massive structure, stretching her body against the black stone, and singing holy words Arn'd used to awaken its spirit.

"Blood of the earth,
Flow through me.
Bring forth your shadow."

She lifted a shred of thorn apple to her lips. *The vision herb,* Arn'd called it. Taking it under her tongue, she sucked the sour taste then folded her hands, prayer-like, and waited for the volcanic vibration. No energy emerged. She repeated the words again. Nothing. What was she doing wrong? By this time, Arn was so filled with power that he appeared twice his true size. Delta had only watched him perform the ceremonies, but they'd worked for him. With this ritual he'd saved Fork Ridge from violent Wampus attacks; and another time, he made the entire valley disappear and so confused an investor group that they left without buying a single parcel of land. This had to work. Both her and Lafette's futures depended on it.

Trembling, she stared into the darkness of the water. "Tell me," she said. "Tell me what I need to know. Tell me how to rid this mountain of my enemies." Dead to her touch. No glow came. No voice spoke. No smoky light appeared as when Arn read the future. She blew her breath onto it and waited. Her hands trembled, nervously rubbing the smooth stone. No life, no spirit, offered aid. Delta kicked a mound of tobacco. She fled to her house, unable to cry, unable to think. Failure.

Her house smelled of smoke and yew leaves. "Kate. Kate!" She half expected to find the old woman. Her presence was in the house even if she was not. Delta flung open windows and doors. "Get out!" She grabbed a blanket and shook it, imagining her hands gripping Kate's throat. She bounced on the bed and buried her face. Dust from the corn-shuck stuffed mattress filled her nostrils.

She concentrated on Kate, probing deeply into her own mind. She needed more than she could see and pressed her thoughts into a dream. An insect buzzed. She drifting dreamily, following a hollow ring, and woke on waxy surface. She climbed upward in a giant beehive. An enormous queen with large black eyes followed her, wings vibrating a wind. The queen took flight, knocking her aside. Delta watched the whirls and leaps of the queen bee with her army of workers and drones following her like a cape.

The queen bore down on Delta. She turned, no place to run but into the hive. She crawled into a five-sided chamber just as a new queen emerged. Delta screamed, caught in the path of the new queen's birth. A blood bath would follow when the queens met. A sappy substance stuck to her, preventing movement. She could not reason with forces that did not speak her language. Why had she even attempted to awaken the power of the volcano? She was out of control. Unable to save herself. The two queens faced off. Their buzzing burst inside her head.

She jerked awake. Her skin itched as if covered with insects. Yes, Kate was after her. And Kate was winning. Delta sensed her in every corner of the room. She found drawing paper and sketched, frantic and without thought. Her hands moved across the paper with a purpose not her own. When she'd finished, she held it out. A beekeeper's bonnet.

How could she hope to stop Kate, who knew so much more about the workings of the mountain? "When bees fill their hives, I rob them and sell the honey," Delta thought aloud. If the queen flies, I smoke her back to the hive and the other bees follow. The beekeeper controls the bees through the smoke. That's it!" She jumped up and struck her fist in the air. "The mountain is all Kate knows."

Delta would get help from the outside, just as a beekeeper controls bees. That had to be what the vision was telling her. "Kate only knows the mountain, but I know the outside world and how to deal with its people." She fished out a mirror from a chest and combed her fingers through her hair. At daybreak she would travel down Shadow Mountain and re-enter the world.

ѱ 12 ѱ

"JOHN SWIFT'S SILVER!" Lafette mimicked peddlers who set up wagons around the Cumberland Gap Trading Post. "Maps from the same scholars that unlocked the secrets of the pyramids!" The vendors arriving early in the morning were forced to stay at least fifty feet from the store or the owner, Bill Linville, would shoot at them for stealing his business.

So far the boys hadn't sold a single map. "Let's head down by the courthouse." Valentine pointed at yet another ox cart teetering sideways with weighty cargo shifting into position. "These people ain't buying nothing."

"Folks over there won't believe in Swift's silver. Better off selling to peddlers or Kingsley lumberjacks."

"Bejezus, bet I could sell a map to ole Judge Treadway himself."

"Bunch of lumberjacks got laid off this week," Lafette said. "Heard the Quinntown coal job is stalled. They'll be looking for ways to make money."

Pots and pans clanged, mixing with a clamor of foreign languages. Lafette could distinguish Italian and German accents but still had trouble with Irish and deep South. "Look yonder." A heavyset peddler with red sideburns growing down his cheeks locked arms with a much shorter, dark-skinned Italian.

"You take too much room!" the first man said in a crusty and unyielding Irish brogue. The Italian shot back a curse no one could understand except his wife, who wailed at the top of her lungs. Two lumberjacks pulled the traders apart. The Irish man cussed and the Italian spat.

"Wonder why them lumberjacks tore 'em apart?" Valentine murmured. "I'd like to've seen a good fight."

"Them's our first customers." Lafette steered Valentine toward the Trading Post steps and had him hold up the maps for the men to see as they passed.

The sun heated the air to an uncomfortable stickiness. Two horses tied to a hitching post swished their tails at flies buzzing circles around their hind legs. One whizzed past Valentine's nose and he swatted it with a map.

"Don't damage the merchandise, cedarhead!" Lafette jerked the maps away and laid them on the porch, smoothing their weathered edges. "Their look is as important as what they are." He pointed at the Trading Post window where drab brown overalls lay stacked next to tin buckets and shiny axes with cherry red handles.

"Dumbest thing I've ever done." Valentine scratched the crown of his head. "Standing here all morning and ain't sold nary a one. They ain't gonna buy a map. They just want to stuff their faces." A lumberjack passed, wolfing down a hunk of cornbread. "Bejezus, if we had a lick of sense we'd follow this map ourselves."

"Ain't no Swift's silver." Lafette scrunched up his face.

"Heard talk there's not only silver but gold, jewels, all sorts of treasures."

Lafette watched the lumberjacks inspect saws hanging on a nearby wagon, and thought, if there'd been silver on Shadow Mountain he'd have found it by now. He knew every inch of that mountain, except the northeast end beyond Kate Huston's cabin where he'd only been a few times because it was so dark and spooky. Every time he ventured there, he had nightmares for weeks afterwards. It bothered him that Swift's map seemed to lead to that area. Still, couldn't be silver there. Old story was only a legend.

"Make it interesting," Lafette whispered, "make 'em want to follow the map, sell 'em a dream, and don't be a cedarhead." He spread the maps in his hands like cards.

As several lumberjacks approached, Valentine tucked his thumbs through the shoulder straps of his overalls and cleared his throat. "Gentlemen," he said, "might I interest you in a life changing proposition?"

The tallest, a boy with curly black hair, wore a blue checked shirt with a rip in the sleeve and had the biggest hands Lafette had ever seen. The other man, considerably older, wiped cornbread crumbs from his chin and chuckled. His cheeks were checkered with pox scars, and he narrowed his eyes at them.

"It's not just anybody we'd offer to sell John Swift's Silver Map," Valentine said, "We followed it ourselves and found us a pot of silver."

"Darn shootin'," Lafette added, "had some put in my tooth." He stuck a finger in his mouth and pulled back his cheek. "See, right there," he mumbled. As the man with the pitted face leaned down to look, Lafette let go and nodded as if to confirm that they'd both seen the silver in his tooth. "Makes bad teeth good," he said, nodding again. The man nodded along with him.

"Reckon there's really silver at the end of that trail, Kenny?" the tall lumberjack asked his friend. Kenny shrugged his shoulders.

"Yes, sir," Valentine said. "Ole John Swift found it, right here in these mountains." Kenny took a map from Lafette and started to open it.

"No sir-ree." Lafette shook his finger and snatched back the map. "Have to pay to get treasures beyond your dreams."

"Lumberin' ain't enough for you, Kenny?" asked the tall man. "You wanna go on a treasure hunt too?"

"Otis Knuckles, it ain't your business if I buy myself a silver mine map."

"Greedy, ole Swift was," Valentine said, scratching behind his ear. "Kilt all the people who knew where he hid the silver." He squeezed his shoulders up into his neck, rose on tiptoes and whispered into the men's faces, "Cut their throats with a hack saw."

"Why don't you boys go get the silver yourselves?" Otis asked, his lip curling up like he might burst out laughing.

" 'Cause I ain't strong as you, Mister. Can't carry it down the mountains. 'Sides, we got enough already. Too much trouble to go get more."

"Kenny, let's go. Don't be so ignorant as to fall for silliness."

"Otis, you sound like an ole lady. Just 'cause you're working, and I ain't, don't mean I'm stupid. Everybody knows Swift's silver is a true story."

"All legend is based in truth," Lafette quickly volunteered, letting the map waft through the air, tempting the two men.

They followed it with their eyes as if it were a bouncing ball. Both traded a glance, trying to gauge the other's reaction.

Otis fingered the blade of a wide-toothed saw he'd just purchased. He flipped the saw and swatted Kenny on the rear. "Sorry, kids, another time."

Valentine stepped up on the porch and pulled Lafette aside. "They ain't buying! What the hell you trying to do, having me talk to these ole geezers?"

"Do it again," Lafette insisted.

Valentine focused on Kenny who stared, mesmerized by the map, and wiped sweat from his brow. Lafette wiped his own brow with the same gesture. "Walk away and you'll never find silver," he said. "Buy this map and your life could change forever."

The boys held the map high, staring silently as if holding a fallen star in their hands when whistling broke the stillness. *New Orleans Woman* wafted lightly behind them.

Lafette's shoulders stiffened and he saw the same frozen fear in Valentine's eyes. An inch at a time he turned his head and looked into the store. Polk Owens was sharpening his ax on a granite wheel at the side of the trading post.

"We gg... gg... gots to cc... cc... close up shop, Mister," Lafette stuttered.

"Now, hold on a minute, boys." Kenny pulled a dollar from his pocket. Valentine grabbed the maps and jumped off the porch. Lafette tried to do the same but Kenny held his arm. When Lafette twisted to escape, Kenny tightened his grip, focusing on the map. "Another time," Lafette whispered, praying Polk didn't see him.

"Sure would like to show Otis a thing or two. Be nice to be rich. I believe in what you said. I believe in the legend."

Another whistled verse of *New Orleans Woman* floated through the air. Lafette thrust a map at Kenny who released

Lafette then bent to chase the map as it fell between the cracks of the stairs. Both boys sprinted down the road, raising a dust cloud.

He called after them, "Hey, boys, don't you want your dollar?"

Neither looked back. The July heat filled their lungs but they didn't stop running until they collapsed a quarter mile away on the courthouse steps. The concrete was cool against their skin and Lafette rested his forehead between a step and the front wall.

"Bejezus," Valentine grumbled, huffing and puffing. "Why didn't you get his dollar, fool?"

"Why didn't you lay your cedarhead down at Polk's feet?" Lafette's side hurt and he wished Valentine would shut up.

They stared at the dirt, elbows propped on their knees and chins buried in their hands. A few adults passed but no one paid them any attention. An hour later they felt safe. Polk had not seen them, nor did it seem that he'd be coming this way today. The boys took turns drinking from the sulfur springs that rose up through a pipe beside the courthouse, spitting out the last drink to rid their nostrils of the rotten egg smell.

"Ought to follow this map ourselves." Valentine slapped the paper in his hand.

Lafette groaned, remembering every nightmare he'd ever had about the northeast side of the mountain. Fire burst from the ground. Twisted monsters crawled out of holes. Dead people flew through the air, crouching in trees like birds waiting to swoop in on children who'd stayed out too late. Wampus probably lived there as well. "I know where it leads," he said. "Ain't no treasure there."

Valentine glared at Lafette. "See, you're already keeping secrets." He scratched his neck and twisted his mouth into a disgusted wrinkle. "You're gonna go without me?"

Lafette rolled his eyes and pointed to the courthouse door. Half dozen flies circling the entrance scattered as they entered. Valentine approached a lady knitting a shawl and held out a map. "Wanna be rich, Ma'am?" he asked in a frank voice.

She read the map's lettering over her wire-rimmed glasses, then quickly covered her mouth with a hanky. She was laughing and Lafette wished Valentine would tone down his smart-aleck attitude.

"Makes a great souvenir, Ma'am." Lafette looked at her with all the earnestness he could muster. The lady shook her head and her shoulders trembled from laughter as she stood and disappeared into the office behind her. "Let's stay away from women folk," Lafette said, annoyed.

"Why? They're foolish. I could sell bunches to them." Valentine huffed and struck a map against his thigh. "You've always known where this map leads and didn't say a blasted word."

Lafette's eyes widened as he stared out the door at a bench across the street. "Get ready to prove yourself."

"What are you blabbing about?"

"Yonder sits Judge Treadway and King Kingsley. Think you can sell the judge a map, let's see you do it. And if you can't, you have to do things my way from now on." Treadway's reputation as a skinflint guaranteed a rebuff. Lafette relaxed, no longer worried about being forced to go to the dangerous side of Shadow Mountain.

Valentine marched toward the men determined as a politician. Lafette followed. The Judge and King, focused on their discussion, did not notice the boys.

"You're not listening," Treadway said. "It's too complicated. You'd have to file suits in Kentucky, Tennessee, and Virginia, and each state has different laws."

"Under the law of miscegenation—"

"Tennessee's law." The Judge emphasized with a sharp hand motion.

"Blast it! You on my side or not?" King clenched his arms chest-level and leaned back until bench tipped.

Treadway gripped the bench seat. "Sure hate to do that woman wrong. Only one of her family that wasn't a bad seed. Streak of meanness runs all the way back to the Devery clan."

King sniffed and looked down at Valentine. "Out of my sight, boy!"

"Buy a souvenir, Judge Treadway?" Valentine asked.

The Judge shook a finger, warning Valentine to back off and Lafette looked at him victoriously.

"Kingsport case ain't about land," Judge Treadway said to King. "It's about marriage between a colored and a white." Treadway ran his hands through his white hair, frustrated with placating King. "That's the only reason miscegenation was cited."

"Worked, didn't it?"

"No, it didn't," the Judge said, exasperated. "Court found that Melungeons are free people of color, and they can marry whites legally."

King's face scrunched like a rotten pumpkin. He clasped his hands and leaned forward, staring at the ground as if he might find an answer to his troubles. "Ain't how we do it around here!"

"It's still the law." The Judge tapped his cane against the bench, causing mint green paint to fleck off like snowflakes. "You tried being nice to her?"

Valentine edged up and pointed at the map. "Valuable as gold. Map, Sir?" he asked again.

Lafette snickered at Valentine's folly, but he also felt sorry for the poor soul that King and the Judge were trying to outsmart.

"Can't we enact a law?" King asked, ignoring Valentine.

"She still might not follow it."

"And why not?"

Treadway shook his head, staring at the sky as if his thoughts were on the cloudless blue rather than King. "That woman follows her own kind of law."

"So did her old man, or so he thought 'til I taught him a lesson or two."

"Even if we tested miscegenation in court again, all she'd have to do is marry a white man and have her son adopted to ensure her title and keep the land."

"Confound it!" King slapped his hands together, "I'm asking for solutions, not ways to save her hide."

Valentine crooned, "You, too, can be rich as John Swift—richer, 'cause you'll have his silver!"

"Let me think on it," Treadway said to King, "Might come up with something."

"Map, sir?" Valentine jumped up and down.

"Stop this tomfoolery!" The Judge swung his cane and Valentine leaped sideways but the end caught him on the backside. "You young'uns go play elsewhere! Out of my sight with this nonsense!" He raised his cane again, stared directly into Lafette's face, and the judge froze like a statue. "You!" he said. His pupils shrank until his eyes looked like exploding stars.

As long as Lafette had known the Judge, he'd never seen such a look on his face, an expression that bordered on fear but still, a thinking man's face. Their eyes locked into each other's. The Judge still posed his cane to strike but instead lowered it and whispered, "Run!"

Lafette didn't wait for King to recognize him, and both boys bolted. They ran up hill and down until they reached the foothills of Shadow Mountain, finally falling, panting against the Elisha Tree.

"Maybe now you'll listen," Valentine said. "Ought to follow this map ourselves."

"You didn't win the bet," Lafette fired back. "Besides, I don't believe in the legend."

"Why would there be a map if there's no silver?"

"Anybody with any sense knows there ain't no silver in these hills. We gotta go to a bigger town where city folk don't know any better."

"I'm tellin' ya, we oughta follow the map, and I'm aiming to."

"No, you ain't!"

"Want me to beat the tar out of you?"

"As if you could. Hush your mouth and let me do some figuring." Lafette opened a map and traced the path with his finger. The route led straight to Shadow Mountain's worst part. He'd been warned never to go there by his mother and by Kate. Both had told him the Wampus lived there. He glanced up at Valentine, lips pursed defiantly. There'd be no stopping him if he thought he'd get money out of it. Lafette considered meeting the Wampus. He knew not to look into its eyes, and he was a fast runner. "Meet me here in an hour. Gotta get Blue."

"Fine, an hour."

"Ain't making no promises," Lafette said. "Get food. It's a long walk and I ain't eat today."

He hadn't seen Valentine this happy unless he was beating somebody up. Valentine bounded downhill, stopping once to throw a rock into the air. When he was gone, Lafette crawled into the Elisha Tree and huddled inside with his legs pulled to his chest and arms wrapped around his knees. His muscles trembled and his heart beat furiously. He couldn't understand why that small patch of land scared him so. He might not be so scared with Valentine. Maybe it was truly haunted and they should stay away rather than risk being swallowed whole by the Wampus. He wasn't sure what to do but he felt safest burrowed inside his tree.

The wood's spicy odor smelled like his bed. His father had built it before he was born, from Tyme timber off the Elisha Tree's top branches. Maybe if Arn came home they could go to that part of Shadow Mountain together and he would explain the monsters away.

Lafette stared at the carved names above him, *Arn Marlon, Elisha Thunderheart*. He ran his fingers over the indented letters, wishing he could sense his father. One day, he'd carve his own name in that wood. Maybe his father would see it and know that his son had been here. But first, he needed to prove himself worthy of his name beside theirs. Now, time to go home. If he were going to the mountain's dark side, he sure wanted to have his dog with him.

⩛ 13 ⩛

AS SHE TRAVELLED down the mountain, Delta thought she saw Kate a short distance away. She slowed Ole Sal to a walk and peered into a giant Tyme forest. Ancient trunks, layered one behind the other, created a fortress. She'd never regarded the trees as threatening before, and the image startled her. Hummingbirds fluttered among the leaves. Honeybees and dragonflies lit on purple irises and orange tiger lilies growing along the creek. The pollinating bees' mesmerizing flight meshed with the frightful queen bee vision and she shivered.

Lafette's Elisha Tree, so large it seemed like the grandfather of all the others, towered into the sky. Falcons perched in the top branches and cast wavy shadows on the ground. She trotted the mule forward, letting it drink from the creek. A cackle like an angry hen broke the stillness. Upstream Kate danced a dervish, her mouth forming a spiteful pout, arms out over the creek. She sprinkled a red powder into the water. *She's poisoning the creek!*

Delta jumped from Ole Sal's back and ran at Kate, but where she'd stood was only a Tyme branch, curved like a woman's body, bent out over the stream. The silvery leaves, shimmering in the wind, flowed like the waves in Kate's long hair. She touched the Tyme branch. "I'm imagining ghosts in the woodwork," she said to the mule. "Worst than an old granny." She closed her eyes, thinking, *Get hold of yourself.*

After remounting Ole Sal, Delta came to the main trail in minutes. She left behind Tyme's cinnamon fragrance and the peaceful, isolated mountain. Other travelers appeared, two solitary riders then a preacher's wagon with red cursive letters scripted on each side: HAVE YOU ENOUGH FAITH? Slowing the mule, she let the wagon pass. No need to rush, she told herself, calming her nerves about what she would say to Judge Treadway. A train whistle blared. The mule spooked and Delta pulled the reins firmly.

"Not used to all these sounds, are you?" She patted the mule's neck. Down the hill appeared the outline of a tiny town. Harrogate, Tennessee. English-style manor houses nestled between giant white oaks. Rising above the community, the deserted Four Seasons Hotel was the biggest waste of lumber Delta had ever seen. The huge building sported a peaked roof and triangular arched windows, and one side supported a castle tower. Completed only a few years before, the building was already scheduled to be demolished for salvage.

In the yard of one enormous mansion, a woman anchored a basket of wet laundry on her hip. She dropped the basket and shook out a wet sheet to hang on a clothesline. Delta recognized her school friend Meg Morrison who worked as a domestic. Meg looked up, waved, and Delta waved back. It felt like a good sign. She continued on, feeling less nervous. People knew her and not all were hostile. Ron Shackly and Bennie Conway slumped on the steps of the King George Saloon. Both nodded as she passed. She smiled back and began to feel hopeful. Kate could never stand against me here, she decided. Wouldn't stand a chance against these people.

Soon the courthouse loomed ahead as imposing as an English manor house. A central tower added an air of importance and round arches crowned all its doors and windows. Its redbrick formality made Delta feel like a roughly hewn log. She tied the mule to a hitching post, then wiped sweat from her brow onto her sleeve.

A circle of men gathered in a corner laughed boisterously. Delta glared defiantly, but no one looked her way, and she realized she'd only imagined they were laughing at her. Nervous tremors rippled through her stomach. Think straight, she thought. These people know you. Kate's an old mountain woman. They'd never side with her.

She hurried up the center staircase through the brick arch and wandered down the hall, ciphering the gold leaf lettering on each door. Judge Thomas Treadway's name was printed old English script. Her shadow looked like a child's against the large oak entrance and her peck on the wood sounded equally small. No answer. She knocked again.

"Come on in!" shouted a gruff voice.

Delta smoothed her brown skirt and took a deep breath before entering. Earleen Mason stood on a chair, dusting bookcase shelves. Judge Treadway, bent forward over his desk, stared at her legs. But his expression was distracted, as if his thoughts were on another matter. His massive size rounded his back like a turtle's shell. Sweat dampened his long, white sideburns, giving them a yellowish cast.

Delta stepped through a rain of dust from the top shelf.

"Delta Wade?" The surprised judge extended his hand in a friendly gesture, indicating for her to sit on a couch across from him.

"Mrs. Treadway doing well?" she asked. "Sure wish she was still the schoolteacher. I'd've never learned arithmetic if not for her." She bit her tongue, unable to control a nervous tremor.

"Bad thing, what happened to Lafette last year." The Judge rose and moved beside her. "Be glad to speak to the schoolmaster. Get him back in school."

"Judge, that's not why I've come."

Earleen stopped dusting after the judge cleared his throat, and she left the office by a side door. "Go ahead," he said, patting Delta's hand.

"I'd like to know about having Arn declared dead and me legally named his common-law wife... widow."

The judge leaned back and a puff of air sneezed from the couch. "I see." He tapped his fingers against the knuckles of his other hand, eyes darting in thought. "Raises questions for the court."

Delta looked out the window at children playing tag. "I have to protect his claim." She turned back toward the judge. "In case something should happen to me."

Treadway inhaled deeply and exhaled with a wheeze. "Sure sympathize with your trying to protect Lafette." He rose with effort and drew the curtains across the window. "It's a hard position you're in, Delta,"

Something about his attitude bothered her. He'd never been a fearful man, and more than once Mrs. Treadway had spoken in her defense when church people condemned Delta for living with Arn. Part of her felt ashamed and she lowered her eyes as she spoke. “Sir, you’re the only person I can turn to.” The room heated and sweat dripped down her back. She waited for him to speak. He didn’t and she figured his hesitancy meant trouble.

Finally, he said, “Let me suggest an alternative.”

Dread wound up her spine and she held her breath.

“Sell the mountain. Invest the money for Lafette.” He stroked his chin and nodded. “That’s the safest way. I can make inquiries about prospective buyers.”

Delta’s stomach burned as if gripped by an unseen hand. The selling idea shattered her confidence. “Could never see my way clear to part with the mountain.”

Judge Treadway massaged his neck and wiped sweat running down his face. Once more he sat beside her. “Delta, now’s the time to trust me. Some people you can’t fight. You’ve known me long enough to know I’d never do you harm. Selling that land is the best thing. Shadow Mountain is isolated. Anything could happen to you up there.”

Dust floated like minnows in a stream and the musty book odor made her want to sneeze. Surely a solution existed in one of his law books. Silence shivered between them like winter. “Arn would want me to stay. I’m sorry, Judge. Appears you can’t help me.” She rose to leave.

He took hold of her arm above the elbow and pulled her back to the couch. “I’ll do whatever you say with yours and Arn’s relationship. You want to be named his common-law wife, it’s done. But don’t hold to that land. Sell it before somebody discovers Arn’s heritage and buys it out from under you.”

Delta felt her cheeks warm. The judge’s intent stare was too fixed—the blue irises too dull, pupils squeezing tighter each time he spoke. What's he really thinking? she asked herself. What's he really mean?

"Some investment company could get title to your land for no other reason than they want it. You can't win against these people. They'll use this Melungeon thing against you and Lafette." He lumbered to his feet and paced. "Life's a'changing in these mountains. They're changing it. In years to come they may want to mine that mountain, get lumber from the trees, build a road across it. Government will side with them. Nothing you can do. Eminent Domain, they'll call it. Get the money now, while you can."

The outside world changed into as fierce an enemy as Kate Huston, but anger surpassed her fear. She was unable to doubt Arn's belief that the Watcher would always rule the mountaintop. "The land belongs to Lafette. It's got to stay that way."

"Think how good it'd be for him, living in town, being among people. He'd be more socialized. Wouldn't get in trouble selling Swift's Silver Mine Maps with that stinky, little Valentine Tolliver."

"He's not allowed to play with that boy."

"Saw him this very morning selling treasure maps to unsuspecting folk, and Tolliver as smelly as ever. Don't believe that heathen's had a bath in his life."

The room closed in on her. Lafette spent his time with Kate and Valentine, the two people he'd been forbidden to see. She stumbled toward the window, desperately needing fresh air. She pushed aside the curtain and gulped deep breaths. One truth was now clear to her... she had failed her duty to train the Watcher.

Children outside galloped happily at play. Judge Treadway pointed at them. "Lafette should have a childhood like these kids. He'd grow up healthier in town. More social. I'd take him under my wing here and teach him law."

With the effort of lifting a log, Delta steadied her voice. "Your offer is more than kind, but I need to go home. Much behind in my work." She held out her hand to him.

"I'm afraid for you, Delta. Don't reject my help just yet." He squeezed her hand as if to press his words into her skin. "Think on it." A ball bounced against the outside wall, causing a George Washington painting to fall. The Judge leaned out the window and shouted. "I told you young'uns to watch where you're throwing them balls!"

Delta silently slipped into the hall while he hollered at the kids. Earleen leaned against the wall outside the door. She turned away as Delta passed.

Outside, the sun pulled her sweat until her blouse stuck to her back. Delta rolled her sleeves to the elbows. Her head ached terribly as she stood by the hitching post where Ole Sal and two horses were tied. Delta's thoughts focused on her son. She'd told Lafette time and again to stay away from Kate and Valentine. To discover that he saw both of them, and to find it out in one day, was more than she could stand. She could deal with enemies on Shadow Mountain or in the outside world—but loss of control over Lafette made her seethe.

Today, she swore she'd pull him back to the mountain. One way or another he would forsake the world, the way all Watchers did. He'd learn his duties and become the most powerful man in the mountains. But he was only a boy, so it was up to her to guide him. Now more than ever, she would take the firmest hand possible with him—the job that should have been his father's.

Part of her cursed Arn's absence. He was the Watcher, not she. The duties of teaching were his. If Arn were here, Lafette would be his father's apprentice. Kate would never have started trouble with him. King Kingsley would feel wrath like God's fury if he challenged the Watcher.

"Damn you, Arn," she muttered under her breath. "Damn you for staying away." She mounted Ole Sal, struck a hind thigh and galloped past the stores and houses without acknowledging anyone who waved or called out. All she left behind was a cloud of dust.

♆ 14 ♆

THE MAP LED the boys past the tattered Grandley Mill. Charred wood still smelled smoky after nearly twenty years. No one had ever bothered to clear away the crumbling frame and, piece by piece, it had fallen like a rotting skeleton. The muddy ground around the burnt structure swelled with spiky weeds around swamp holes. Ten feet from a collapsed porch, no plant survived.

"Supposed to be haunted." Lafette pointed at a shattered window frame, partially buried in swamp sludge.

"Don't believe in ghosts." Valentine said, eyes white all around his dark irises.

"Me neither." They gave the mill a wide berth. Glad they hadn't come later than mid-afternoon, Lafette planned to be home by sunset. "You know we're headed to the dark side of Shadow Mountain?"

Valentine shivered, then glanced side to side as if the mountain was already too dark to suit him. "Good thing you brought Blue," he said. The puppy yelped, aware of recognition.

Above them, giant Tyme trees spread towering butterfly branches, and sunrays lit the ground in sparse strips. Lafette was reminded of the hollow where he'd met Kate's strange sister, Polly. No flowers bloomed there either, grass grew sparsely, and the ground was spotted with saucer-sized holes brimming with slimy, green water.

"Hear something?" Valentine glanced backwards.

"Blue'll let us know if a'body's behind us." A hollow echo of footsteps followed them, stopping when they were still, moving as they stirred. The dog's ears perked up, but he acted confused, as if the sound ricocheted from a distant ridge. Lafette tried ignoring whatever might be following them through the moist forest.

Blue trotted ahead, sniffing the air and picking gingerly through the woods. Valentine stopped several times and looked behind him, finally taking out his pocketknife to notch a tree. Lafette smirked. " 'Fraid I might run off and leave you?" he asked, leaning down and scratching Blue between the ears.

"No, 'fraid you might get us lost."

Lafette pointed upward. "Long as you know to find sky, you can find home. Wait 'til dark, find the big dipper and the handle'll lead you to Arn's Volcano. Least in summer."

Valentine wrinkled his nose, unable to comprehend the directions. "Still daytime. Can't see stars and in the dark you'd never see up through these blasted branches." He swatted at a fly buzzing his head then cut into another tree. "I'll depend on my notches."

"Almost there." Lafette pointed on the map. As they journeyed on, stuffy air smelled like rotting meat. Neither mentioned the odor. "Gonna buy myself factory-made dungarees with my silver," Lafette said.

"I ain't buying nothing!" Valentine sliced a hand through the air. "Nothing but a train ticket out of these hills."

"Your daddy'd never let you do such a thing." Lafette picked up Blue after he jumped a large, sunken dip in the ground. "Don't get near that hole, Valentine, snakes live in it."

"Doubt that." Valentine danced a jig around the opening. Lafette shrugged like he didn't care whether Valentine fell in or not. "Gonna get rich off my silver and live far away in California!" Valentine sang. The brown, murky water bubbled. He leapt vertically, yelping, "Yeoow!"

They raced through dense trees seven feet in diameter. The silvery bark cast a blackish sheen that in certain lights appeared indigo. Branches grew low on the trees, some sweeping the ground. They hopped over thick protruding roots. Blue scampered underneath the brushwood and Lafette whistled to keep track of the puppy. Soon, offshoots of the larger branches twisted and twined around limbs from surrounding trees. They swelled upward like a wall, twice the height of either boy.

"This is it." Lafette looked from the map to the mass of trunks and limbs.

"This is what? Don't see nothing." Both boys stared among the leaves while Blue dug at the roots. "There!" Valentine squealed in excitement. He pulled a leafy branch. It opened into an aboveground tunnel created by the interwoven limbs of dozens of trees.

Lafette helped snap the branch and peered inside. "Never seen anything like this," he marveled. Blue stood on his hind paws, sniffed and barked.

Slices of light cut through the crisscrossed branches, illuminating the tunnel in a crossed swords pattern. The interior was high enough to stand. Lafette stuck his head in, waited for his eyes to adjust then gingerly stepped inside.

Valentine followed, clutching Blue to his chest. From the main tunnel a maze of twisted Tyme tree branches spread off into corridors. The light, barely breaking through the silver leaves, guided them onward. The temperature cooled a degree at a time as they progressed deeper, stepping on a solid base of branches. "No wonder old Swift couldn't retrace his steps. I'd never've found this place again, either." Valentine's voice trembled in a high-pitched, strangled tone. "Smart of me to mark the trees, just in case we can't carry it all out tonight." Leaves to the left of him shook. A black rodent the size of a squirrel jumped out. "Bejeeezzzus!"

Blue growled and chased it into another branched wall.

"Only a rat," Lafette said smugly, then patted Blue on his hind leg. "Probably a nest of 'em in there." Valentine's lips trembled although he walked with his back straightened, chin out as if nothing frightened him.

Then, the tunnel's end cocooned them like a beehive. They looked up, down, around, then stared at each other. Lafette held the map in a blade of sunlight.

"Gotta be here somewhere." Valentine tore through the nearest patch of branches and leaves. He stopped to scratch his head. "I don't like this place."

"What's that?" Lafette pointed at a silver sparkle among the leaves.

"I'll get it!" Valentine rushed forward, pushed him aside and ripped away a mass of cobwebs to reach for the silvery sparkle just as the ground gave way and he disappeared in a puff of dust. "Aaarrrrgh!" He clung to a slowly collapsing branch. "Help!" Unable to get a more secure hold, he swung back and forth over a pit of darkness.

Lafette lay on his stomach and stretched out an arm. He couldn't reach Valentine. The branch dropped another foot.

Frantic, Lafette stood up to look for something to use as a pole. Blue whined and wagged his tail. The branches were too thick to break. He ran back about ten feet, then turned and ordered, "Stay here, Blue."

"Don't go," Valentine yelled. "Don't leave me here to die!"

Mid-tunnel, Lafette found a smaller branch and tugged at it. The wood clung to its parent tree but broke after he stomped it. He dragged the branch back. Blue sat obediently at the hole and jumped up when he saw Lafette.

"Valentine? You there?" He peered into the crevice. Darkness. "Valentine?"

"I'm here," said a small, weak voice.

Lafette flushed with relief. "Gonna lower a branch for you to climb."

"No."

Lafette thought he'd heard wrong. "Here comes."

"Don't lower it!" Valentine's voice quivered with desperation. "There's copperheads all around me," he moaned, "If you stir 'em, they'll be on me."

Lafette fell back and ran his hands through his hair. Copperheads. He hated copperheads. Worse, he couldn't think of a way in the world to save Valentine's life. He looked over toward the silver sparkle that Valentine had reached for. Nothing. Probably an illusion created by the silvery leaves and sparse light. Why had they ever come here?

"Valentine," he said, "can you hear me?" A small moan came in reply. "I'm coming down to get you."

"No!" Valentine broke into sobs. "Don't! You'll shake 'em loose on me!"

"It's the only way."

He stepped cautiously onto the web of branches latticed down into the hole. With each move he pictured Polly Huston's cabin and the long, reddish-brown copperheads lying on her porch. He closed his eyes, took another step and dirt cascaded all around him. Valentine hung on a vine attached to a rocky ledge. Beside him, a thick, fat snake coiled on a rock. Up above, Blue whined.

"Give me your hand," Lafette said. Valentine put out his hand, but pulled it back when the coiled snake unwound and knocked loose a shower of pebbles. "Come on," Lafette encouraged him. "I can see on all sides. Ain't no other snakes around." The copperhead was so close he could make out the diamond-shaped brown markings on its back.

Valentine stretched to reach him. They gripped each other's wrists and Lafette jerked him forward. Valentine latched onto Lafette's back. Their combined weight swayed the root lattice back and forth. Dirt from above spewed over them. The snake whizzed past his ear and landed on his shoe. Lafette kicked it off, then, steady as a plow horse, he climbed, pulling Valentine out behind him. When he rolled his chest over the top, Blue clamped his teeth onto Lafette's shirt collar and tugged.

"Thought we was dead," Valentine said as they rested against each other. His eyes formed wide circles and mouth a thin line.

Blue licked Lafette's face then went to Valentine and licked his.

Lafette rubbed his eyes, unable to rid them of grit. He rotated his shoulders, loosened the tightness in the muscles, and rested his head on his knees, arms wrapped around his ankles. Something wet dripped onto his fingers. He lifted his hand overhead to a spot of light. A bloody streak ran across his palm and splattered onto his cheek. "I've been bit."

☫ 15 ☫

KING APPROACHED THE barn, thumbs tucked in his pants, "Son?" Henry adjusted a stirrup, then led Zeus from a stall toward the opposite door. King paused beside the grain bin. "Too hot to exercise your horse, Son." He rubbed his chin with the back of his hand. "Going to see her?"

"Meant what I said, Daddy." Henry turned halfway. "Drop that lawsuit against Delta."

Nancy entered, carrying a bucket and stool, and sat beside the milk cow. King waved her away. "Run into a spell of bad luck, Son," his voice softer than Henry had ever heard. "All this today, the party, bringing the Pratts here." King leaned against a stall and patted a burgundy-colored mare. "All I've left you should be carried on for more generations than those limey Quinns ever dreamt."

"It wasn't Rebecca's fault she couldn't have children," Henry said.

"Surely you don't believe I held that against her?" King held his hands, palms open. "But all the more reason to choose a wife with more care this time."

Henry slapped the reins against his hand. "You held Rebecca's health against her. You'll find something to hold against Delta. All because she doesn't toe your line."

King stepped into a blade of sunlight running the length of the barn. His shadow stretched over Henry's. Hands deep in his pockets, he studied the ground, then kicked a black stone so hard it ricocheted against three stalls. "I'm about to lose all we own."

Henry dropped the reins. The horse shifted to a grain bin and chomped on corncobs. An old rooster strutted across his boot toes. The birthday cake churned in his stomach. His father didn't move and Henry found that he could not go toward him either. "Lose everything?"

"We don't get this Quinntown job, that's it. Banks'll own me." King's tone was matter-of-fact, as if describing a particular way to saw a tree.

"W... we... We could go to the banks, Daddy. Explain things. They'll give us more time." His stutter unnerved him and his heart throbbed in waves of sensation that prevented him from understanding the gravity of his father's words.

"Ain't just me. It's happening all over. Times not so good anymore." King's hand rubbed a circle just below his chest. "It'll kill me to lose what I've built. All that'll be left to me is to die an easy death. And all I can think of is how much I need to see grandsons before I die, but not with Wade blood in their veins."

"Delta never took after her kin."

"It's in the bloodline, son." King grabbed Henry's arms, pulling him close. "You know that from breeding horses."

"I don't believe in that, Daddy. I never have—"

"Her family's trash. She bore Arn Marlon's bastard. You marry a family, Son, not just a person."

"Delta has nothing to do with her family."

"Henry!" King's shout stilled every creature in the barn until finally an owl flapped its wings. "Her father and two uncles are jailbirds!"

The musky horse odor closed in around Henry. "I'll prove it to you, Daddy." He broke from his grip and pulled Zeus to him.

"Plenty of pretty little girls around for you. Can't you honor your father's wish?"

Henry's chest ached as if he were being pulled apart. He mounted and trotted the horse beside his father. Leaning down, he squeezed King's shoulder. "I'll get the Tyme trees for you. Then you'll see the kind of woman she is." He looked deeply into his father's eyes, hoping to see the slightest trace of faith. King's cold, hard expression spoke his hatred for Arn Marlon. "When I get the trees, you'll see in her what I see."

"Be a dead man 'fore I see good in that woman." King shoved his son's hand away.

Without another word Henry gripped his thighs against the horse and galloped toward the Tennessee road to Shadow Mountain, the quickest route and the one Delta kept clear all year round.

Near the top, the road dipped sharply and circled jagged rocks Zeus could barely get around. The temperature dropped. A cool, light mist hung under the giant Tyme trees. He looked out over the weave of ridges, softly cursing to himself that Tyme trees had to grow on this land. White, rocky cliffs and green tree-lined crests struggled up from the earth, each trying to outgrow the other.

As he neared Cat's Crossroads, dizziness flooded his ears. He shook his head and sniffed the air. A multi-floral odor blended and became oddly intoxicating. Purple vetch and wild indigo curled up the middle of the road. Red clover grew among the rocks lining the south side of the crossroads.

Henry dismounted and picked a clover flower. The pale purplish-red matched the color of the dress he'd buried Rebecca in, and he breathed in the memory of her, Squeezing the flower to his chest he unintentionally crushed it. Nesting whippoorwills whistled above him. Two flew uphill toward Arn's Volcano. When the birds stopped singing he figured someone was watching him. Walking his horse, he swept the trees with a glance.

No one appeared, but he couldn't shake the strange feeling of being observed, especially when the birds didn't return to their nest. He thought of Macbeth's witches. An English scholar traveling through Eastern Kentucky was said to have named the crossroads after one and the name has slowly devolved through the years to Cat's Crossroads. The still air and sickly sweet smell made him experience the land's haunted quality for the first time. He remounted and trotted his horse up the hill.

Delta leaned on the porch rail, staring down the Virginia road so intently she seemed unaware of his approach. He swallowed hard, realizing how nervous her manner made him. *Ask for ten trees,* he told himself. Surely she'd not deny him that few.

"Waiting on me?" he asked, trying to sound friendly. The shock of his father's impending ruin still bubbled in his mind and he feared it would seep into his voice.

"On Lafette," she answered, not looking toward him. She held a hickory switch against her chest. Sunday shoes lay on the porch, and she wore a brown skirt and white blouse that were more formal than her usual gray dress.

"Ankle's all better now." Henry grabbed the banister and swung onto the porch. "Recall getting a few swipes across my legs with one of these." He touched the spear of the switch but she continued to stare intently at the road. "Always thought it made Momma feel worse than me." Delta didn't respond. After an uncomfortable silence he continued. "Been thinking, Delta, 'bout Tyme trees."

She ignored him as he dusted his boots, her whole focus on the road.

Down on one knee he began, "Been thinking, must be a way me and you could work something out. There being so many trees and all." Her mouth pressed a tight, thin line and Henry's back soaked with sweat. "Delta?" He touched her arm to see if he had her attention. She intently rolled the switch between her fingers.

Blue barreled up the Virginia road, yelping and turning flips in the air. Delta jumped off the porch and hurried forward. The dog met her then ran back down the road.

"Want me to come?" Henry asked. She didn't answer. He waited until she stopped walking, then followed, standing a few feet beside her.

Delta puffed quick, erratic breaths. Eyes wide, she stared down the road as if expecting someone long lost and Henry couldn't help but think of Arn. Lafette appeared at the crest of the road, an arm slung over Valentine Tolliver's shoulder.

Both boys stopped to stare at Delta. Valentine turned and ran. Blue sniffed at Lafette's ankle, whining and wagging his tail. Lafette timidly walked forward, favoring his left leg.

Delta hid the switch in her skirt folds. "You avoid Kate Huston's part of the mountain, like I told you?"

"Yes, Ma'am," Lafette said. "But I—"

"You didn't fight with Valentine Tolliver, did you?"

"No, Ma'am."

Delta struck Lafette with the switch so hard he tumbled backwards, tripping over his own feet. "You been with 'em both today," she shouted, "and you come home and lie to me!" She switched his shoulder.

"No, Momma, no!" Lafette rolled on his stomach, taking the blows on his back. "I been snake-bit, Momma," he sobbed into the grass.

"Lying to me!" She drew back to strike again.

Henry grabbed Delta's arm and ripped the switch away. "Didn't you hear?"

"Let go of me!" she shouted, twisting from his hold.

Henry knelt beside Lafette. "Where's the snake bite, son?"

Lafette pointed to his ankle and Henry rolled up the boy's pant leg. Large, pearl-shaped tears rolled down Lafette's face. He stared at the sky, afraid to look at his ankle, clasping his calf with one hand and wiping his nose with the other. Henry picked him up, shoving past Delta. "Not swollen much. Probably means dry venom snake. You're mighty lucky, Lafette." He kicked open the cabin door, laid the boy on a corn shuck bed, and covered him with a patchwork quilt, folded across a rocking chair.

"Reckon you and me are destined to always have ankle troubles," Lafette said, sniffing and managing a smile.

"Reckon we are." Henry smiled back. "Rest a spell. Your momma'll tend to you." He turned, but Delta had not followed him. Outside, she stood beside Arn's Volcano.

"You oughtn't to've done that," he said.

"I'd thank you to mind your own business and get off my mountain."

Henry growled in frustration. From the slight shoulder tremble he suspected she'd been crying and knew in his heart she loved Lafette more than any soul on earth. But she carried mistrust in every part of her. "Why! Why do you have to be so contrary with every living soul that tries to help you?"

"Who's trying to help me?" She turned toward him, her eyes swollen and red but ripe with fury. "You act like you want to help Lafette, you pretend you want to help me, like you're doing me such a favor! All you really want are my trees!"

Henry put a hand to his forehead. His head ached from the heat. He leaned against Arn's Volcano, wishing the cool rock would pull him inside and ease the painful pulse in his temples. "Delta, there are things you don't know. Things that could happen if you don't sell me the trees."

"You stand there and threaten me."

"I'm not threatening you. I swear I want what's best for you."

"And you're the one to decide that!" She walked around him. "Listen to me, Henry Kingsley. I didn't ask you to come up this mountain. I didn't ask you to kiss my lips. I don't want your money or help. And I will decide what's best for me and my boy!"

"Sure doing a sorry job of it!"

She struck him across the face with the switch.

He knew she'd drawn blood and quickly covered his cheek with a hand. "You and my father are two of a kind," he shouted, "you both deserve whatever comes!" Henry whistled for his horse and stomped toward the Tennessee road. As he mounted, he heard her behind him.

"I'm not afraid of King Kingsley! Of anybody! Just the way Arn wasn't afraid!"

"You're scared as a hunted rabbit, Delta! It's written all over your face, and when you realize what I can do for you, it might be too late!" He tugged Zeus' reins and made him rear, "And Arn is dead! You hear me? Dead!"

Henry galloped in a fury and didn't slacken the pace until he reached a green fern field. As leaves brushed against his horse he could hear spores dropping. A bee cluster clung to the Tyme trunk. He listened to the steady hum, barely noticing the sting on his cheek. "King Kingsley," he said bitterly, "you were right again."

His chest tightened and he dropped the reins and wrapped his arms across his stomach. Zeus stopped at a clover patch. Henry let himself fall forward onto the horse's neck. The sickness in his gut moved to his chest bursting upward into his throat, his mouth, nose, and eyes. He sobbed into the horse's mane, feeling somehow that it was Delta's hair entwining his fingers. One thought obsessed him: he had to get away from this cursed mountain. He had to think, and he had to get Delta Wade out of his heart.

♆ 16 ♆

DAYS PASSED AND an orbit of calm settled on the land. Once more life became the daily chores that started and ended with the sun, giving Delta a measure of safe feeling. What shadows haunted her thoughts were reined in by an undaunted belief that she stood in the right.

In the cool of morning, a young Indian girl hopscotched across eight rocks lining the edge of Delta's cornfield. Her pigtails flopped with each jump and one sleeve of a brown-checkered shift slid off her shoulder. Delta stopped rubbing a shirt against a metal scrub-board and squinted to see the child better. Rosy Thunderheart stood in the long shadow cast by Arn's Volcano, unable to take her eyes from the rock.

"Rosy?" Delta let the shirt slip into the washbasin of gray, sudsy water.

The girl stepped toward the volcano, absorbed by its shadow. Her arms folded on her chest as if chilled and even a yellow butterfly darting past her nose didn't stir her attention. "It's the darkest thing I ever seen." Rosy raised both arms to measure her height on the rock. "Seems liable to reach out and grab me."

Delta shook the water off her hands as she sauntered toward the little girl. Rosy inched away from the stone formation but did not turn her back to it. "You've seen it enough times. No reason to be scared, child."

"Aunt Nancy says for you to come." Rosy rubbed her stomach.

"Too soon for that," Delta said, instinctively touching her own stomach.

"Baby ain't comin' yet," Rosy said, counting off the phrases on her fingers as instructed. "But Aunt Nancy wants you to make the baby come today 'cause Uncle Amos's liable to bring that town doctor otherwise." She paused and blinked twice. "Aunt Nancy don't want no town doctor. You're to come in the back way, and, uh, Uncle Amos ain't expected home till past sundown." She bobbed her head, proud to have remembered all she needed to say.

"Can't leave now." Delta glanced toward Lafette, slumped down in a cane-backed chair at the edge of the porch, his hands thrust deeply into his pockets and his lower lip stuck out. He stared at Blue, curled in a ball with his nose between his paws as if he were being punished too. It pained her to suspect he'd be over the mountainside the minute she left.

"So come before then," Rosy recited, her eyes fluttering up and down as she tried to remember exactly what to say, "so it can be done with 'fore the men folk have any say in the matter." She dusted her hands together while eyeing the blackberry bushes that grew intertwined with a wooden fence.

A honeybee buzzed around Delta's head. She swatted at it, wishing she could sprout wings and fly as quickly. Causing the baby's birth might last into the night, and it was a route she hated to take. Too many things to go wrong. She looked back at her son in his moping slouch. "Go tell Nancy to wait one week," she said.

The little girl shifted from foot to foot. Her face crinkled into a frown and she jiggled her hands in front of herself as she shook her head. "Can't do that." She pulled Delta's arm, making her kneel, then whispered in her ear. "Aunt Nancy says if you don't come, she's gonna do it herself... come what may."

"Lafette," Delta said sternly, turning toward him. He didn't answer. She had to go. Nancy would never survive if she induced the birth by herself. Her son didn't acknowledge her as she approached the house. "Lafette, I have to leave." From behind, Delta put her hands on his shoulders. He twiddled his thumbs forward, then backward, and shrugged his shoulders to escape her touch. She caressed the back of his head, hoping he'd warm toward her but Lafette squeezed his eyes closed and refused to look up. "Enough sulking, young man," she said sternly, at the same time wishing she could take him in her arms and tell him how sorry she was for whipping him.

She cleared her throat, hoping he'd at least look at her. Lafette's forehead wrinkled. He rolled his eyes, popped up, and shifted himself through the front window and bounced onto his bed. "I'm going to Nancy's. Time for the baby." Delta huffed a deep breath and went to the kitchen to pack herbs and salves. "Don't leave this house," she called. A bobwhite whistled, and Lafette answered it. "I expect you to be out of this mood by the time I get home. Hear me?" She stood in the doorway of his room. Lafette whistled again like a bird.

Rosy skipped forward, blackberry juice staining her lips. She bounced berries in her hand and sat gingerly beside Lafette. With a teasing smile she held them out to him. Delta knotted the bag closed and slung it onto her shoulder. Rosy popped all the berries into her mouth and grinned, squirting the purple juice between her teeth.

"I don't allow girls on my bed!" Lafette hollered, stomping his foot.

"Come on, Rosy," Delta said when the little girl's face broke into a pout.

"Why is he so mean?" she whimpered as they left hand in hand.

"He's being a baby." Delta looked back and shook her finger at Lafette before closing the door.

The two cut a path through aromatic wild roses surrounded by field daisies and Queen Anne's Lace as they hurried down the mountain. A sour odor wafted around them. Rosy squeezed her nose between two fingers and looked up for guidance. Delta wrapped a hand around the little girl's wrist to pull her along. The path ended at a wooden fence covered with fragrant honeysuckle vines. The sickening smell mixed with the floral sweetness. Something near them was dead. She slid over the fence and turned to lift Rosy across.

In a patch of flattened weeds behind the girl, a swarm of flies covered the corpse of a rotting dog. Her heart jumped. The dog's coat glistened with the same gray sheen as Blue's. A female, and so much like the puppy she might be his mother. Regret for having whipped Lafette surged through Delta as she thought of him on the mountaintop with only Blue at his side. *I'll buy sugar-rock candy on my way home*, she decided, *and get a bone for Blue.*

∞

Nancy lived in a clapboard shack King Kingsley had built to house the men who worked for him, two rooms with a front porch built up on poles and the back fastened into the mountainside. Most had a corn patch with bean vines twisted around the stalks. Outhouses dotted the creek bank and an assortment of shirts, dresses, and sheets hung on clotheslines nailed between hearty elm trees. Delta studied the sky. A gray cloud drifted across the sun.

"When I'm alone with Nancy," she told Rosy, "bring in the clothes from her line." The little girl nodded. Delta pointed at the creek. "Right now, grab yourself a bucket and carry water up to the house north of the outhouses."

"Yes, Ma'am." She skipped off toward a tool shed behind Nancy's house.

Delta wiped sweat from her forehead and upper lip. The sun hung low in the sky, yet the afternoon sweltered. Another gray cloud drifted by. She hoped it would cover the sun and cool the air, but it dissipated into white stripes that vanished into the horizon.

When Delta entered Nancy's yard, a hand pulled back the blue linen curtain. She couldn't see who stood inside the house. The door opened before she reached it. Amos faced her. "What you doing here?" he asked.

Alarm spread through Delta's chest. "Come to see Nancy." She swallowed hard, keeping her voice friendly. "No harm to that."

His eyes narrowed and face tilted sideways as he rubbed his chin between his index finger and thumb. "Nancy's not up to company."

Amos blocked the doorway and Delta couldn't see inside. "Just say a word or two." She smiled.

Amos's gaze bore into her suspiciously. "Took to her bed. Doc's on the way."

"All the more reason to have woman folk around, Amos."

He thrust his head forward and whispered, "Already told Nancy the town doc is delivering my baby. I don't hold to these old mountain ways of yourn."

"All I'll do is keep her company."

Amos bit his lip and looked at the ground. His eyes locked onto a black coal bucket turned upside down beside the bottom step. "I mean to be firm on this." His jaw looked cut from iron and he shook his head.

"Amos," Nancy moaned from inside in a small, feeble voice.

"Maybe if you stood on the doorstep," he said, turning around part way.

"Amos!" Nancy pleaded. "Please let her in!"

Shreds of pain filtered through Nancy's voice so clearly that Delta knew she had induced her own labor. She had to get into the house. "I'll send Rosy to see what's keeping the doc."

"Suit yourself." Amos spat out the words in a trembling tone.

Quickly she found Rosy and sent her running, then stepped inside the house when Amos turned toward his wife.

Amos shook his finger at her. "What are you and my woman up to? Baby ain't due for another month. I'm supposed to be supervising a logging operation for Mr. Kingsley. I come home early and find this."

"No need using that tone with me, Amos."

"Just stand in the doorway. Don't come no further." Beads of sweat appeared on his forehead.

"If Doc don't make it in time, maybe I should help out a little."

Gripping the back of a kitchen chair, Amos shifted from foot to foot. "You best leave." Nancy moaned again. He pushed her toward the door.

"Wait!" Delta grabbed onto his shoulder.

"Don't touch me, witch!" Amos shook her off and raised an arm over his face as if to ward off a hex. Nancy's piercing scream came from the bedroom.

"Let me sit with her 'til Doc comes. Could be hours."

"Amos, for Godssake!" Nancy sobbed and screamed again.

Amos's eyes grew red and glassy. His lips pressed together as he glared at Delta. "King Kingsley says you're the danger in these mountains. I believe him. Things'll be all right if you just leave."

Delta could tell by his heaving chest that he didn't know what to do for his wife. A dozen men on horseback galloped by, and Amos perked up to see if the doctor was among them. As they passed, his chin trembled. She sensed his resolve weakening. "I'll keep my hands in plain view. Anything needs doing, I'll tell you how."

He nodded. She hurried to the bedroom into the acrid smell of blood and sweat. Nancy's hands were tight wads of flesh around the metal bars of the headboard. Her eyes rolled up and her mouth bled from having bitten her tongue. Delta smacked her cheeks. "How much did you take?" she whispered.

Nancy focused her eyes and her lips trembled as she mouthed words that made no sense.

"You said you wouldn't touch her." Amos stood like a statue at the door.

"Wash your hands," Delta told him, "then I'll tell you what to do."

He left at once. She unwrapped a mound of cloth on the floor and found the bottle of peony and pennyroyal medicine she'd given Nancy the previous week. Empty. "Why?" she said, sickened. She slipped the bottle into her pocket. "You drank it all?"

Nancy squinted her eyes, panted through parched, cracked lips. Another wave of contractions convulsed her body. She whined like a cold puppy, squeezing her eyes shut and gripping Delta's hands as if a lifeline. "Momma," she cried. "Momma, help me."

Delta cringed. She'd witnessed women in childbirth utter prophecy, claim to see the souls of their infants, and enter a spiritual state so peaceful that it might be called holy. But Nancy's voice sounded unnaturally like Lafette's. She groaned and twisted toward the open window, gaze focused on Shadow Mountain's rugged peak. "Tell me what you see," Delta said urgently, "Something wrong with Lafette?"

Nancy let out a low, throaty laugh. "Don't do it boy, the worms'll get ye." Her swollen lips made her look disfigured. Her agitated state wasn't the same as other women's. Nancy was on a frightening edge of insanity. Delta wanted to run to Shadow Mountain as one thought filled her mind. *Something's wrong with Lafette. I have to get to my son.*

Nancy reached out, grabbing her hands. Their gaze locked into one another's. Delta could see how much Nancy and the unborn child needed her. Her cousin's eyes seemed to be saying, *I'll die if you leave. I'll die.*

Amos returned holding up his freshly washed hands, his pale face was tense as he asked, "What's she laughing for?"

"She has no idea what she's saying. She'll say lots of things, don't pay her no mind." Delta motioned him to the bed and tore Nancy's gown up the middle.

They took turns holding her hands through contraction after contraction. Nancy spat up twice, and Amos came to tears, sure his wife was about to die. Delta didn't dare tell him it was best she throw up the medicine she'd taken.

During the quiet periods, she paced by the window, staring at Shadow Mountain and thinking about Lafette. As clear as water, the feeling descended on her that she should be with her son now, but each thought was followed by Nancy's moaning. If only Rosy would return with the doctor. She looked down the road for them. The late afternoon heat wafted up from the ground. A rabbit hopped across the road. Katydids sang like a church choir.

Nancy's head drooped until her chin touched her chest. She tried to speak, eyes wide, gasping air. Delta pressed Nancy's shoulders, helping her with the strain of pushing. Pools of blood gushed from Nancy's body. Blood vessels broke beneath her cheeks in spidery webs. Delta pressed her fingers into Nancy's temples and whispered so Amos couldn't hear. "Become the baby, Nancy. Let the baby ease its way out. Your body will do what it has to. Become the baby." Nancy's body relaxed and her muscles rhythmically responded to the child's birth.

Amos blinked back tears as his baby's head dropped into his hands. "Told you I didn't need you," he said to Delta, a smile spreading across his face. "Easy as pie." He held up the infant to show Nancy but she barely lift her head.

Delta doubted her cousin could even see the child and knew that the medicine she'd taken would now make her sleep until the next day. "When Rosy gets back, you tell her get some goat's milk and then—"

"I know what to do from here on out. I delivered him." Amos laid the baby on a sheet and wiped him with a towel.

"Reckon you did at that." Delta took advantage of his euphoria, figuring his resentment would return if she didn't leave. "I come for a visit and end up with a new relative." She stood slowly as if her spine ached. "Best get back to my own young'un. Let Nancy sleep and tell her I was by."

Amos shook his head, preoccupied with the baby.

Delta slipped out the back door. Rosy lay curled like a cat on the steps, her cheeks red and tear-stained. Delta pulled her up, "Where have you been?"

"Had to go to that fancy hotel in Middlesboro. Doc was at lunch with Mrs. Pratt."

"I don't care if you went to China! Why didn't he come?"

"I tried everythin', Aunt Delta. Promise I did. They wouldn't let me inside. Then, Mrs. Pratt comes to the door and said Doc couldn't interrupt his lunch for the likes of people like us. Said we had to learn to take care of our own."

Delta kicked the coal bucket next to the step. Rosy burst into tears and covered her face with her small hands. "It's all right, Rosy. I'm not mad at you."

"But we do take care of our own, don't we, Aunt Delta?" she said between sniffles.

"That's something we'll always do, child." As Delta spoke, the voice she'd heard from Nancy's throat still haunted her. Shadow Mountain loomed ominously and she couldn't help thinking as she hiked up the road that she'd not taken care of her own. She'd stayed too long. Lafette needed her.

She concentrated on the mountaintop. "Lafette," she whispered, "where are you?" She could not sense him. *Should've left sooner. Should've gone to my son.* The higher she climbed, the deeper her feeling. *Something was terribly wrong.*

♆ 17 ♆

UNLUCKY OMENS CROSSED Delta's path all the way up Shadow Mountain. Tree leaves turned up their undersides, a dead limb blocked part of the trail, a span of spider webs attached between two Tyme trees swayed in the wind, empty. Means rain, she told herself, to keep from dwelling on the scent of dire fortune.

The grueling climb hindered her thoughts, ricocheting between her fear for Nancy and her premonition of her son in danger. A pearly gray dusk settled in the trees. The fragrance of honeysuckle didn't calm an urgency tugging at her. A stick cracked beneath her foot, popped up and smacked her arm. Another bad sign.

By the time she reached Cat's Crossroads, Delta panted, her muscles cramped as she forced herself up the hill. No light shone from the house and Blue didn't howl at her approach. "Must be asleep," she said to ease her apprehension. The door opened stiffly. Lafette was not slouched in his chair nor was he in his bed or the backyard.

"Lafette!" she hollered from the front porch. She called again. No answer. As she paced the length of the porch, the sky darkened to evening blue. Thunder sounded in the direction of Creation Ridge and the rumbling triggered chills inside her.

Delta tried believing he was anywhere except with Kate. But the probability came to her again and again until she could ignore it no longer. Can't sit and wring my hands, she decided, and sprinted down the path to Kate's house. *More his mother than you are,* Delta remembered her saying. She squeezed a fist so hard her nails dug into her skin.

Kate's rocky property was marred with cliffs and crags. Delta grabbed to rocks and vines, climbing in the shadows created by massive trunks and layered branches. Out of the dense grove, Kate's cabin sprang up like a boot jammed in the fork of a tree.

Delta peered through a window at a floor carpeted with Tyme leaves. *A spell to steal Lafette and the mountain!* Her jaw tightened as hatred bubbled. Crickets ceased chirping and she slipped around the side of the house, halting at the sound of a rip like a hide being skinned from an animal. Near the edge of the cliff, Kate knelt over a hole in the ground. Delta crept into the soft crab grass. Kate's arms and shoulders moved as she worked intently. "Old woman."

Kate whipped around, slinging droplets of blood onto Delta. "Who're ye?"

The wet drops jolted Delta. Kate's lap was matted scarlet, as was the hunting knife she clutched in her fist. Pink and blue entrails filled the hole. A strong, salty odor stuck in Delta's throat, making her gag. "What have you done?"

With blood trails streaming down her arms, Kate wiped a strand of white hair from her forehead and chuckled. "Think I kilt something other than my dinner?" She pointed at the smooth, tan flesh of a half dozen skinned squirrels.

"Don't mock me!" Delta had gutted and cleaned animals all her life, but Kate, bloody from the hunt, made her feel like death had stalked her across the mountain.

Kate cocked her head to one side. "What troubles ye?"

"You know who I've come for."

"Ain't seen *Who* in a month of Sundays." She shrugged her shoulders.

"Don't lie to me." Delta fought the urge to wrap her hands around Kate's throat. "Where's my son?" She bolted to the house and swung open the door. "Lafette! I know you're here. Time to come home. Stop fooling with Momma."

No answer. Nor did Delta see any sign of him.

Kate followed her into the house, shaking a finger. "Told you hard luck was coming." She still held the bloody knife in her hand. "You've run him off, ain't you?"

Tears welled in Delta's eyes. Where else would he go? Her feet scattered the Tyme leaves in a wide circle around her. Someone had to know where he was. Someone had to help. She glared at Kate, loathing the gleam of triumph dancing in her eyes.

"He's left you," Kate said.

"He'd never leave me." She spoke as much to herself as to Kate.

"Just like Arn." Kate dropped the bloody knife into a pan. The clang of the two metals jarred the room. She stared hard at Delta as if knowing all along this would be the conclusion of a saga written years before.

"Just like Arn," Delta repeated, some cruel logic floating in her memory. She pressed her hands to her cheeks. Her stomach churned. Turning away from Kate did not relieve the sensation of the woman's eyes burning into her back. Delta bolted out the door and dove through the bushes, the words *Just like Arn* screaming in her head.

∞

Delta headed to the main road. He wouldn't run away, she told herself wildly. I'll find him if I have to search all night. Sharp claps of thunder silenced the clamor of crickets, katydids, and bullfrogs. As she reached the mid-point down the mountain, a misty rain hung in the ribbons of fog. She called out Lafette's name and whistled for Blue, but neither answered. Got to get light, she thought. Can't hunt in the dark.

Her fear struggled for control of a stream of images: Lafette falling off a cliff, being chased by a panther, drowned in a creek, even hunted by the Wampus. But her boy could take care of himself, she also told herself. Knew his way around the mountain better than she did. Could find his way home in darkness as black as pitch.

At the base of the mountain rain sprinkled and a ghostly fog shrouded the coming darkness. A thick carpet of leaves left a rotting smell in the air. Delta followed the glow of oil lamps in the Cumberland Gap Trading Post. Breathless and drenched, she staggered onto the porch.

Raucous laughter erupted. She pushed open the door. A dozen men, their boasting cut off sharply, stared at her. King Kingsley straddled a chair at a card table. Henry sat opposite him, shuffling through a deck of cards.

"Want your lantern," Delta told the cashier.

He glanced toward King before answering. "Ain't none for sale."

Henry stood and cast the handful of cards onto the table. "None for sale?"

She pointed at a lantern above the cashier's head that lit the room with a vivid orange hue. "I'll take that one." She narrowed her eyes until he couldn't meet her gaze.

"We're using it." He swallowed hard unsure whether to be intimidated more by King or by Delta. King tapped his fingers on the back of his chair, stared at Henry and steadfastly ignored Delta. Henry stood, reached up and pulled the lantern down, and thrust it into her hands. The cashier gave King a helpless shrug.

"What's the matter, Delta?" Henry asked, following her out onto the porch.

Her wet hair matted against her face. Part of her wanted to collapse in his arms and beg for help, but her pride hid the shame of responsibility for her son running away. She gazed at Shadow Mountain, circled in fog with only the tip of Arn's Volcano sticking up like a fist shaking at the gray sky. "Lafette's run away. Just like Arn." She put a hand to her throat, trying to still the tremble in her voice.

"Wait here." Henry reentered the store and called to the men that a boy was lost. None of them stirred. Only the click of boot heels on the wooden floor. The steps halted beside Henry. Without turning, Delta knew the boots belonged to King. She knew the faint whispers were his. She knew what he said was poisonous as rattler venom.

Henry burst out the door. Behind him, King hovered like a wasp. "I'm ashamed of you," Henry told him. "Ashamed to be your son!"

King glared at Delta, his eyes hard and reflecting the lantern's flame. His creased forehead looked like layers of broken slate. She sensed his hatred aimed sharp as an Indian's arrow.

In the store, men shuffled, watching the porch but mostly stared at the floor. Good, Delta thought, let them be ashamed too. How could they be so ornery to refuse to help find a little boy?

"Come," Henry said to her. "I know where he might hide." He took the lantern, helped her up on a sorrel mare and mounted behind. With one arm around her waist, he pulled the reins to the side and they galloped toward Shadow Mountain.

The rain drizzled, slapping her skin with the sharpness of bee stings. Trees flailed, ripping leaves off their branches. The lantern flickered wildly. Shadows of tree limbs shot back and forth across their path, creating a jail-like barrier on all sides.

The horse trotted to the edge of a roaring flood in Tyme Creek. On the opposite side, the Elisha Tree stood like a warrior against the storm. Rain swelled the creek to twice its normal size. Henry spurred the horse as it slide onto the muddy bank. Delta lurched forward, gripping its mane. Water reached the horse's belly and Henry's boots dipped into the surge. The horse stumbled and creek water splashed into her face. They slid sideways against a torn tree limb barely clinging to its shore roots.

The horse's high-pitched neighing screeched with the howl of the wind. She pushed against the thick limb and Henry grunted as he kicked it. Her dress slipped under the log, threatening to pull her under. She flung an arm around the horse's neck. Henry's gripped her waist. She remembered Arn saying, *a horse will obey, if you know the right words.* As he had done, she pressed her lips to its skin and whispered. “Muscles of iron, brave steed.” The animal surged forward, its strong limbs undulated through the deluge, staggering until its hooves struck the opposite bank and heaved them onto solid ground.

Delta slid from Henry’s grasp, landing in a heap. Above, the branches of the Elisha Tree created a roof against the rain and only the steady drops from the leaves pelted them. She reached up to Henry to pull herself back onto the horse, but he raised his hand and dismounted.

He pointed at the roots. “Little boys always have their secret places.”

The pond beyond the Elisha Tree had risen but did not have the roaring overflow of the main creek. The tree glistened with crystal raindrops dripping around the knots of its ancient bark. They sparkled like stars when Delta raised the lantern. A popping sound echoed on the other side of the tree. She stepped across a woven mass of gnarled roots bulging from the ground, leaned out over the water and peered around the tree.

On the far side, Kate stretched out, her legs and feet hooked into protruding roots, her arms lengthened over the pond, rhythmically slapping its surface.

Henry pressed against Delta’s back, both hands clasped her shoulders. “Careful,” he said. “Got to be careful.”

She glanced at Henry, confused by his pale face. “She’s working a silly spell. Can’t hurt you long as you’re with me. Let’s find Lafette.”

“Delta, we found him.”

Delta looked again at Kate as she slapped the water, making the pond’s surface choppy. She stretched her neck toward the moon and howled. “Wampus, Wampus, break this tree. Wampus, Wampus, break this tree.” Revulsion filled Delta. The water bounced to and fro as Kate’s pounding created waves. She tipped forward gripping the tangled roots more tightly with her legs.

Delta shivered. “Let’s leave, Henry.”

Henry held her firmly. “The tt... tree,” he stuttered. “The tree has him.”

♆ 18 ♆

THE ENORMITY OF the Elisha Tree froze Delta's breath. Her focus zoomed to an arm-sized hole in the wet brown bark and a white hue beyond. Lafette's spiked, cotton-colored hair. "My son! She's calling the Wampus to get him!" Delta lunged toward Kate. "You're trying to kill my son!" She clawed at Kate, dragging her away from the water.

"Delta! No!" Henry yelled, tugging her back.

As the two women fought, the pond shot up into the roots of the Elisha Tree. Henry released the struggling women and leaped into the water. "Got to get to Lafette under the tree," he said. "Only way." He dove into the tangled roots.

Delta concentrated on Kate, intending to block any curses. "You called that creature to do your will on my son?" They grappled, balancing precariously on the tightly woven roots. Kate's pale blue irises flashed wildly. Her chest panted for breath. The icy skin of her arms felt hard like a dead animal's. Delta realized she was shaking an old woman and loosened her grip. "Stay away from my son."

"You stir my hate, Delta." A strong wind blew Kate's silver hair from her face. She twisted free. "Take my place and learn what I can't teach you." She pressed herself against the tree. "I'm gone, boy."

"Don't leave, Aunt Kate, please." His voice shivered and he jammed a hand through the hole, his fingers spread in the space between Delta and Kate's eyes. The women stared at each other, Lafette's fingers forming bars between them, then Kate bolted. Delta squeezed her son's hand between hers. "Momma!" he cried.

She reached into the Elisha Tree, breaking bark around the squirrel hole, and felt his hair, his forehead, his nose, his chin. "Lafette, honey, come out of there."

"I can't, Momma. I'm stuck."

His voice quivered pitifully. Delta leaned out onto the roots to locate Henry under the tree. Water looked about six foot deep. She heard bubbles and a flush of mud sent slivers of wood to the surface. "Henry? Are you there?" No answer. She rushed back to the tree. "Lafette, watch for him! He's trying to get you out."

"Momma, I'm scared."

Her heart pounded and fear twisted throughout her. Again, she tore at the bark around the hole, but the hard wood bit splinters into her nails. Under the roots came coughing and gasping. Henry's head emerged and he yelled, "Lafette's lodged between the tree and some rocks he's stored in there. Wood's too strong to break. Gonna take some time." He spat water and showed her his pocketknife. "Best you can, keep the water out of the tree." Inhaling deep breaths, he disappeared again.

Delta anchored the lantern between two roots on high ground. She shrank from the looming shadow and solid stillness of the ancient tree. The water churned like a thresher against tall grass, an unending sound that unnerved her.

At the tree base she splashed away the water in waves, terrified that the Wampus might appear behind her any minute. Out past the rim of the Tyme branches, rain pelted the creek, driving the water level higher. Already it lapped at the hem of her dress. "Quick, Henry, it's rising," she shouted, but couldn't tell if he'd heard.

A brown, stick-like body slid by. Delta slapped the water and the snake darted off. She looked into the woods, trying to anticipate from which direction the Wampus might jump. The coppery back of another snake humped out of the creek and she smacked the water as hard as she could, drenching herself.

The flood kept rising, and she dragged a tree limb into the water to divert the stream. She anchored the log with the largest stones she could find and tore up a solid hunk of grassy sod from the creek bank to throw on top. Another snake slithered toward her. She wound her legs around a large root and leaned out to slap at the water. Her body formed the same position as Kate's, striking the water to keep the away the snakes. Only then did Delta realize Kate had been saving Lafette.

"Look for Henry!" she yelled back. "He'll get you out." If the water rose another inch, it'd be up into the tree. But how could he drown? *How could the Watcher drown? How could the mountain allow this?*

"Henry?" she called out. She heard no sound. Judge Treadway was right—she should take Lafette and leave the mountain. If Henry died underneath the tree trying to rescue her son, who could she blame but herself? Were their lives worth trying to protect land that only caused her strife? Arn... Arn was the only reason she stayed.

She struck the water until her hands stung. The pond inched up around her, cold as winter snow. The wet wood of any other tree would have broken apart in her hands. She could have pulled the tree down with a rope and horse. But Tyme wood was so strong only the Wampus could smash it. "The Wampus," she whispered. *Kate had called the Wampus to break the tree.*

The pond lapped through the roots. "Lafette?" she called back. "Do you see Henry?" She jerked around and reached through the hole. Her hand plunged into icy water. Her sight fell black and air seemed to suck from her lungs. "Answer me!" Delta's stomach cramped and she clung to the tree to keep her knees from giving way, then in frenzy she tore at the wood. The ragged bark scratched her cheek. All she saw inside the tree was blackness. "Lafette! Henry!" she shrieked, her entire body shaking.

She hung by one arm, trying to force more of herself into the tree. Her strength gave out. The bark burned her hands as she slid to the ground.

The rain ceased. Pond water calmed. Between the tree branches the sky showed through, tinged a subtle gray. The unsettling aloneness was like a cape around her shoulders. Her teeth chattered, yet she could not feel the cold. The outlines of the trees came into focus, standing like silent witnesses.

Empty. She just felt empty. "Oh God," she groaned, "no, no, why would you do this to me?" She stared up at Shadow Mountain. Gripping the roots of the Tyme tree, she screamed, "I'll pay any price, just give me back my son!" The echo of her voice stretched to the mountain peaks and down the ridges, through the saddle of Cumberland Gap, past houses and graveyards, and the overgrown paths of the Wilderness Road. But Nature could not, or as she believed, *would* not, answer her.

The world spun, losing all form. The night of Lafette's birth, she'd felt the same dizziness. *Arn's face drifted in front of her.*

Kate gripped her hands. Lafette struggled inside her, spilling out between her legs, then his cry, an angry shout from a creature hardly bigger than a sitting hen. Now he was gone… and all creation with him.

Tree roots quivered beneath her. Instantly she crouched, ready to fall into the earth. A roar howled through the Elisha Tree. Branches rattled. An explosion of mud washed beneath the roots and a wall of stones crumbled into the water. Sludge sprayed across the pond. The center bubbled like a cauldron. Henry surfaced in the middle of the mire with her baby held tight against his chest.

Delta pulled herself onto her knees, too tired to speak, and opened her arms. Henry stood waist-deep in the pond. Blue paddled behind him. He waded out and laid Lafette in her arms. She cradled him as if he were newborn, kissing his muddied hair and hugging him so tightly that he struggled against her for breath.

The rush of the creek died and the pond cleared just as sun broke through branches of Tyme trees. Henry wrapped a blanket around Delta. A robin chirped and a patch of red and purple morning glories opened toward a ray of sunlight. Blue jumped on Delta's lap, trying to lick Lafette's face. Henry picked up the dog and helped her onto his horse, cushioning Lafette into her lap with Blue resting on the backend of the saddle. The puppy licked its jowls as if grateful to be riding up the mountain. While Delta hummed Lafette to sleep, Henry led the horse through the misty forest.

Except for the muddy ground, the mountain looked merely rearranged: boulders wedged between trees, grass mashed down from the flooding creeks. The air smelled new. When they reached Delta's house, the mugginess of early morning heated up the ground causing a grassy odor to fill the rooms.

"Momma, the Wampus chased me," Lafette said sleepily as she tucked him into bed. Blue jumped up and settled in beside him.

"He can't get you here, honey." Delta smoothed his forehead and brushed a bit of dust from his eyelashes. "Momma won't let nobody get you."

"The Wampus was gonna tear me apart and crush my bones against White Rocks." Lafette pulled his legs up against his chest. "I kept thinking of Daddy. Kept thinking the Wampus had kilt Daddy, and he would never come home."

"Just sleep." She kissed her son's forehead, waiting until he closed his eyes. Henry watched as she pulled the curtain across the window. His hair had dried in spiky strands against his forehead and mud caked every seam of his clothing. His unshaven face looked rough, and for the first time, Delta saw the age around his eyes. She held his hand and led him toward the porch. "Henry, there's no words to thank you." Her arms circled his waist and she hugged him with all her strength. When she raised her gaze to his, his brown eyes shone with the loneliest expression she'd ever seen in a man, and she cupped his face in her hands.

"Delta, I... I want to know you."

She peered deeply into the web of that russet color, until finally he let his head fall back onto his shoulders. Her arms came from around him and curled like kitten paws on his wide chest. She felt like a small animal against him, and the warm, safe feeling he created was one she knew could only last for a few seconds.

From his throat came a sound halfway between a laugh and a cry. "I love you," he said. "I don't know how to hide it anymore. I love you. I want you to be my wife. I want Lafette to be my son. I want to protect you, and do for you. I want to..."

She stepped away, looking toward the green rows of corn growing higher than she could reach. White straw-like webs spotted the stalks, a sign that the cobs were strong and healthy this year. Her gaze took in the beehives, the barn and the chicken coop, then Arn's Volcano that cast a shadow over half the mountaintop. She cleared her throat, feeling weak about what she knew she must say. "Henry, you're one of the richest men in the county and better looking than anybody I know."

He blushed faintly.

"When your daddy came here, people in these mountains lived by hunting, farming and barter. He gave 'em something by which to change this land. For a long time, I hated him for it. Just like Arn hated him. Thought he was an evil that'd come. Maybe sometimes I still do. But it's yours to continue that, come what may."

"You can be part of my world, Delta."

"No... I can't." She pointed at Arn's Volcano. "I'm his world. No changing that."

Henry rubbed his fists against his eyelids, but before he could speak she placed a hand on his chest and held him at a distance.

"Don't know how the world you and your daddy brought on us is gonna sit with these mountains," she said. "So far, the land has allowed your people to stay. It's the change that worries me, even as the mountains tolerate your lumbering, mining and such, so the people have begun to accept it as well."

"Delta, you talk nonsense."

"Arn taught me things you don't understand. Things that make me different from other women, and because of it I could never be a wife to you."

Henry looked away, his eyes darted back and forth, unable to express himself although his lips parted to speak several times.

Worker bees made a steady hum in the background. Dragonflies darted past them and the chickens clucked to be fed. The day began like every other. "I thank you for saving Lafette. I..."

"I'd never try and replace Arn in your life or Lafette's." He touched her shoulders. "I only want to love you."

"You could do that, Henry, without marrying me."

"Tell me what Arn did that was so different."

She looked at the sun, staring until spots floated in the air in front of her. When she answered, Henry's form was dark like a shadow, and for the time he stayed, her sight was never quite the same. "Arn treated me like hisself and expected no less from me." She took Henry's icy hand between her palms. "Tell me I could be equal in your world. I'm the mother of the Watcher, Henry. The Watcher guards the pulse of the earth. The Watcher keeps the balance. In your world, men would laugh at such notions."

His lips stretched into a thin line and his large dark pupils pulled inward as if a bright light had suddenly been cast into his face. He stepped to the edge of the porch and whistled long and low for his horse. The mare edged up to the porch and Henry mounted. He clicked his tongue once and the horse stepped forward so he was below Delta, looking up at her. He reached for her hand and pressed it to his lips. "I'll never bother you on it again. But if you ever need a thing, you know to come to me. Say that you will."

"I will, Henry," she answered, but made a vow in her heart never to pain him for the rest of her life.

Henry squeezed his calves against his horse's sides. She withdrew her hand and held it high in the air, waving to him until he was out of sight.

ᐯ 19 ᐯ

THE RHYTHMIC PLODDING of Ole Sal's hooves against the cakey soil of a Virginia mountaintop echoed through the valleys of Tennessee's Hancock County. Delta traveled along Powell River, then crossed over into Tennessee. The strong mule carried an adult, two children and overstuffed sacks of ginseng, rhubarb, and Tyme leaves.

Delta held Rosy around the waist so she wouldn't slide onto the mule's neck. Lafette rode comfortably behind them. He'd been quiet, almost solemn, since his experience in the Elisha Tree, and Delta worried about what this meant. He'd begged to make the journey with her. His ankle, wrapped with a bandage soaked with fennel, witch hazel and sarsaparilla, seemed to trouble him with an annoying itch from the healing snakebite, and he swished it back and forth against the mule's side.

They crossed over Powell Mountain and came upon a long, winding trail. It bridged one peak to the next, almost as high as Creation Ridge and as wild as Shadow Mountain. Many travelers gave its blue darkness a wide berth. They avoided these ridges because Melungeons lived there.

"There it be, Aunt Delta!" Rosy pointed up at the rocky peak. "Newman's Ridge. Reckon Aunt Verdie'll remember me?"

"Why would she remember a piss ant girl?" Lafette smirked. "Aunt Verdie meets hundreds of people a year, probably thousands."

"Lafette," Delta said, turning around as far as she could. "Be good. We trade here once a year and I don't want to leave the impression you're a hooligan."

"He *is* a hooligan, Aunt Delta."

"I swear, next year, I'm leaving you young'uns home."

Both children snickered, then fell silent. Delta heard the echo of a horse resounding through the valley. Its hooves beat the ground in a gallop. She stopped Ole Sal.

"Somebody's following us, Momma." Lafette cupped a hand behind his ear and closed his eyes to listen. "Comin' fast, so they ain't got trading sacks about 'em."

Instantly Delta thought of the coming trouble with King Kingsley and Kate. She jabbed her heels into Ole Sal's sides and the mule quickened her pace. The morning sun rode along the top of the ridge where Ole Sal shifted to stay in the shade. Dragonflies whizzed atop purple irises along with yellow and white butterflies, honeybees, and hummingbirds darting in and out of the flowers with the precision of a human hand. The moist air hung heavy, each intake of breath smooth as velvet. Delta no longer heard the galloping horse but sensed someone still following.

The landscape grew rocky, so whoever was behind them would also have to ascend slowly. Over the past few days she'd begun to hope Kate and King would cease to disturb her. As soon as fall arrived, the Tyme wood would be too wet for his use, and winter's snow would keep Kate holed up for another season.

A rifle blast rumbled in the valley below. The sound ripped through Delta as if it were the bullet itself. Both children stiffened, watching her response.

"Have to walk to that ledge," she said, pointing at the path's sharp grade.

Lafette slid off first and reluctantly helped Rosy down. Delta led Ole Sal as they climbed up a crooked washed-out trench formed by rain that drained off the mountain. Dry earth crumbled under their feet, and the children pulled themselves up on the vines that grew along the ground.

At the top, Delta stared out at the valley, hoping to spot the traveler behind them. Lafette repositioned the sacks on Ole Sal's back, then pulled out his squirrel rifle. "In case we see a squirrel." He studied the carpet of trees below them. "Could be somebody coming to buy Aunt Verdie's moonshine."

"Most likely." Delta brushed his hair from across his eyes, trying to reassure him.

The clopping of hooves neared and a patch of gooseberry bushes swayed. A bolero hat appeared, then the nose of a brown and white horse carrying a big man. The hat shaded his face. He took it off to wipe his face. "Judge Treadway," Delta murmured, and her heart pounded. Her fingers trembled, she held her hands together so Lafette wouldn't see her nervousness.

"Somebody's in trouble," he said. " 'Course, the Judge knows how to help people, especially women."

"Why women?" She looked at him, puzzled by his statement.

"Heard him say it to King Kingsley. Marrying 'em off."

"What?"

"Wonder if it's Aunt Verdie he's coming to see."

"Lafette, why would you think such a thing?"

" 'Cause me and Valentine heard Judge Treadway discouraging Mr. Kingsley from filing a lawsuit against some woman. He said the way to stop lawsuits is for a woman to get married. Seems awful easy. 'Lessen you're Rosy Thunderheart. Who'd want to marry her?" He hesitated and continued, "Got me a whippin' for being with Valentine that day, so I ought to remember what I heard."

Delta's throat dried up and she coughed. "Young man, where's your manners? You be nice to Rosy."

"Ain't Aunt Verdie too old to get married?" he asked.

"Get up the hill. Judge'll follow if it's us he needs."

They passed through a lush, well-tended cemetery decorated in Melungeon fashion, flowers planted at both ends of the graves, grass trimmed as on a house lawn. Some graves had shelters to protect the mound from harsh weather. Rosy dropped honeysuckle blossoms beside each tombstone as they passed. Goins, Mullins, Bowlin, Collins, Washburn, Lucas, and Mull, families who'd settled this ridge in the 1700s. They had been forced to live in isolation because genetic quirks colored some of them a reddish brown shade while others were pale-skinned, and because they were poor and unknowledgeable in the ways of fighting businessmen.

This Melungeon settlement consisted of six cabins built on rocky, uneven terrain. More people were said to live farther up the ridge, but Delta had never met them. As they approached the settlement, a couple of children ran to their mothers bent over gray tin wash tubs, their arms elbow-deep in soapy water. The black-haired women stared guardedly at Delta until they recognized her. Then they nodded and shooed their children from around their legs.

Delta led the mule to a trough of water and pointed to some kids playing hide-and-seek. "After we deliver the goods, you two go play."

Lafette scrunched up his face. Delta glanced back. No Judge Treadway. Golden corn grew on the sloping hillside. The garden gave off the rich aromas of greens. Delta yelled at the house, waiting for admittance.

"I hear ye." Aunt Verdie replied. "Come on in, you'ins know I can't leave the house." Her high-pitched voice sounded like singing.

Lafette unloaded the sacks from Ole Sal and dragged them up to the porch. Aunt Verdie's hound dog, Rip, was trained to pull open the door and he stood at attention, sniffing the air. Before stepping up to the porch, Delta turned and looked out at the mountain's edge. Judge Treadway's horse staggered up the embankment. Her pulse accelerated as if she were running a race, and part of her wished she could vanish. Rip sniffed her feet when she stepped into the house and she petted his head.

Aunt Verdie, all four hundred pounds of her, rested in a custom-made chair, fanning her face with a dishtowel. Her skin was maple brown except for darker, reddish circles under her blue eyes. " 'Spected you'd be along any day now."

"Got you a good mess of rhubarb, and my best ginseng patch matured this year." She touched Aunt Verdie's hand, noticing the grassy smell of collards simmering in a caldron outside the window. "And of course, brought some Tyme leaves."

"Why, Delta, your hands is a'tremblin' and you're cold as the dead." Aunt Verdie leaned forward, her thin lips pressed together so they disappeared into the fleshy folds of her face, and she stared unblinkingly.

"I'll have Lafette throw some rhubarb in that mess of greens you got cooking yonder." Delta started out the window.

"Verdie Lucas?" Judge Treadway called out in his booming voice.

Delta whirled, her hand clutching the collar of her dress, and fought the impulse to drop to her knees.

Aunt Verdie inhaled deeply. "Don't you worry none, girl. Aunt Verdie's here." She winked and wiped her forehead with the dishtowel, then called out in the same sing-song voice, "I hear ye. Come on in, you'ins know I can't leave the house."

The Judge's footsteps shook the porch as he entered with an air of an important man. Wasting no time, he took a paper from his pocket. A shiver shot up Delta's spine as she detected the tightness of his mouth and glassiness of his eyes.

"Like to've never found this place," he said. "Seems like the roads change every time I come on this mountain."

"Likely they do," Aunt Verdie said. "Impressive to see a'body try."

The Judge arched slightly forward, and it seemed to Delta that he forced a polite sternness he did not actually feel. He swallowed and stared at the floor, the paper passing from hand to hand. When he handed it to Delta it was moist with his sweat. She slipped into a chair beside Aunt Verdie. He hung his hat on a nail behind the door, then rubbed a hand through the thick front curls of his white hair, shifting uncomfortably from foot to foot. "I want you to know how bad I feel about what happened. Those men not helping you find Lafette was a disgrace."

Delta unfolded the paper without looking up at him. "Is this legal?"

"Heard you was headed to Newman Ridge and figured I could use a nice ride." Treadway took a canteen from his pocket and looked knowingly at Aunt Verdie.

"Yonder in the corner." She cocked her head at an oak barrel.

Delta followed each sentence with a finger so she'd miss none of the meaning. Some words she didn't know. Others stood out like a blaze at midnight. Melungeon, she read: *Arn Marlon, a Melungeon.*

The Judge bit a corner of his mouth as he filled his canteen with moonshine. "It ain't a recorded legal document," he said, "but it could be." Taking a drink, he nervously jiggled coins in his pocket. "Delta, you got to consider the best interest of your child."

Aunt Verdie looked from one to the other, gestured at the paper, then leaned back until the chair creaked. "Reckon it says what they always say." She shook her head and smiled bitterly. "Honey, them farms you passed on the way up, that fertile bottomland, used to belong to my granpappy. Land around it belonged to the Mullins and the Goins. White folks come with papers saying by law we couldn't own it, saying we had slave blood in us, and couldn't vote or bear witness. Now they own the good land and we's stuck up here on the ridges."

"Delta, I beg you, sell that mountain before this gets out of hand." Judge Treadway stepped forward, his towering body a shadow that almost consumed her.

"Lafette's to be the Watcher."

"You consider anything I told you last week? Raise Lafette in town. Get him an education. He's a smart boy. Forget this Watcher nonsense. That's old times. It's 1894! Six years, it'll be the turn of the century."

"Is this or is it not a legal document?"

Judge Treadway inhaled deeply and exhaled through his mouth as if expelling an unpleasant taste. "No, Delta. It won't stand in a court of law." He paced a few steps, hands clasped behind his back. "If King submitted court papers claiming Arn is Melungeon, and further claimed that Melungeons are descended from the Negro race, therefore, as a Negro, he could not own Shadow Mountain, he would lose that law case. It's been proven Melungeons ain't descendants of slaves. Though, frankly, we don't know what they are." He paused and looked at the big woman. "No offense, Aunt Verdie. What happened to Aunt Verdie's grandpappy couldn't happen again." He spoke as if he stood in his own courtroom. "But if King files anyway, you still lose." He glanced out the window where Lafette stirred the greens, and breathed in the mouthwatering aroma. "Be no way to protect Lafette from finding out his daddy was Melungeon, and so would everyone else."

If this knowledge became known, Lafette would have to live as a Melungeon no matter how white his skin. As badly as Negroes and Indians were treated, Melungeons were treated worse; shunned, forced to avoid contact with the rest of society, as feared a people as the Wampus was feared a beast. This was not the life she intended for her son. She had no fear of Melungeon ancestry, but the outside world did. "Henry Kingsley part of this?"

The Judge wiped his forehead with the back of his arm and his jaw muscles flexed, increasing the depth of his dimples. When he spoke, the same muscles quivered with nervous tension. "I told King if you married and had Lafette adopted, he'd never be able to get the mountain from a white man. King don't give a damn who he has to fight! You're just a woman,

Delta. You won't win against him. Time to think of Lafette. If you won't sell the mountain, for Godssake, give him the trees." His hands clutched at the air as if to hold her shoulders and shake sense into a willful woman.

"Married?" She chuckled faintly and fanned herself with the paper.

"Is there anybody? Is there even a possibility of a man to fight him and keep him from making this public? If you're accused of miscegenation, all these people who've moved here in past years will never forget it. It's a new breed come to these mountains. They'd always hold it against you and Lafette. Think, now."

Delta stared at the floor, knowing he meant Henry. How many years had she watched the invasion of timberers, coal operators, con men? They came. They went. Taking more than they ever gave back. These were people the Watcher fought. The Kingsleys, including Henry, were part of them. "No, there's no one."

"Been a Judge thirty years now and glad this ain't a decision I got to make. Don't want to see you lose the mountain to him for nothing." He staggered back to the doorway, shaking each leg as if it were cramped. "Don't fight him, Delta. Hate thinking what would come of it." He nodded his head at both women. "Mrs. Lucas, my respects. Hope you didn't take offense to my using the word Melungeon."

Aunt Verdie stared at his canteen until finally Judge Treadway took a bill from his pocket and left it in a jar by the door.

Delta sat quietly, her fear threading through her limbs. Judge Treadway mounted his horse and yelled back that he'd be in his office late, should Delta need him.

Aunt Verdie pushed herself up on her hands, straining and huffing like a woman giving birth. With a critical squint she peered out the window at Lafette. "Could be the boy's a Watcher. Could be being a Watcher ain't what it used to be." She dropped back down in the chair and put a hand on Delta's shoulder. "Kate Huston is an old fool. There ain't a Melungeon alive that'd ever identify Lafette as having dark blood. We know what it's like. We'd never pin that life on another. If the child don't know, then don't you do anything that might wise him up. Settle that feud with King Kingsley. Don't let him hurt your boy. That ole mountain ain't worth it. You want Lafette to end up like me? Sitting way up here, not a blamed thing to do with myself 'cept make moonshine and wait on company." Her eyes watered and she wiped her nose on the dishtowel.

Delta wrapped her arms around Aunt Verdie's shoulders. Such doubt rose within her that she thought she might cry too. "If only Arn was here."

"Don't say it, girl." She shook her finger in front of Delta's nose. "Arn ain't here. Yer the one that's got trouble. Best think that Arn Marlon's dead... and been dead these five years. Fool yourself into thinking he'll come back and save ye, and you foster a lie."

"But nobody knows what's become of Arn."

"That right. Nobody knows. Comes down to a matter of what you're gonna believe. Best you start believin' he's a dead soul."

Doubt flooded through Delta. Her dry throat felt cottony, and her voice cracked as she started to speak. She tried again but found she could not. Giving up, she kissed Aunt Verdie on the cheek and went outside.

Lafette had brushed Ole Sal and was loading her with the jugs of medicine Aunt Verdie had prepared to trade. "You've been a real help today," she said, but wondered how she and a small boy could hope to fight.

The top of his head grazed her chin. He had grown, and she hadn't even noticed. His movements had a maturity and adeptness as he readied the mule for the trip home. But he was still a boy. Someday he'd be the Watcher his father wanted him to be. The will inside her felt strong as iron, and she looked up at the heavens and in her heart, thanked Arn for giving her this son.

ⅴ 20 ⅴ

LAFETTE RESTED HIS face rested against Delta's back as they journeyed down Newman's Ridge. His mother's muscles tensed and relaxed like fists ready for a fight. He worried that she might be in trouble. When Rosy stopped chattering and finally fell into a quiet spell, he asked, "Judge Treadway doing good?"

Delta slowed the mule at base of the ridge near the flat bottomland where twelve or so farms marked their boundaries with split rail fences. Each had a barn, smokehouse, and some had icehouses. One had a bee-hive shaped iron furnace built of creek rock. Fields sprouted row upon row of corn and tobacco. She let a long, slow stream of breath flow out of her body, as if expelling evil thoughts. "Miscegenation..."

Lafette leaned around her and peered up at her face. She seemed more upset than angry. "What did you say, Momma?"

"Nothing, son. Talking to myself." She spurred the mule forward, not speaking again until they rode in sight of Shadow Mountain. Stopping where a small waterfall formed a bowl in the rocks, they and the horse drank their fill. Delta left Rosy with the mule, took Lafette by the hand, and walked out of hearing range.

"Momma, what vexes ye?" Lafette stepped onto a stone so he was the same height as Delta. She shot him an amused smile. Annoyed, he thought, she's funning me. Thinks I'm too little for her troubles. Since he'd come tumbling out of the Elisha Tree he no longer felt like a boy. Something inside him had changed.

"We have an enemy trying to steal the mountain, Lafette. Momma's gonna have to settle it." She hugged her chest and shivered as if December knocked on the door. "Might be hard to understand, but I need you to be as much a man now as your daddy. Be brave and strong as him."

"Then, I should defend the mountain." Lafette looked over at his rifle, strapped to Ole Sal, and thought maybe it was this Watcher story Mamma always told. An iron-like resolve formed inside him. Its fierceness beat in his chest, knowing Shadow Mountain was threatened. No longer just a boy who lived on the mountain, partaking of its fruits, he was the mountain. The land was his body; the trees were his limbs; the paths, his bones; the creeks, his blood. No foot would set on his mountain without his say so. "Let me go, Momma. It's mine to do. Tell me who's trying to steal the mountain from us."

"Too soon for you, Lafette. Too soon for you to fight like a—"

"A man?" He swallowed, fighting off the embarrassment that filled him. "I thought this was what you wanted."

"It is, but Lafette, your daddy didn't start out being as powerful as he was. It took much work. He studied under Pappy Thunderheart for years. And when he did take his place, he was stronger than any Watcher that ever lived."

"But Daddy's gone. How can I ever learn?"

"The mountain itself will teach you."

"The mountain?" He cocked his head sideways in confusion.

"When the Watcher calls to it, the mountain responds. It'll teach you its ways more surely than any living man." She held his chin between her fingers. "Right now, I need you to see Rosy home safely."

"Can get there by herself." He scowled, thinking here he was, saying he'd give this Watcher business a chance, and his first duty was to escort home a girl. "Baby Rosy Thunderheart," he said in disgust.

"Lafette! Where's your manners?"

"Left 'em hanging on the clothesline."

She gave him an uncertain look, then went down on one knee and drew him to her. "I've a secret to tell you, Lafette."

He leaned closer. His toes tingling as the expectation of what she might say. "A secret Daddy knew?"

She pressed her mouth into a thin line, gazing at him, searching for the proper words. "A powerful secret. Probably the strongest magic you'll ever know."

Lafette's eyes widened. "Secrets change everything, Momma."

She studied the ground, hesitation deepening the lines around her eyes. "A dragon lives in Arn's Volcano. I saw your daddy raise it." She paused, gauging his reaction before continuing. Her voice was church-song smooth as she described her memory, "Pale as mist it flowed out the cracks of that rock, billowed from the top, even seeped up from the ground. It hovered like a cloud over the mountaintop, and Arn said we were invisible to anybody looking our way." Nervously, she wound her fingers through the unbraided part of her hair. "Bad people had come searching for a place to settle, and Arn hid us." She watched Lafette, unable to decide if he believed her.

"The dragon shook the earth beneath their feet, scared them off from these parts."

His eyes narrowed as if he'd been told a fairytale. He pointed at the gun. "That's how Daddy would have handled a bad person."

"He told me Pappy Thunderheart once used the dragon to confuse a Confederate regiment. It can kill, too. The dragon protects the mountain and the Watcher."

"Then why don't we call it now, Momma?"

She exhaled in frustration. "Because we don't know how. Even Kate's not powerful enough. You have to be strong enough to control it, send it back when need be, and call it forth to do the mountain's bidding." She stroked his head, then stopped, realizing that was what one did to a child.

"I'd have to see this dragon first. I ain't too sure."

"For now, take Rosy home. I've another journey to make. Won't be gone long."

"What'cha gonna do, Momma?"

She smiled and turned away. He suspected she didn't know what she would do. It made him afraid for her. If he was not yet strong enough to fight as the Watcher, there had to be another way he could fight. He banged his hand against his head. "But how?" He looked up at Arn's Volcano. He was like an ant below it. To think his father controlled the power in that rock. If it was there, he knew he could do it. *If it was there.*

The dragon weighed on his mind as he walked Rosy home, even taking her inside to make sure her house was safe. Her wide eyes watched every move he made. "Don't go getting in no trouble," he ordered. "Your folks'll be home past sundown."

"I won't, Lafette. I'd never do nothin' to upset ye." She smiled, then frowned when he didn't smile back. "You need me to help you with anything?"

"Naw, just don't tell nobody where you went today." When she didn't respond he shot out the door.

"Wish you did need me for something, Lafette," she said.

He heard her, but pretended he didn't. He meandered back toward the mountain, walking through Harrogate and past the dismantled Four Seasons Hotel. Pieces of the ornate wood lay on the grass. He touched one, its finish so smooth and shiny he could see the reflection of his face. *There ought to be something I can do.*

From where he stood, Arn's Volcano looked like a perched eagle, ready to swoop on a farmhouse for its evening meal. If only he could summon the power of the dragon now. For the first time in his life, Lafette felt the need for a teacher. Not the kind he'd had in his short time at school, but one who understood the knowledge he must learn. All the same, he was unsure he believed in this Watcher story.

He picked a crab apple from the Kingsley orchard. Past it, he could see Henry exercising one of his horses in an oblong enclosure. The horse did what looked like a little dance, prancing up and down, its clipped tail held up like a baton. Henry shifted his legs back and forth while the horse moved in a way Lafette had never seen before. He was reminded of how Kate Huston controlled her hawk, making it fly to wherever she demanded just by thinking of the destination. How's he do that? Lafette wondered. Was it possible Henry knew the magic of controlling animals? And if he did, could he help control the magic of Shadow Mountain?

Lafette cut through the apple trees to hide beside the horse paddock. Henry was shirtless, and the tanned muscles of his back rippled as he stiffened his spine to stay vertical on the horse. His arms are big enough to carry a log, Lafette thought.

Henry cooed a low, "Woooo," and the white filly stopped as if frozen. He whistled. She lifted a hoof, holding the position like a picture. He kept his back straight and his heels well down, pressing into the horse's sides. She hopped into another little dance. Lafette could hardly believe what he was watching. He decided that whether Henry knew it or not, he understood magic as well as Kate.

After Henry dismounted, he stood in front of the horse and kissed her nose. The filly snorted and nudged his pants pocket. Lafette cleared his throat. Henry turned around and his face reddened. Lafette pretended not to notice. "Thought I'd let you know I ain't feeling so poorly no more."

"You look a dang sight better than last I saw you, son." Henry came to the fence with the white filly trailing behind him. He picked Lafette up and slung him across his shoulder, affectionately whirling him around.

Lafette giggled and beat on Henry's back causing a sound that vibrated like a drum. Henry sat him back on the fence and rubbed the top of Lafette's head. The sweaty smell of the horse swirled in the air and mixed with the grassy odor of a nearby pile of hay. "I know a woman who converses with a hawk the way you talk to your horse," Lafette said, arching his eyebrows, teasing. "She can make it do most anything"

Henry laughed and wiped his mouth with the back of his hand. "Takes a sight more than talking to put a horse through dressage." He took a carrot from his pocket. "Can't recall one that ever did something just by being told." He held the carrot under the horse's mouth. "This is how you put these critters through their paces. All bribes. Right, Cotton?" He patted her neck, and she chomped on the carrot.

"Dress... age? Second time today I heard a word I never heard before."

"That a fact. Smart boy like you. Figured your momma taught you lots of words."

"Judge Treadway said the word, mis... seggie... nation? Wasn't supposed to be listening, but how else would I know anything. He tried to get Momma to get marry and have me adopted so she wouldn't be accused of it. Mis... seggie... nation, that is. 'Course, Momma being like she is, would never give in to that. Though I'm a mite sorry she never took to you." Lafette realized he was babbling and bit his lower lip. He wanted to get Henry back to the subject of magic and how he really got his horse to do tricks. If a man could make a horse dance like a bow-legged woman, how much harder could it be to coax a dragon out of Arn's Volcano? "Reckon you could teach me the magic of dress... age? Wheeeh, powerful word to have to say, ain't it?"

Henry's face paled to a shade as ivory as his horse, making his tan body look darker, and Lafette realized the true power of the word he'd uttered. Dressage must be a secret Henry was intent on keeping because he tightened his hands into fists and began to pace. His boot prints sunk deep in the sandy ground.

"You forget that word, Lafette. Forget you ever heard it."

"I hate to be so direct, but it's real important for me to learn how to talk to animals like you do. I can't go to Aunt Kate but I don't think Momma would mind me coming to you." He tried to smile. It felt forced so he alternated looking at the ground and up as Henry as he pleaded. "If you could teach me your kind of magic, then," he leaned in and whispered, "I'd be strong enough to tame a dragon."

Henry smiled faintly and rubbed Lafette's shoulder with the same affection as he'd massaged his horse's neck. His hands were warm and strong. The skin had a rough texture that

Lafette's liked. "Son, controlling a horse ain't magic. It's all up here." He tapped Lafette's forehead. "Ain't no such thing as magic, and if you use your noggin you'll figure that out." Henry looked deeply into his eyes. "Someday, I'll teach you all you need to know about horses."

Having said that, he stared down at his boots and idly kicked at the sand with a distracted frown. The black toes of the fine leather soon lost their shine. Lafette worried that Henry thought he wanted free lessons in magic and wondered what he might offer as payment to make Henry change his mind. "What can I do to get you to teach me?"

Henry held him by the shoulders and again looked deeply into his eyes. "Tell your mother to marry me." His brow was as deeply furrowed as the bark of an old tree. He held his breath, making his chest muscles bulge out.

Lafette pulled back, both startled and curious. The ghost of his father loomed in his thoughts. Delta never admitted Arn was dead, but Lafette's heart told him it was so. He'd known Henry loved his mother from the first time he'd seen him kissing her beside Arn's Volcano. He had purposely interrupted them when jealousy exploded within him. He didn't feel so resentful now, not since Henry had saved him from drowning. "Wheeeeh, you're asking a lap cat to take on a panther. Ain't you heard of being careful what you wish for 'cause you might get it?"

Henry chuckled. "I know your Momma's weaknesses, son. But there's a powerful lot good about her too."

Lafette twisted his shirttail around his fingers and thought harder than he had in his whole life. Marrying Delta might save Shadow Mountain. After all, Judge Treadway had said so. If Henry lived on the mountain with them, all the quicker he could learn animal magic. All the sooner he could control the dragon, just like his father had done. He sucked in a deep breath, unsure he was doing the right thing. "Reckon I could do the asking, but if she starts to knock me in the noggin, you better be there to take the blow."

Henry smiled widely, lifted him under the arms and swung him onto Cotton's back. He climbed behind and clicked his tongue, steering the horse out of the training paddock. As they started toward Shadow Mountain, he hummed a nursery rhyme familiar to Lafette; one his mother used to sing. He hummed along, then remembering the words, joined in and sang the last part of it.

Who looks like the devil?
He looks just like me.

The sun beat hotly upon their backs. Henry let Lafette hold the reins while his own long, strong legs gripped its sides and controlled their pace. High above, Shadow Mountain blocked the horizon like a wall of black clouds. Their voices meshed with the sound of katydids and bullfrogs.

Who looks like the devil?
He looks just like me.

♆ 21 ♆

DELTA PAUSED AT the Elisha Tree to choose the words she'd say to King. Had only a week passed since she lay on the roots of this enormous tree fighting for her son's life? A green patch of clover already sprouted at its base. She slipped off her shoes and curled her toes in the soft grass. Despite the near tragedy, she associated no bad feelings with this place. How many picnics had she and Arn shared here, how many arguments underneath these branches, how many times had they made up and pledged their love on the tree their son had named Elisha? *Arn, are you really dead?*

She leaned against the trunk, letting her hands drift down the crinkled bark. "First time I laid eyes on you, couldn't stand the sight of you, Arn Marlon." He'd towered over her, his hair a tangle of black curls, jaws sprouting a two-day growth of beard. "Strangest looking critter I ever saw."

"Sure would like you to draw me a pretty picture, Delta-girl," he answered.

She stood, her imagination opening like a morning glory. Slipping on her shoes, she walked the last half-mile with her missing love. "What would you say to King?"

"Got nothing to say to him. I'd say to you, never let an enemy up once you got him down."

"Fine thing! Why didn't you kill him years ago and save me all this trouble?"

Her Arn laughed, throwing back his head like a rearing horse. His smile glorious, eyes blue as chicory. *"More poetic to see King Kingsley done in by a woman."*

"Since when did you become poetic?" She smiled at the thought and stared down at the Cumberland Gap Trading Post. Ant-sized figures sauntered in and out, no one in a hurry, no one with a care in the world. Beyond the store, the rolling hills of a green valley marked the entrance of King Kingsley's land. "I've failed you," she whispered, "I want to protect the mountain, but I have to protect Lafette first." In her mind she heard no answer. "You understand? Folks can't know Lafette carries Melungeon blood."

"Don't go do something foolish, now, Delta-girl."

"If I give him trees, he'll leave us alone."

"Like a cat napping under a nest of baby birds."

"I'll give him an acre. It'll hold him off."

"A year at the most."

"A year longer than I've got now."

"Mistake, Delta. It'll haunt you."

"Only a few trees, Arn!"

"Then Kingsley wins! He's beaten you."

"Our son is more important than those damn trees!" She turned sharply to face her Arn. But there was only a northward breeze that pushed along a billowing white cloud. It shaded her face for the briefest moment. "Hope you understand."

Delta traveled on, determined to barter for time. Judge Treadway was right, she had to deal with King, even at the cost of a few trees. If she gave him an acre now, by the time he demanded more Lafette would be older, stronger, wiser, more cunning than his father. A true Watcher would know what to do even if she did not.

∞

The dusty road to Kingsley's land curled like a snake over sand. Delta wiped her cheeks, hoping her face wasn't dirty. The two-story house, painted white as snow, was lined with flowering plants in burnt orange pots. A horse barn off to the side was the same shade of orange, and beyond were fields of tobacco and orchards of apple trees. She approached the main stairs as if sneaking up on a sleeping animal. Her heart raced as she mounted up each step. The top half of the front door was a stained glass window with the design of a white stallion racing into the wind.

Delta raised her hand to knock, then instead reached for the cold doorknob. She turned it and the door opened. Before her stretched a wooden floor shiny as a pool of water in the afternoon sun. She stepped carefully onto a woven rug running down the center of the hallway, the multihued colors so beautiful she figured it was not meant to be walked on and stepped off to the side. Above her a round fixture of gold-colored limbs was hung with what looked like melting crystals. The sun shining through the door touched the hanging icicles and created rainbows. She stretched an arm, hoping to touch them, but could not reach high enough.

Against a lavender wall a mahogany table glistened as polished as the floor. On it sat human figures that looked to be carved out of ice. Delta picked up a lady posed in a flowing dress, one leg pointed and arms gracefully extended in a bow. Her frock billowed as if she twirled, hair lifted in the breeze and delicate lips kissed the wind. Delta held the figurine up to a window. Strangely and wonderfully, the lady's features favored her own, the most beautiful object Delta had ever seen.

The whole place shimmered like a fairy palace and she was only as far as the hallway. Her dingy brown shift felt horribly out of place. She touched a lace doily lining one side of the table and got the sense of a female: Henry's wife, soft, clean smelling, a woman whose heart hid her fear of the curt, masculine presence threatening the edges of the room. Delta recognized a pair of mud-crusted boots scooted under the table as the ones Henry had worn the night he saved Lafette.

Her fingers slid down the slender figure of the dancer again. She admired the way Henry's wife fit herself in among the strong-willed men of this house. Even after death, she remained like a sweet breath.

"What in blazes are you doing in my house?" King Kingsley stood in the center of a room to the left. Books lined the wall from floor to ceiling. A desk bigger than Judge Treadway's filled the far end. Two oversized chairs opposite it were covered in a shiny material the muted color of dried blood.

Delta dug into her skirt pocket and pulled out the paper Judge Treadway had showed her up on Newman's Ridge. Forgive me, Arn, she told herself, for Lafette's sake. She held the paper waist high.

King's eyes glittered. "Got my little recommendation?" He pointed at the paper, then looped a thumb into the top of his pants. With his other hand, he flipped a silver coin into the air. He missed the catch and dug it out of the plush carpet. "You know," he said, flipping the coin again and catching it this time. "Treadway is only a Judge 'cause I allow it." He stroked the back of one of the red chairs, left to right, right to left, as if it warmed his hand.

Delta concentrated, furiously determined not to be intimidated. The heavy smell of tobacco choked her and she coughed to clear her throat. "You still want trees?"

One side of his mouth curved upward in a half-smile and he scratched his chin. "Naaaw," he drawled. He reached out and tugged the paper out of her hand. Flipping it open, he ran one finger down the edge. "Don't need to buy any tree of yours." He ripped the paper down the middle. Turning it sideways, he ripped again, letting petals of paper flutter to the floor.

Delta inhaled deeply, relieved and astonished. The burden that had plagued her all the way down the mountain vanished. "I'll be grateful as long as I live."

She hurried to the hallway. The arms of the crystal figurine opened toward her. The sparkling chandelier tinkled as a breeze wafted through an open window. In an instant, she froze. Here she stood in King Kingsley's house, thanking him. Every nerve in her body signaled she balanced on a cliff. She returned to the library, feet sinking into the plush carpet.

King's eyebrows peaked and his mouth sported a taunting sneer. He flipped the silver coin in the air, catching it and flipping it again. Delta's eyes followed the coin. She sensed lies surrounding him as if they were his clothing.

"Miss Wade, dear." He spoke in a nasal whine, flipping the silver coin then using that hand to indicate his red chair. "Don't need to buy trees from you 'cause I already purchased them from the rightful owner of Shadow Mountain." From the red chair a small person stood and turned sharply. A vengeful glint in Kate Huston's pale eyes pierced Delta like glass.

"What trickery is this?" Delta's hands balled into fists.

"Miss Huston has provided evidence that she is legal owner of Shadow Mountain." King picked up a yellowed paper from his desk. "Bought the trees from her."

Delta's face heated from cheeks to forehead. "Don't mind it being legal for a Melungeon to own property when it suits your purpose."

King tapped his chest with a finger. "When it suits *my* purpose," he said as if she should memorize the words.

Delta tipped her chin at Kate. "Arn owned Shadow Mountain and this woman wouldn't dare dispute it." Kate's already pale skin became a shade lighter and Delta knew she had the old woman trapped. Kate'd never deny Arn. He'd been like her own son.

Kate bit her lip. She appeared dizzy and placed one hand on the chair to steady herself. "You're right, Delta. I would never dispute that Arn owned Shadow Mountain."

"Enough of this!" King waved the paper at them. "Miss Huston, or should I say Mrs. Marlon, was Arn's wife. Got a marriage certificate to prove it. In Arn's absence, she has say over Shadow Mountain. Not you, not your bastard son."

Delta was so startled she laughed out loud. "You believe her? She'd tell any lie to get what she wants!"

Kate took the paper from King and held it out to Delta. Her hand shook and her blinking eyes made her appear almost sorry. "See for yourself."

Delta swiped the paper. At the bottom was drawn a curly, forked Y that she recognized as Kate's mark, and the scripted name Arn Marlon. Delta felt as if she'd been hit on the head with a log. Arn's name—the only words he knew how to write. A marriage certificate with Arn's signature. No wonder he always put her off when she brought up marriage. She raised her eyes and glared at Kate. "Arn would hate you for what you've done."

Kate's lower lip trembled. Her forehead wrinkled as she pressed one hand against her cheek and leaned back against the desk. She turned to King. "May I speak to Delta alone?" He shrugged his shoulders, put his coin on the fireplace mantel and strode toward a pair of floor to ceiling windows that opened like doors to the outside. When he closed them, Kate pulled the curtains.

She held to the fabric and spoke without turning around. "We got you for the Watcher. I was past childbearing. You were a vessel. We needed you to birth the new Watcher. Arn said it was the best way. I let him do it. I shouldn't've." Kate stepped to the fireplace, picked up the silver coin and stared at it, her mouth twisted with a bitterness she could not hide. "I believed him. I always believed what he said. Every damn word."

Delta pressed both hands to her stomach, feeling she might vomit. "Not true," she managed to say. "He loved me. He courted me."

"And paid a handful of silver for you."

"That was my Daddy's doing! Arn did it because he loved me. He wanted to get me away. You know how mean Daddy was."

"Arn never fell for you. He loved me the way a man loves a wife." Kate circled around her. The line of her jaw sagged and skin under her eyes looked as if she had not slept for days. "I was stupid in love enough to tell Arn how to make Pappy believe he was the next Watcher, but never told him where the silver was. He had to get it from me. I had to agree to the whole thing."

"A lie," were the only words Delta could get past her lips.

"The truth." Kate's hoarse voice scratched the air around her slow, feeble movements. "All of it started with Pappy Thunderheart's vision. Men trapped in the bowels of the earth, rising as dark spirits, devouring all that was good. His last words, *'We've betrayed the land,'* bore into my bones. Me and Arn watched him die. Buried him in a cave. Then, we bought you, had you start out as my helper. Slowly, you come to know him, trust him, love him. Me and Arn couldn't measure up to Pappy Thunderheart's power. We didn't have the skills. Couldn't walk in the world of men. By that time people hated Melungeons. It was a thing to hide, a secret for all your life. Arn said the new Watcher had to command both worlds, had to journey in spirit and in flesh to defeat the darkness. We would train him in what we knew, and hope he could break the wrathful tide," she paused and licked her lips. "We needed your white blood."

"Even if some of what you say is true, he came to love me."

"Maybe."

"Why sell the Tyme trees to that man?" Delta asked. "Arn treasured them. He said they were the measure of the mountain's power, growing up from the magic earth."

"I did it because I don't have faith in the old ways no more."

"Arn would strike you dead."

"When the earth almost swallowed Lafette, I realized the forces had turned against us. Polly's prophecy would come true. Shadow Mountain was trying to reclaim Lafette. It'll soon reclaim the Tyme trees. I dreamed them folding up and slipping underground."

"Fine! Fine! Why sell them?"

She placed the silver coin on top of a small box painted with a portrait of King. "Because I hate you."

"You're a pitiful creature, Kate Huston."

"Accept what you've brought on yourself. You've lost the mountain. King'll take it from you and give it to me. Lafette's welcome to stay if he chooses. I'm old and I'm tired. I only want a piece of land where no human will plague me. To spend the remainder of my days untroubled by the likes of you."

"Well, you chose a sorry devil to join up with. King'll betray you."

"King has his own destiny. I'm not afraid of him." She cast a glance at the piece of silver she'd replaced on the painted box. "My sister's bad luck coin. I was too late. It's out in the world, and now all that's left is to live my life away from its curse. I've learned too late, you can't stop the wind."

The uncertainty on Kate's face didn't give Delta the satisfaction she craved. She glared at Kate, then opened the curtains and left by the glass doors. Ahead of her Shadow Mountain edged up against the sky like the head of an ancient god. *Arn Marlon, I hate you. I hate you.* The words repeated as Delta walked toward what had been her beloved home.

ѱ 22 ѱ

THE ROAD MERGED into a blur. Branches of trees barred Delta's way like pointed daggers. When a wagon rolled up behind her, she jumped into bushes to hide, afraid whoever saw her would see her abandonment, the ache, the humiliation. Arn had married Kate. He was her lawful husband. He'd never truly belonged to the mother of his child.

Delta's body turned on her. Her arms seemed too long and she whipped them about aimlessly. Her feet felt clumsy, her head dull. Her muscles tensed and her inner organs burned. She looked down at her hands; skin showing age; rough, short nails, a scar where she'd been scalded as a child. "Ugly," she said. "Ugly hands!" She kept going, putting one foot in front of the other without caring where she stepped. "I hate you, ugly hands, hate you!" At the Elisha Tree, she collapsed.

The muscles of her abdomen and chest contracted into knots. She beat the ground with a fist and buried her face in the crook of her arm. "Why? Why did he marry her?" she cried into the earth. Her sobs wailed like the howls of a wolf.

When she had no more tears and her voice could barely sustain a whisper, she stared into the black ground. As the hour passed, the warmth of the sun moved up her legs. The smell of dirt and grass lingered as a taste in her mouth. The snap of a twig, a thud of a walnut falling from a tree, an animal tramping through the water as it crossed the creek—it didn't matter what passed by. It just didn't matter.

She sensed a small presence but had no will to lift her head. Soon a wet lapping on her forearm caused her to look up. Blue turned his head sideways and licked her face. She sat up and hugged the puppy so tight he yelped, then loosened her grip but kept him close, rocking back and forth and listening to the sound of the creek.

Blue continued nuzzling her. She wiped her swollen eyes, her cheeks so chafed they stung. She leaned over the creek and splashed water on her face. "She can't have this mountain," she said to Blue between splashes. Blue barked as if agreeing. The ground vibrated with the thump of horse hooves. She wiped her cheeks with the bottom of her skirt and turned as Henry and Lafette, riding the same palomino, sprang into view.

Blue yelped, and Delta prayed her face didn't reveal her tears, but her red eyes stung with every blink. "Stay where you are," she said as they dismounted. "Don't come closer." Lafette started to run to her and she held out her hand, palm outward. "Stop!"

"Wait, Lafette," Henry's eyebrows knitted together as he studied her. "Delta?" He gently patted the air. "Me and Lafette want to talk to you." He put his hands on Lafette's shoulders. "Delta, I know about the miscegenation charge. I had no part in it."

"So you say!"

"Momma, what's wrong with you?" Lafette twisted his head sideways. "I've requested Uncle Henry here to marry you." He nodded up and down as if it were the most natural suggestion in the world. "And he's agreed."

Tears welled in Delta's eyes again. "Seems who I marry is never up to me." She chuckled and shook her head in angry amazement. She sensed their impatience with her stubbornness, but what did they care about her feelings? No time to think this out. With so much at stake, she must decide now.

"Momma, it'll save the mountain. I heard Judge Treadway say so." Lafette pleaded in the same tone as when he wanted a cookie. "Told you I could help. Told you I could act in Daddy's place. It won't be so bad."

Delta raised her hands to her face. Her fingers smelled like the grass she'd been lying on. "It's King Kingsley that's trying to steal the mountain."

"All the more reason to marry me!" Henry's voice took on a fierce edge. He wadded his hand into a fist and shook it in emphasis. "I'll adopt Lafette. I'll fight for this mountain as surely as you have, and no one will ever touch the Tyme trees."

Delta stepped toward them, her shoulders tightening. Wide-eyed, Lafette tried to smile, afraid he might have angered his mother. Henry stood like his tall reflection. She was unsure how far she could trust him. "You'll fight your father? You'll fight Kate?" He nodded and held out a hand. She stared at it, motionless in the air next to Lafette's head. In her mind, she saw Arn. Saw him kiss Kate, hold her, make love to her. *I hate you, Arn. I hate you.* Her heart thumped like a drum and her hand trembled as she clasped Henry's, so much larger than hers, the skin warm and the muscles strong. He pulled her toward him. She resisted until she could speak. "You betray me and I'll cut your throat as you sleep."

"Momma!" Lafette exclaimed, slapping his cheeks. "Where's your manners!"

Delta and Henry traded a long stare, then both broke into nervous laughter. Henry tousled Lafette's hair, swung him around while Blue yelped and jumped, and the palomino snorted out and tossed her head.

∞

Judge Treadway's office smelled musty, and Delta sneezed twice. Mrs. Treadway gave her a handkerchief, then motioned for her to keep it.

"Something borrowed, dear."

Delta nodded, unable to speak. The book-lined walls blurred and a harsh glare through the window gave the room an orange tint. Every impulse urged her to bolt.

Judge Treadway stood in front of her with Henry at her side, hands crossed in front of him. Mrs. Treadway smiled as her husband recited the marriage ceremony. Delta couldn't concentrate on the words, couldn't even hear them as the English language.

Henry took her hands in his and pulled her toward him. She stared as if he were a stranger. She'd have given her life to be looking into Arn's eyes. *He had married Kate. Arn is her husband.* The rage inside Delta threatened to burst, and her arms trembled.

Henry tightened his hold on her hands as if sensing her misgivings. *I'm marrying Henry Kingsley. I'm marrying Henry.* The idea seemed unreal, the room as foggy as a dream. Judge Treadway asked her a question and she looked at him without answering.

"Momma's a mite nervous," Lafette whispered up to Mrs. Treadway, and she smiled kindly and wrapped her arm around his shoulders. Blue yelped a yodeling bark. Everyone in the room laughed except for Delta.

"I do," she said. She didn't remember another thought or movement until they were well on their way back to Shadow Mountain.

♆ 23 ♆

HENRY'S STOMACH RUMBLED from hunger. He breathed through a sharp pain in his ribs, attributing it to his excitement of a new wife at his side. They hiked along, he and Delta leading, Cotton following with Lafette and Blue on her back.

From the corner of an eye, he noticed Delta gaze up at him then glance away quickly as if embarrassed or afraid he'd look back. When he'd found her at the Elisha Tree she looked like a rag doll shaken by a bear; eyes swollen from crying, hands clenched in fists. She'd tried to conceal her emotions, especially from Lafette. At times she'd turned away until she regained composure. Usually, she walked with her head down, pressing one hand to her mouth. He didn't mention his father, except when her eyes teared, then he reassured her that the mountain would always belong to her.

Henry realized she'd look to him for a solution, but facing his father with her as his wife scared him more than being cornered by a pack of wolves. Confronting King about Shadow Mountain would be another battle. He hadn't expected to be so afraid.

"Momma, let's sing a song," Lafette said brightly.

"Don't feel like singing." Absorbed in thought, she didn't look back.

Her indifference seemed cruel, and Henry nodded for Lafette to sing if he liked. Lafette stayed quiet. Their footsteps were the only sound until a loose rock spilled down the hill. Thoughts tumbled in Henry's head like children rolling in the grass. Delta had married him not for love but to save her mountain. No other reason. Why hadn't that thought bothered him before? He'd wanted her so intensely, he hadn't considered it. In time, he told himself, she'll love me. He cleared his throat and turned toward her. "Be wanting you to stay at my house for about a week."

"What?" she exclaimed, her voice stunned. She stared at her feet as she walked and gripped fistfuls of her skirt.

"Part of my plan..." Henry patted her shoulder. "Drive home the point that you're my wife and Lafette's my son."

"I couldn't." Delta crossed her arms at her waist.

"Only way he ever accepted my first wife. Momma moved Rebecca in a whole month before we married."

"A whole month?" Lafette scrunched his face and rolled his eyes. "We don't have to stay that long, do we, Uncle Henry?"

"No, a few days. Daddy hooted and hollered about me marrying Rebecca 'cause she was poor, but Momma knew how to make him accept her." A blue jay landed in front of them, pecked at the dirt, and flew away as they came close. Delta's silence made him so uncomfortable he wished he could spread his arms and take flight like the bird. He could hear her breathing and sensed her thoughts flapping like wings.

She inhaled deeply and blew out her breath in a hiss through clenched teeth. "I don't know, Henry."

"Trust me, Delta. It won't be pleasant, but it'll work. Momma's the only person I ever saw beat Daddy down."

Delta stared into the green leaves of an oak tree, hiding the face of a rocky cliff. Her eyes were still swollen, the whites veined with red. She twisted to and fro, shallow breaths spoke the uncertainty seeping through her body. "Maybe you're right."

"Awwww, Momma, do I have to?" Lafette moaned.

"Teach you to make a horse sidestep," Henry said, wiggling two fingers in the air to imitate Cotton's movements.

Lafette's eyes widened. He bit his lower lip as if considering Henry's words in the light of his own hidden agenda. "And how to talk to the horses?"

Delta rubbed her temples, staring into the distance. In a voice tinged with resignation she said, "Only for a day or so."

"Take the horse. Get your things." Henry handed her the reins. She brushed his hand aside. "Faster on foot. Lafette knows short cuts." She pulled her son off the horse, holding him in front of her almost as a wedge between herself and Henry. "We'll come in by the kitchen and wait with Nancy 'til you say it's okay."

"No." Henry shook his head firmly. "Come in the front. I'll be waiting."

She nodded and turned to leave. Henry reached out and touched her shoulder. She looked at him with narrowed, uncertain eyes. He leaned down and pressed his lips to her cheek. Her soft skin smelled like fresh milk. When he straightened up she shaded her eyes with a hand. He could not gauge her reaction.

Trembling spread through his chest as she and Lafette stepped off the trail and onto a path. Why can't she love me? he thought. Why? He watched until they disappeared into a lush grove of Tyme trees. A wind blew the fragrant cinnamon smell of the leaves into his face. He mounted Cotton, holding his calves firmly against her sides, and trotted toward Kingsley land.

The sun flashed high over the orchards as he approached home. The barn sat empty. Surprised, he tied Cotton to a post, pulled off the saddle and looked to the tobacco fields. Deserted, as were the cornfield and peach orchard. Veins in his neck pulsed as he marched toward the house. He concentrated on his mother and prayed for strength.

But Delta doesn't love me, a voice inside him said. *She married me to save her mountain.* He rubbed his face, feeling the bristles of his whiskers. *She's always loved Arn.* Stop thinking it, Henry, he warned himself, confused that these thoughts would come to him now that he had what he wanted. Will she want to make love to me tonight? Share my bed? Will she ever touch me, kiss me, say the words one hears from a wife? *That damn mountain!*

He looked toward the peak. Arn's Volcano loomed over him like a ghost. "She'll love me," he told it. "Someday she'll love me more than you." Part of him saw her love as the next goal. If preserving her land was what it took to win her, then that's what he'd do. Why did he need so much from her so soon? He had her as his wife. His selfish thoughts embarrassed him.

Jumping on the porch, he swung open the front door. His father's laughter crackled from the library. Henry touched the crystal ballerina and invoked the spirit of his mother. A woman's voice spoke. Please don't let Diane Pratt be here, he thought.

The cool house dried the sweat on his brow, tightening his skin. He paused in the library door. King looked over, expecting him. Henry's shoulders tightened into his neck. Kate Huston stood with King, holding a crystal goblet of wine, grossly out of place in her work shirt and trousers.

King motioned him inside. "Can see by that ornery look on your face—"

"I've beat you," Henry snapped. "And there'll be no fuss about it."

"You're right about nothin' to argue on. Know who Kate here was married to?" King picked up a crystal goblet from his desk and sipped.

"All that matters is who I'm married to." Henry concentrated on Kate.

King opened his arms and announced, "Arn Marlon. Been his wife all these years." Kate's pale skin reddened and she swallowed a gulp of wine. King hurried to refill it. "Now I ain't being judgmental," he said, gesturing with the bottle before putting it down. "These ain't the times to judge your fellow man."

Kate emptied her glass in one swallow and watched Henry. "You married today?"

"Married?" King echoed, eyebrows peaked and forehead wrinkled.

"Married Delta," Henry said. "Adopted the boy as well."

King grabbed him by the shoulders. "How could you do this to me?" He tried to shake Henry, but the son stood taller and King released him with a shove. "What's that woman put you up to?"

"I love her." Henry faced Kate "Intend on protecting her land. Takes more than a certificate to make a marriage." He stared into her pale eyes and couldn't imagine why people were so frightened of her. Shrunk from age, Kate's jaws sagged, and the puffy eyes gave her a fish-like appearance. If some saw her as a mountain witch, in his house she was just an old woman.

"Too late." King threw his arms into the air and let them bounce against his sides.

"Spoke to Judge Treadway. I've stopped you."

"No, no, no." King paced, shaking his head each time he said the word. He flipped his silver coin and caught it.

Kate shrank into the corner, eyeing the coin and looking like a fox hiding from hounds. "Best go," she said, making for the doorway.

"Treadway assessed the land," Henry told her, "marked off boundaries, and I paid the taxes. I own Shadow Mountain, Kate. It's in my name and my wife's name. No one will ever touch those Tyme trees."

King slapped his thigh, threw back his head and laughed. "Wonder how much you'll want that mountain when it's as bald as an old crone."

Kate whipped around, eyes shifting nervously. "You said you'd take a few trees. What have you done?" She leapt so close to him they could have inhaled each other's breath, then she gripped the hair on both sides of her head as if she knew something unspoken. "You betrayed me! Just like Delta said you would!" She spun around once, twice, and whirled like a dervish. Her frantic expression melted to terror almost as if she heard a voice from beyond. "Got to stop it, got to!" She burst through the windowed door, shattering one panel against the outside of the house.

"That woman's crazy," Henry said. He picked up the goblet she'd been drinking from and put it on the liquor cabinet.

"Father, we need to come to an understanding. You'll come 'round to my way of thinking if you take time to know Delta."

King stared into the fireplace, pressing his lips firmly together. "Understand perfectly well. That slut's tricked you. Now I have to figure a way out of it for you." He nervously rubbed the silver coin in his palm, then put it in his pocket.

Henry picked up a paperweight from the desk and smashed it into the liquor cabinet. Shattered glass shot across the room. "Her and the boy are coming here. You'll accept them or you've seen the last of me."

Looking astonished, then wary, even fearful, King tapped his fingers on the fireplace mantel. "Henry?" His eyes, glassy with tears, he fought to keep from shedding. "I'm your father, No one cares for you the way I do. No one ever will. You know a lot of people in your lifetime, but no one can look out for you like a parent. I want that mountain for you and our descendants."

The same misery that had consumed Henry when his mother died filled his stomach and felt heavy as a bag of rocks. "Daddy... I..." He inhaled a deep breath, trying to ease his quivering voice. "I'll wait for Delta outside. We'll stay at the mountaintop." He shuffled broken glass with the toe of his shoe, wishing he could leave the room without having to look at his father. "Talk to you in a couple of weeks, when we've both had a chance to rest this out."

King put a thumb and forefinger to the bridge of his nose and squeezed. He sniffed, coughed, struggling to keep control of his trembling hand. "By end of day, ain't gonna be a mountaintop."

Henry jerked his father's arm from his brow. "What do you mean?"

King face flushed bright red. "Sidewalks. Need the volcano rock for sidewalks." Tears caught in his lashes and wet the skin around his eyes. His voice spilled hoarsely from his throat. “My men‘ll get ’em off the mountain. They won’t set off no dynamite ’til they’re sure her and the boy are clear of it.”

“Didn’t you think?” Henry raced for the barn, feeling about to choke, wild with panic.

☫ 24 ☫

DELTA AND LAFETTE packed what they needed, then hurried down the mountainside. As they approached the Kingsley house Delta fought the suspicion of having made a terrible mistake. This was not her world. Ten years ago, she might have made a life for herself here, but by now she had seen too much and knew too precisely the powers that shaped these hills. How could she walk into this house and be a wife? No more than two days, she promised herself. By the end of the second day, she and Lafette would be gone.

"Don't see him, Momma," her son said, scouring the front yard. "Think Uncle Henry changed his mind?"

She squeezed Lafette's hand, heart thumping like a captured rabbit's. *Said he'd be waiting at the door.* She pulled Lafette along and stepped up on the porch. "He won't change his mind. Probably inside."

Delta tapped lightly on the stained glass window. The white stallion rattled in its frame. No answered.

Lafette frowned. "If we live here, why don't we walk on in?"

She smiled at his simple, logical way of thinking. "Because it's not polite." She rubbed the top of his head then peered through the stained glass. The blue-tinted hallway stood empty. The library door hung open and a gentle breeze created a faint chandelier's musical tinkle. She glanced at Lafette then turned the doorknob.

"Wwwoooow!" Lafette said, stepping onto the multicolored rug. He leaned back to look at the chandelier, twirling underneath it, then bent and rubbed the carpet, tracing a flower pattern with a finger. His expression beamed both awe and fear. "Momma, I can't live here. I'll make a mess of this place in a day's time."

Reminding herself as well, Delta said, "Remember what Henry's done for us. We got to work his way." She stroked the glass figure of the dancing woman, again noticing the resemblance to her own face. "Be back on our mountain by week's end, promise."

"Okie-doke, I'll tie my pinkies." He hooked his little fingers together in a clinch.

"Come see." She pointed at the crystal figurines on the table.

"Look like they might melt, Momma."

"Reckon they're glass. I like this dancing woman. Which one you like?"

Lafette poked a finger at a deep blue figurine of a man on one knee, his rifle pointed toward the ground, and one hand extended in the air. "Must be pointing at a duck he wants to shoot. Don't you think?"

"Always thought he was pointing at the sun," King bellowed from the library. He had turned a maroon-leather chair toward the door and hunched down in it like a bear. Drawn curtains darkening the room to the color of dusk. His eyes caught a gleam of light from the hallway and shone like an animal's at night. "Sitting here wondering if you actually had the nerve."

Lafette stepped inside, squinting to see. "Afternoon, Mr. Kingsley."

Sensing danger, Delta pulled Lafette behind her. Lafette leaned sideways, curiosity pulling him around her waist.

"Don't hide the little feller," King said, his childlike tone brimming sarcasm. "After all, this place, all my trinkets… be his someday… you have your way. Ain't that right?" He smirked then drew on a cigar, sending white streams of smoke toward the ceiling. His eyes narrowed to snakelike slits, dark pupils focused on her.

She tensed. "Where's Henry?"

"My son?" King leaned forward, planting his elbows on his knees. His expression hardened like petrified wood, pupils shrank to pinpoints. "Got yours there beside you, and now, you want… my son."

Her confidence shrank like a dying flower at sunset. Lafette took her hand and laced his fingers through hers. His touch gave her strength. "We'll leave," she said, trying with all her might to believe Henry had not abandoned them.

"But Uncle Henry told us to wait." Lafette tugged at her skirt.

"Uncle Henry is it?" King slapped his knee. "Thank Jesus you ain't used to *Papa Henry*, little boy."

Lafette's grip tightened on Delta's hand. Loathing swept into her chest. "You're scaring my child," she said through pressed lips.

King shot up, his lower jaw protruding, eyes glaring. "Don't let the words Papa Henry get all warm in your heart, child."

In the distance, a rumble rose like the sound of a train, clattering the hallway chandelier as if someone had reached up and shaken it. She looked at the ceiling, expecting it to collapse. Pulling Lafette with her, she backed away.

King grabbed her arm. “No, no, no,” he said, smiling, his eyes wide and almost joyful. “Don’t leave. Stay, see my treasures.” He gestured at more figurines on his desk. “After all, you’ve sought so hard to make what is mine into yours.”

Delta trembled. His iron grasp hurt her arm as he tugged her into the library. Lafette followed uncertainly, waiting to see what she would do. King reached around Delta and shut the door, closing them in the darkened room. She spun around, out of his reach, but keeping King at arm’s length, then demanded, “Where’s Henry?”

“Momma! I know what it is,” Lafette said, his voice full with hushed amazement. His eyes widened as round as coins and his lips curved in triumph like a boy who’d just won a foot race. “It’s the dragon, Momma. The dragon’s come alive.”

♆ 25 ♆

COTTON REARED AT the flash of an explosion, nearly causing Henry to topple over. He straightened, heels down, and at the second rear pulled the reins tight. The horse calmed. He patted her neck and stared up at Arn's Volcano. Grateful relief spread through him when he saw it still stood. He trotted Cotton until she was ready to gallop.

The first workers appeared a quarter mile from Cat's Crossroads. Henry slowed and demanded, "Who's in charge?"

"Amos's up by the fork. Should've seen it, Mr. Kingsley. Best idea your daddy ever had."

Henry smacked Cotton's shoulder with the reins and sped toward the crossroads. Splintered tree trunks, rocks, and piles of dirt forced him trot the horse to the rounded plateau where Amos stood. Dust and wood shavings hung in the air. Henry coughed and held a handkerchief to his nose as he crossed through the dusty cloud.

Amos shielded his eyes with one hand, studying three fallen Tyme trees. Dynamited trunks were blown clean through. Men busily sawed the length into chunks and attached chains so logs could be pulled down the mountain. Twenty or so mules tied to a fence waited to be hitched up for hauling.

"Hold off!" Henry yelled. "Halt dynamiting now!" He looped Cotton's reins to a supply wagon piled with crosscut saws, picks and double-bitted axes. The horses shifted and a shotgun propped against the front seat slid sideways.

Several timberers made their way to the plateau when Henry called out. Amos waved his hands, motioning for them to keep quiet. "Expected you earlier," he said, stepping down to Henry's level. "Clear 'em out faster this way." He proudly pointed to the shattered Tyme trees. Broken roots stuck up from the ground like torn body parts.

The blasted trees looked like war casualties and Henry found their wounds difficult to face. In his mind he could hear them moan. "I bought this mountain."

"King always intended you to have it." Amos stared at the ground as if to hide a jealous streak. "Told me he'd name it after his only son. Put a big resort up here." Amos propped a shovel against the wagon as Henry eyed the gun and folded his arms across his chest, shifting his weight to one leg. "Mount Henry. Don't that sound fine?"

"No more blasting," Henry said in a commanding tone.

"King won't go for that." Gathered men mumbled among themselves. Amos growled at them, "Don't stir yourselves up."

"I quit a job at Jellico to come over here," a black-haired man said.

"I got more than that to worry about," said Ty Lowe, who'd worked all his life for King. "Ain't crossing the big man."

Amos leaned toward Henry and whispered, "You're rattling my bones, Mister. If you don't care about your daddy, then think how you're putting these men out of work."

"My decision," Henry said. "There'll be work. Just won't be using Tyme trees."

"King put me in charge. Not you." Amos studied the wagon.

Henry followed his sightline to the shotgun. He shoved Amos aside. Both men scrambled for the firearm, but Henry got hold of it, swung around and aimed at Amos. "Go against me! This is what you'll get."

Amos and the other men stood silent, still as stone. Let 'em be unsure, Henry thought and stepped up on the wagon so he'd tower above them. "I own this mountain! How would you feel if hooligans plundered your home!" The black-haired man pulled a pistol. Henry shot at his feet.

The man dropped the gun. "You damn—"

"Enough!" Amos faced the men, his back to Henry. "Nobody jacks a bullet without my say so!" He bore down on the black-haired man, fists up as if about to pound him into the ground. "Get the hell off this mountain."

Henry stared at Amos, thinking he was either a fool or a fox to turn his back on a man with a shotgun. He lowered it, keeping a finger on the trigger. "All of 'em off."

Amos shifted his weight to his back leg, then turned, jaw clenched and cheek pulsing, looking angry enough to slug Henry. "Awww hell!" he said, poking him in the stomach. "I shoot you, who'd I have to argue with?" He huffed out a breath. "Men, put down your tools." They obeyed and Amos waved them off. "Henry, you got a powerful lot to explain to your daddy. And so do I."

"Don't worry, Amos," Henry smiled, relief spreading through his chest. Stopping the blasting was critical to forcing King to reconsider. Some deep part of him knew his father would not see him hurt or go against him, no matter how much King carried on. "Gonna get Delta and Lafette," he said, pointing toward the volcano.

"Can't go up there." Amos said. "Detonation's set."

Henry dropped the shotgun and scrambled over the giant fallen trunk. Wood dust filled his nose, and he coughed as he climbed up the mountainside.

"Come back!" Amos hollered. "Blasting power all around that rock!"

Henry waved Amos away, his only thought to get Delta and Lafette. If the volcano was blown, they'd be buried in rock. He had sent them up here. *Please, let them already be gone!*

"Nitro around that powder!" Amos yelled after him.

Henry's heart pounded when he caught sight of the cabin's roof. "Delta! Lafette!" No answer. He bounded onto the porch, kicked open the door and searched the rooms.

Outside the cabin a voice moaned like a fatally wounded animal. "Noooooo!"

Henry followed the sound outside toward the volcano. The flash of a woman's blondish-white hair disappeared behind the cone of rock. Delta? Had to be! He raced around Arn's Volcano. "Don't touch nothin'!" he shouted. He saw the woman leaning down, digging at the ground, and struggling to lift a baseboard rock. "No!" he screamed.

She looked up with eyes of a cow being led to slaughter, her mouth a ring of empty blackness, jaw slack with horror. Her smooth forehead held together a disintegrating body. Kate Huston's face was the last sign of humanity Henry saw—then—the sky, blue like his mother's eyes, blue like Rebecca's eyes.

Then—the sun—white, white, white.

♆ 26 ♆

A SECOND EXPLOSION rattled the chandelier so violently Delta thought it would crash to the floor. Walls vibrated. A vase tipped over. Lafette flung his arms around her waist and buried his face in her skirt. Another explosion followed. She pulled her son closer, and shouted at King, "What is that?"

His eyes widened as he lifted his arms in triumph, a tense joy creasing his features. "The might of a King!" As the vibration died, he centered himself and flipped his silver coin high into the air, catching it with his other hand. "Comfort your son, Delta. Sons, after all, are the most important commodities in the world to a parent." He narrowed his eyes, opened a tobacco-filled chest and dug through the shredded leaves until he found another cigar.

Lafette's shoulders trembled and he hiccupped through his quivering voice. "Momma, dragon might eat us."

Delta rubbed his shoulder with one hand and held her other arm tightly around his back. Her heart pounded and her voice scraped through her throat in a rough whisper. "Shhh, no dragon will hurt you." Yet in her entire life, she'd never heard such a sound. If it wasn't the dragon, what was it? The suffocating odor of tobacco filled the room. King appeared too sure of himself, not afraid at all, in no hurry to see what had happened. "Let us out," she said, stepping to the side to go around him.

He mirrored her movements and dropped cigar ash on the floor. "Don't be so eager to leave." He blocked the doorway holding his arms wide. "After all you've done to assure your place in my household." He spat out the words, his breath smelling of wine and tobacco. "Stay. Tell me the good times we'll have."

Delta swallowed, her throat, parched. She glanced at a door behind him. Curtains billowed with a breeze. If they ran, they'd escape, but Lafette still clung to her, too afraid to move. She studied King, trying to judge his reaction. "Don't want to stay here," she said. "It was Henry's reasoning. Never meant to offend you." King stood silent, self-satisfied, one fist, clenching and unclenching. Delta fidgeted, eyeing for a way around him. "I did this to protect mine. You must understand?"

"Matter of fact, I do." He pointed to the window. "See for yourself what I would do to protect... mine." His hand trembled, then his entire arm. "See how well you've protected that pile of dirt."

Delta pulled Lafette toward the door. Once the fresh air hit them, she released him but couldn't shake the feeling that something crouched, ready to attack if they hesitated. "Hurry, let's get home." Lafette stopped short. His jaw dropped and he mouthed words soundlessly as he pointed up. Delta staggered, then fell to her knees. Shadow Mountain was encircled with smoke clouds. The top of Arn's Volcano had disappeared as if whisked into the heavens by a whirlwind.

"Dra, dra, dragon." Lafette held a hand to his throat and the other clutched her shoulder in terror, afraid to let go or lose sight of her. The wind blew their direction and the harsh smell of smoke consumed them.

She stared helplessly. "I don't understand," she murmured.

"Nitroglycerin," King announced, coming up behind. He perched on the porch, hands resting on his hips. "No dragon, little boy. Nitro on either side and Arn's Volcano is sidewalk." He chuckled, baring his gritted teeth, daring them to confront him.

Delta stood, pulling her skirt from Lafette's hand. She marched toward King unsteadily, afraid of falling. He towered over her like Goliath. "How can one man answer for such destruction?"

His face lost its sinister joviality and his fixed, unyielding eyes glared into hers. "Not destruction. Creation. When we're all dead and gone, history books will call King Kingsley the creator of the modern South. There'll be towns named after me, monuments erected, a national park in my honor. Books will tell my life story!"

However foolish he sounded, Delta realized she was dealing with a dangerous man. He would stop at nothing. Neither his son, nor Judge Treadway, or the law itself would stop King Kingsley. He raised his arms toward the smoking mountain as if paying homage to a god. She backed away from him. "You're crazy."

"And you're small, Delta Wade. Little-minded, ignorant, stupid mountain fool."

"Don't call my momma that." Lafette's voice edged hard as stone. He stood like a little soldier, feet planted, arms at his side, head held high. All at once, horse and rider galloped up and halted so close to Lafette he could have been knocked down, but the boy didn't flinch.

The rider jumped to the ground, collapsing at King's feet. "Accident... too close to the blast. Doc's been sent for. Wagon's bringin' wounded here."

"See what you've done," Delta said.

King glanced toward the mountain. "Probably that fool Huston woman."

"Dead," the rider coughed, struggling to clear his throat. "Not much left of her. The rest... don't know how to tell you, Mr. Kingsley..."

Delta twisted away, stunned to think that Kate no longer lived. She raised a hand to her heart, suppressing a hurtful throb. Kate had anchored her, been a crutch; a painful revelation. She reached for Lafette. He stood firm as any tree, staring at King with eyes so full of hate that Delta could have sworn they were Arn's eyes.

A wagon raced onto the Kingsley road, the driver cracking a whip at the backs of two mules. The smoke at the mountaintop turned black, giving it the appearance of a belching train engine.

"Nooooo!" King moaned. The rider held King back, forcing him to sit on the steps. King dropped his face into his hands.

The wagon clattered to a halt. Amos jumped out, his face bloodied, one arm wrapped in a sling. Delta ran to him saying, "Amos! How many hurt?"

He grabbed her arm and dragged her into the rear of the wagon. "He's dying."

She knelt next to a man wrapped in a blanket. His body spasm and jerked. Another man held him steady. She pulled the blanket from his blackened face and gasped, "Lord Almighty."

Henry's back twisted in a way she'd never seen. His limbs, gashed with gaping wounds, were bound in rag strips. She bent over him, careful not to jar his head or neck, and pushed up his eyelids. His eyes rolled back into his head. The sight made her heart feel like lead. "You men tear off a door from the house! Biggest one you can find."

Henry's body began to convulse. "Steady him so he doesn't hurt hisself," she said to the men. As the spasm ended, Henry opened his eyes and stared at her. She sensed the full burden of his pain. He wheezed and pointed to his throat. "Lafette," Delta called. "Give me your pen knife." Her son was quick, and Delta tore open Henry's collar then touched the soft, raw skin of his throat. Henry wheezed again, lips turning blue. She cut into his throat, opening a star-shaped wound. With her skirt bottom she wiped bubbling blood and forced a finger into the incision to open a passage. Henry stopped wheezing. His eyes, sparkling with the little life left in him, seemed to acknowledge her efforts.

"You're killing my son!" King grabbed Delta by the hair and pulled her backwards. Her dress ripped as she fell to the ground at his feet. "You see her, you men? She tried to kill my son!"

Lafette ran at King, all fists and feet, flailing on King.

King backhanded him and knocked him six feet. "Get off my land before I kill you both!" Amos clapped King on the back, trying to calm him. "Get off, you murdering whore! Get out of my sight!"

"Curse you, King Kingsley! Curse you 'til the day you die!" Delta grabbed at Lafette and stood up, then snatched a look into the wagon but Henry lay out of her sight. The men backed away as if her curse might fall on them as well. Amos's eyes brimmed with tears streaking his blackened cheeks. He waved Delta away, then dropped his hand so it hit the wagon with a thud. The resignation on his face angered her. Why wouldn't they stand up to King? Why wouldn't they fight him? Amos's expression, she realized, was the face of the future.

But there were those who would fight. They would spring from the earth itself, if need be. Arn had fought. Now it was her turn. She knew where to find an ally as dangerous as King, but did she dare use the forces Arn had always cautioned her against?

Mother and son marched from the Kingsley house, holding onto each other. Lafette, silent, stared straight ahead. His pink cheek swelled and carried King's mark. Looking at his tender bruise, she made a decision. Yes, she resolved, one path left. Arn would have warned her off, maybe even forbidden it, but now there was no choice. Arn had fought his way, now she would fight hers.

ꓯ 27 ꓯ

AS HE AND Delta walked, Lafette stared into the sun. Inky black spots floated before him and he angrily swiped at them. Delta led him through Cumberland Gap, where sun hung high enough to give them several hours of light. They caught a ride on the back of a wagon pulled by two oxen and entered gray, foggy Midnight Valley.

Midnight Valley had a swampy, decaying smell that Lafette thought might come from the coal mines. He'd watched from distant ridges as long chutes called tipples were built with a railroad underneath leading away like a long tongue. Teams of blinded mules were sent into a dark hole in the earth driven by men blackened with soot. He hoped he never had to see such a place because it sounded terrible.

He and Delta jumped off the wagon, thanked the driver and wished him good fortune, then pulled Lafette along a dirt road leading into the darkest hollow he'd ever seen. He recognized Polly Huston's property and exclaimed, "Can't go up there! Snakes! Big, long copperheads!"

Deliberately she stepped back and looked at him. "You know the way?"

He realized he'd given himself away and stared at the ground, thinking she would tan his hide for straying so far from home. "Yes, Ma'am."

Delta lifted his chin, locking into his eyes. "Then, you'll show me. I can only guess and we haven't time to waste."

Lafette's relief dissipated as he peered into the hollow where a creek latticed through a sour-smelling swamp. Broken reeds stuck up from muddy banks islanded in shallow, slime-cover water. Spider webs tangled what grass there was and all he could think was *snake country.*

"This is the most important journey we've ever made, Son." She knelt and waited silently for his answer, stroking the back of his head.

He dreaded having to see the strange little woman and her spooky cabin, especially knowing her sister Kate had been killed when Arn's Volcano exploded. But it was still daytime, he reasoned, they could get there and out before the sun went down. He swallowed hard, wishing he could absorb his fear as easily. They stepped off the road and circled the swamp, aiming for the wildest part of the hollow.

He stomped down briar patches, but Delta's skirt still snagged and they untangled it several times. Trees grew thick and dense, giving the forest a sulfuric smell. Animal life seemed limited to lizards, screech owls, and a solitary fox that followed them in the distance. Nary a squirrel or rabbit, Lafette thought. He was sure the critters must be somewhere, *probably hiding from snakes.*

When the cabin came to view, he walked on tiptoe, scouring the ground for copperheads. Still a ways from the porch he turned to his mother and said, "Better holler from here, less'en we disturb her pets."

Delta cleared her throat and cupped hands around her mouth.

"Stand there!" cracked a woman's voice from up the hill. Polly stepped from behind a stack of logs, crisscrossed for a bonfire. Black hair hung loose to her waist and hid her long arms, so disproportioned to the rest of her stunted body. She held flint along with a piece of brownish cotton. Kneeling in front of the wood, Polly placed a pinecone in the center of the cotton, striking the flints until the fluff caught fire. The flame lapped the wood into a blaze. "Come to mourn my sister's passin'?"

"How'd she know, Momma?" Lafette whispered. He didn't like the sound of Polly's voice, spewing bitterness just salty enough to mock his mother.

Delta stepped forward, but the leaping flames forced her back. She licked her lips and swallowed as if fire burned in her throat. "Come for your help to take vengeance on those who killed her."

Polly did not turn, but her back undulated in a way that made her seem like a much younger woman. "Maybe I think you kilt her."

"My momma did not!" Lafette sprang forward to his mother's side.

Polly faced them and wrinkled her nose, sniffing the air in his direction. Her sharply angled features seemed to soften as her lips curled into an amused smile.

Lafette's body tingled under her stare, then a breeze urged his gaze upward toward tree branches, so tall they blocked daylight and shading the forest in twilight.

He strove to find the sun, but leaves filtered the light like lace. What rays made it through danced on all sides of him, bringing his eyes downward again, to Polly. The fire brimmed golden around her, its heat reaching out to him. Her body, which he knew to be misshapen, loomed huge on the hill and was as well formed as Kate's. Her eyes bore down on him like a hungry cougar's. He could taste her meaty breath. Her full lips sucked the air from his lungs.

"Lafette?" Delta shook his shoulder then pulled him under her arm like a baby chick under its mother's wing.

His mother's touch was all that kept him from floating up to the sun again. The bonfire crackled, lighting an oblong circle around them. Polly was again herself, a misshapen dwarf, and Lafette retreated behind Delta. The heat of fire didn't seem to affect the old woman, but as far away as he stood, it scorched his forehead.

Polly rubbed her hands together and paced in front of the bonfire. She stretched her fingers backwards, cracked her knuckles, then traced the outline of Delta's body in the air. "Always told Kate you were a mistake. A Watcher can't choose love *and* destiny."

"What do you know of Arn?"

"He failed as Watcher."

"He did everything that was asked of him."

"Not the first Watcher to try and outwit darkness by drinking it in, thinking the fight was his alone, figuring he could walk away afterward and live an earthbound life. Probably won't be the last."

"Is he dead?"

An unsettling glint of sparks flashed in her eyes. "He's cursed."

"Speak plain, woman."

Her bobbing head tilted to one side as if listening to something unseen. "Your belly understands me."

Lafette felt his mother's leg muscles tighten. Her grip on him changed from firm to protective as Polly's eyes roamed over his face.

"But perhaps," Polly studied Lafette, "perhaps his miscalculations can be set right." She reached into a sagging dress pocket and pulled out a jar filled with sand: black at the top, then purple, blue, green, yellow, orange, red, and white on the bottom layer. Lafette recognized all the colors he'd collected at Sand Cave, but the order had been reversed. She held the jar in the firelight for Delta to see.

Lafette suspected it was the same sand she'd shaken and turned white, and now, they were separate again, surely a feat only a witch could do. Now he understood. Polly Huston didn't live way out here because of her deformed body or to study magic like Kate and his mother. She already had the conjuring in her. She didn't strive for power. She was a born witch. His knees trembled.

Delta reached for the jar and Polly pulled it back. "What payment do you require?" Delta asked with a steady stare.

"An easy price." She reached down the front of her dress, ripping the neck of it. A coppery, diamond-shaped head slid between her breasts and through her black hair, looping its body around her neck. "The boy has to pet my little friend while I tell him stories of the old days."

Lafette's knees buckled. He fell against Delta and would have sunk to the ground if she hadn't caught him. "Lord Almighty, he passed out." She smacked his jaw as she lowered him into her lap. "How could you do such a thing to a little boy?"

"Ain't no child." Polly perched cross-legged in front of the bonfire and placed the jar of layered sand on the ground. The copperhead slid through the sleeve of her dress, down her arm and curled around the container.

"Honey?" Delta rocked him in her arms as Lafette moaned into consciousness.

"Momma?" He raised his head, unaware of his surroundings, then saw the bonfire and Polly, and scrambled upright. He brushed his arms, frightened a snake could be on him. "We have to take the sand from the copperhead?"

"If I'm lookin' at a vengeful woman," Polly said, "you sure don't seem willin' to pay the price." She pointed at the jar, now hidden by a serpentine coil. "Dispense one color of sand at the base of Shadow Mountain, another color an eighth of the way up, and so on until the last layer of white sand is emptied into the rocks of Arn's Volcano. Then, vengeance will birth through the legs of the earth." The snake flicked its tongue with eyes like fiery slits reflecting the bonfire.

"I am a vengeful woman, but the price is mine, not my child's." Delta gripped Lafette's hand. "Honey, you don't have to touch the snake." She veered toward Polly. "I'll do it. I'll take retribution from the viper." When she reached out, her hand went through the bottle and snake as if it were a dream. She tried again, and both the sand and snake disappeared, fading like an illusion of heat.

"You can't touch the serpent. Didn't you ever figure that out? Only a guardian of the gate can rule that power." Polly shot Lafette an indifferent look, not caring whether he paid her price. Waiting to see what he would do seemed a game to her. "Fine, I'll empty reckoning into the fire."

"I'll touch the snake." Lafette's insides felt hollow as a corncob doll's. What this witch wanted with him was a mystery spiraling around him, filling him with the fervor of fire. A maze of sparkling blue spun before his eyes and he thought he'd passed out again.

"No, Lafette." Delta grabbed for his arm, but as he stepped out of reach she could not move. "Polly Huston, stop this!" Delta fist-pounded her thighs. Her planted legs could not lunge forward. "Lafette, don't!"

He knelt in front of the snake. Its tongue flicked and its head wove back and forth, measuring his body. He figured to grab its neck, and raised his hand shoulder level. Think of it as a frog, he told himself. He stared at the viper and imagined a big toad.

Bonfire heat scalded his cheeks. Sweat dripped down his face and perspiration beaded his upper lip. Inching his hand over the snake's head, he cupped his fingers. Behind him his mother breathed in short gasps. Polly hunched still as a rock. The snake's tongue flicked out again.

He plunged his hand down, fast as a striking serpent, Polly's hand shot up and clamped onto his just as he would have taken the snake. "Ahhhhh," he called out. Delta gasped but did not speak. Polly was strong as any man and Lafette pulled against her but couldn't break her grip. He twisted sideways to give the reptile less target.

"Quit strugglin', boy," Polly hissed, "or that serpent'll bite you in half."

Lafette trembled all over. He exhaled a shiver, teeth chattering. The snake lifted its head onto Polly's hand and crossed over onto his, gliding like a ribbon. He felt about to pass out, watching the copperhead's flickering tongue, headed toward his face. It coiled around his arm, coming up under his armpit and onto his neck.

The tightening and releasing of its skin was gentler than he'd expected, not unpleasant. He remembered capturing a baby chick and holding it in his hands, refusing to let go despite its determination to free itself.

The snake crawled to the top of his head and Lafette's vision went dark again. He stared into the bonfire while visions of the old days melded into him, muscle and bone. The snake's tongue flickered against his ear and woke him. His breathing relaxed, inhaling with the constriction of the copperhead's body. It slid down his other arm and curled its head in the palm of his hand.

"What'cha see there, boy?" Polly asked.

He looked into her slit-like eyes. Firelight danced in her pupils even though the flames were behind her. "A snake," he answered.

"A dragon," she said. "She holds the stories until Kingdom Come."

The copperhead wound down onto the ground and slid off into the grass. Lafette stood and returned to Delta's side. "Not so bad," he said, proudly.

"You shouldn't've had to do this." Her eyes flashed angrily at Polly.

Polly opened both hands toward the jar of sand. "In this cup lies vengeance. You've earned it." A gust of wind shot splinters of fiery wood into the air. "One warning. Do not leave the mountaintop for a fortnight once the spell is in place. Walk away from the mountain and you'll drink death."

Lafette grabbed the jar and they hurried away. Two foxes followed them, baying until they were out of sight of the cabin. A burnt wood smell soaked their clothes, and his nostrils brimmed with the odor long after they exited the hollow. Dusk watered in when they reached Shadow Mountain and poured the first layer of sand.

By the time they reached home, night was pitch black, and

they could not make out what was left of their house or Arn's Volcano. The barn, on the far side of the mountain, left its outline in a sliver of moonlight. Ole Sal and their cow banged against their stalls, letting Delta and Lafette know they were alive. She hurled the empty jar in the direction of the Volcano and heard it shatter.

"We'll sleep in the barn," she said. "Daybreak will show us what is left."

They curled in a stall. Ole Sal snorted until she was sure of the visitors and their cow mooed a couple of times. Crickets chirped in a tandem with the coos of barn owls and then hushed until all that remained was soft, empty silence.

Sometime during the night, Blue found his way into the same stall. Delta lay awake wishing the day had been a dream. Perhaps Arn's Volcano still stood. Their house survived. Henry's injuries weren't fatal. They could go on living as they always had, protected by the strength of Polly's spell.

Lafette dreamed that his toes and fingers were baby snakes, and he played with them, romping with Blue through a field of soft clover. Once he awoke, thinking Polly had whispered in his ear that tonight would be the last peaceful evening he would spend for many years.

♆ 28 ♆

BETWEEN THE CRACKS of the barn's rough gray boards, a white dawn striped the stall where Delta slept. She yawned and stretched aching muscles. Grassy hay tickled her nose. A rooster crowed and she bolted upright, remembering where she was. Lafette curled a few feet away, his arms folded around Blue. The dog's eyes popped open but he did not stir. A foreboding filled her as she recalled yesterday's events.

The scent of fennel and rue seeped through a crack at the bottom of the barn. The same kind of yellow flowers had grown outside the window when she awoke after her first night with Arn. Today might have been her first morning as Henry's wife. She'd watched Arn sleeping that morning, memorizing his features and hoping that all she'd do in life would bring him pleasure. Henry's twisted and bloodied body was imprinted on her memory as firmly, but this wedding morning she huddled in a horse stall, terrified of what she would find outside. Henry's injuries haunted her, especially knowing she could not be there to help. "Pray that your daddy got a doctor in time," she whispered, feeling the need to apologize.

Delta brushed hay from her skirt. Her skin was sticky from old sweat, her hair so tangled she couldn't run her fingers through it. Gulping deep breaths, she stepped toward the barn door and pressed a hand against it, fingering the rough texture of the wood. Why don't you open it? she asked herself. Can't change what's outside. She pushed, flooding the doorway with morning light. What she saw whipped her breath away. She covered her face with both hands. Several seconds passed before she could look again. Instead of the massive black wall that shadowed half the mountaintop, she stared at air—fine, misty white morning sky. Black rocks, some as small as pebbles, others the size of a wheelbarrow, littered the mountaintop. Arn's Volcano lay in pieces.

The cabin had fared better than she'd expected. Poles holding up one side of the porch had snapped, and the roof over Lafette's room had collapsed under a tide of rock and dirt. In time, she knew they could clean up, re-support the porch, rebuild Lafette's room. But the volcano... the volcano was gone. *Was the magic gone, too?*

She climbed onto a jagged fifteen-foot tall boulder and looked over the mountain. The explosion had spread rocky debris nearly an acre down the slope and covered every living thing in its path. The creek flowed through the rocks creating a wide stream. Trees lining the ridge below were shorn away, some snapped in half. Cornstalks from the garden had been yanked up by the roots and strewn into distant trees. The dusty smell choked her.

"Almost pretty," Lafette said, coming up behind her. "Like nothin' I've ever seen before, like a dream of the moon."

"All that's left of Arn," she said, feeling guilty because she wasn't grieving and realizing she felt shock but not pain.

Lafette took her hand. “We’ve still got this.” He showed her his fist with the silver ring on his middle finger. He twisted it off and held it out to her.

“Keep it.” Her tongue thickened and she swallowed again and again. Unsure what emotion her features might betray, she stared out at the mountains to keep Lafette from seeing her face. Impossible to tell him she didn’t want the ring back or that she was relieved that the volcano was gone. No longer would she cut the shrubbery, consecrate the stone with magic words and rub it with sacred herbs. She hardly knew how to explain her feelings to herself. How could she explain to Arn’s son?

He closed his hand around the ring and rubbed it against his ribs. Climbing onto one of the larger boulders, he stared out over the blasted rocks. “Glad we went to Polly Huston, Momma. Anything’s worth keeping this mountain away from King Kingsley.”

A ripple of nerves went up Delta’s spine. Good rarely came from a practitioner of snake magic, but what choice had there been? With Henry hurt, Polly Huston offered the only way.

A faint clacking sound caught her attention. Lafette cupped his ear. “Could be somebody banging pans to stop a bee swarm,” she said, and pointed toward the south. The sun shone hotly on the Tennessee side. “Weather’s right.”

“I could go look—” he said.

“No!” She grabbed his wrist and squeezed. “Polly said stay on the mountain all this day. No matter what we hear or see.” She pulled him down from the rock and placed him squarely in front of her, shaking him by the shoulders. “Promise, Lafette. Promise me you won’t sneak away. No telling how Polly’s curse will come to be.”

His lower lip trembled. “I promise, Momma.” He looked down at his hand, pink from her grip on his wrist. She released him and he shook his hand to restore the blood flow. “Reckon I’ll milk the cow.” As he turned to leave, a faraway explosion rocked the ground beneath them. “Is it the curse, Momma?”

Delta looked the direction of the sound, but an echo bounced from ridge to ridge and she was unsure where the explosion had occurred. Then, a plume of smoke rose at the base of the mountain just as another explosion blossomed a half mile away.

She squinted. Polly’s curse, or was this King stealing more of her trees? The second mushroom-shaped smoke cloud rose upward, black and dirty. The clacking she’d heard earlier grew to a hushed, whooshing sound like someone lightly snapping their fingers. As the day progressed explosions occurred again and again, but the clacking didn’t seem connected to them.

By noon the sound vibrated, loud as a swarm of insects. Explosions steadily worked their way around the south end of the mountain. King stealing trees, or Polly’s curse? Delta could look no longer and threw herself into drawing picture after picture to halt her fevered thoughts.

From time to time she leaned against a tree stump, sometimes staring at the sky, sometimes at the ground. Lafette went back and forth, feeding the mule and hog, spreading feed for the chickens. He stopped now and then to watch her, and she would concentrate on the spread of charcoal against the page, pretending not to notice him.

Finally he went inside, dug through the ruins of his room, and came out with his squirrel gun. “We got to do something!” he shouted, pointing the gun skyward, pockets jingling with bullets. “King’s blowing up every Tyme tree we got!” Delta kept drawing, obsessed with the movement of her fingers across the page. He stalked over and grabbed one of her arms. “Momma!”

"Stay here. Do as I say." Her voice grated like shattered glass. The sound of it frightened her. She folded her legs underneath her. Grass stuck to her flesh, and without the shade of the volcano, the air was as hot as fire. Thousands of anthills between the blades of grass looked like intricate castles crushed by black stones. She stared at them, thinking her house had been crushed just as easily.

She picked up a black stone and tossed it between her palms. "Hear that clacking noise?" Lafette shook his head. She squeezed the stone hard and wondered if the sound was in her mind, maybe she was going mad, maybe everything she'd tried to do was for nothing. "Barn looks fine to me," she said. "Start clearing the dirt and rocks out back. Then we'll rebuild the porch."

Lafette stared and shook his head, not understanding her lack of concern. Sullenly he walked toward the house, turning to look at her twice. The clacking was all she heard. With each new explosion it grew louder. That has to be the curse, she decided. Has to be our salvation. Believe it. Have faith.

She began the laborious task of picking up one stone at a time and heaving it over the mountainside. The clacking came and went depending on how she focused her attention. She worried about Henry. The passage she had cut in his throat for him to breathe should have been cleared with more care. The rest of him had been so twisted and mangled, it hurt to think of him. She tried to divine his spirit far down the mountain, but could get no sense of him.

"Momma, we'll never get this cleaned up." Lafette leaned back against an oak tree that'd somehow been spared. His face was streaked with rock dust and he squinted against the bright light of the sun.

"Never's an awful long time." She bent to roll a medium-sized stone over the hill, grunting as she pushed. Her back ached, and each new explosion vibrated her to the bone. "More rocks, come on now," she encouraged him.

Lafette's eyes saddened, wide and almond-shaped like a puppy's, the soft brown faded to golden in the afternoon heat. "I'm afraid, Momma. Yonder's King taking our Tyme trees and nobody's even trying to stop him." He waited for a response, then looked at his rifle leaning against a rock.

Another explosion farther up the mountain rocked the house and they jumped away. After that it was quiet for a long time.

Delta wanted to answer Lafette's questions, but her thoughts swirled into one another like tangled vine. A sensation of emptiness filled the air. The circle of power that had once surrounded Arn's Volcano had begun to dissipate. The rock's massiveness was gone, mountaintop splayed open. In the sunshine and warmth, honeybees whizzed back and forth, confused by the new terrain. Dragonflies and butterflies lit on the broken stones. It was not the same place as it had been the day before. She was unsure if this was for good or for evil.

The clopping sound of a horse startled her. A chill swept through her and the clacking became a faint background noise. She grabbed Lafette's hand and they ran to the front of the house.

King Kingsley rode up, his cheeks dark with stubble, jaws bloated and shoulders hunched over. Behind him, Amos rode a sorrel mare, his left arm in a sling and his forehead bandaged. A burlap sack lay across his lap.

King's black and white spotted horse reared to a halt and he flung himself out of the saddle. "Scorpion," he said to her. "That's what you are."

Skin on her neck prickling, she felt like a hen ready to flog an intruder. "Got me a few names for you, too." Her knees trembled and it took all her strength to keep from striking him.

"Come to tell you that you got your way. Won't be bothering you about your damned Tyme trees." King's eyes bulged like a bug's and his mouth hung slack as a carp just pulled from the water.

Delta regarded him as she would a wild animal. King's face had reddened to the color of smashed beets. He'd spat words venomously, lacking his usual superior attitude. She realized his anger was touched with madness. She backed farther away and spoke cautiously. "You've come to see Henry's way of thinking?"

"Henry's dead," King said matter-of-factly. "You killed him." His eyes watered with despair, but some force of will held back the tears from sliding down his face.

"Don't believe it, Momma. He's lying. Another of his tricks." Lafette stepped forward. "You're saying that 'cause Uncle Henry was gonna stop you from hurting us."

Delta stared up at the sky where Arn's Volcano had stood. Every nerve in her body burned with numbness. She watched Lafette, surprised at how tall he was next to her. His jaw clenched with anger as he glowered at King. She touched her lips, afraid she would be unable to talk, then she spoke to the sky as much as to her enemy. "If he's dead, it's no doing of mine."

"More 'en that," King said. "Henry knew you was the one who kilt him."

An anguished cry escaped her throat and she clamped the back of her hand across her mouth. She knew not to believe him, but grief slipped up her spine and wound around her heart until she told herself it was true.

King pursued her as relentlessly as a treed animal. "Doctor said the hole you cut in his throat suffocated him."

"No!" She stamped her foot. "I cleared his air passage so he could breathe."

"Breathe he did. Inhaled into his lungs, drown in his own blood." King panted for breath. Every muscle tensed and he struggled for control. "Weren't no easy dying." He crossed his arms tightly on his chest. "His last words were of you. Said he couldn't believe he'd died at the hands of a witch. Said if there were a way to do you the justice you deserved, he'd find it. He'd return and haunt you to your dying day." King spoke in a hard-edged tone as if he'd finally learned to fight her on her own ground.

Delta dropped to her knees and clapped her hands over her ears. She wanted to die. "The puncture in his throat kept him from suffocating."

"You knew exactly what you were doing." King remounted his horse. "You should hang for it."

Amos trotted his horse to her side and leaned down to whisper, "Sorry to tell you, Delta, but it's the truth." One of his eyes was swollen shut and it had taken a great effort for him to make the trip. "Best you not come to town no more," he said, his voice wavering. "Stay up here for your own safety and his." He nodded at Lafette.

King reached over and snatched the burlap bundle from Amos's lap, and heaved it at her. "Henry begged me to avenge his death. But I don't have to." He pointed at the bundle. "This is vengeance enough. Don't know how you did it, but now you got your rottin', stinkin' trees. They're of no use to me." He turned his horse. "Scorpion, that's what you are, scorpion."

Within seconds both men had disappeared. Neither Delta nor Lafette could move, both numb from the encounter. Henry was dead. They stood still, trying to comprehend his absence from the earth, breathing softly, lost in thought.

Finally Lafette asked, "Why did he call you a scorpion, Momma?" He knelt down, threw open the burlap sack and emptied it onto the ground. A thick Tyme branch landed in front of him. "Why it's only wood." He inspected closely as if he expected some trick from King. "Yeowww!" He jumped back as the branch crumbled and a large insect flew up and bounced against his chest.

Delta touched the wood with her foot and it broke in two, revealing brown wormy larvae embedded like bees in honeycomb. A slimy gel clung to her foot. She wiped it on the grass and leaned down to study the worms. One emerged from its cocoon, breaking open the orange shell with jagged legs like a grasshopper. Long wings resembled a dragonfly's and it clacked loud as a katydid.

Delicately Delta touched the inky purplish wings. The insect popped the rest of the way out of its shell and flew up above her along with two more. They spiraled around each other until she lost sight of them. The clacking was the same sound she'd heard the entire day. A sinking feeling merged with fears piling in the pit of her stomach.

Polly's curse, Delta had to admit, was truly Polly's revenge. *She must've blamed me for Kate's death. Must hate me bad as Kate hated me.*

An insect landed on the porch rail built entirely of Tyme wood. Delta whacked at it, knocked it to the ground and crushed it under foot. Thank God most the house is white oak, she thought.

It was truly a demon insect, the likes of which she'd never seen, with a body lime-colored as a green snake and bulbous eyes of a bumblebee. Hatching as quickly as it did, it wormed its way through the wood faster than a termite.

"What's this mean, Momma?" Lafette's soft voice was fearful, clearly aware of trouble they'd invited. "What are we gonna do?"

"I don't know." She climbed on one of the boulders, and stared at the mountains layered like a braid of hair into infinity. The insects would surely infect what Tyme trees hadn't been blasted away. Arn's Volcano lay in pieces. Henry Kingsley was dead. If she stayed here, didn't move, she couldn't hurt anything else.

She heard Lafette scuffing his shoe against the stones. "Momma, they're in the house and in all the Tyme trees." His voice cracked and he sobbed out the rest of his thoughts. "They ain't attacking any other tree."

His conclusions were unavoidable: she'd killed the Tyme trees. Done more damage to them than King's blasting would ever have accomplished. Polly had said she must lose everything to gain everything. King would trouble her no further, but the price had been the Tyme trees. The clacking insects whipped around them like diving wasps. No stopping them. Damn you, Polly Huston, she thought. You're more bitter an enemy than Kate ever was.

She slid off the boulder and confronted her son. "Don't maintain the roads, Lafette."

"Momma?"

"Let Shadow Mountain turn wild. Let the paths overrun with briars. Let the roads fill with rock and mudslides. No man will be able to climb this mountain for the rest of our days." Lafette was silent. When she turned around, he was gone. She heard him throwing things in the house but lacked the strength stop him.

∞

Nightfall. Stars bloomed like flowers. She'd never seen the sky from this angle, like a sparkling veil draping the world. Had it not been for the horrible clack of insects destroying the Tyme trees, she might have known peace. When would they stop? Would they eat every sliver of wood? She prayed they'd not attack the remaining trees once they finished with the Tymes. Lafette had torn out the destroyed mantel over the fireplace, her ruined kitchen cabinets, and all the door and window frames. Only the porch remained and sometime after dark, it fell, dislodging itself, too weak to sustain a connection to the white oak house.

Lafette had stubbornly stayed out of sight, avoiding Delta. She found him in the barn loft, petting Blue. "Momma, you fooled yourself. You can't see what's real."

"I've done the best I can, Lafette."

"Henry had it right about women and their silly sorcery. I'll never again believe something as false as a Watcher. There's no magic, only tricks. King dynamited our trees and woke up an insect that's been hibernating for years. And you attach some senseless meaning to it. It's nothing. Nothing."

Delta turned away from him. What could she say?

The insects continued their feast into the night. Delta stood like a sentry near the edge of the scattered volcano stones. When would she understand? Why had she no answers to the senselessness of all that had happened? Lafette came up behind her and kicked a spray of pebbles out into the air. "Just a bunch of rocks," he yelled. "A bunch of dang, dirty rocks! No dragon! No magic!"

A pain shot through Delta's heart. Lafette took off running, his feet chafing on the gravel. She clasped her hands to her chest and called after him. "Lafette, come back." He bolted into the barn, stopping at the door to turn and glare at her, his face so full of anguish and disappointment she knew any words from her would be a lie. He slammed the barn door and another pain crescendoed through her chest.

She understood nothing. What purpose was there to all of this? What purpose did their lives have? Arn had always told her that the magic had meaning and worked with an intention that grew and developed. She could see none in this. Her efforts had gone unrewarded for too long. And now, she was a Judas to the Tyme trees, the scorpion that stung itself. She had destroyed everything.

The clacking insects drowned out the usual night sounds. She heard no crickets chirping, no owls hooting, and no soft, evening hum. One by one, lanterns in the hamlets below went dark and became black spots amid ridges covered with foxfire. Fireflies beamed off and on like shooting stars. Her eyelids grew heavy and her will weakened. She opened her arms to the stars. There was no task left to perform, no tomorrow to hope for an easier life, no magic to save her, no Spirit to which she could appeal. She had lost her Eden and the sin clung to her bones like muscle.

An owl spanned its wings across the white crescent moon, screeching and aiming its feet toward the ground. Bullfrogs croaked in unison with crickets, and creek water gurgled over the rocks. The clacking had stopped. Their sticky, suffocating presence was no more. Delta sniffed the air, and honeysuckle and cinnamon wafted around her, bathing her in scent.

Fireflies glowed like buttons of light, weaving through broken rocks and spiraling around her.

An ache in her chest blossomed like a rose opening one petal at a time. What exactly was it that she'd done with her life? She had bandaged cut fingers, soothed bruised knees, grown corn and tomatoes, planted flowers and trees, given passage to birthing infants, cooled the foreheads of their mothers. She'd created, and when what was born was wounded, she'd healed.

This, she decided, was what she would do for the Tyme trees. This was her purpose. She would heal them from the blight just as she might treat any plant growing in her garden. She would restore the trees to their ancient and venerable state. That was all that was left for her. A requirement of her death. To this cause, she would dedicate the rest of her life, then perhaps she could sleep without heaviness in her heart.

"Arn Marlon is dead," she said aloud. "Only me now."

A pale aurora spread across the night sky as if confirming her conclusions, then whipped through the heavens like an arrow, upward toward the moon and disappeared into its light.

Part II

∞ Eight Years Later ∞

Prologue II

ONE NIGHT IN OCTOBER, at the peak of Indian summer, a shadow blacker than pitch eclipsed a bright Hunter's Moon. As the specter darkened the white disk, a wild dog howled at the figure of a second man creeping across Creation Ridge. This one sniffed the air, inhaling the scent of newly forged iron. Both men boiled with an ancient, angry lust that had been their undoing, but their day was done, and they walked as ghosts in this world, trying to reclaim some semblance of former glory.

The Shade spat dirt and shook his body to test his corporeal limbs. He paused to perceive a cool wind. The eyes of a fox reflected in the bush and a snake slithered across his boots. The season was ripe with witchery, but he hadn't the hours to consider what devil had brought him into being. He had one chance to set destiny aright before returning to dust.

King Kingsley's throaty growl disappeared under the clanking L & N train being loaded in the valley below. Voices echoed through the ridges as the railroad workers yelled instructions and the heavy cargo screeched against the metal cars. Where once only the panther's scream set terror in a wayfarer's heart, these new sounds were painful as scalding oil to King's ears. Painful—not because they were foreign, but because he was no longer master of all he surveyed.

King stalked the lush Tennessee farmlands he'd once owned and spat at an abandoned timber company no longer belonging to him. He wandered through the shell of a mill and a stable that had housed the best mules a teamster could want, then he crept through a deserted blacksmith stoop. He kicked a half buried hammer, spreading sooty ash that wafted a burnt smell in the air. At the corner of a rickety building hung a faded sign: Kingsleyville.

His town had not sprung into being as he had intended. It had fallen victim to rumor and hope just as star-crossed lovers trust the predictions of fortunetellers. Like so many other *Pittsburghs of the South*, Kingsleyville was built on the expectation of successful steel, timber, and coal industries.

Families moved from their back-mountain farms to the towns. They searched for a better life. No longer would they cultivate the land for their sustenance. Their children would never watch the sky for rain, or crumble dirt clods between their fingers to gauge if the soil was ready for seed. Their sons and daughters would learn to read and write, and judge their worth not by the quality of their crops but by the money in their hands.

Yet the towns conceived in 1900 were stillborn by 1902. No one bought the natural resources ripped from the earth. The ore was labeled an inferior grade. The trees didn't grow back as large as in centuries past, and they were branded an unhealthy lot.

So fell King Kingsley's timber company, mill, quarry, stable, blacksmith shop, farm, and a dozen other businesses. Not long after, rumors spread that Delta Wade's curse had swallowed him whole. In these hard times, bad luck rubbed off on a person. Best to avoid anywhere ill fortune had walked.

If anyone fared better than his town, King knew it was Delta. With no challenge to her ownership, she lived silently on Shadow Mountain. She hunted her food, made her clothes, her needs so minimal that she never need leave. No word came from her for years, and the only signs that she existed were her son's frequent comings and goings as he grew into a wild, unruly youth.

The Tyme trees slowly rotted away. Shadow Mountain looked like an ice cap when the ghostly fog engulfed it. Hardly a plant survived in the Tyme soil, and it seemed Shadow Mountain was poisoned forever.

Lafette sometimes spoke of his mother's efforts to restore the land. In the past few years, the mountain became dotted with ferns and mountain laurel. Perhaps, people would say, Delta Wade could bring back the Tyme tree. Others said there was no such thing, and as more time passed, the Tyme tree joined the region's folklore.

Angrily, King stomped through Kingleysville's ruins, his focus always returning to Shadow Mountain. He covered his face with both hands as if to shield himself from it. Someone seeing him might have assumed he was finally afraid—or had nothing to lose. Perhaps he was only tired. He flipped his silver coin in the air. Besides his house, the coin was all that he had left in the world.

A cat hissed as King moved through his lost empire. A harsh, cold wind whipped his coat from his chest, but he took little notice and marched from the deserted town without looking back. In the distance, a train whistle blended into the wail of the wind as he turned toward home. A stray dog, its ribs bearing against its skin, trotted beside him a ways. He cast a long shadow in the disappearing moonlight.

King approached his house, carefully stepping onto the porch, to avoid further damage to the rotting steps. Holding to a column, paint chips flurried into his face. He choked and wheezed when the dust reached his lungs. Amos came out to help, a loyal servant after so many years, but King pushed him aside, the walk through the deserted town hardening him against human contact. He needed an iron heart. He looked past Amos and into the hallway. “She here?” he asked.

Amos nodded, his eyes narrow with concern, taking in every nuance of King’s mood. “She don’t want nobody to know she’s come off the mountain.”

“I sure as hell ain’t likely to tell.” King flipped his silver coin, then squeezed it tightly. He held breath in his lungs, willing the air to support his frame, pulled his shoulders back and pressed his chest forward. He would not walk into that room a broken man.

The library was awash in firelight. Delta stood at the mantle, facing away from King. Thin, hair more white than blond, she retained a solitary stance, feet wide apart like a man, hands on her hips and a dip to her head like a snake coming up under its prey. As King approached, she turned sideways but did not stare at him directly.

“You’ve bewitched me,” he said.

Delta’s face was lit with the fire’s gold tone and shadowed by the eclipsing Blood Moon shining through the full-length windows. Her lips curled, cruel and taunting. “You were never one to believe in witchery.”

“Take your curse off me.” He squeezed his silver coin, then flipped it as if the skill kept his world under control. “Remove it or I’ll find a way to level that mountain.”

Delta's eyes followed the coin as it spun. Before he could stop her, she slipped her hand over his and caught it. "The curse is no longer with you."

"That's my good luck coin." He grabbed her wrist. "Give it back."

"It's my price for removing your curse."

"That coin's worth a thousand dollars." He released her and paced past the burning logs. "It'll give me a new start. I need that money!"

Delta held the coin out to him. "Here then, take it back."

He stared at the coin, then at her face, focusing into her eyes. "It has no value to you?" He shook his head, hardly believing she had gumption to ask so high a price.

"You wanted your curse gone. It's gone. You want your coin back. Take it—but the bad luck goes with it."

King's focus bore out the window toward the black mountain overshadowing his dead town. "You're a lurking snake, Delta Wade." Pressing thumbs against his temples, he pondered whether his fear of the curse outweighed his need for the coin.

She dropped the silver piece into a mantle dish and the striking of glass vibrated in the room. "A curse from a bad luck coin ain't a thing I'd wish on anybody." She stepped to the windowed doors and pulled aside a sheer drape streaked with runs. "I came this time because of Henry. I owed him that much for my part in his dying. I'll not venture off my mountain again." She stepped out the long glass doors, darkness swallowing her as if she were the eclipsed moon.

King left the house quickly, stopping only for a barn lantern. He arrived at the Cumberland Gap Trading Post in need of strong drink to make him forget Delta Wade's words. He also needed to concentrate on his plans. "Gonna rebuild Kingsleyville," he told Bill Linville, who slid whiskey in front of him.

"Yup," Bill said, paying him no mind.

"Be bigger than ever. Make Contrary look like a piss ant town."

"Contrary is a piss ant town." Bill went about his work without acknowledging King.

"People'll listen to me again. Stand aside when I walk down the street." King held out his cup.

Bill rolled his eyes and filled it before returning to arrange merchandise. A decade ago he'd sold farming hoes, wide-toothed saws, or corn and bean seeds. Now he stocked sturdy shovels, sharpened picks, caps with eye-like contraptions on the forehead, and carbide flasks for coal miners. The store itself had changed, too. Gone were the ancient iron lanterns permanently set into the walls; instead, light shone from a single bulb hanging over a side table used for poker games.

King tapped his cup. "Another." Bill pointed at a sign. NO CREDIT. Hunting through his pockets, King had only his silver coin. His future. A destiny Delta Wade stole from him. *That witch won't steal my fate, he swore. Not long as there's breath in me.* In the window behind Bill, a face appeared. One King hadn't seen in a generation. He chuckled, blinked, and the visage was gone. "Can't be," he said aloud. "He's dead."

King grinned and stared at Bill, gesturing with palms up, "Remember it was me that give you the business to keep this place afloat during hard times." Bill filled the cup and leaned against the counter as King gulped it down. "Another?" King asked, as if his very life depended on it.

♆ 29 ♆

A STARK LIGHT BULB hanging over a poker table glared into an inventory of shelved pots and pans, sending out jagged blades of distorted light. Flesh appeared whiter and card players' pores dark pits. Cigarette smoke ribboned around men ripe with sweat.

Lafette cleared his throat as Valentine cut the cards and shuffled an ace to the bottom. If he'd observed correctly, that made three aces Valentine had dealt himself. A tap on the window behind him caused Lafette's shoulders to tense. He glanced around to make sure they weren't being spied on. A tree branch scraped against the pane.

A burl counter crossed the back corner of the Cumberland Gap Trading Post. Lafette leaned on one end and, on the opposite side, a heavyset prostitute rested against Nolan Johnson. She stared over Nolan's shoulder toward Lafette, her large eyes blurry from drink. Lafette turned his back, propping on his elbows. That way he didn't have to look at Rosy Thunderheart. The card game called for his attention.

Ted Butterfield scratched his whiskers, eyes shifting from card to card. Lafette read his nerves. Clark Yates and Garrison

Weaver shuffled their cards, mimicking aloof milk cow faces, while Frank Devery tapped his foot. Lafette rubbed his left eye to signal Valentine that Clark, Ted, and Garrison held unlucky hands. Still unsure of Frank. His foot tapping made Lafette feel lucky. He rubbed his chin, telling Valentine to bet high.

As they placed bets, Lafette stepped out a side door to look around. The chilly wind moaned. Tree limbs tossed in a rushing noise. The sky around the Hunter's Moon misted with bluish clouds.

A pine branch bent unnaturally toward the ground, then shot up as if released by an unseen hand. *Somebody's behind that tree,* he realized and ran his hand along the pistol in his pocket. He circled the pine. No one. The moon's luster spread enough light to distinguished trees and buildings. The night before it had eclipsed, and Lafette looked up, wondering if it might do so again.

An overturned wheelbarrow was tipped beside an apple tree, and a sickly decaying smell mingled with pine scent. He wiped sweaty hands on his pants then kicked the wheelbarrow, feeling very much a fool when a bony dog yelped and trotted toward the hills. He scanned the darkness. No one.

Before reentering the trading post, he hid in the shadows, holding himself like stone. One by one, he eliminated sounds: wind, crackling leaves, cricket chirps, howling dog. *Someone's out there.* He could sense a vibrating presence. Why was this person hiding? Could someone have seen him and Valentine cheating?

Lafette returned to the store and inhaled a lung-full of cigarette smoke. He wrapped both hands around a tin cup to steady himself. Billy Jr., the owner's son, refilled it with moonshine after Lafette turned down the more popular brewery beer transported over from Kentucky. Valentine fidgeted, catching Lafette's nervousness, and his chair squeaked against the floor.

Ted, Clark, and Garrison had folded and leaned back restfully, slowly drawing on stubby cigarettes. Frank bit his lower lip as he threw in his last dollar. Valentine leaned forward. "You're sure a-wearing me down," he said, and bet again. "If you ain't got money, I'll bet you for that pearl-handled pistol."

Lafette choked on moonshine. He glared at Valentine and called out, "If we're gonna talk about going to California, better hurry 'fore I fall asleep." Valentine wanted that pistol so much he'd almost stolen it one night when Frank was drunk. Lafette had pointed out that anyone who saw the distinctive gun would recognize it and the Devery clan was not one to fool with. Valentine still set his mind to scheming how to get it. Lafette could have kicked him for betting for the pistol.

Frank studied his cards, then laid them face down. He reached into a shoulder holster and pulled out a silver pistol with a gleaming pearl-colored handle. "Supposed to've belonged to a fancy whore from New Orleans. Hate to lose it." He studied his cards, picking up the top one for a last check, then pushed the pistol into the pot. "Momma passed it down to me."

The smoke hung thick enough to ignite as Nolan struck a match to light cigarettes for himself and Rosy. A loaded gun on the table is the last thing I need, Lafette told himself. Raising the cup to his lips, he prepared to distract the men without his eyes straying from the gun. He swallowed a big gulp then coughed, spewing out moonshine on the floor. He clutched his neck and cleared his throat.

All the men turned. "You alright, Lafette?" Ted asked.

"Just swallowed wrong." Lafette waved Billy away as he thumped him on the back. Valentine stared steadily at his cards, and Lafette knew the winning cards were now in hand.

A forceful wind shook the building and the side door slammed against the wall. Two tin skillets knocked, making a sound sharp as a gunshot. Lafette's heart pulsed in his throat. Just a clanking skillet, not pistol fire. He tensed his torso, wishing he could calm his jittery stomach. The wind somersaulted a handful of crinkled brown leaves across the floor. The night had a bad smell to it

Billy ran to shut the door, but stopped and looked out. "Sorry, sir," he said to someone outside. "Take your time."

Lafette slumped on the counter, rubbed his forehead, and stared through the gaps of his fingers. Whoever's outside was the one, he figured. Must have seen us cheating. Why ain't he coming in? Lafette's dry mouth fought a scratchy throat. Feet scraped the porch steps, and Lafette hunkered down, ready to move.

Valentine laughed loudly, throwing three aces and two queens on the table. He swept up the pistol and gave it a kiss. Frank covered his face with his large, square palms then rubbed his scalp as if he did not understand.

A porch floorboard squeaked. Lafette's muscles tensed and he knew anyone who might make a move would do it now.

A tapping noise on the porch closed in on the open door. Someone touched Lafette's arm. He froze. Caught. His sight blurred, then focused, though he was unsure if that was caused by moonshine or fear. A hand reached over his shoulder and pointed toward the door.

"Look yonder," a voice whispered. Canes were poised inside the doorframe.

A frail man leaned on two walking sticks. His shirt hung on bony shoulders, making the sleeves bunch around the wrists. His bent body held like a crooked post, and across his back, he'd strapped an English saddle.

Lafette could hardly believe the man stood under the saddle weight. As he stepped into the trading post, everyone snuck glances at him. Cane taps across the floor broke the awkward silence. His legs dragged along after them, scraping the wood planks with a sound louder than the whistle of the wind.

"Can't I help ye, sir?" Garrison asked, standing up as the man inched past him.

"No, no, I'm fine. Just fine."

The man stared intently at the counter. Sweat dripped down his forehead to his cheek. It pained Lafette to watch this cripple walk with less speed than a terrapin. It was more painful to think that perhaps he was the one who had seen Valentine cheating.

"Who is that?" Lafette whispered aside. The man was oddly familiar like someone remembered from a childhood dream.

"You mean ye don't recognize him?" asked a voice behind him.

"Looks a mite..." Lafette paused. The crippled man raised his chin and gazed directly at him. For a moment the man's eyes were like a snake hypnotizing a bird. *He knows! He knows we been cheatin' at cards.* Sweat beaded on Lafette's neck. He looked for an escape. Out the side door! He'd grab Valentine, and they'd head straight into the tall trees. Nobody could catch them once they were on Shadow Mountain.

"Looks feeble as a wounded hare," the voice behind him whispered. "Don't ye recognize Henry Kingsley?"

Those words jolted Lafette. "Henry Kingsley's dead. Can't be him." The crippled man continued to stare at Lafette, then looked away.

"Kingsleys need money. Falling on such hard times and all."

"How can this be?" Lafette stared intently at a skeletal body, not close to the tall, square-shouldered Henry he remembered. The man's sunken eyes resembled holes in his face and his nose had taken on a beakish look.

Some part of Lafette wanted to deny that Henry Kingsley stood in front of him. The determination with which he shifted the saddle off his back and onto the counter reminded Lafette of being a child and the many times Henry had thrown him across his shoulders in just the same way.

"Ole Kingsley might be a good stooge for a silver map," the voice whispered in Lafette's ear. "Hear he ain't right in the head."

"Need to hear his voice," Lafette said under his breath.

"Sure would serve 'im right. After all the Kingsleys done to you."

"The Kingsleys didn't do nothing to me!" Lafette grumbled more loudly than he'd intended. He turned to confront the man behind him, but all he saw was the hem of a ragged coat and a tattered black hat leaving by the side entrance. At first, he'd thought it was Nolan behind him, but now realized someone had followed him in the side entrance. "Ornery fool," Lafette spat toward the door.

Lafette inched toward the center of the counter so he'd be in Valentine's line of sight, then nodded toward the crippled man. Valentine's eyes widened in a questioning look and Lafette signaled him by stroking his shirt collar.

Slowly, Valentine stood, sliding a folded paper from his jacket. He sauntered to the counter. The crippled man caressed the shiny saddle. Lafette noticed an interest sparkling in Valentine's eyes when he realized saddle's value.

"Howdy," Valentine said, smiling. "Awful night to be out and about, especially toting a saddle on your back."

"That it is," the man said.

Lafette tried to catch the inflection of his voice but couldn't hear enough to make certain if it was truly Henry.

"This one's old." Valentine touched the saddle's seat. "Good condition, though."

"It's for sale," the man said, "on consignment... they still do that here?"

"Reckon so," Valentine answered, "but not many got cash in these hard times."

"Seems times are always hard." The man gazed at blurred reflections in the hanging pans.

"That they are."

"Bill Linville still run this place?"

"His son. Bill Senior don't work most nights. Said he felt too tired and old for all this. Junior's out back. Be around in a minute."

The man adjusted the saddle straps and neatly wrapped the stirrups over the seat.

"Tell you what." Valentine ran a finger around the brown leather hump that formed the rear. "I have here in my hand," he tapped his finger against the folded paper. "Something I might trade for this saddle. Sure save you some trouble."

Lafette wished Valentine would shut off his sales speech and let the man talk.

"Swift's Silver Mine Map?" the man read. He glanced at Valentine. His drooping cheeks warmed to a peach color and his eyes sparkled as if he'd heard a joke. Then, he laughed as heartily as a young child.

"What funny?" Valentine asked.

"This." The man dropped the map.

"Be glad to read it to you, if you can't read," Valentine said, sounding sincere.

"There's no silver mines in these mountains." The man nudged the map with his cane and sent it flying.

"How in hell would you know?" Valentine shifted his weight to one leg and gripped his belt loops so tight one broke.

Lafette had never seen his friend so goaded, especially by someone so helpless. The other men watched from the card table. Their eyes glittered with amusement. Frank mimicked the crippled man's stance behind his back and shook a crooked finger. Valentine whipped around with fury as if to shout that any other man except a cripple would have been lying on his back with a bloody nose.

The man's face softened into a serious but sorrowful mask. He studied the dusty brown floorboards and tapped the scuffed boot against the counter, then his lips curved into a smile reserved for an errant child. The expression looked comfortable on him.

Lafette's stomach knotted. Henry Kingsley stood before him, and this knowledge chilled him like a dying man's touch. His former friend alive, yet all Lafette could think was that Henry still had the same cheerful smile.

"Son," Henry said, his expression altering only for his words, "don't do this." He stepped on the map and pushed his saddle to the side counter, dragging his canes with him. Bill Jr. came back, and in the several minutes it took to make the transaction, Lafette hung on every word. Then, in an awkward shift, the man thrust the two canes out and aimed for the door.

"Need help?" Frank asked.

"Me and my canes have learned to make do. Thank you, though."

Lafette waited until the door closed behind Henry. He straightened up from his crouched position on the counter. The men laughed while Frank shook a finger to indicate Valentine got exactly what he deserved.

"Teach you to start that foolishness." Clark ripped the Swift's Silver Mine Map in half. "Cheatin' a crippled man is a sin sure as shootin'."

"It's that varmint's fault." Valentine pointed at Lafette. "Why in hell did you get me started on this with him?"

Lafette stared after Henry as he inched down the steps. "Had to know if it was really him."

"If it was who?" Frank asked.

Lafette grabbed the moonshine jar and drank deep. "Fella standing behind me," he said between gulps, "claimed it was Henry Kingsley. I had to hear his voice to be sure."

"Henry Kingsley's dead." Frank huffed. "You sayin' a ghost trotted into this store, totin' a saddle 'cross his back."

"Well, if a cripple can do it, I don't know why a ghost can't." Valentine took the moonshine from Lafette and swallowed a mouthful.

"Never saw any dang man behind you." Frank suspiciously inspected the area.

"Come to think, I didn't neither." Clark looked at Ted and Garrison, who nodded in agreement.

"Ain't a wise thing for a man to hide hisself during a high-stakes poker game." Frank rested a hand on his empty holster. "Somebody might think there's more goin' on."

"Curly-headed feller," Rosy said from down the bar, her legs intertwined with Nolan's. "Tall, black-haired, pretty blue eyes. Weren't hidin'. I saw him plain as day. Came and went by the side door."

The men surveyed the room to find some clue of this second visitor. Only Rosy had observed the man who'd stood behind Lafette. He figured she had probably lied to protect him. Yet Lafette knew someone had stood behind him.

Rosy curled a ringlet around her finger. "I'm telling you it was a curly-haired man," she said, turning away from Nolan and pointing to the place where Lafette had been standing. "I noticed 'cause he had such a twinkle in his eyes, the kind that makes tingles run up your spine."

"Hey!" Nolan pulled her back toward him. "Don't make me jealous, woman."

Lafette thought on the voice he'd heard. He'd concentrated so much on the card game and who might have seen them cheating that he hadn't given a thought to who'd hid behind him. Not like him to be so careless. Whoever stood there could have been the one he'd sensed when he was outside. He leaned on the counter and focused, hoping to jar a memory.

"Don't know how you missed seeing him, he was tall as a tree," Rosy said.

Valentine snickered, elbowing Clark in the side. "Anybody'd notice, it'd be her."

"A curly-headed man ain't the only thing to disappear." Clark motioned to the card table. Instantly, they gathered around, looking at the scattered cards and the empty box in the center. All their money was gone.

"Sonnvabitch!" Valentine slammed his hand against the table. "Why don't you codgers ever watch what goes on around this sorry place!" The pearl-handled gun lay on Valentine's chair as if placed just for him. He stuck it in his belt.

"We were all watching you, fool," Clark said.

Lafette cracked open the door. Henry stood beside a black horse—not as perfect a horse as the Kingsleys had usually owned in times past, but a strong, well-muscled animal. He slipped his canes into leather loops on the saddle. The stirrups hung low, and he lifted one thigh and placed his foot in one, then he hung by his arms and pulled as the horse shifted in a circle. The display looked like a dance the horse had been taught and gave Henry the momentum to shift himself onto its back. Lafette cringed. Henry had once been the best horseman in the county. He'd had a way with horses that seemed magic, and it appeared he still did.

A cane slipped from its loop and dropped to the ground. Henry stared down at it, his mouth strained in frustration at the prospect of dismounting to retrieve it.

Lafette stepped onto the porch and called out, "I'll get it."

"Thank you kindly." Henry steadied the horse with a pat on its neck.

Lafette picked up the cane, noticing at once that it was carved from Tyme tree. Tyme wood hadn't been strong enough to use since the insect blight eight years ago. He rubbed his fingers down the sleek, round cane. Light caught the honey-colored grain, making it shimmer like gold.

"Tyme?" Lafette asked.

"Surprised somebody your age remembers Tyme trees. Things are forgotten so quickly nowadays," Henry said.

"They were special to me." Lafette looked into his eyes to determine if this man he'd loved like a father recognized him. If he did, he gave no sign. Lafette slipped the cane through the saddle loop and scratched the horse's neck.

"Thank you again." Henry pulled the reins and the horse circled, its hooves clapping in dull rhythm against the dirt.

As they disappeared into darkness, Lafette could hold his tongue no longer. "Don't you know me?" he called after him. Henry did not look back, and Lafette realized Henry couldn't turn his body. He plunged into the darkness toward the vanishing outline. Henry gazed down on him, eyes slanted in sadness, mouth curved in a frown, choking back feelings.

"Don't you know who I am?" Lafette repeated.

"I know you, Son." Henry's hands folded across his lap and his stooped shoulders trembled. "Had to be sure you'd take me to her."

"You knew I'd follow you out here," Lafette said, annoyed he'd been so naive. "Curiosity might've got the best of me, but no way I'd take you to Momma."

"Is Delta well?" Henry's voice softened when he spoke her name. "I've tried to find my way up the mountain and I can't make it."

"It was unlucky the first time I helped you up that mountain. I'll not help you again." Lafette crossed his arms over his chest. He turned to walk away.

"It would mean everything to me. Please take me to her."

Lafette froze in place, feeling awkward and undecided. Then he waved Henry away and walked on. Henry followed him until Lafette stepped off the road, into a thick poplar grove. Lafette knew Henry would get lost in this forest, especially in the dark. He leaned against a tree, holding in the ache of thinking this man dead, and the sour fragrance of wet leaves nauseated him.

Seeing Henry made him want to say all the things he'd believed years ago. *Liar. Betrayer. Let us believe you were dead. Let us be blamed for your death.* He could hear Henry calling out to him.

"I beg you, Lafette. I beg you. Take me to Delta."

The pleading in Henry's voice sent shivers up Lafette's spine. He walked a few steps in the Henry's direction. Thoughts of his mother and her years of being shunned and alone on Shadow Mountain stopped him. He put his hands against his ears to block out Henry's voice. No, he thought. Last thing Momma needs is a Kingsley's bad luck.

Henry and his horse formed a silhouette against the bright, full moon. The wind moaned, and before long, the whistle of the L & N passing through Cumberland Gap drowned out the sounds of nature. All the while a shadowy phantom, tall and tattered, hid in the darkness, watching.

ᐯ 30 ᐯ

SILVER TYME SPROUTS shimmered under a Hunter's Moon. The orb hung low in the sky, so large it seemed close enough to touch. Delta raised her palms toward the white disk then emptied her hands over the potted Tyme plants as if watering them with moonlight. She wiped the buds with gauze soaked in a solution of witch hazel and willow bark. These buds were the first in eight years to live without succumbing to disease. She was so pleased that she slowly twirled in place, dancing in the moonlight.

The lavender buds dangled like bellflowers. Night after night, she nurtured the stems, soaking them in starlight under the full moon. A good light for them. A warm Indian Summer allowed her to work late. She sprinkled crushed yellowroot while waving ginseng in a figure eight just above the plants.

"Grow, little stems," she whispered. "Make trees as strong as your ancestors."

This time, she prayed, *let them live*. In her mind the seeds became fiery trees, burning hot as the summer sun. She imagined the entire mountain flowered with Tyme trees. "Just like the old days," she said and opened her eyes. It seemed the Tyme spouts stood a little taller, with a healthy sheen.

A shadow grew into the moonlight and the sudden darkness made Delta think something was upon her. She picked up a stone. "Who's there?"

"Your son," Lafette slurred, stepping out. Moonlight lit his face, hair mussed and eyes red-rimmed. The crease between his eyebrows deepened when he was troubled. "Your only son."

Delta stared at him. "Valentine Tolliver's gonna get you into trouble some day." She dropped the rock then shifted the plants out of Lafette's shadow. "Trouble you might get stuck with."

His lips pressed together, eyes sheepishly darting from her face to the ground. His clothes smelled of smoke and his breath carried the sharpness of liquor. "Why do you bother with these ole things, Momma?" He touched a Tyme plant, flicked it with his finger and sighed as if to comment on its sorry state.

Delta pointed at one. "It'd help if you'd take these and plant them in the corn patch."

"Give the corn a bad taste."

She knew his tone was meant to annoy her. If she mentioned how often she'd watched him checking the shrubs' progress, he'd only deny it. Once he'd even kissed a leaf, though he'd insisted he'd only smelled it.

She grabbed his arm to pull herself up. He'd grown into such a big boy, almost tall as his father but muscular like the men in her family. She smacked him lightly on the cheek and shook a finger underneath his nose. "You'd do well to stop roaming these hills like a hooligan and spend a little time learning what I can teach you."

Lafette rolled his eyes then dropped his gaze to a caldron, fragrant with wild roses and marigold. A fire burned low in a smoldering heap. He tossed in wood chips to add light. “Smells good enough to drink.” He sniffed the steam like smoke from a pipe. “What’s in it?”

“None of what you been drinking, for damn sure.”

“Momma!” He put a hand on his chest as if shocked to hear such language.

A bullfrog croaked, and he puffed out his cheeks and imitated the sound. When he did it a second time, she pressed two fingers into his cheeks and deflated them. “I’m tired of jokes.” She waved her arm to encompass the chicken coop, pigpen, barn and beehives. “The barn stinks! The mule needs brushing, the hives need new combs, and if you’ve not noticed yet, we are in desperate need of a new outhouse.”

The bullfrog continued to croak, and Lafette croaked once with it, but ceased as the wind shifted and brought the outhouse’s acrid smell past his nose. “I’ll get to them things, Momma. I always do. Easier to break ground in the spring.”

She picked up a plant and placed it gently in his hands. “More’n that. Bringing these Tyme leaves to life is the task I really need you for.”

He held the plant as he would a baby chick. “Get Nancy to help you, or better yet, get Rosy Thunderheart. She’s not doing much these days.” He stared at the far mountains even though the black night made them impossible to see. Dark veins criss-crossed the moon and its light dimmed. “I don’t know what to do in these matters.”

“They’re not Watchers, Lafette.” She touched his shoulder. “You know what I need.” He marched to the mountain edge and set the Tyme plant on a rock pile. From the back, his figure seemed like Arn’s. Only when he turned toward her could she get the sense of the man he’d made himself into. He laid an arm across his stomach and touched his other hand to his chin, his thoughts disturbing him. Delta could only hope he was considering the prospect of becoming the Watcher. "You're the only one who can breathe life into the dead."

"Don't start that crazy stuff, Momma." He crossed his arms defensively.

"Got your daddy's blood, but sure don't have his brains."

"Valentine says Watcher stuff is nonsense. Started by some old Indian who wanted to scare people away from the mountain."

A rush of anger filled her whenever he quoted Valentine as an expert. "Feel the power, just once, then you'll believe the things I say."

He kicked a rock and sent it flying into the darkness. It cracked against a tree then thudded to the ground. "Momma, ain't no power up here. It's make-believe."

Delta pointed toward the corn patch. She bit her tongue, knowing if she said more, she'd drive him further away and deeper into that silent place he escaped to when something troubled him. He picked up a plant and waded into the garden.

It seemed to her the straw-colored cornstalks parted for him, or was that her imagination? Lafette has got to be the Watcher, she thought desperately, but was exhausted from trying to convince him. Now, it was up to the mountain itself. She'd done the best she could to kindle his interest, but her son was stubborn. "Cornbread and hog meat for supper," she called out.

"What'd ye say, Momma?" Lafette looked up from where he knelt, hands covered with dirt as he pulled a cornstalk by its roots and planted the Tyme twig in its place.

Remind him of when he believed he was the Watcher, she decided. Let him remember those feelings and he'll start trusting them again. “I said you must think it was make-believe that chased you through the woods that time Henry Kingsley saved you from being stuck in the Elisha Tree.”

Lafette was silent. The dried corn leaves crunched as he moved toward her and took the second plant from her hands. Silently, he stared at the ground, lines around his mouth deepening. “Why would you bring up Henry Kingsley tonight?”

“You said the Wampus chased you.” She knew she’d angered him. “What is it, Lafette?”

He did not answer but stared upward at the moon. His lips parted as if to speak, then clenched against his words. Air whistled through his gritted teeth as he dropped his head, still struggling to talk. Suddenly, his shoulders jerked backwards, “Momma, this plant is dying.” He loosened his hold, and the plant broke and dropped to the ground. Gingerly he picked up the stem.

“Not again!” A leaf yellowed and fluttered away like a snowflake. White spores dusted the bud. The stem drooped rubbery. “Bring the rest inside, quickly.”

She hurried ahead to open the kitchen door. A rush of warm air enveloped her. She hopped over Blue, napping on a throw rug, and, in one swipe, cleared her table. The limp plant hung like a rag doll. She spread it on the table, carefully arranging branches as if they were a human’s broken limbs.

Wall shelves were stacked three jars deep. She tossed several containers aside until she found wintergreen leaves and a pouch of wolf’s fangs. Emptying both into a caldron, she spoke into it, “Purity and strength. Purity and strength.” Lafette entered with the other two plants replanted in their pots. Only one was infected. “Take the healthy one to the other side of the room,” she said urgently, “and heat up the fire.”

He stood behind her like a lost child, his large frame looming awkwardly in the small kitchen. He fumbled with the coal bucket. A burst of sparks fluttered upward when he tossed coal and a block of black locust into the stove. Blue nudged him with his nose. “Not now, boy.” Lafette pushed the dog gently with his boot.

Delta worked with a doctor’s precision, firmly shoving a hickory twig into potted dirt and gently lifting the limp plant. She wrapped the top part around the twig so the Tyme plant would stand upright. Sweat beaded her forehead.

The caldron bubbled, then erupted into a boil. She held the plant over the steam and the heat reddened her arms. White spores dropped like melting ice. Her arm muscles cramped as the steam burned hotter. She gritted her teeth as her skin cooked.

Blue lapped spilled water from around Delta’s feet. He sniffed her legs, then looped around to nudge Lafette behind his knees. Lafette stood still until Blue nipped his pants leg and pulled him toward Delta. He bent over her shoulder and took the plant. Ignoring her red, swollen arms, she began working on the other Tyme bud.

“Sure this is gonna work?” he asked.

“Hold it near to the water as you can.” She cast another handful of wintergreen into the pot and the room filled with a minty aroma. Lafette hissed as the steam seared through his sleeves. “I’ll take over,” she said, reaching for the plant.

He blocked her with his shoulder. “I’m fine. Just work on the other one.”

“It’s gone.” Delta pointed to the limp stem, bent over its pot, the browned bud touching the table. She wiped his brow, pushed wet hair from his face flushed from the heat. Once more she tried to take the surviving plant from him. Again he refused to give it to her. "I can stand it, Momma."

She wrapped wet cloth around his arms to lessen the pain. "If I could get one healthy piece of Tyme wood to tie to these plants. I could make 'em live."

Lafette grunted from the burn but his voice conveyed more than physical pain. "Must be something else that'll work."

"Everything I lived for these past years has come to nothing. Why can't I find one healthy piece of wood?"

The plant drooped over Lafette's hand, hugging his fingers. "Oh God," he said, his voice brimming anguish. "I'll get you the wood, Momma. I'll get it somehow."

She lifted his arms higher out of the burning heat. "Honey, you'd be hunting an animal that don't exist."

"I know where to get some." He groaned again and exhaled to relieve the pain of his scalded arms.

"Not a fit slice of Tyme in the Cumberlands." She poured cool water over his arms so he'd be able to stand the steam. Her own arms stung when the steam hit them.

"It exists. Never mind where. Just know, I'll get it for you."

Arn immediately came to mind. "Tell me who has this wood." She massaged the muscles above Lafette's elbows.

The plant's main stem began to turn a bright green. The white substance had nearly disappeared.

"Who?" She pushed his arms closer to the water and held them while the bud popped open, its lavender color returned.

"AAAwwwww," Lafette's head dropped backward onto his shoulders. "I got to take my arms out now!"

"Who?" She held his arms in the steam. The plant perked up, waving in the hot, moist air.

"Henry Kingsley! Henry Kingsley has a walking cane of Tyme wood!"

Delta released him, her mouth dropped open though unable to speak. Lafette whipped his arms out of the steam and dropped the plant on the table. Her limbs felt limp as the Tyme seedling. "Put your arms in here." She pointed to a pail of cold water, though her mind could focus only on his proclamation.

Lafette grimaced, plunging his arms into the water. Sweat dripped down his cheeks and his breath was heavy as if he'd run a long distance. "Wasn't gonna tell you. I saw him. Talked to him. He's alive."

"And so is our Tyme bud." She gestured at the table. "It'll flower now. You saved it, Lafette. I knew you had the power." She reached into the bucket of water and took hold of his hands, smiling at him proudly.

"I shouldn't've told about Henry Kingsley," he murmured.

Delta lifted his arm and dried the reddened skin. She applied salve, smoothing it on generously.

"It's a mistake," he said. "What you're thinking."

"This'll keep you from blistering." She massaged the crooks of his fingers. His stillness reminded her of the child he'd been, hardly ever a tear for physical pain; crying only when she'd fussed at him and hurt his feelings. "This is good," she said, showing him his arms weren't swelling. "You won't feel any hurt in the morning."

She'd healed his arms, and with Henry's walking cane, would make sure the Tyme tree survived as well. Touching Lafette's shoulder, she pointed out how the bud opened into a delicate pink flower. "It's not a mistake, Lafette." She looked up into his eyes, so narrow with doubt. "I know exactly what I'm doing."

"Momma, your arms!" He held them out, shocked she'd spend so much time on him and neglect her own burned skin, blistered from wrist to elbow. "You'd do the same thing with Henry Kingsley. Put him before yourself."

"First thing tomorrow morning, fetch Henry Kingsley to me."

"But Momma!"

"And make sure he brings that Tyme cane."

"Ain't gonna do it!" Lafette jerked away from her. He whistled to Blue and they left the house. She ran after him, but he disappeared into the corn patch. When she called out he did not answer. The snapping sound of a katydid and the trill of a cricket mingled with a dog's howl somewhere below them.

The moon hung over the house. Henry Kingsley alive, she repeated to herself, feeling stunned all over again. How could it be? She thought back to the night Amos had arrived, begging her to come off the mountain and meet with King. After she'd agreed to go, a plague of inner voices reminded her of his past deeds. Then when she'd seen him, her heart filled with pity—King's gaunt face showed the bitterness in his soul. The world had done to King Kingsley what he had done too often to those less fortunate. Now she could barely stand the thought that she'd offered to help him. *He could've told me Henry's alive. Kept it from me even after all these years. Lied to me. Lied to my face.*

She went to the creek and dipped her arms in the cold water. The moon glided over her as she treated her skin for the next hour. All she could think of was Henry, and seeing him again. *Is Lafette right? Will it only bring pain and sorrow?*

Deep in her heart she admitted wanting more than healthy wood. Yet the only certainty she trusted was the rhythms of nature: the moon setting, the sun rising, the creek drying out in summer and swelling in spring. Sometimes to know certainty seemed like a God's benevolent favor. If faith was spiteful, it was all she had. If she chose wrongly, life would let her know soon enough.

Lafette was not home when she returned. Her stomach fluttered so nervously she hardly felt the sting on her arms. She looked into the darkness. Out in that same dark night, Henry Kingsley was alive—living, breathing, and probably hating her as much as she now hated him. What little was left to do in her life depended on Lafette bringing Henry to her. She could only hope her son would obey. Although she stayed awake until the moon disappeared behind the farthest mountains, she did not see Lafette the rest of the night.

31

GOT EVERY REASON not to trust him, Lafette thought. He kicked his boot on a step, impatiently waiting outside the Kingsley house for Henry. The front wall was blistered gray from age. Window frames, cracked from neglect, had shed yellowed paint peelings in the dirt. He remembered this house when the exterior preened and flowers bloomed year round in the pots lining the steps. Now, broken terracotta lay where the plants had grown. Old house is broken like Henry Kingsley's body, Lafette thought, feeling halfway sorry for the man.

King Kingsley hunched in a rusted lawn chair where he'd stomped a dirt patch. Whenever he looked toward the house, Lafette pretended to adjust the horse's stirrups. King poked in the dirt with a whittled walking stick, staring at the horse he knew was his son's. When Lafette heard the stick tap against the metal chair, he groaned. King was summoning him.

Lafette approached and saw the old man's name scraped in the dirt over and over. Unshaven, his eyes darted around like a bird's, following every movement, a mannerism that made Lafette nervous. "What do you want?" Lafette asked, while King scratched his name again.

"Blast ye." King glared, grinning as if drunk. "Blast ye, I said."

Lafette rolled his eyes. "Crazy old man." He returned to the horse, leading her farther from the house so he wouldn't have to look at King. "Crazy ole fool gives me the jitters." He'd hated the Kingsleys for so long that any grief that befell them was okay with him.

The front door's stained glass window had been smashed. A jagged crack dissected the galloping stallion, and through the shattered pane, Lafette saw Henry limping down the staircase.

He leaned on Amos, his body dropping one step at a time. By the time he opened the door, he panted like a treed opossum. Holding a hand to his ribs and his other arm draped around Amos's neck, he saw Lafette watching and strained with all his might to straighten his back.

Lafette found it difficult to look at his twisted body. Amos held a wide-brimmed hat and fussed with Henry's coat collar. Henry shrugged him away. Amos waited in the doorway, nervously holding to the frame.

Lafette led the horse closer for easier mounting, and Henry adjusted his hat and stepped rigidly onto the top step. He gripped the porch rail to pull himself along. Lafette looked away, embarrassed to watch such pitiful determination in such a helpless body. Then he realized, *God Almighty! He don't have them canes.*

"You'll need your sticks." Lafette's voice squeaked and he cleared his throat.

Henry paused to look at Amos, who stood poised to rush in and help. "Don't need 'em this time."

A flood of anxiety filled Lafette and the hairs on his arms rose straight as pine needles. No point in this, he decided, if'n I can't get the canes. "Might need 'em in case I have to walk the horse up a sharp ridge and then come back for you. The higher ridges are worse than you remember."

Henry looked down at the gray porch floorboards, then without lifting his head, raised his eyes to Lafette. "Don't want her to see me walking with canes." His voice rang firm and unyielding, with no hint of pleading.

Lafette scratched his neck and turned toward Shadow Mountain. Fog inched up the west slope. Bare, sharp ridges protruded like gnarled fingers. "Only take a minute." Lafette stepped toward the door. "I'll leave 'em on the horse, just in case."

"Don't you step foot in my house!" King marched over from his dirt patch, looking like a hornet ready to swarm.

"He'll need his canes," Lafette said.

"You heard me." King pulled himself onto the porch as if to guard the door.

Lafette backed away, knowing the old man was dangerous. Henry took Lafette's arm to steady himself for mounting. He balanced on his toes in perfect symmetry then stared at the saddle. The horse neighed as if it understood some unspoken order. Henry grabbed fists of mane while cooing toward the horse's ear in a high, soothing voice and stroking its throat. In one sweeping movement, he straddled the animal's back.

"I'd've helped you," Lafette said, feeling a bit insulted.

Henry pointed to the mountain, ready to go and wanting no conversation. Lafette could think of nothing else to say that might make him bring the canes, so he grabbed the lead line and started off, thinking his mother would have to figure this out herself.

When Henry looked at his father. King stared at the porch, jabbing the wood with his walking stick and said, "Don't think ye'll interfere with my plans!"

King's angry tone worried Lafette. When they were a quarter mile down the road, he asked, "What'd King mean by plans?"

Henry waved his hand. "Nothing. He's an old man."

Lafette couldn't rest as easily about it, and purposely chose the route past the Elisha Tree. He'd let Henry see what King's last plan did to Shadow Mountain. The gurgling creek flowed evenly. A startled lizard slithered across sandstone rocks and disappeared into a log. He led the horse to water, letting her drink, and pretended not to notice the splayed Elisha Tree. Then Lafette stretched his arms and rested his head against a bent limb, knowing it was where King once tried to hang Arn.

Henry bunched his hands into fists and rubbed his eyes in disbelief of the destruction. The Elisha Tree stump stood five feet high, so black it looked burnt. Its thick limbs were withered, half of it blown open. The squirrel hole that had once been upright was now sideways, and the entrance under the trunk was submerged in the pond.

Henry coughed into his hands, then panted quick breaths. The inner wood was still golden as polished pinewood, but white worms had burrowed through it, leaving a rotting smell. The outer hull, gray and black like a stormy sky, crumbled at the slightest touch.

Lafette was secretly glad when Henry squirmed uncomfortably in the saddle, figuring he was remembering his father's evil doings.

"I remember you getting stuck in that tree," Henry said.

Lafette fidgeted, not expecting to hear about the time Henry saved him, and especially not wanting to be reminded of it. "Lots of things happened at this tree," he mumbled. "Even before I was born. This tree is a mountain sentry. Something's gonna happen, it happens here."

Henry slapped his hat against his leg and stared at the sun, annoyed and impatient. "Can we move on?"

"This is where King hung my daddy." Lafette chuckled before taking up the lead line, glad he was needling Henry. "Now that's something to remember."

"Who is that smiling man yonder?" Henry pointed into the trees across the creek.

Lafette looked into a maple grove but saw no one. "Where?" he asked. A breeze rippled the creek water.

"Tall, with curly, dark hair." Henry shaded his eyes, his cheeks paled to the shade of a white pumpkin. "It looked like..." The horse spooked and he gripped the reins when Lafette lost the lead rope. "Whoooa! Whoooa, boy!"

The steed tossed her head and would have bolted if Henry hadn't jerked the reins. Lafette grabbed the leather throatlatch, stroked the horse's shoulder and patted her jaw. He peered across the creek, but only the trees stood gate-like along the bank. "Nobody there. Must've been a shadow."

The horse snorted and tried to back up. Lafette couldn't help thinking that the man Henry described matched the stranger Rosy Thunderheart described at the trading post. He wondered if King had sent someone to follow Henry.

Lafette began the ascent up Shadow Mountain, feeling that whatever ghost Henry saw or imagined was well deserved. Deliberately he chose the most difficult route so King's son would miss none of the destruction inflicted by his father. They passed acres of rotting Tyme trees with the same black bark, furrowed until a breath would render it into dust. A slimy gel fermented in the tree crannies and smelled so pungent one might swear a dead body was hidden inside. Every quarter mile, craters formed by dynamite blasts left barren hillsides where no plant would yet grow.

In several places, giant Tyme trees blocked the road, criss-crossing it like a fence. Lafette inched the horse through hills of splintered wood and blasted rock. The air, once aromatic with the cinnamon scent, now hung heavy under skeletons of dead trees. Each time he looked, Henry sank farther into the saddle, and Lafette smirked.

Yet Henry's stamina amazed him. When the horse slipped on the steep paths softened by morning dew, he straightened his back, gripped the horse with his thighs and stayed astride. His once muscular body had deteriorated into this frail shell, but his inner energy rallied. He asked Lafette to stop only once, near Cat's Crossroads, then seemed more interested in staring over the mountains than resting.

"Never thought I'd see this again," he said, pointing at distant ridges of maple, hickory, oak, ash, and poplar. "Could swear that yellow is gold as the sun, and the oranges and reds... I remember a girl who used to wind red Tyme leaves through her hair. She was beautiful as the mountains."

"Best be on our way." Lafette found Henry's memories as distasteful as this chore his mother had forced on him. *He can see the glory in the mountains on the far horizon,* Lafette thought angrily, *but can't say a word about the destruction at his feet.*

The final ridge took them below the remains of Arn's Volcano. Henry cried out when he saw it, and Lafette felt the horse tense. Impossible to guess if his cry was a response to the memory of the explosion or the horror of the shorn mountaintop. A river of black rocks spilled where once a ledge spouted with every shade of morning glory, narcissus, and daffodil. The mountaintop caved inward, hollow as if God's hand had scooped it out. The yellow-brown earth mixed with a vertical coal seam and disappeared into rubble.

Lafette led the horse until the crumbled ground became treacherous. "Have to walk the mare from here on in" he said, "I'll come back and carry you up."

"I can walk it." Henry studied the scattered black rocks that had once been Arn's Volcano.

Annoyed, Lafette blew out a breath. "You can't, it's too hard."

"Allow me to judge what I can do." Henry's soft voice had an indignant edge.

Lafette tossed the lead line aside and shifted his weight. "If you cared about what's happened to this mountain, you'd have the sense to leave us alone."

"When I want your opinion, I'll ask." Henry leaned forward to dismount. His thin leg crossed the horse's back, catching on the saddle. With his other foot in the stirrup, he fell sideways. The horse shifted, and Henry slid toward the ground.

Lafette rushed to catch him, saying, "I got you! I got you!" Henry landed in Lafette's arms. The bony ribs, sunken stomach, and crooked spine felt like an animal burrowed beneath Henry's skin as Lafette lowered him to the ground. The deformity of the frail body sickened him. Lafette struggled to steady his voice, "That far path, yonder where the rocks are small, you can hold to gooseberry bushes and pull yourself up. It's the one I always use."

"It was a mistake to come." Henry steadied himself on the horse, resting his head against the saddle. "Shouldn't've come eight years ago and shouldn't be here now."

Lafette swallowed, awkwardly reaching out to touch Henry's shoulder—now so skeletal and thin—this shoulder he'd once been tossed across and had ridden like a horse. "Well, we come this far, might as well go the rest of the way."

Henry stepped toward Lafette and hung onto his arm. His head fell onto Lafette's chest and he inhaled three deep breaths, clearing his throat, trembling slightly. "I'd appreciate it," he finally said, "if you'd let me lean on you."

Lafette nodded, and with his arm around Henry's waist, they picked their way through Arn's rocks and upward to the top of Shadow Mountain.

♆ 32 ♆

DELTA CRACKED WALNUTS and gently picked the kernels from the shells. The porch boards squeaked beneath her as she rocked to and fro. "Wonder how far up the mountain they are now?" she said to Blue, who lay on his back, paws dangling above him.

She firmly held a walnut against a flat rock and tapped it with an apple-sized stone, then peeled away broken shell. "If Lafette thinks he can ignore me and not do this thing, he'll have the devil to pay." She smashed a finger, dropped the rock and shook her hand. Blue jumped and licked his jowls. "I'm not mad at you, boy."

A flutter in her stomach caused her to stop work. She stood at the porch edge and looked out over the hill. A black bird lit on a bare branch and a fern patch shook from the movement of an unseen animal. No sign of Lafette or Henry. She rubbed her hands together. Surely Lafette would not disobey her.

Blue stood at alert then leaped off the porch. He vaulted to the fern bed, sniffed the ground, let out a yodel and dove straight ahead. A wild hog squealed and darted from the bushes with Blue nipping at its feet.

Delta swallowed to relieve the dryness in her throat. Henry Kingsley alive. Her heart beat at hummingbird pace. What would he think of her after all this time? She picked up the walnut basket and looked once more toward Cat's Crossroads. No plants grew on that slope so she could see to where the land dropped. "Can't even get a sense of them."

Inside, she placed the basket on the fireplace hearth and curled into an overstuffed blue velvet chair. Lafette had won it in a card game the year before and given it to her for her birthday. Her fingers wandered over the soft material and she shut her eyes, letting the smoothness comfort her.

I'm ready for this, she told herself, forming the words she'd say to Henry. *I'll be as clear as day. Say I'll purchase his Tyme canes. What if he won't sell? I could say for old times sake. No. Best to be honest.* It struck her that once he'd wanted to buy Tyme trees, and now, she needed his canes just as badly.

Old bitterness invaded her thoughts. After the newspaper story of Henry Kingsley's death, rumor spread that she had been the cause. No one bought her herb medicines or came to her for doctoring. Some stopped speaking to her. A few would not even acknowledge her existence.

Yet King had forbidden anyone taking revenge. He'd seemed pleased enough having her blamed for Henry's death. How he must have laughed, she thought. Henry alive all this time. *Henry must've known what his father did. I've a mind to tell him off if I didn't need that Tyme wood so bad.* But it was more than that. Henry had loved her. Was it vanity to wonder if some affection might still live in his heart. He had allowed much of the unhappiness of the past eight years just as surely as King had caused it. Affection or even respect would be the last kind of feeling between them.

She cracked two walnuts against each other. As she chewed the nut, the hollow shells reminded her of the wasteland she'd lived on all these years. At first, she had stared at the rotting trees and diseased earth, agonizing about what to do. The brown, barren land obsessed her, and, it seemed her very blood drained into the earth in an effort to sustain the least bit of life. No one could reach her. Even Lafette spoke softly and didn't play boyish pranks. Only Nancy had visited her regularly, bringing seed for the small garden that grew stunted vegetables, and occasionally Rosy Thunderheart came with news of the outside world. Delta listened, rarely speaking, and finally told Rosy not to return after seeing black welts on the girl's arms from her father's beatings for coming to Shadow Mountain. Delta could not bear the guilt of causing more pain.

Someone knocked on the door. Delta jumped, heart beating wildly. Every vein pounded with blood, and she felt flushed and heated. She slowly opened the door.

A rippling tingle charged through her body as if struck by lightning. His gaunt face was deeply lined around the mouth with wrinkles sunburst around the eyes. He leaned to one side. Spaces between his square teeth had flattened his lips, but he had the same wide smile that helped Delta to smile back. Yes, it truly was Henry Kingsley.

She gestured for him to enter. He moved in an awkward sideways motion and she strained not to look at his legs. *The canes, she thought, he didn't bring the canes.*

"Room still smells of lavender," he said.

He faced away and looked toward Lafette's bed, the area that had been rebuilt. She glanced at his legs. He leaned forward, steadying himself with a hand on his thigh, but he didn't seem humpbacked. Shifting his back to move his legs was an awkward movement, not the limp she'd expected of a man who walked with a cane.

Lafette stood in the doorway. When Delta gave him a hard look, he shrugged to indicate he didn't have the canes. "Wait outside," she said. Lafette's eyes flashed with hostility. As soon as the door closed, Delta lost all thought of what she'd wanted to say. Henry looked at her as if she were a crystal figurine she'd seen in his house so many years ago. She wondered if he still had the one that looked like her. "I'll make us some tea," she said.

"No, no, I don't want any." He lowered himself on the velvet chair arm and looked her up and down, not a lecherous look but comparing her to his memory. "House looks good," he said, eyes still on her.

She sat cross-legged on the hearth, stretching her legs across a rag-rug. Henry arranged himself fragilely, then gestured at the willow wood furniture. "Looks like you now, instead of all the people who lived here before you." He pointed at her drawing of a dark night with Blue howling at a full moon. "I like that one," he said.

"We hauled oak and cedar to rebuild the rooms that used to be Tyme." Her hand cracked two walnuts in a tight grasp. She tossed them into the basket, feeling him study her every movement. Nervously, she laced her fingers together and wished he would not look at her so directly.

"Wood's beautiful," he said. "Lafette's become quite a carpenter."

"He's always been more than he knows." Her face warmed at the compliment.

"Your hair's lightened to the color of ash. Remember that time we plaited red Tyme leaves in the strands? Sometimes, I can't help wondering..."

"Wondering can make you crazy, and remembering can almost kill you."

He looked at his hands, studying the palm lines. "You thought I was dead." He did not speak for almost a minute. "Was Daddy's way of not being shamed."

"Shamed?" Delta leaned forward to look into his eyes, waiting for him to accuse her so she could let him know what the last eight years were like for her.

"Was just his way. Like it's yours to close yourself off up here."

She stared at the rug and balled her hands in tight fists, thinking he still blamed her for what had happened to him. "Wasn't like I had a choice." She dipped her head, forcing him to see her eyes and understand that she'd been shunned.

"Daddy put me in a private hospital in Richmond. For the first few years, I couldn't move below my neck. Just stared up at the ceiling."

"I'm sorry, Henry."

"Every night for eight years, all I saw on that ceiling was your face."

Delta squirmed, repositioned her foot and knocked over the basket of walnuts. They spilled on the rug, partially covering Henry's shoes. He stood, towering above her, and for a moment she wasn't sure what he meant to do. His gaze was unfocused. He fell forward and she broke his fall as best she could but he swerved away. "Don't touch me!" he said, grabbing the chair.

She jumped at the hard edge in his voice. He eased down on his knees and lowered himself to the floor beside her, gasping for breath, face drained of color. She took hold of his arm. He didn't try to stop her.

"Lafette, come in here!" she hollered.

"I'm okay," Henry said. "Just get faint when I tire myself out." He tried to smile but needed his energy to slow his wheezing lungs. He wiped spittle from the edge of his mouth, eyelids fluttering as he concentrated on controlling his body.

Lafette opened the door but halted at the sight of them on the floor. He looked away, embarrassed.

"Reckon you was right, boy," Henry said, pointing up at him. "Reckon I need my canes after all."

"Lafette shouldn't have let you come without them." Delta seized the opportunity. "Go get them right this minute."

"King'll set the dogs on me." Lafette glared at Henry on the floor.

"Call for Amos. He'll get the canes for you."

Delta waved Lafette away. He seemed relieved to have somewhere to go and whistled for Blue as he backed out, knocking his shoulder against the doorframe.

"No telling what that boy must think," Henry said after Lafette was gone.

Sprawled on the floor, she knew they must be quite a sight. "I'll help you up." She held out her hand.

He laughed softly. "Naw, just as happy down here." Still chuckling, he looked at her and then spread his legs out. "Reckon we're a couple of big kids."

For the first time, Delta got a sense of the old Henry, the man who'd been her friend. Yet she still cautioned herself: *He blames you for his being crippled.* She cleared her throat and wrapped her arms around her knees. "Henry, I've something important to ask." Her lower lip trembled and she wished he'd stop looking so directly into her eyes. "It's about the canes."

"Silly thing," he said. "If I hadn't been so vain, I wouldn't have fallen flat and made a fool of myself."

"I want to buy the canes."

He stared as if he'd misheard. "Why?"

"I'll make you some new ones of oak and fix you a year's worth of salve to rub on your muscles. Whatever price you name." She swallowed and waited.

He couldn't look at her. When he did, his eyes were so dark brown they rivaled the earth at spring planting, and part of her wanted to tell him how beautiful they were.

"You know about the canes, do you?" Henry looked out the window, up toward the sky. His lips pressed into a thin line and he inhaled slowly before speaking. "Can't sell you the canes."

Her gaze wandered to the potted plant in her kitchen. Part of her didn't have the heart to continue watching the seedlings die. Another part of her knew that if she died without trying to right this wrong done to the Tyme tree, her soul would burn in agony worse than hell.

"I can cure you," she said with every ounce of sincerity she could muster. "I'll heal your legs if you give me the canes." The words came from so deep within her that she knew she must possess the power to do it.

He took her hand between his and squeezed it. His brow wrinkled and his eyes closed as he brought her fingers to his lips. When he opened his eyes, the doubt that marred his thoughts was readable as scripture. "Delta," he said, "much as I want to have hope, there's none. This is the body I'll die with." A familiar stubbornness filtered in his voice but it was gentler, without the arrogance of youth.

"Let me try," Delta argued. "All I ask in payment is the Tyme canes."

"Not a matter of that."

"What then?"

"Arn. I can't give them to you 'cause of Arn Marlon."

A wave of shock ran through her. She stood, opened the door and let in cool air. A thin layer of fog had yet to burn off the mountain, and her thoughts felt equally clouded.

"Lafette did all he could to keep me from coming here," Henry said, his voice almost a whisper, "even rode me by the Elisha Tree where Daddy hanged Arn. Even rested his head against the branch." He adjusted his legs by lifting his knees, sucking in air and gritting his teeth. "Lafette doesn't know the branch he touched isn't the one where Arn was hanged. I sawed off the real branch. Sawed it off the morning after Arn rode into our barn alive."

"I don't understand." She sat beside him.

"Couldn't get out of my mind how Arn survived. I felt so bad about Daddy hanging him for something I'd done, I was gonna cut down the whole damn tree. Found something real different when I got out there."

Delta breathed shallowly, resisting what she was about to hear. She put her hands to her ears but Henry's soft voice still came through clearly.

"It was a trick Arn'd pulled." He leaned toward her and jerked an arm loose from her head. "I ploughed my ax into that tree and the limb nearly fell on me. A thin wire ran alongside the wood, holding it in place. When Daddy hanged Arn, the branch gave just enough to let him balance on his toes. Who looks at a dead man's feet?"

Delta jerked her arm free. She stalked out onto the porch, refusing to believe what she'd heard, but also knowing that Henry had no reason to lie. Delta sweated despite the cool morning air. She wiped her forehead. Her vision blurred and she saw a tall, dark-haired man walking up the mountain toward her. When she blinked, no one was there. These were bad omens.

Henry followed her. “When Arn gave his full weight, the branch snapped,” he said. “That day when I found the trick, I heard a man laughing. Arn, standing uphill. Said I was stealing his wood and maybe he ought to shoot me where I stood.”

“You were a boy, Henry. Arn would never’ve hurt you. He was scaring you.”

“Well, I don’t like being scared!”

Delta’s back arched like a defensive cat’s. “What would you know about being scared? Arn lived his entire life in fear! Folks like you and your daddy were always hounding him. He was a revered man before your kind came to the mountains.”

Henry leaned back and rubbed his chin. “Arn said long as I kept the wood that me and mine would die in fear and suffering. I’d seen the trick he pulled with the hanging. I knew his secret. So I wasn’t about to ever let him scare me again.”

“And look at how you and yours have died. Your Ma, your wife, your daddy’s craziness. Look at yourself, Henry.”

“Coincidence!”

“He wasn’t cursing you. He was warning you. Tyme wood should never leave Shadow Mountain.”

“He was scaring a little boy into believing lies he used to hold on to this mountain. And I said to him that I’d be buried with his Tyme wood before I’d let him threaten me.” Henry looked into the ashy hearth. “I wrapped that Tyme wood in burlap and buried it deep in an iron box outside my bedroom window. When I needed my canes, I had them made from that wood. It’s the only thing I have left to prove in life.”

“You’ve paid a pretty sorry price.” Delta couldn’t be angry at Henry. If only he could understand. How much different his future might have been.

"I don't have much life left, but the one thing I'll stand by is the truth about Arn Marlon." Henry pounded his clenched fist on the porch rail. "I know you loved Arn, but I hated him. I don't believe he did you fair. I don't believe he did Lafette fair. And it made me sick to see what it did to both of you."

"I came to love Arn," she said, raising a hand to calm him. "I didn't at first. Then I saw him raise the volcano's power in giant vapor, long and curved like a snake. I knew then he was no ordinary man."

Henry took hold of Delta's shoulders. She dared not look from his face even though she heard a horse galloping in the distance. "Arn was no magic man," Henry said. "He was a smart man, a mean man, maybe even an evil one. He liked to scare little boys. And I don't believe that's a thing to be proud of.

"If I could give you cause to be proud, would you give me the Tyme canes?"

"Those canes'll be buried with me. It's the only way I can feel even against a man like Arn Marlon."

"If you give me the canes, I promise you a coffin of Tyme wood. Whether Arn was right or wrong you never needed to compare yourself to him. You were always more than his equal in your own way." She waited for him to answer, but Henry's brow tightened. She pulled him inside toward the kitchen. "I've something to show you." Once again, she heard horses and knew it was too soon for Lafette to return. She looked out the window. Mist danced in the treetops. The air was dry as summer. She listened but no horse appeared. "I'll show you why I need Tyme wood."

He followed her, favoring his right side, his back bent so his head was even with hers. Henry had once towered over her. Now, each step seemed to pain him and Delta did her best not to notice.

"You and me can make the trees live again," she said, pointing at the Tyme blossom. "And I can make your legs live again." He cast his eyes downward, not believing her, but she felt his disbelief was of little importance as long as he stayed. "For my sake, let me make our lives back the way they were."

"I never thought I'd see a Tyme blossom again." He traced a finger along the delicate petal, so much smaller than the early spring tree flowers of long ago. "You are indeed a lady with a special talent."

"Then you'll stay with me for a while."

"Delta, if you could make Tyme trees live again, it'd sure right a basketful of wrongs."

"I can't do it without your help, Henry."

He smiled. The lines around his eyes deepened and he raised a hand to touch her cheek. "I do need to be close to you, Delta. It's burned inside me for years now." She tensed, and he stepped back, giving her space.

"You'll let me work my magic on your legs?"

"Nothing's gonna help these ole limbs."

"Let me show you." She approached him. "I need to hold you. I need to feel the sickness."

His brows pinched together and he looked down at his chest. "It's an awful thing, Delta. I don't want you to."

"Trust me." She stroked his cheek, stared deeply into his eyes, and the friendly feeling between them strengthened. Then she wrapped her arms around him, letting her hands rest on his back. She closed her eyes and imagined her mind wandering into his. Again she heard galloping horses—and knew it wasn't a trick of her imagination. It had been Henry's spirit reaching out for her in a way that he could not.

She concentrated, pleased with her discovery. He sprang into her thoughts: a strong stallion galloping through a rocky terrain. Her hands drifted down his back. His spine twisted into his side, pushing out the skin as if the bones were breaking through.

“Oh, Henry.” Her voice weakened as painful emotions reached up through her throat, and she lost the image of the horse. “I feel you. I feel you.”

“I promise, Delta, I’ll ask nothing of you. Be so kind as to allow me to stay here for awhile... to be near you, and be a part of this.” He leaned down and breathed in the Tyme plant’s cinnamon sweetness. “Our differences are something we’ll work out.” He gestured at the seedling. “A worthy cause,” he added. “Something I can be proud of.”

♆ 33 ♆

LAFETTE CHEWED HIS lower lip and ground his teeth, unable to rid himself of the image of his mother and Henry spread out on the floor like playful pups. Should've told 'em how foolish they looked, he thought abruptly, irritated at a sight that made his stomach turn. He patted Blue's head and received a lick on the hand that made him feel even lonelier. I'm the blamed fool, he thought. But in his heart he recalled his mother's face. He couldn't remember the last time he had seen her eyes bright with excitement; her smile so fragile it seemed it might tear as easily as an autumn leaf. She'd been happy to see Henry. The crisp, frosty mid-morning air chilled Lafette's lungs. He exhaled a stream of white breath, imagined he was the dragon of the mountain and thought, *Wish I was a-blowin' Henry Kingsley away*.

When he reached the house, King was back in his yard chair. I'll sneak in and steal those canes, Lafette decided, eager to make a game of it.

"Boy! Boy!" The gravely voice rose in the air like an irritation made visible. King Kingsley twisted around as though his hearing was sharp as a cat's and tapped his walking stick against the ground, wildly gesturing for Lafette.

"I've come for Henry's canes," Lafette said. "He wants them."

"This is more important." King held out a silver coin, polished until it glistened, and shook it at Lafette. "Take it."

Lafette drew back, uncomfortable and then mistrusting, figuring King might say he'd stolen it and get the law after him. "Don't want it."

"Ain't for you, ignorant!" King jammed his hands onto the chair and pushed up.

For the first time Lafette noticed King's bare feet, covered with festering sores, the hard, yellow nails curved over the front of his toes. The sight disgusted him as King flipped the coin in the air and caught it with the other hand, some memory stirred in him that he could not fully retrieve.

"Take it to your Momma." King rubbed the coin between his fingers as if to remember the feel of it. "Promise me, boy."

Lafette kept his eyes on the coin, mesmerized by it. "What do I tell her?"

"Just say that I beg her." He clamped his lips together to keep them from quivering. When he held out the coin, his hand trembled.

Lafette strained to resist but couldn't help but take the silver piece. King fell back into his chair as if a weight had been unhinged from around his neck. Could it be, Lafette thought as he pocketed the coin, he means to pay Momma back in some way? *Only a fool would trust King Kingsley's goodness.* Still thinking this might be a crazy old man's trick, he slipped around to the rear kitchen where he and Blue snuck into the house and took the Tyme canes.

∞

The smooth shafts, polished until they glistened like lake water in the sunlight, were yellow-gold and flared on the bottom to grip uneven ground. Henry's handprint was worn into the curved tops, and Lafette measured it against his own. The canes were indeed a beautiful piece of handiwork.

Blue had sniffed them out, and Amos didn't know until he was out the door. "Probably wouldn't've known at all if you hadn't got your tail caught." Blue's ears spread to the side and his head angled. Lafette laughed, partly at the dog's human expression and partly recalling Amos's howl as he hollered for the canes. "Can't do what people expect, now, can we? 'Cause we're mavericks." Blue panted, like a smile. "Have to let ole Henry set him right."

Near the hilltop, Lafette used the canes to ease himself down underneath a willow tree. It rose above a clover field, a sluggish creek, and the rotted Elisha Tree. He could remember when his childhood hiding place had stood higher than the willow. Now, it was a jagged stump, its gray wood as ugly as moldy food. Henry Kingsley's fault, he thought.

Suddenly he jumped up, bolted down the hill and kicked the Elisha Tree. Part of the trunk caved in. On the inside wood the carved names Arn Marlon and Elisha Thunderheart saw sunlight for the first time. Lafette leaned in and traced the letters. The interior wood was as hard as rock. He stepped into the truck to see if he could fit inside as he had as a child. The bark crumbled underneath his boots when he slid one leg into the hollow interior. He slipped in as far as his hips, but the tree seemed to have shrunk. "Outgrowed you," he said. "Outgrowed you like a pair of shoes."

He pulled himself clear, breathing in the woody smell of the core, unlike the sour odor of the outer bark. For a few seconds the whiffs of mold and cinnamon made him dizzy and he coughed through a queasy fume. The two carved names gave him a connection to a past he would never know; an ancestry he wondered about endlessly; a time that through all its mistakes, heartaches, and miseries had produced him. "Ahhh, Daddy," he sighed, "Why did you never come home?"

Three grouses pecked in the dirt, and the creek water gurgling over sharp bird chirps. The cloudless sky rested, but Lafette could partake of none of its peace. Henry had saved him from drowning at that very spot. Maybe it was wrong to be so jealous. Henry couldn't hurt them now. He was a broken-down, old man.

He turned to leave and saw a fisherman on the creek bank with a pole dipped into one of the deeper ponds. No one had been sitting there a few seconds ago. And who with any sense had the gumption to traverse Shadow Mountain?

"Hey!" Lafette hollered. "You there."

The man remained motionless and Lafette wondered if he was hard of hearing.

"Don't you know you're on Shadow Mountain?" Still, the man didn't respond. Lafette propped the Tyme canes on the backside of the Elisha Tree and held to yew bushes as he slid down the hill. "You lost?" he asked, coming up behind the man.

His back was broad, legs jacked up in front on him with an elbow propped on each knee.

"You know where you are?"

The mass of curly hair jiggled as he nodded.

"And you've the nerve to come up here anyways?" Lafette patted the pistol he'd slipped into his pants. "Most folks are scared of Shadow Mountain."

He waited. The stranger didn't reply. Lafette cleared his throat. " 'Course I reckon that might be the best reason for fishing up here."

The man pinched bread from a loaf lying beside him and rolled it between his fingers, making a dough ball. Blue growled. The man's back straightened. Lafette reached for his pistol. The man stood slowly then picked up his fishing pole. He was unarmed. "Sit, Blue." Lafette ordered.

This stranger looked to be a good six or seven inches taller than Lafette's own six feet. "Not many fellers in these parts would carry such a dislike of dogs," he said, narrowing his eyes in a half-challenge and stepping around to look at him. A wisp of salt and pepper hair blew across the man's wide forehead, and his bow-shaped mouth turned up slightly at the corners as if to say he'd meant no harm.

His eyes twinkled brightly as he pushed the wad of bread dough onto the hook then dropped it back into the pond and turned away.

Lafette thought he looked like a praying mantis, the way his big-boned body folded into itself. His clothes were dark, not quite black, not quite gray, with a worn, loose look as though he'd been wearing them for a long time. "Got a name?"

The man didn't answer.

"Well, ain't you as quiet as the Wampus."

His eyes brightened and he nodded as if he recognized the beast, then one long finger pointed at the creek bank.

" 'Course, I ain't heard of nobody sighting the Wampus in years." Lafette moved in the direction the stranger pointed but kept one eye on him, half expecting an attack. He balanced on his tiptoes and peered at the smooth, brown mud between the rocks. A three-pronged bird track and the curved path of a snake were all that he saw.

He bent down. A deep, part hoof, part padded imprint curved in the sand—just the way he'd always heard Wampus tracks described. An electric shock jolted his chest.

The soft bank barely sustained the track mold. He leaned out over the water to see if there were others on the moss-covered rocks, and in the same moment, the man jerked his fishing line. The hook whizzed past Lafette's nose, making him lose his balance and fall to his knees to keep from going into the creek.

"Look what you've done! I mashed half of it." Lafette pressed his hands into the sand.

He studied his boot and measured the paw pad against it. Five holes like claw marks of varying sizes were cut sharply in the mud. Could it possibly be true, or was it just a big cat track? Lafette's stomach churned as he spread out his large hand. Even spread-fingered, it measured less than half the size of the Wampus track.

He wiped sweat from his upper lip. "Panther must have stepped twice in the same place," he muttered," making it look like one big track."

The man anchored his fishing pole into the ground between his legs and slowly wound the line around it.

Lafette got cold all the way down to his toes. His empty stomach growled for food and he found it hard to focus on this trespasser. The dust he'd inhaled in the Elisha Tree caused him to sneeze. Colors sprang more brightly to his eye and sounds crisped in a way he'd never heard before. He turned to the man who looked directly into his eyes with a piercing gaze that shot through Lafette like a sharp pain. "More 'n likely this is a big momma cat that ain't none too friendly. I'd track it, but I only got my pistol and you ain't got no gun at'all."

The man stretched out his legs and picked up an old black coat and hat that lay beside him. A Winchester rifle was underneath, hidden so well he could have shot it before Lafette had the chance to aim his own pistol.

Lafette swallowed hard. His gun was no match for a rifle. "Momma's waiting on me," he said, immediately wishing he'd used different words. "Got a guest in our home."

Nervously he twisted the ring on his smallest finger and looked up the hill where Blue romped carelessly in crusty brown leaves. He whistled for the dog. A voice inside warned him not to turn his back on this man. Blue sniffed the ground and bared his fangs, but did not growl.

The stranger stared at Lafette's ring.

The ring had grown warm from twisting it and he curled his hand into a fist to hide it from the stranger. His chest tightened. "Who are you?" he asked, bracing himself against the Elisha Tree with one hand. His stomach churned and he felt about to vomit.

The man continued to stare at the ring, then he pulled the old hat onto his head, shadowing his face. His eyes beamed the blue of blue jay feathers.

A cramp seized Lafette's gut. He tried to see exactly where the rifle was, then had to turn away. He coughed, gripping his stomach with both hands through wave after wave of nausea. Blue sprinted toward him. Lafette vomited, holding to the Tyme tree. Its craggy bark made an imprint on his cheek. He took deep breaths, trying to control his lightheadedness. Finally, he turned toward the man.

Gone. He looked up at the sky. The sun showed an hour had passed. How could that be? Had he fallen asleep? Had to be, he thought. The mixture of bark and grit he'd inhaled from the Elisha tree must have knocked him out. He might even have imagined the man he believed was here. Maybe it had been a dream or the effect of breathing in the moldy Tyme dust.

"You here?" Lafette called out. Embarrassment wavering his voice. He was glad when no reply came. Spitting, he wiped his mouth, stepped down to the creek and splashed water on his face. No footprints led away from the bank. Must've rock walked, Lafette figured, if he was real. Lafette blinked his eyes, trying to clear the fog from his mind. Had he really seen someone here? If so, why would a feller leave him here, why would he have jumped rock to rock, lessen to hide his direction, make him hard to follow? More to him being here than fishing, he thought. Best keep a heedful watch out the next few days.

Lafette leaned down, touched his lips to the cold water and washed out his mouth. His head cleared and only his throat felt raw. Except for his embarrassment in front of the odd stranger, he again felt in control of his mountain. He stomped surefooted up the hill with Blue trotting behind him. "Let's get home, dog," he said, and reached behind the tree for the Tyme canes. One was missing.

"Blue, did you carry off a cane?" Lafette looked around the other trees, through the leaves where Blue had been playing, then along the creek bank. In the soft sand, where the man had pointed out the Wampus track, was a new, unusual print. He knelt, studying, but already knowing what he would find. "Sonnavabitch!" He measured the Tyme cane's base against the oval print, a match. The prints led up the creek and disappeared as the mountain became rocky. The stranger had strolled away with one of the Tyme canes. He had been real. He hadn't imagined or dreamt the odd encounter.

"Well, why didn't you do something!" he yelled at Blue. The dog cowered. Lafette slammed his fist against his other hand, wondering how he would explain this. Why would that dern fool take the cane? Why just one and not both? "Quick as a hare."

Acted feeble as a hare, he said to himself, tapped his temple and squeezed his eyes shut. He'd heard those words before, *feeble as a hare*, and for some reason associated them with the stranger. "At the Trading Post!" he hissed through clenched teeth. The dirty black coat, the tattered hat, the man he'd seen leaving by the side door the night he and Valentine were cheating at cards. "That varmint pointed out Henry Kingsley to me!" He looked down at Blue and his mind raced with thoughts of conspiracy. "Knew more was goin' on here, Blue. I'll be damned if Kingsley'll pull the sack over my head!"

Henry must be in on this, Lafette thought. That stranger probably stole our poker money too. If Henry had sought him out at the Trading Post, then he must have set up this fella to seek him out now to delay him. King must still want the mountain and Henry's helping him. Why else would he go to such length to get Momma alone?

Lafette raced toward home with Blue at his heels. By the time he reached Cat's Crossroads, he was sweating and stopped to catch his breath, still fighting the queasiness in his stomach. He wondered if the fungus on the Elisha Tree had made him sick. He coughed, determined to get hold of himself for what he needed to do. If he confronted Henry and made his mother see Henry'd set this whole thing up, she'd throw him off the mountain faster than she could pitch water.

Blue leapt on the porch. Lafette grabbed a pole and swung up. Through the window he saw Delta and Henry entwined in an embrace. His grip tightened on the cane as he watched his mother's hand slide up Henry's back and heard her moan. Henry's face was tilted toward the ceiling, eyes closed. Slowly his head dropped onto Delta's shoulder, and when he opened his eyes he looked directly at Lafette.

Henry gently pushed Delta from him, still staring out the window. She turned around and also saw Lafette. Her face flushed slightly, but she disappeared from view, and he knew she was coming toward the door. Part of him wanted to run. Part of him want to yell at them, *How could you do this to me?* She stepped outside but Lafette couldn't speak.

"Henry'll stay here a spell." Delta's eyes beamed green as ferns. "I've offered him your bed." She stepped closer to him and whispered. "I need your help with this."

Lafette had never heard such gentle pleading in her voice, and swallowed hard, wishing for distance or fury, yet neither broke forth within him. She looked at the golden-colored Tyme cane, her eyes sparkled and she took it, holding it up toward the sun.

Henry came to the doorway. Lafette glared at him. Henry stared back, but his gaze was questioning, almost asking Lafette's permission to stay.

Lafette decided he would not be fooled. Henry Kingsley was up to more than he was willing to say, and Lafette would not sit by like an obedient hound.

"We are saved!" Delta said, throwing the cane into the air and catching it. Henry smiled as she began whirling around with his cane. He seemed happy as a boy on the Fourth of July with Delta as his playmate.

Lafette's stomach cramped once more and he felt as if he were back in the Elisha Tree breathing the revolting Tyme fumes. He clenched his teeth together and bit his lip. He squeezed the coin in his pocket, refusing to give it to Delta or even show it to her. At least he could interfere with this much of King's plan. He'd stay silent for the time being. But he'd not let Henry Kingsley ruin their lives again. Of this, he was certain.

☙ 34 ☙

GRAY MIST HUNG in front of a crescent moon, making it a fuzzy chip in the sky. A blazing fire burning in a circle of black rocks didn't warm the icy air of Shadow Mountain enough for comfort. Orange embers sailed up like fireflies. The smoky smell of the burning wood competed with fragrant rose oil Delta rubbed across her chest.

She raised both hands, summoning the image of fire into herself. Standing so close to the heat, her skin dripped sweat under a bearskin cape. Only her bare feet were cold against the hard ground. Reaching through jagged slits in the cape, she placed a feather wreath on her head.

Henry sat at the mountain edge, staring at the starless black sky. Delta approached him from behind and placed a similar garland upon his head. It annoyed her that he wore his everyday clothes. At least he'd consented to having the panther skin over his shoulders, but she suspected it was only for warmth.

A tuft of feathers came loose from Henry's headdress and floated past his nose. He swiped at it. "Blessed damn, I feel stupid!" he explained.

"Shhhh! You'll ruin the spirit." She pulled a pouch from around her neck and emptied it into the fire. Smoke blossomed in a mushroom cloud and a cedar aroma circled them. She grew dizzy from inhaling.

"Delta, I felt like a fool two weeks ago when you tried this, and still do."

She clenched a fist against her stomach, trying to regain her spiritual composure. "Would you hush up? I swear to God you're as ornery as Lafette."

"Sure wish I was at the cock fights with him." He bit his lip, regretting the complaint because Lafette probably hadn't mentioned where he'd gone. Delta was liable to pitch a fit. "You know, it's a little hard to take seriously a woman with chicken feathers sticking in her hair."

"Owl feathers!" She swung around and poked his shoulder. Henry snickered. "Be respectful or I'll kick your bad knee." She squared off with him, having learned that treating Henry as if he weren't crippled was important to him. He seemed to stand a little taller whenever she asked him to carry wood or fetch water. She admired his determination to seem normal as much as she hated his disbelief that she could cure him.

Henry cleared his throat and rubbed his face to erase his grin. He stood erect even when a mouse leaped over a boot and darted into the weeds. "Okay, Delta," he said, his voice edged with sarcasm. "Here I sit... respectful, but not too serious."

"Not being serious enough almost lost me everything." She looked over a rocky waterfall of what used to be the volcano. Pieces of Arn, she thought and took in their muted blackness. Sometimes, concentrating on the stones brought her his strength; other times it only depressed her.

" 'Fraid I take issue with that." Henry limped up behind her. "Everybody being too serious caused the destruction of this mountain... and other things." He looked at his legs. The oak walking stick she'd given him was sturdy enough to hold twice his weight, but he avoided using it in front of her. In his three weeks here he'd tried to keep her from seeing how much walking pained him. He touched her shoulder. "Shouldn't've said that."

"I'm going to heal the hurt, Henry. Whether you believe me or not." She took his hand and they sat near the fire. She closed her eyes, determined to show him what her magic could do, break through to him so he could see the possibilities. Tonight she had to make him see as she saw, if only for a moment. But that meant trusting him enough to enter him and be him, to possess his deformed limbs.

She balanced her breathing to match Henry's, inhaled the misty smoke and strove to maintain her posture as it unbalanced her. In her mind she reached through the owl wreath on her head, and as her arms stretched upwards, they became covered with feathers. Her body swooped up into the black night sky. She flapped her wings as her wide owl eyes scoured the ground.

Angry winds tossed the treetops. She bared her breast against it and flew into the wildest part of the wind. Under the trees she saw a mud hole. In it, a stallion struggled, as strong as a god, yet its hind legs were hopelessly buried in the mire.

She landed, sharp talons clutching the stallion's mane. The horse struggled, panicked. Fear sparked like lightning in its liquid brown eyes. Its neighs as painful as birth. She pulled the steed like a cub, stepping back again and again... but falling... A giant insect dragged her into the hole. She sank into the mire. The stallion shook mud from its mane, reared and galloped away. Sludge filled her mouth and covered her eyes, nose, gritty, black earth swallowed her. She choked out, "I'm dying."

A hard whack stung her cheek.

"Delta!" an angry voice shouted. Arn had just hit her.

"Help me, I'm dying!" She felt her body rising, floating in the air. Her chest constricted. She saw a hazy crescent moon and knew that Arn must be carrying her.

Footsteps tapped against a wooden floor and then a feather mattress cushioned her. She struggled as hands held her down. For a moment, she was forced into the mud again and struggled against the black mire. Arn stood over her. Pressure against her forehead made her relax. *No, not Arn, but Henry.* The taut lines around his eyes, concerned and worried. He patted her hand. "It's your fault!" she screamed, causing him to back away. "You blame me for your legs! You've always blamed me!"

Henry's mouth dropped open and his hands spread like a minister's asking for souls to come forward. He reached out to her. She slapped at his hands and twisted away, jumping away from him.

"I didn't want that to happen to you!" Tears dripped down her face and she gasped for air. She realized she had been moved to her bedroom.

"I don't blame you." His face cramped in a painful grief.

"Your father said you wished me dead!" She sobbed like a frightened child, hunched in the corner with years of pent-up sorrow that would not be held back.

"I didn't." Henry's expression drew inward like someone betrayed. Each time he moved closer, Delta jumped like a scared rabbit. He backed away but stayed beside the bed until her body relaxed and she could sit without trembling. "I never said I wished you dead," he told her, gently. "Never."

She looked up at him but could not speak. Her throat, parched. Her swollen eyes stung when she blinked. His hands clutched to his hip. Delta was ashamed that she'd been afraid. She moved to the center of the bed. He blinked and looked away, uncertain what to do. She motioned for him to sit. "Well, there it is, I guess."

"Good God, Delta, the thought of you kept me alive all those years." He wrenched his head in a slow, deliberate nod. "In the sanitarium, Daddy told me you'd said you had no use for a crippled husband. And that you'd deliberately destroyed the Tyme trees so he'd have no reason to go after the mountain. He tried to get me to sign divorce papers."

Anger welled in her throat and she struggled to hold it back. "No surprise to me he'd tell such a lie."

Henry's lips tightened in a thin line, and she knew he was sick of the hate between her and his father. Yet she could not stop herself from despising King Kingsley.

"When I came home," Henry said, "Nancy told me that it'd been you who'd saved my life. Funny thing about all the years, thinking I'd never walk again or leave that sanitarium... was when Daddy lost Kingsleyville I started to get stronger. I had to find out if you truly said I'd best stay at the sanitarium 'cause you had no use for a cripple. I knew the answer the minute I looked into your frightened eyes, Delta."

She inhaled deeply. "To think what his words did to us." All the years she carried the guilt for killing Henry were gone. She dropped the bear cape from around her shoulders and pulled her nightgown from the bedpost, slipping it over her head.

Henry touched the lace collar, then let his hand drift down her arm to entwine his fingers with hers. "I'm not so lonely anymore." He smiled, eyes glistening.

"You're also not so crippled." She smiled back, feeling their friendship blossom like a rose.

Confusion filtered through his eyes. "Not so crippled?"

"You carried me in here, silly. Since when could you have done that?"

He looked at his legs, stood up, and shook one at a time, then laughed, throwing his head back and beating his chest like a drum. She slid off the bed and held out her hands to him. He waltzed her around, awkwardly, whirling in a circle, barely avoiding chairs and dried herbs hanging from the ceiling. Their laughter filled the room, and a white cat, sleeping by the fireplace, slunk away from the odd couple.

"I feel like a different man," Henry said.

"Let's not overdo it." Delta pushed her shoulder under his. "Told you my magic would work."

"I don't give a mule's rump what it was. I feel good as ever!" He briskly paced to the next room with her following. His stride energetic as a young man's but he held one hand to his right hip to keep from arching his back. "Best improvement since I left the sanitarium." He pulled her to him, touching his lips to hers, softly at first, then ruggedly.

She hugged him as he gripped her even tighter, and her memory raced back to the mighty stallion. Heat rose up in her. She pushed back on both his shoulders and said, "Stop."

He sat on the arm of the velvet chair and rubbed his eyes with his fists. "Don't know what got in to me. It's not like I'm eighteen and anxious."

"No matter." Delta smoothed her nightgown, unable to look at him and suppressed a smile. "When you start hopping like a hare and running like a horse, I'll start to worry."

He chuckled, seeming grateful for her understanding. "Reckon I got new respect for spells and cures." Wild rose fragrance filled the room. The fire made the air toasty, and they breathed it in as if it were a warm drink of milk.

For a while Delta felt young again. She remembered the nights like this when she and Arn lived here alone. To have discovered this full, cozy feeling again was a joy she'd never believed could be recaptured. She sat by the fire, watching the flames and hot embers burn themselves out.

Henry caressed the top of her head, letting his fingers comb through her hair. Arn used to do it just that way, she thought. She leaned her head against Henry's knee, closing her eyes on the edge of sleep. She would give Henry back his life. Even if it cost her own.

The quiet was interrupted by footsteps coming toward the house. They sounded too slow to be Lafette's. Blue barked, and Delta and Henry pulled apart. The late night visitor replaced the warmth that had filled the room seconds before. They held hands and waited for the knock. A chill ran up her spine.

A male voice yelled out Delta's name. "Who's out there?" she called back.

"Amos!"

Henry opened the door and let him in. "What the devil made you climb Shadow Mountain this late at night?"

Amos looked like a windblown sailor. He set a lantern on the floor and stood, weaving slightly in place. "Couldn't wait 'til morning." He held a walking stick covered with the name "King" whittled in the bark and looked at the floor as he spoke, panting for breath as if he'd run the last several hills. "It's your Daddy."

"Go on." Henry rubbed Amos's shoulder to calm him.

"He disappeared a week ago. We looked everywhere."

"Well, he can't've gone far. Has the law been called?"

Grunts and squeaks escaped from Amos's throat as he tried to control his emotions. "Should've come and got you, but every day I thought he'd show up. Just come walking down the road, blowing off steam and chewing on a cigar."

"It's okay, Amos," Henry said. "You're right, Daddy'll show up."

"I found him." Amos wiped his eyes, still huffing breath. "He was so close. My son noticed the smell." Amos looked up at Henry, then over to Delta.

She knew what he was about to say. She saw King in her mind and couldn't keep the words from bursting forth. "He took his own life." She clutched her throat as if hers slipped away as well. *The bad luck coin*, she thought, horrified.

Amos stepped away from her, shocked at her knowledge. His voice tumbled in a high-pitched whine. "Crawled into the chicken coop. Shot hisself." The words seemed to drain him, almost as if saying them made it real for him. "We had to bury him. I tried to make them wait, but Doc said he'd been dead too long and made out like it weren't healthy. The hens had been at him."

Delta moved to Henry's side, afraid he might fall. He put an arm around her shoulders and lowered himself to velvet chair. The silence marred only by the crackling fire. After a while he took the stick from Amos, snapped it in half and threw the pieces into the fire. "Well, it's finished."

Amos excused himself, saying he wanted to get back to Nancy, but Delta figured he was uncomfortable around her. When he left she spread a blanket on the hearth and threw more logs into the fire. "Come down here," she said, looking at the burning walking stick, carved just as her son's name had been all those years ago. "Just rest in my arms."

Henry lowered himself onto the floor, pulled her to him and buried his face in her shoulder. He cried until he fell asleep.

Delta rose while he slept and walked out onto the porch. The night air pressed on her like wetness. She stared at the sky, looking for a star to wish upon, something that had a hint of happiness or hope. “May your soul travel fast, King Kingsley.”

♆ 35 ♆

POLK OWENS' SUNDAY evening cock fights had been a tradition since the War Between the States. His grandfather built the cockpits despite skirmishes for control of Cumberland Gap. When soldiers raided farms for food their commanding officers ordered them to keep away from the Owens' fighting cocks. It was said that men on both sides put away their blue or gray uniforms to sneak away in the dark night to drink Papaw Owens' moonshine and bet on game roosters, only to return to the war the next day.

The main pit, a ten-by-ten dirt circle, was surrounded by a yard-high pine fence. Built at the base of a hill, so onlookers sat above, it saved Papaw Owens having to construct a seating section. Two smaller square rings anchored the main pit. If roosters fighting in the center ring tired or began ducking one another, they'd be moved to a smaller one—a disgrace owners hoped to avoid.

The matches started in the late afternoon. Now that night was coming on, spectators were aroused to a fever pitch at the sight and smell of blood and the thrill or pain of winning or losing money. Lafette stood away from the crowd, exercising Valentine's best rooster, a Rhode Island Red named Slim. He spread some oats across an unfinished pine table and the bird scratched vigorously in them as if they were dirt. Valentine moved among the men making private bets on Slim, stopping only to bring Lafette a cup of moonshine that he swallowed in one gulp, then turn his concentration back to Slim.

A brown-haired boy with slate-colored eyes looked Slim over before placing his bet. "Pretty good rooster you got there, Mister," he said to Lafette. A tall stranger in a black coat pushed through the pack, hovering behind the boy. The man's iris-blue eyes blinked beneath a tattered black hat low on his forehead. The boy shot him a once-over then swallowed nervously.

Lafette let the rooster strut back and forth for a cluster of men making wagers. Slim lifted his head high, eyeing those who studied him. He crowed and arched his neck backwards so his scarlet-colored crown tilted on his head. His copperish neck feathers spread down toward a gold and black body and out to a tail of long black feathers.

The boy's gray eyes sparkled as he fingered money in his pocket. Lafette slipped his hands under Slim's wings, firmly holding his breast, and flipped the bird upward. The rooster flapped for balance and swung out his claws. Lafette exercised him like this a half dozen times then gave him a bit of raw ground beef. "That's enough, Slim," he said as the rooster gobbled down the meat and pecked at his hand for more. "No water either 'til you win your fight." He lifted the bird with one hand to judge its weight one last time. Just right, he thought, not too heavy. The rooster hadn't been watered in three days and only fed a scratching of oats and bits of beef. He began running Slim around his arms in a figure eight, the final exercise to give a fighting cock just enough tension to kill an opponent with one strike.

"Mighty fine stag."

Lafette looked toward the voice. Behind the boy, the tall man in the black coat removed his hat, revealing a mass of curly hair—the stranger who'd been fishing at the Elisha Tree the day before. *The Kingsleys' man!* He protectively pulled the rooster close. Had the stranger spoken, or was it is boy? Lafette wondered.

Polk pushed behind Lafette to light another torch, one of many that dotted the hillside with diamond-shaped flames. They exposed the stranger's face in deep shadows and gave his cheekbones a skeletal look even though he was full-jawed.

"Ain't a stag." Lafette held the rooster's claw to clip a pointed spur on its leg. He was unsure if the stranger had made the comment, but his coming around surely meant trouble. "Been fighting this cock for near three years now." He stared directly at the man.

"Mighty long life for a fightin' rooster," the gray-eyed boy said.

"That's 'cause I train 'em." Lafette spurred the rooster's other leg, keeping the stranger in view. The tall man fingered the spare gaffs lying on the table.

Lafette squinted to let him know he did not appreciate the invasion. "You sure disappeared awful fast the other day." The stranger dropped the spur on the table and spun it with his forefinger and thumb. He reached out and deliberately petted Slim's back as if he were a fat lap cat rather than a fighting cock. Now's the time to warn him off, Lafette thought. "Had a cane disappear at the creek the other day," he said. "If I find out who took it, he'll be one sorry feller."

"Three-count!" the referee yelled from the ring. A cheer rose from three men sitting on the hillside and Lafette knew that a rooster was about to give out. Slim would be next in the main pit. The stranger drummed his fingers on the table and clicked his tongue as if calling a horse, then glanced sharply in the direction of Shadow Mountain.

Even though Lafette sensed a deliberate attempt to make him nervous, he shivered inwardly. Again, the man looked toward Shadow Mountain. Lafette decided to create some nervous tension of his own and asked, "Got somebody to meet?" and waited to see if doubt crossed the man's face.

"Hope you ain't against that yellow stag," the gray-eyed boy said, his face blank as if he were talking in his sleep. "That's the one I bet will win."

The man smiled a mocking grin, and Lafette knew that a moment before, the boy had been all set to bet on Slim. He turned to the stranger, fists clenched. "Mister, our rooster ain't lost a fight yet. He's the meanest chicken in Midnight Valley. He don't duck. He kills in one stroke." With a glare Lafette added, "I bet every cent I got he'll win."

The stranger's eyebrows peaked in amusement at the challenge. He dipped his chin into his coat until only his eyes showed. "Would you bet your mountain?" The voice was tinny, as if he spoke from inside a cave.

Lafette's heart raced. "Mountain don't belong to me," he replied, eager to test Henry's friend. "Belongs to my ma. We made sure of it a few years back." The stranger buttoned his tattered coat and rubbed his hands together as if the night chilled him. "I'd've thought you already knew this," Lafette said, "since you seem so eager to be on Shadow Mountain." Lafette tucked Slim under his arm. "Didn't I see you a few weeks ago with Henry Kingsley? Over at the Cumberland Gap Trading Post. Believe I did."

The stranger reached out and touched Slim's red feathers. The rooster clucked and hid his beak in the fold of Lafette's arm.

"Or maybe you're more familiar with his pa, crazy ole King Kingsley?" Lafette shifted Slim to his other arm, spooked by the way this man avoided speaking. A cold wind blew grit in his face. He staggered and the stranger opened his hands, offering to hold Slim. Lafette shook his head and rubbed his eyes.

The gray-eyed boy was gone. The nearby torch had burned out, covering the surrounding ground in a dark circle with the stranger on the opposite side. Lafette moved over the uneven ground toward the main arena. The stranger waited in the darkness, his head fading into the shadows.

"Slim and Darla's Beau in the center pit," the referee shouted. The challenging yellow rooster belonged to Joey Garlin and had ducked its opponent the only time Lafette saw it fight. He was surprised Joey hadn't killed Darla's Beau himself.

"That's the one you think'll win!" he jeered. "First time a rooster ducks, it's ruined for life." He hurried to the main pit with Slim cradled in his arms.

A dozen of the forty or so men around the main pit turned to watch Slim scratch in the dirt at the ring's edge. The rooster clucked, absorbing the spectators' excitement. Lafette picked him up so he wouldn't lose all his fight. He glanced back to make sure the stranger had followed him. A plan began to form in his mind. "How much you want to bet me Slim can whip Darla's Beau?"

A giddiness filled Lafette when he heard a man putting eight to two odds on Slim. Polk was giving six to four odds but reserving rights to pick the rooster, hedging bets for the house. The gray-eyed boy put his money on Slim, then looked over at the stranger, quickly stepping away to give him a wide berth as if the nearness made him itchy. Soon talk blended into one sound and Lafette focused on the tall man who seemed as luminous as foxfire in the torchlight.

The stranger slowly pulled his hands from his coat pockets and stared intently at the ground. He twisted a ring on his left hand, hiding it from Lafette then, slid it off his finger and laid it on the betting table.

"Done!" Lafette said, pulling out all the money in his pocket and dropping it beside the ring. He'd show this fool friend of the Kingsleys that if he tangled with Lafette Marlon, he'd have a reckoning on his hands.

The silver ring glinted in the torchlight.

Valentine came running over and took Slim. "Of all the bad luck!" he complained. "Can't get a'body to give me odds. Everybody knows Slim'll take that chicken out in one run."

"I got a bet going that'll be worth it." Lafette stroked Slim's smooth back for good luck, then stationed himself at the main cockpit. Valentine stood opposite Joey Garlin, who gulped deep breaths, believing his rooster would soon be dead.

"Hey, Joey!" Valentine called out. "Sure you don't want to give up now?" He hooted an edgy, mean laugh. "That scrawny poultry's just good for stew!"

Men abandoned the side rinks to watch Slim. They smelled blood. A lanky kid in blue coveralls swung on a low tree branch and whooped with expectation. Canteens and moonshine jugs were left aside. Shorter men climbed higher on the hillside to get a better view. Polk lit three more torches that brightened the pit with an orange glow.

Joey Garlin's rooster squawked and flapped wings like a scared hen wanting to bolt for a bush. Valentine and Joey held the opponents chest high. Slim's copper-colored neck feathers began to puff out. Darla's Beau lifted its claws, trying to scratch Joey and free itself. The referee pulled a tobacco plug from his pocket and bit off a piece.

Lafette wished he'd hurry before Slim got too excited.

The referee raised his hand. Valentine and Joey watched him intently, then the referee's hand fell, and both roosters flew in the air. Slim's wings spread wide, his claws high. A good sign, Lafette thought. The fight would be over soon. His rooster's shrieks were like war cries. A cluster of boys shook their fists and shouted.

"Come on, red rooster! Make me a millionaire!" the gray-eyed boy yelled.

Men struggled to see over the shoulders of those in front. The drunker ones, trying to move forward, were pushed back and a fight broke out, but Polk quickly stopped it by shoving his shotgun between the two men slugging it out. A cold wind blew in and someone handed Lafette another cup of moonshine. He sipped this time. Jacking one foot up on the pit rail, he glanced at the crowd. The stranger's head rose above everyone and his black curly hair flew over his face. He watched Lafette more than the cockpit.

The roosters landed face-to-face. Slim didn't even attempt a hit. Lafette could hardly believe his eyes. Usually he aimed his claws instantly, puncturing an opponent's lungs or heart fast as lightning.

Slim and Darla's Beau ran at each other, beating their wings, both puffed up far as their feathers would stretch. They danced around each other, bumping chests and shrieking angrily.

"Get 'im, Slim! Kill 'im! Kill 'im!" Valentine punched at the air with his fists.

Suddenly Darla's Beau ducked. The long yellow neck curved downward, then up, avoiding Slim's beak. Half of the spectators groaned. Polk slapped his head, bitterly disappointed. The roosters withdrew to take another run at each other. Valentine's back jerked, copying Slim's movements but Lafette fought the stiff tension that spread through him. If Darla's Beau got Slim to duck, he'd be ruined. "Kill 'im, Slim," he whispered to himself. "Don't give 'im a chance."

"Come on, boy!" Valentine yelled. The crowd quieted as the roosters flogged at each other. Red, brown, black, and golden feathers exploded into the air and blood wet the yellow feathers of Darla's Beau.

Lafette bit his lip. He'd spent more time with Slim than Valentine over the last three years, and this was like watching an old friend drown and being unable to help. Valentine shot him a worried look, as if he could read the future. In the next instant, Slim ducked. His shiny neck feathers curled in a wave that Lafette never thought possible. Groans poured from the crowd.

"One count!" the referee called out, indicating the fight was going nowhere. He pointed at a boy, who began counting to ten. The roosters danced in a circle, wings spread, necks waving in the ducking motion that meant both would avoid attacking. Valentine covered his eyes. Lafette's heart pounded as if it'd fallen to his stomach.

"Two count!" the referee yelled, this time pointing at a heavyset man standing opposite him. The man quickly counted to ten. The roosters still battered at each other, ducking in and out with only an occasional hit. Slim staggered. Lafette thought he might have taken a blow to his lungs, and motioned to the referee to bring him over. He pulled up the rooster's neck so its beak fit into his mouth, then blew once, twice, filling Slim's lungs with air and put him down again. Slim stumbled around the ring, then dove toward Darla's Beau with new fury. If Slim didn't finish him off soon, the referee would call three count. Valentine's face had gone stony.

Lafette's head throbbed and he pushed through the men behind him. Most old timers strolled to the smaller rinks or to the beer keg manned by Polk's son. It seemed they, too, could not stand to see a champion fall.

At the betting table, the stranger stared at the money and the silver ring, his arms crossed at his waist. His grin was gone and the torches reflected in his eyes looked like golden spikes. Lafette looked hard at him, warning him not to speak. The man pointed at the roosters. Darla's Beau had lost an eye and the soft dirt was muddy with blood. Slim pecked over and over at a gaping wound.

Polk patted Lafette's shoulder. "Bad break, boy," he said and moved to the betting table to collect and pay off the bets. At the "Three Count" call, the stranger watched Lafette with eyes that seemed to laugh. He wanted to wrap his hands around the man's throat and crush the breath out of him. Even though Slim would be ruled as winning the fight, he'd ducked.

Finally Darla's Beau battered against the ground, a thin line of blood shot up across the dirt, and his claws kicked weakly at the air as he died.

"Yeeesss!" yelled the gray-eyed boy. He threw his cap up in the air and whistled through his fingers.

Valentine jumped into the rink, grabbed Slim, and headed directly toward a tree stump next to Polk's smokehouse. An ax, its blade buried in the center of the stump, stood ready. He grabbed the handle and jerked it free.

Lafette implored, "We can breed him." He touched Slim's back feathers. The rooster trembled.

"Ain't gonna have no duckin' blood in my roosters."

"Turn him loose, Valentine. No need to..."

Valentine's expression hardened. Slim lifted his head and pecked at Valentine's hand, so weak he could hardly squawk. Part of his red crown was torn off and his wounded wing bled. Valentine held him upside down against a dogwood tree.

"I'll take him," Lafette said, "I'll turn him loose in the mountains." He felt sick, thought he might throw up as the moonshine he'd drunk whiffed into his nostrils. "Don't! Just don't!" Slim's eye stared at him and Lafette's knees started shaking.

The ax came down, severing Slim's neck. The body spasmed, flailing in a circle, soundless except for the flap of wings. Lafette put a hand to his throat and squeezed to make sure nothing came up. Slim's body fell at the stranger's feet.

"There," Valentine said, with as much pain as anger in his voice. "My best fightin' cock. All yours." He dropped the bloody ax on the ground. "It was the only thing to be done, and you know it." He sniffed and wiped his eyes.

Lafette stared at the yellow claws curled like dried twigs, the sharp gaffs still around the legs. The feathers were shiny and blood stained only the golden wing feathers. The rowdy crowd had turned to another fight, with wagers and odds being made on a new rooster. The smoky smell of the burning torches wafted past and he felt scorched inside.

The stranger touched Slim with the toe of his boot and leaned down to pluck a long, black tail feather. He brushed the feather against the back of his hand, then slid it behind his ear into his curly, black hair. His face was half hidden but his eyes still reflected the long, slim torch flames.

"Won your bet," he said, his voice hollow and unreflective.

Lafette drew back, punched him in the jaw, and the stranger's hand flew up and circled Lafette's neck. Instead of strangling him, he rubbed back and forth, sending a shock down Lafette's spine. They held each other in a clinch, unable to let go.

Lafette thought he was being electrocuted and thrashed so hard they both fell to the ground. The stranger did not fight back. Lafette struggled to his knees, intent on punching him again. Polk and Joey Garlin caught hold of Lafette, and he coughed and sputtered, trying to break free.

"Take it easy," Joey said. "Nobody feels as bad about this as I do." Lafette shrugged away. Polk knew better than to talk. He patted Lafette's back, giving the stranger an irritated look, then bent down and carefully picked up Slim's body, indicating with a nod that he'd handle the burial. He shook his head as if the death of this prize rooster upset him as much as it did Lafette.

Lafette coughed to clear his throat. The black sky, filled with white specks of stars, seemed to surround him like a cage. Cold night air made his fingers stiff and hard to bend. The stranger's ring sparkled with a white glint like a star in the sky. Lafette picked it up along with his money. He had won it. He had beaten the Kingsleys' friend. He tossed the ring in his hand, then turned sharply toward the stranger.

The man stared back with a knowing look; a taunting look that said they would meet again; a look that acknowledged a worthy opponent. "If I was just anybody," the stranger said softly though lips that seemed not to move, "I'd've bet on your rooster." He dusted his pants and turned toward the mountain behind him. "Nothin' like a little challenge to gage a man's gumption." His huge size seemed cumbersome as he arched his back, causing the spine to crack. He seemed to know exactly where he was going as he faded into the darkness, then disappeared.

♆ 36 ♆

AT THE COCKPITS, black smoke spiraled from low burning torches. Men hooted and hollered but without the same enthusiasm shown for Slim. Money changed hands, spectators consumed moonshine from kegs and jugs, the night grew cold, and their breaths exhaled like fog. Valentine studied two roosters Bill Sutton had brought to sell.

Lafette rolled the ring in his hand then slipped it on the fourth finger of his right hand. It fit perfectly. He held his hand next to a torch. The thick silver ring matched the one on his little finger. The ring his mother had given him years before was a thin silver band engraved with a starburst where a diamond might go. *"Your Daddy had a matchin' one," she'd told him. "He never took it off."* Lafette twisted the stranger's silver ring around. As it revolved, he came to a starburst cut perfectly in the center of the band.

He whispered, "This can't be." Thunder clapped loudly and shook the ground. Lafette stumbled backward against the torch post, certain he'd been struck by lightning. Orange embers fell on his sleeve.

Some men pointed at the sky and several packed up their roosters, expecting a thunderstorm any second. Polk promised to move the fights inside his barn if it rained. A few spectators changed their minds and stayed. Lafette swallowed. A lump in his throat pulsed over the loss of Slim and the excitement of finding Arn. "Polk," he asked, "you remember what my daddy looked like?"

Polk scratched his graying beard and thought for a moment. "Hmmmm. Seems I recall." He dipped a tin cup into a water bucket, gargled and spat. "Used to buy moonshine from my daddy. For his magic work, he always said."

"Did he favor that stranger any?"

Polk scratched his chin, brushing loose hairs from his chest-length beard. "Reckon a mite. Tall, curly headed. Long time ago. Reckon he might be kin?"

Lafette peered into the darkness and walked the direction the stranger had gone. He listened for footsteps. An owl hooted and a bat silently wove through tree branches, but no sight or sound of him. "You still here?" he called. No answer.

He held to the slender birch branches and pulled himself up the hill. Polk's cabin, the cockpits, the endless rooster squawks, faded. He listened to his own breath. The lump in his throat throbbed like a cramped muscle.

At the ridge crest, the crescent moon offered little light for the way home. Oak and spruce trees cast sinewy shadows. The stranger might be hidden among them. *If he's kin, he might call out to me. If he's an enemy, I could be dead before I even see him.*

Lafette thought back, hoping to stir some memory of his father: a touch, a smell, a blurry dream of being thrown high in the air and landing in large hands that cushioned him and jiggled him in his laughter. His memory would not form a face.

He followed the ridge to Shadow Mountain. Black clouds raced high in the air against a navy blue sky. His feet fell onto familiar ground and he climbed the mountain easily despite the darkness. Red, iridescent eyes reflected; owls, rabbits, a startled deer bolted.

The rotting smell of Tyme wood filled his nostrils. The higher he climbed, the more he was forced to take shallow breaths until he reached the mountain peak where the air was fresh. He came upon his house, windows glowing like a golden lantern. As warm and inviting as it looked, he knew he was not part of that home anymore. Delta's and Henry's silhouettes shadowed the curtains as they sat in front of the fireplace.

Watching the pair filled Lafette with disgust. He leaned against what was left of Arn's Volcano, a jagged boulder, rising from the earth like a blasted tower. The creek behind the house, redirected in the explosion years ago, ran over part of the stone and cascaded over the mountain in a gentle waterfall. Lafette dipped his hands into a pool of cold water, thinking, *If only it was you, Daddy. If only it could really be you. If only you'd let me bring you here.*

Blue began to bark, and he saw Delta rise and walk toward the door. In another second, she would come out onto the porch. *Dare I tell her Arn's returned?*

She cracked open the door and Blue bolted toward Lafette, his tongue hanging to one side. Lafette held his hands out and Blue jumped up, forepaws on his waist.

"That you, son?" Delta asked.

Her voice was hoarse—probably from the resin she burned for magic ceremonies, he thought. "Can you come out here, Momma?"

"It's cold as the hills out there, Lafette. Come on inside, honey." She ran her hands up her arms, her long hair catching in her fingers.

He stayed a distance from the house, watching her. She moved toward him, nothing about her expression giving away her feelings. Of all people, he thought, she should have known Daddy would come back. *Used to tell me he'd come back. Promised me he would.*

"What is it?" she asked. Her furrowed brows peaked as her eyes bored into him.

"Everything you ever wanted." The words almost bruised his throat.

"What do you mean?"

"Daddy's come home."

Delta folded her arms across her stomach, stared at him blankly, then turned away. Lafette wanted to jerk her around and wanted to read her face. Even in the darkness he would know if his father still meant anything to her.

"You're mistaken, Lafette." She looked at the black sky with millions of stars hidden by swarthy clouds. "Honey, your father's dead." She walked away, then turned back. "I know Arn Marlon through and through. If by some odd chance he is alive he'd never return here. He wouldn't be able to face me, for reasons that are not your concern."

"If it's not him, it could be his kin, or somebody who knew him," Lafette said as she continued walking. "Don't you even care?"

"I already know what I need to know."

"He gave me his ring. The one that matched yours."

She stopped, wrung her hands together and stared at the house. Lafette wasn't sure if she was cold, or nervous that Henry might hear. "Show it to me."

He raised his hand as she walked toward him. The ring was gone. It had disappeared as if it'd never been on his hand. Only the slender silver band Delta had given him as a child remained. He searched his pockets, his jacket. He ran his hands over the ground where Blue had jumped on him. "I could've lost it anywhere on this blasted mountain!" He looked up, his eyes pleading for her trust.

"The ring isn't important," she said softly. I believe you're telling what you think is truth." She pulled her long blond hair to one side and twisted it tightly in one hand. "Whoever you saw, he wasn't your father."

"How can you be so sure, Momma? It's only been the last few years you've said he was dead. How can you be so sure?"

"I refuse to live in the past, Lafette. Not for the rest of what life I have left." She gave him a sharp look, her eyes hard. "Don't upset Henry with this talk, and if you ever want peace with yourself, best trust my words. Your Daddy is dead. So, best you stop seeing what you want to see. Hear me. Dead."

He searched his pockets again and felt something cold and metallic. "Here it is!" He pulled out the coin King had told him to give to Delta before he had died. Quickly, he closed his hand around it.

"Where did you get that?" She grabbed his wrist.

"No, no, nowhere," he stammered, refusing to open his fist.

"Give it to me, now!"

He opened his hand and she took the coin. "Momma, can't you see they're up to something?" he whispered. "King sent it to you when I went for the canes. I believe the Kingsleys still want to steal the mountain."

"Don't even say that." She held up a hand to silence him. "You should've given this to me quicker than water runs." Delta face twisted with worry. She looked back at the house again, then lowered her voice to a whisper. “King is dead. The past is finished. Henry said those very words tonight. He told me it was finished. Now, you be respectful. You act like King Kingsley was a bad dream.”

“Even dead, I don’t feel safe from him. Not ’til Henry Kingsley is off this mountain.” Lafette kicked a grass mound. “Momma, listen to yourself. Those people tried to kill you.” He pointed at the rocks of Arn’s Volcano.

She shook the silver coin at him. “And it just may be you played the biggest part in King’s leaving this earth.” She walked around him, one hand stroking her chin. “This is what you’re to do. I’ll make a sachet to rub on your body for the next few days. On fourth day, wash yourself with onion peelings and rinse off in the creek. In the creek, now, you hear? Not a tub, the creek. So the bad luck’ll wash downstream.”

“Daddy’s come back, the Kingsleys are at their old tricks, and all you want is to stink me up like an onion!”

“Promise me you’ll do as I say. This is a bad luck coin. You need to get shed of its poison.”

“I don’t believe this.”

“Promise me!”

“I promise!” he yelled.

“Don’t ever hold back from me.”

Lafette dropped to his knees and rested his head against a boulder’s grainy surface. He didn’t want to watch her walk away. “Just because she can’t believe Daddy’s alive,” he said to himself. “Doesn’t mean he might not be watching me right this minute.”

He whistled for Blue and scratched him on the head. The folds of the dog’s skin wrinkled above his eyes. Old Blue, he thought, older than me now. As old as my Daddy. Tomorrow I'll find him, he promised himself. Tomorrow, I'll know who this man is and what he wants from us. "And if it's you, Daddy," he said to the web of stars breaking through the murky clouds, "I'll bring you home to Shadow Mountain. I'll be your son, and we'll conquer these mountains in ways the Kingsleys could never have even dreamed."

♆ 37 ♆

LAFETTE AWOKE TO hammering above his head. He sat up and wiped away hay stuck to his forehead. Sleeping in the barn for the fourth week in a row was wearing on his back and he arched sideways, stretching sore muscles.

Through the roof slats he saw Henry on his hands and knees, pounding at loose boards. The sun behind him created a shadow across Lafette's face. Almost noon, he figured as he stood up, shaking life into each leg. Was gonna fix those boards in the next few days, he thought. He swiped resentfully at wood flakes showering from above.

The roof jarred as Henry crawled across it and climbed down a ladder. He staggered across the yard like an animal dragging its own trapped leg. If Daddy came back Henry'd be shamed into leaving, Lafette told himself. *It had to be him last night. That man has to be Arn. Won't be long now, he thought. Henry Kingsley'll be out of Momma's life.* A restless energy soared through Lafette. He stroked a black horse on his way outside and stopped by the water bucket on the back porch to gargle a drink. Inside, Henry puttered around the sink. Lafette quietly stepped into the doorway. Nails lay scattered on the table and several herb and potion jars had been moved. Henry slid his hand across the top shelf. He latched onto a small box and pulled it down.

"Momma wouldn't like you going through her pantry." Lafette leaned against the doorframe and folded his arms high across his chest.

Henry looked over, "Looking for horseshoe nails." He opened the palm-sized box and a strong tobacco whiff rose into the air.

"Some's out in the barn."

"I didn't want to wake you." Henry stared into the box of shredded tobacco.

"I'd've gotten to that roof." Lafette dropped into a kitchen chair and propped his feet on the table. "No reason for you to go blundering around." Henry touched the tobacco shreds with his finger, spilling some onto the floor. "Momma's gonna split a gut that you're poking in her herbs," Lafette added, hoping to plant a few seeds of doubt.

Henry picked through the tobacco, pulled out a silver coin, then looked at Lafette as if waiting for an explanation. When none came he set the box aside and leaned against the table for support. "This coin was my father's," Henry said, voice shaky.

Lafette sat up straight. "If'n it's in this house, then it belongs to my Momma." He held out his hand for the coin. Henry flipped the coin in the air and Lafette watched it twirl so fast it seemed like a solid silver line.

Henry caught it and closed his fist around it. "How could she've come by it?" He flipped the coin again. Lafette stood and bad memories flooded in on him. *Standing in the Kingsley library, King's harsh voice belting accusations at his mother. His knees shaking, heart pounding, the plush rug, crystal chandelier, smell of tobacco, taste of smoke in his mouth. Most of all the coin, the silver coin that King ceaselessly flipped into the air.* "Clean your ears, Mister. I said it belonged to Momma. Now put it back or—"

"No." Henry glared up at him. The coin glistered as he rubbed it between thumb and forefinger. "I'll not put it back, Lafette. I'll wait and ask Delta about it."

A black coffee tin on the stove puffed white steam from its nozzle. Lafette grabbed it and threw it against the wall. A gulping pulse of water wet the floor. "Tired of you thinking everything my mother does needs your approval. Just 'cause you're crippled don't give you say-so on Shadow Mountain! Maybe you ought to consider who's got more right to the mountain than you, more right to my mother than you." Lafette thought of his father. Arn might be somewhere close—maybe watching him, waiting to see his son defend the Marlon's territory. "If that coin belonged to King and my Mamma ended up with it, then I'd say that's the least she's entitled to for all he did to her."

"I deserve to know if my father came to see Delta before he died."

"So much for it being finished." Lafette narrowed his eyes, knowing his words had cut deep. "Always knew you couldn't be trusted."

"What's this commotion?" Delta hurried in through the back door. She'd been bathing and her wet hair matted against her forehead. A towel, loosely draped on her shoulders and her dress, soaked the dampness. "I can hear you all the way to the creek."

"Henry's plundering through the house, Momma. Into stuff he's got no business."

She pulled her dripping hair to one side. "Henry lives here, Lafette. He can go through anything he wants."

Her words were like a switch across his back. He bit the inside of his cheek, no longer fighting the resentment burning in his chest. "I was defending you, Momma!"

"Stop it, Lafette!" The dress stuck to her skin, showing her body.

He turned toward the wall, squeezed fists tightly inside his pockets, and wished his mother had on more clothes. "If Daddy was here, you'd stick up for your own."

Henry stared at the floor, then leaned down and picked up the coffee pot. "It's nothing, Delta. Me and Lafette'll work it out."

"No, you two will not 'cause there's nothing to work out." She jerked Lafette toward her. His size dwarfed her. "I'm going to put on dry clothes. When I return, you'll apologize to Henry. Then we'll plant those Tyme trees."

Lafette opened his mouth to speak, but she shook a finger at him. He clenched his teeth and watched her go into the next room. He hoped with all the fury inside him that his father was out on the mountain, watching this house, seeing what he had done.

He and Henry stared at the floor then at each other. Neither spoke. Henry set the coffee pot on the stove, then squatted to pick up tobacco shreds. His humped body made him resemble a wad of clothing without a human form. For all his pitifulness, Lafette could not lean down and help him.

Henry refilled the tobacco box, replaced the coin, and closed the lid. Lafette stared out the window at the cornfield while Henry shuffled across the room and stretched to return the box on the top shelf where he'd found it. "Satisfied?"

Lafette stomped outside, saddled Henry's horse and rode furiously down the rocky terrain. If his father was going to come back, he had to figure a way to get Henry to leave, and Delta to believe him. The best way, he decided, was find Arn and bring him to her whether he wanted to come or not. It annoyed him that his father hadn't come directly home and claim all that belonged to him. He wondered why Arn kept himself hidden. Bring him right to the front door, he thought. Present him like a Christmas package. He snickered to himself. *I'll show 'em.*

♆ 38 ♆

AS THE DAYS passed Delta and Henry looked at one another with more than devotion brightening their eyes. Perhaps they loved each other as they were now—one broken in body, the other broken in spirit; or perhaps they loved the memory of themselves as youngsters—strong, beautiful, wild as the laurel thickets overrunning the mountains in the spring. Whatever it was that came to life, they encouraged it, nurtured it as if it were their child. What did it matter that the world changed and grew and continued around them? They had the mountain where life was as they believed it to be, and where reality was merely a mirror they avoided looking into. Yet after drying her damp hair in the sun, Delta glanced into that mirror and realized it was a shattered glass.

She paced the mountaintop, maneuvering through the black rocks as she had done so often in the past eight years. She stepped over three holes dug between the rocks for the Tyme plants and climbed onto a sharply tilting boulder that looked about to tip off the mountainside. "Arn, are you really out there?" she whispered.

She waited, watching the treetops wave in a gentle wind. Pale green, mixed with emerald and lime, mingled like woven fabric. She pressed her fingers to her temples and listened for a difference in all the sounds she heard, trying to sense a new presence or the appearance of an old one. *Eight years ago when I learned you were Kate's husband, I killed you, Arn Marlon. I made you dead. I told anybody with the courage to ask that you'd died. And in my heart you were dead.* "Don't come back to me alive now."

"What'd you say?" Henry carried the Tyme plants, setting them in plowed dirt.

"Place it in the right light." She lifted the young tree he had positioned awkwardly, cleared away a few rocks and rubbed dirt between her hands to feel the grainy texture. Henry tossed a palm-sized black stone, trying to act unconcerned, then knelt and pulled back a braid of her hair that dragged on the ground.

"Don't see why you plant 'em amid these black rocks anyhow." He picked up a potted Tyme plant, now nearly two feet tall, grown from pieces of the Elisha Tree's roots. Under her supervision he'd tended it as if it were his own creation. A leaf brushed against his nose and he sniffed it. The slender plant was tied to a thin sliver of his Tyme cane. Henry set it carefully in a small, round patch of ground. Despite its growth, the leaves were still curled and yellow on the ends, and the plants had never come to flower again. "Don't see how these'll turn into trees," he said doubtfully.

"With the magic in these rocks." She moved her arm in a wide arc, indicating the thousands of stones that once formed Arn's Volcano. If she squeezed a small stone between her hands and focused her attention on it, she could feel its power pulsing like a drum. The mountain's magic still existed. "Lafette didn't come with you?" she asked.

"He left." Henry avoided looking into her eyes.

She cupped her hands in her lap for a moment as if holding a thought, then resumed working on the plants. "We'll let 'em alone for as long as Indian Summer holds out, then take 'em inside once it turns frosty."

Doubt radiated from him like heat. It made her want to defend all that she believed about the mountain's power, but they had argued about it too many times. He kicked the toe of his shoe against a diamond-shaped black rock. It tumbled over, revealing a brownish-red mass of earthworms. "Maybe Tyme trees were meant to disappear from the earth. We're all meant for the worm. Maybe it's just their time. Maybe they were meant to die eight years ago."

Beneath his eyes was a darkness she'd never noticed. "What's made you talk this way?"

"Delta, can't you see the weakness here?" He rubbed a curled, yellowish leaf between his fingers. "Certain physical laws can't be overcome. Plants as sick as these won't make it." He coughed and held onto his chest until the congestion passed.

She touched his arm, willing her own strength into him. "Lafette upset you. I know the Tyme trees will live again just as I know this mountain is magic, and that someday Lafette will recognize hisself as the Watcher and won't have a resentful bone in his body toward you." Henry took her face between his hands. His skin was cold, and she shivered as she looked into his eyes and wondered why he couldn't believe as she did. "Look how far you've come."

"That's what hurts me most. You can't see the weakness in these leaves no more than you can see the dying in me."

She put her fingers to his lips, hoping to prevent his cursing his own health. A low thunder rumbled and she knew in an instant that change was upon them. From the south, a flock of black birds flew north to avoid the approaching gray sky. A terrapin crawled bravely past them as if they were fence posts rather than people. It fell between two rocks and closed up into its yellow and brown shell. A few weeks into Indian Summer, and in a few seconds, the weather had turned as cold as January—all bad signs.

Henry held her shoulders, pressing his fingers into her back and making it impossible for her to turn away. His shallow features squeezed together like dried fruit; his eyes pits in his head and his lips pale. Moist air fell heavy around them. A few raindrops spattered on the rocks. Color struggled for possession of the sky. Half was a cloudless blue, the other half shaded gray as if a downpour might start any second.

"Last eight years," he said, "there's nothing I didn't come to know about this body." He looked down at his chest, so close to her she could feel his warm breath on her cheek. His hands slid down her arms to her fingertips. An icy wind blew and he squinted against it, then dug his hands deeply into his pockets and faced outward. The sky bowled over them like a wide lake. Clouds raced against each other and the wind whipped around so wildly that the Tyme plants bent toward the ground. Only the Tyme cane held them upright, strong as a piece of iron.

"We should take 'em in," she said, blocking the wind with her body.

"My body's failing me, Delta." Henry rubbed one palm against his thigh. "It shames me so I hide it from you. My twisted bones are weak as twigs and they pain me like rusted nails bolted into joints." She tried to speak, but he shook his head. "All I've done up here is cause trouble between you and Lafette." He walked out to the mountain edge. "It's a hurt I do not want." Towns tiny as pinpoints scattered throughout the three states could be seen below. Instead he stared down at the thousands of black rocks crumbled over the mountainside. "I'm headed home today."

"Henry, I won't hear of it!" She turned away, gripping her skirt edges in tight fists. The tall boulder of Arn's Volcano shadowed them as the sun shifted. Wet stones among the gurgling creek water were slippery, but she crossed them like a rabbit, heading toward the barn. Her pulse pounded like thunder. His expression had been full of shame, perhaps because his body had failed him or that he was leaving her. Her heart denied the idea the instant it occurred to her, but the thought spoke again: *he's abandoning you, just like Arn.*

Henry followed her to the barn. He spoke methodically, counting each point on his fingers as if rehearsed. "With me gone, Lafette'll stop fighting with you."

"I won't hear this!" She covered her ears, but his words penetrated her like the fiery sword of an archangel. She pulled the barn door open. It swung wide and bounced against the wall, making the loose boards clatter. She stood with her hands on her hips, legs spread wide to fight him if he tried to stop her. The grassy smell of hay hit her like a wave.

Henry's belongings were packed in two cloth sacks lying opposite the stall. She realized he'd planned his leaving long before. A gush of pain kept her from stepping into the barn or touching the horse and feeling the reality of his departure. Chickens pecking in the spongy ground by the pig trough scurried into the hen house.

Henry looked out at the distant mountains. "Lafette talking about his father made me realize this is still Arn Marlon's mountain. A Kingsley has no place here."

Sorrow filled her as if she were an empty cup. She looked into his eyes, coppery brown and clear like a fawn's. Her teeth chattered and she bit down. "Your mind's set. Be silly for a woman to try to stop you." *I love him, she thought. I love him.*

He smiled tenderly. "There's no words to thank you for letting me be here with you. It's the first time in all these eight years I've known peace."

"Eight years ago and today," she said, an idea occurring to her. "You're still my husband and it's only right for you to stay with me."

He shook his head and rubbed his face with his slender hands. "It's time you and Lafette started being family again."

"You're part of us now, Henry. Lafette will accept it in time."

Again he shook his head.

She heard the desperation in her own voice, and hated it but could not help pleading. "I'll talk to Lafette. He'll stop his nonsense."

"You've not listened to a thing I've said." He faced away from her.

They stood, back to back, watching the struggle between the blue and gray sky, each feeling the other's trembling and fear of the future. Ancient pine trees lined the base of Shadow Mountain like a river of green. Slowly their growth and the spread of mountain laurel and ferns had made the dead mountain live again. The warm Indian Summer even caused dogwood trees to bud. A few buttercups and violet sprigs inched from the ground. Delta saw it as a cruel trick. In another few weeks winter would set in and they'd have flowered for nothing.

"I'd be honored if you'd ride with me down the mountain," he said, "at least far as the Elisha Tree. I'll saddle your mule."

Delta watched a golden falcon swoop over the timberline and disappear into a grove of tulip and maple trees. There was no more to be done. She smoothed her dress, hands forming fists that she uncurled with effort. Blood pounded in her temples as she reached for his hand. He curled his fingers through hers. "I'll see you home, Henry."

Delta watched Henry saddle his horse and wondered what source gave him strength. He arranged the blanket on the mule's back, then hoisted the saddle as if he'd done it every day of his life. When he adjusted the stirrup, she realized the face she stared at belonged to an old man. His graying hair was thin, reddish circles underlined his eyes, and his cheeks sagged below the jawbone.

She looked away, knowing that she loved this man, and yet hadn't seen his body aged beyond its years. She'd seen the young Henry who had galloped up to her on his horse years ago, cutting as dashing a figure as any storybook hero.

Delta looked at her hands weathered like old leather with nails bitten short and grains of dirt embedded in the skin. Her hair, more white than blond, tangled in her fingers as she ran her hand through it. She was thirty-six. She felt as old as the mountains themselves, and wondered if they were also tired and closed in on themselves. Could this be what's happened to Shadow Mountain, and was she another fungus that would dry up and scatter to the wind when she died?

Henry brought the mule to her. She mounted, keeping her face turned away, suddenly afraid he would see the same aging in her that she saw in him. They headed toward the Tennessee road. Except for one trip to see King Kingsley, she hadn't left in eight years, and only a few times had she ventured as far down as the Elisha Tree. Now she was about to see a world she'd only gazed upon for so long: the world that had shunned her, a world she hated.

A ripple of fear shot through her as they descended past forests of jagged Tyme stumps. I'll not let anybody see I'm afraid, she thought, gripping the reins to keep her hands from shaking, and realized how many times Arn must have said the same words to himself. Now she knew how he had felt.

The road wasn't as overgrown with weeds and briars as she'd expected. Occasionally she saw where Lafette had cleared a path. The mule rocked comfortably beneath her, stalling only when they had to pick a path around fallen logs.

The farther down the mountain she went, the more unreal the territory became. For so many years, the burgs and strings of houses in all three states had looked delicate as doll towns nestled on the hills or in the valleys. Now as the buildings slowly became life-size, she began to doubt her sentimental reasons for coming. Fog rolled like a river through the valley on the Kentucky side. The sun disappeared behind the mountain. The mule hawed and the loud clops of its hooves on the moist ground scared off birds and small animals, sending them fleeing through the underbrush.

As they curved around the mountainside, the rocky cliffs surrounding Cumberland Gap appeared, then the old Trading Post below. Small maple and oak trees sprouted beside a creek. Bushy green ferns lined the roads. Here the mountain had some semblance of belonging to the lower valley, but would its people accept her among them again? She inhaled deep breaths, calming the nervousness in her stomach and decided, *if people still hate me, I'll have no trouble turning my back on 'em.*

Henry motioned for her to follow him to the clover field beside the Elisha Tree.

"We don't have to stop," she said, thinking he sensed her troubled thoughts.

"I need to rest my legs," he told her.

She helped him dismount. The horse and mule wandered to the creek, and their loud slurps of water mixed with the buzzing of a nearby beehive. Clover covered nearly an acre of what had once been blasted dirt piles. The mountain was coming back. If she could only bring the Tyme trees back to life as well, and if only, Henry would stay with her.

He spread his coat on the ground beside the Elisha trunk. "If God had a lick of sense, he'd've spared this one tree," Delta said, letting ragged wood crumble in her fingers. Chips of crusty, brown bark scattered on the ground where woodpeckers had hacked away at them.

Henry pointed at the names Elisha Thunderheart and Arn Marlon carved inside the tree, and laughed. "Always wondered how Lafette come by the name Elisha Tree."

Delta didn't want to upset him with thoughts of the past or of Arn, but she couldn't help staring over Henry's shoulder at Arn's name every time he looked away. "I have something for you." His eyebrows peaked as her hand slid into her pocket and she pulled out the curved handle of his Tyme cane. "It's the only part I didn't whittle up."

Henry smiled and rubbed the smooth wood between his hands. "Keep it. No telling what good it might do."

"You told me once you wanted to be buried with your canes and I promised you a coffin made of Tyme wood if you'd let me cut this one up." She reached out and held his hands, the curved Tyme wood cuffing her wrists to his. "I can't keep that promise, so the least I can do is give back what's left."

"I'm past any bitterness I had for Arn." He looked at the Elisha Tree. "Was a boy's anger."

He pulled her to him, the curve of the Tyme wood still binding their hands. Gently he wrapped an arm around her back so their chests and stomachs matched muscle for muscle. She could feel the curved Tyme wood between them, against her stomach so firmly that it pressed into her. He tilted her chin up and touched her lips with his. She kissed him back, and the kiss didn't end but lingered until they fell back into the clover, his body entwined with hers. She could see Arn's name carved in the Elisha Tree above her and she closed her eyes.

The rhythm of Henry's body on hers felt like chords of music played slowly. Her chest tingled from his closeness. The power of his body on top of her was strong as she remembered Arn's. He pressed the breath from her chest and she pushed against him, biting his bottom lip. The smell of his skin was Arn's, the taste of his tongue was Arn's, the way he held her hands above her head was Arn's. She opened her eyes and stared into Arn's blue eyes. *I'm with Henry, Henry...* A terror filled her and she struggled against a dead man. Arn was on top of her, making love to her. She saw him as clearly as she felt him. Her movements matched his, then she hungrily clasped him tighter against her. She squeezed her eyes closed and gripped Henry's legs with hers, she could sense his heart beating, could visualize his heart inside of him. She held him tighter until his moaning in her ear brought her to herself.

Henry lifted his head from her shoulder. Pink-cheeked, he grinned and couldn't seem to stop. She wiped sweat from his brow, then let a hand slide down to his hips. She didn't feel the least bit embarrassed. She swore to herself she'd never tell Henry that for a moment she'd believed he was Arn. Yet she couldn't shake the feeling that it had been Arn she'd just made love to. She kissed him again, holding him and becoming aware of the hard Tyme wood still pressed between her stomach and his. For these next few moments, where they were going and where they had been did not exist.

She straightening her clothes, thinking people around the Trading Post would be scandalized if they knew what Delta Wade had done now. She laughed and pointed down the mountain at ant-size figures scurrying about. Henry smiled, understanding her amusement. He'll not make it off this mountain, she thought. He'll stay with me.

She turned and held out her hands. He kissed her fingertips. She couldn't remember a time when she'd been happier. In his eyes she saw Arn. The memory of Arn making love to her flooded her mind. Arn touching her, kissing her, entering her body. As disturbing as the thought was, she held it in her heart as if it were a rose from a secret lover. She pulled Henry close, breathing in the woodsy smell of his skin.

♆ 39 ♆

THE SUMMER AFTERNOON sizzled with heat waves distorting the distance. From the saddle of Cumberland Gap, Lafette pointed toward Shadow Mountain. "I'll scout the high peaks," he declared, "you take the side ridges."

Valentine rubbed his chin whiskers. "How in hell do you expect to find a man if'n he don't want to be found?"

"I'll smell him out. He's got a powerful lot to explain." Lafette's throat muscles tightened like twisted rope. "And I need him to rid Shadow Mountain of that cussed Henry Kingsley." He knew as well as Valentine that trying to find his father in these mountains would be nearly impossible. Arn probably had hiding places even the squirrels hadn't discovered.

Lafette had a grievance with a father who'd deserted him long ago, but he also desperately wanted him home. He'd thought of little else since seeing the silver ring with the starburst design. Now he recalled all the times he hidden in the Elisha Tree, staring at his daddy's name, wishing with his whole heart for him to return. He held his hand to his mouth, tasting the silver metal on his little finger. He remembered the day his mother gave him the ring. He'd been no bigger than a tadpole. Delta had called the gift a *memory token* of Arn. That day Lafette had thought he was the luckiest boy in the world.

But what if this man was some relative of Arn's who meant him or his mother harm—some man who only favored his father? He wore the silver ring that matched his mother's wedding band, but the stranger could have stolen the ring, bought it, traded for it. Yet as a child, all Delta had told him of his father said otherwise. *Daddy would never have let the ring from his hand. Only if he was dead would it have fallen into someone else's possession. Only if he was dead.*

Valentine gestured at the Trading Post. Half a dozen men lounged on the porch. They sipped cola, shared chewing tobacco and swapped stories about the old days. "Be quicker if the boys helped look."

Lafette shook his head sternly. "They don't need to know Shadow Mountain business." He glowered when Frank Devery and Arlis McKinsey jumped from the porch and headed toward them. Lafette turned away. "Ain't told 'em, have you?"

Valentine's eyes narrowed as he stared over Lafette's shoulder. "Didn't Arlis shoot a man over in Pennington Gap?" He bit his bottom lip. "Damn." His right eye twitched and his shoulders tensed.

Lafette turned and faced the two men. They walked slowly as if each step were a calculated move and held their arms away from their sides as if expecting they might have to move quickly. Lafette flicked Valentine a glance. Trouble.

"You, Tolliver." Frank's rolled his sleeves around his elbows. Dark rings stained the armpits.

Sweat rolled down Lafette's chest, tickling his muscles. "Me and Valentine's occupied, Frank."

"You'ins probably busy with another little con game." Arlis smirked and winked.

A blade of resentment shot up Lafette's back. "Got something to say, spit it out." He tensed and felt his pistol pressing on his spine, tucked firmly into his pants for the unarmed look he preferred, unlike Valentine whose gun was worn in front against his hip.

"Figured some knavery going on." Frank's hands anchored on his hips, one leg stiff, the other bent at the knee. His boot heel pawed the ground like a horse. Eyes weighed on the pearl-handled pistol he'd lost in the poker game.

Valentine shifted, angling sharply toward both men. That pistol was held against his leg by a leather holster he'd made especially to show off the handle. "Think twice, Frank."

Snow-white fog raced swiftly over the Kentucky mountains. In a few minutes it would reach the Tennessee hills and cascade onto this side of Shadow Mountain. The day would turn cold. An orange-breasted bird batted its wings against a maple's leaves. A fat gray cat sharpened its claws on a cedar log. The remaining men on the trading post's porch disappeared into the store.

The heaviness in Lafette's shoulders spread to his neck. The fog swept in, running past them like a flooded creek. His ears popped from the pressure. His mind was a cauldron of confusion and he couldn't see a way out.

"That's my pearl-handled gun you got." Frank pointed at Valentine's leg.

Lafette's knees quivered. "You're running off at the mouth, Frank."

"You'ins cheated me." Frank cocked his head and his left eye narrowed. "Me and Arlis figured out how you two work together."

"Arlis wasn't even there," Lafette said.

"I want my gun back." Frank held out his open hand. "Unless you want to take on every Devery in these mountains."

"You sorry skunk." Lafette and Valentine shifted shoulder to shoulder, shadows of one another.

"No need to get upset." Valentine motioned with a hand. "Frank can have his gun." He untied one leather straps, unholstered the pistol and held it out for Frank to take.

Frank stepped forward and reached for the pistol. Just as his hand crossed over it, Lafette whipped out his own pistol and pointed it at Frank's head.

"Go ahead," Lafette said, "let's see you take Valentine's gun."

Frank's brown eyes looked as muddy as a flooded stream, the pupils barely pin points. His hand froze just above the pearl handle, fingers trembling slightly.

Arlis shoved Valentine sideways into Lafette, and the gun fired. Frank fell. Blood spurted from his neck. Arlis drew a gun and pulled the trigger the same instant Valentine shot him in the chest. A bullet from Arlis' gun slammed into Lafette's shoulder, and he dropped to his knees clutching the wound, blood squirting between his fingers.

" 'Fate!" Valentine yelled. He dragged Lafette toward his horse, shoved him onto its back, and scrambled up himself. Desperately snatching for the reins, he kicked the horse's sides, and galloped away.

They stopped on an eastern ridge of Shadow Mountain. Valentine shaded his eyes and stared downhill, past the Elisha Tree to people at the trading post running every direction. He slid off the horse, pulled Lafette to the ground and yanked open his shirt.

"Can't feel nothing," Lafette groaned.

"Shoulder's bleeding. Bullet went through." Valentine tore strips from his own shirt and tied them over the wound. "Gotta stop the bleeding."

"Don't hurt." Lafette pulled away from him.

"You're losing blood!"

"I said it don't hurt!"

They drew back from each other and stood like perched eagles scouring the area around the Trading Post. Men came out and covered both the bodies. Two others mounted horses and rode off. A few minutes later the same two came back with three more men. Frank's or Arlis' kin, Lafette realized. The terror in Frank's eyes as he'd fallen to the ground, knowing he'd been fatally shot, gripped Lafette as if the mortal wound had been his own. Today all he'd wanted to do was find his father.

"Don't think about 'em." Valentine stared at the ground. "Don't think about 'em."

"We killed 'em," Lafette said. The tremor in his own voice panicked him.

"You're shivering. Gotta get you home."

"Bleeding's stopped," Lafette mumbled, unsure if it was true but needing to hide his pain. He'd always believed it wouldn't bother him to kill a man if forced into it, but he could hardly stand to think that Frank and Arlis were dead. Shot. Murdered, some would say. He swallowed hard, his head aching more than his wound.

In the seconds of a breath, Shadow Mountain now held no excitement or beauty for him, half barren, half reclaimed with trees turning every shade of red, orange, and yellow. His sight was not focused on the Trading Post, but on the trunk of the Elisha Tree and the people there—a man and a woman. Two figures lay on the ground, one on top of the other. He pressed his hand against his stomach, and made a fist, then slowly opened it one finger at a time. His insides churned. The blond woman was no doubt his mother. Air caught in his throat. He wanted to spit up. "I can get home by myself."

"I'll take you home." Valentine stepped up beside him.

"No, don't want you on the mountain now."

Valentine followed his gaze. He must be seeing 'em, Lafette thought and burned with shame.

"I'll talk to Daddy," Valentine said hesitantly, unable to look him in the eye. "He'll know what we should do. Deverys got lots of kin. We got to be ready."

The wind blew in a dense fog. Lafette nodded for him to go.

"It'll be okay." Valentine turned to look at him. "Daddy'll make it right."

Lafette watched the Elisha Tree as the entwined bodies pulled apart. Delta held the man's hand. Lafette winced. "Henry Kingsley," he said, "Figured you to be a sorry rascal and I was right." Fathers made the world safe for their sons. Why wasn't his father here? In a sudden burst of feeling he swore, "I hate you, Arn Marlon. You should be here with me." Grief competed with the burning shoulder wound. He wiped his eyes and held his breath until the anger passed.

Reluctantly he looked again at Delta and Henry. Something about them was wrong. Henry stood taller, broader-shouldered, sporting grayish, curly hair. Lafette squinted and held a hand over his forehead to block the sun. The man—not Henry Kingsley at all—it was Arn! His father and his mother together!

℣ 40 ℣

LAFETTE PULLED HIMSELF onto the horse. With one hand he jerked the reins and headed for the Elisha Tree. The jarring mountain ride brought agony to his bloody shoulder. It pulsed like no pain he'd ever known. He clenched that arm tight against his chest, steering the horse with the other. His head felt twice its size and the terrain took on a sharp, crisp look. It didn't matter how much his body hurt or the blood he lost, he had to get to his father. What he'd wished for his entire life was about to come true.

The horse jumped the creek, reared, and Lafette tumbled backwards. The taste of dirt spread through his mouth and a painful explosion racked his shoulder. He gritted his teeth and twisted around on his knees. Delta stared at him as if he were a stranger.

Arn leaned over the water, splashing his face. Lafette leapt up and sprinted toward him. "See, Momma! I told you Daddy was alive." Arn stood and turned around. But it wasn't Arn. It was Henry—water dripping down his pale, lean face, shirt unbuttoned to the waist.

"Noooo!" he yelled.

"Lafette, you're bleeding!" Delta covered her mouth with a hand.

The bandage Valentine had fashioned from his own shirt was spongy with blood. Lafette sputtered, his throat tightening. "How could you whore-off with that man?"

Delta's eyes flashed, the green color brilliant around the brown iris. "I'll ask the questions." She raised her hand, circling it around his shoulder. "This is Valentine Tolliver's doing."

Lafette stared back, confounded. In that way of hers, she had divined his actions and he hated it when she slid through his mind like a lizard, making off with his innermost thoughts. He huffed an angry breath and stepped back from them. His face burned hotly, vision distorted as if he were under water.

"What happened, Lafette?" Henry stared at him like a judge. Lafette stepped further away and Henry took a stronger tone. "We can't help you, son, if you don't tell us the truth."

His stooped body, shrunken and withered, swayed like a fragile fall leaf. How could I mistake him for Daddy? Lafette wondered. It didn't seem possible. He'd been so sure Henry had been Arn. "Did you run Daddy off?"

"Your pistol's gone," Delta said, staring at his shoulder. "You've been shot." Terror flooded her voice.

He backed away as they circled him like a sick, caged animal. They'd stepped apart, each trying to come up beside him. "I ain't a dog you can command to do tricks!" His shoulder throbbed. Staring at his mother and Henry, he saw them in a new light. They were as dangerous as Arlis and Frank. They wanted him off the mountain as much as they wanted his father never to return. His eyesight darkened for a second. Blood snaked down his arm, dripped off his fingertips and spattered the ground. "Neither of you's gonna tell me what to do again!"

Lafette leaped into the creek, splashing to the other side and plunged through a thick fern bed. Henry's horse bolted, causing his own steed to rear and gallop off. Only Ole Sal calmly maneuvered away from the disruption. Lafette ran, ignoring the sharp jabs in his shoulder. His body broke out in sweat. His forehead burned with fever.

He followed the creek, climbing the rocks as if he didn't feel the throbbing pain. Stumbling through the water to Kate Huston's land, he waded across her bathing pond. Her cabin had fallen to shambles. A pig lay inside a pen, its carcass only bones and leathered skin.

Lafette leaned over scraggly weeds tangled at the pond's edge. Water spiders glided gracefully across the surface and mist rose up like steam. He tossed a pebble into the pond and watched the spiders ride the ripples. As the waves subsided, he stared into his reflected eyes. Pussy willows and cane shafts darted up behind his head like a spiky crown. He cupped a hand and splashed water on his lips.

When the pond settled, his reflection had changed. Weeds behind him parted and slowly, an image formed: almond-shaped eyes blinked, a grin bared long, sharp fangs, two pointed ears spread sideways. The panther smelled his blood.

Lafette held himself still as a dead man, He'd never seen a panther this close and thought wildly that they'd all been killed off in these parts. If it sprang, he'd rush forward into the pond. Maybe it wouldn't follow him into the water. He prayed there were no young cubs nearby. That would change every reaction he could expect from the cat. Against his common sense he inched around for a better look. *Make a big noise. Scare it away.*

A throaty purr thickened into a growl. He swung up, ready for the pounce.

Instead, he stared up at the figure of his father. Arn stood on the hill above. He stepped back into the shadows, his black coat blowing in the wind, curly hair shooting out every direction beneath a weathered black hat.

Lafette's muscles petrified like ancient wood. His mouth dropped open. At first he couldn't speak, but a volcanic tremble grew deep inside him and burst through with a murderous violence. "Why didn't you come? Why didn't you stay? You been here the whole time!"

He raced toward Arn, smashing down thick cane and briar patches, intending to tackle him to the ground, to kill him, or at least beat the tar out of him. *Drag the bastard to the mountaintop. Make him account for everything. Arn Marlon would apologize to Delta for deserting her; for not being a husband... or a father.* When he reached the hilltop, there was only a tree. Arn had vanished into the mist. Lafette squinted, peering ahead. A swish of color, the dark patch of his coat, and Lafette gave chase, hollering after the man. "Damn you! Talk to me!"

No answer returned.

On the far side of the mountain, Lafette quit running. He panted, shaking, realizing his father knew the mountain as well or better than he. Angrily Lafette held one hand to his aching shoulder and leaned against an oak tree to catch his breath. His feverish eyesight made the forest a blur. He focused only on Arn, who stayed ahead, always out of reach. They had come to what was once the dark side of the mountain.

Arn rested against a twisted maze of rotting Tyme limbs. Where he stood looked familiar and Lafette tried to place it in his memory. He looked up at stars, barely showing in the evening sky: Orion's bow, Mars, the Dipper. That was it! Arn stood at the end of the tunnel where he and Valentine had searched for Swift's Silver and fallen into the snake pit when they were boys. The years had worn it away, making it look like a deserted beehive. It smelled of stinking, rancid insect larva. The back end was torn open as if a great beast had broken through. And there he stood. Arn Marlon… the snake pit behind him, dusk hiding him in a curtain of darkness.

Between sharp throbs in his shoulder, Lafette limped toward his father. He reached out to touch him, then pulled back when he saw Arn's eyebrows like sharp peaks over his blue eyes streaked with yellow in a starburst pattern. The sight unnerved him but he forced himself to speak. "Daddy, come home. Momma needs you. Don't run from me. Don't fight me."

Arn raised both arms and pulled the missing Tyme cane from a lattice of branches. He hooked the end into the dried-out limbs forming the tunnel ceiling and shook them furiously. A swarm of June bugs pelted Lafette. He batted his hands at the insects, protecting his eyes. "Daddy, please. I don't hate you. Please come home." He stepped forward, shielding his face, the June bugs' drone loud as a choir. Stubbornly he pushed forward, staring at his father through the black curtain of insects flying at him.

Arn's hair turned white, his skin wrinkled like dried fruit, blue eyes still and empty. Lafette reached out, wrapped a hand around Arn's neck and pulled him into his arms. The June bugs disappeared. "It's me, Daddy. I've wanted to know you for so long." He hugged his father so tightly that he seemed to melt into him. "Don't go away again, Daddy." He sobbed like a child on his father's shoulder.

Although Arn remained still, heat burned between them like a fire scorching their shirts and struggling within their chests. Lafette felt it so clearly, he could have warmed his hands by it. He hugged his father even more tightly. Then came a gesture he'd longed for his entire life: his father wrapped his arms around him.

The musty odor of Arn's shirt filled his nostrils, but it was his father's smell and he didn't care. He was touching his father for the first time he could remember; the man whose seed created him; the man who loved him; the man who'd finally come back.

Lafette loosened his grip on Arn's shoulders. "I'll take you to Momma. I'll take you, now. Please Daddy, come home with me." His father's body hung on him for support. Lafette looked into Arn's face and found that he was staring at a skull—empty eye sockets, gaping mouth with square, brown teeth, grinning at him.

The skeleton and clothes crumbled, falling to his feet in a pile of bones. Lafette stared into the murk of the snake pit. "My father... my father... my father..." he repeated again and again, his voice rising. A silver ring shone on the skeleton's left hand—the right hand clutched a yellowed, rotting paper. Even in the dim light, Lafette could make out the letters, *Swift's Silver Mine Map*.

"Daddy!"

♆ 41 ♆

BLOOD AND BROKEN foliage marked Lafette's trail. Easy as it was to follow, by the time Henry and Delta reached the opposite side of the mountain, she nursed thorn scratches on both arms and he had fallen twice while steadying Ole Sal on the rocky, uneven land.

"So much blood," Delta said, trying to keep calm. "How does he keep going?"

"It's like he's chasing something and not giving in to it."

"No," she said to mislead Henry. "He's hiding from whoever shot him." She couldn't forget the way Lafette had called out for his father as if Arn stood before him. Her son's face had twisted with such anguish she didn't know how he could bear it. There was more to this than a bullet wound. She had to find him soon. He'd not survive long with the blood loss and no telling where the desperation of his mind would take him.

Henry helped her down a steep, treacherous embankment. They held to gnarled fern roots that snapped under their weight and made them slide on loose pebbles and dirt. When Ole Sal jumped to the bottom, Henry cursed in frustration.

"Your hand's skinned." She wiped off the embedded pebbles with her dress hem.

He pressed his cheek against hers. For a moment, they rested quietly. "We'll find him," he said.

His assurance calmed her but each time they came upon a red-stained patch of foliage, fright ran through her body like a disease. *This is my child's blood.*

Near the base of the mountain Ole Sal stopped as if propelled backwards. "Listen," Henry said. A faint whisper rose in the air. "Someone singing." He steered the mule toward it, but she balked again. "Come on, Sal!" He kicked her sides.

"That's the Grandley Mill," Delta said, and pointed at the burned ruins. "Take that path around it."

He pulled the reins tightly and bounced his feet into the mule's side. Sal snorted, then leaped forward into the marshy land, not slowing until they were on the opposite side. Delta held her breath the entire time to keep from inhaling cursed air. Quickly she glanced back, hoping no haunts would follow them.

The area ahead had been the land of the Tyme trees in the old days. Now it was clear far as they could see. The singing grew fainter. The male voice crooned again—something familiar, from long ago. "I know that song," she said.

They followed the singing, stopping only to get a fix on the location. "I'm not seeing any blood," Henry said. "That's good."

She wasn't as sure. The melody kept slipping away from her, lost in the mule's clomping. The farther they went, the fainter the voice became. She hummed a few bars then tugged at Henry's sleeve. "It's Lafette." The only other person who knew that tune and those words was Arn Marlon. *It was The Watcher's Song*. The voice sang out:

"Who looks like the devil?
He looks just like me"

She pounded Henry's shoulder, urging him to hurry, afraid of what she would find. The sun dipped low in the sky. If Lafette were alive, it'd be after dark before they could get him home to her medicines. She squirmed impatiently as Henry searched for a trail. A crackling sound beneath Ole Sal's hooves turned out to be the shells of thousands of dead June bugs.

"What the hell?" Henry said, perplexed at such an oddity.

"There!" Delta caught sight of Lafette, jumped off the mule and sprinted toward him. He sat cross-legged in the arched opening of a cave of interlaced branches. His lips moved, barely forming the words. He stared straight ahead and didn't acknowledge her as she ran toward him. He held tightly to a Tyme cane, thumping it against the ground in rhythm to his singing.

"Who looks like the devil?
He looks just like me."

Delta fell on her knees, tenderly touching the bloody cloth around his shoulder. Henry came up behind her, bringing the mule as close as he could. The ground around them was spongy and each step made a ripping sound as if the earth beneath them were tearing apart. Startled she looked up at Henry, unsure what was happening.

"Cave underneath us," he said. "Ground could give way any minute."

She pressed the cloth on Lafette's shoulder. "Somebody's packed the wound with this grit and stopped the bleeding." She rubbed the bloody substance between her fingers, thinking its unfamiliar texture seemed like corn before it had been ground fine.

Henry leaned down beside her as a strong breeze blew dusty sand around them. "It's bone," he said, and sifted his fingers through the mound beside Lafette. Bone fragments speckled it, and when the wind blew again the dust pile evaporated, leaving only a tattered paper somersaulting into the sky.

Lafette's gaze followed the scrap until it disappeared and he laughed as if a joke had been played on him. Yet his features twisted angrily. His teeth clenched.

Delta peered into her son's eyes, whispering the words, "Swift's Silver?" She caressed his cheek then looked to Henry, her worried thoughts broke through to her face.

"He's out of his head," Henry said. "Lost too much blood. I'll get him from behind and you pull."

The ground beneath them swayed like a swinging bridge. Henry got Ole Sal to kneel. They arranged Lafette, one limb at a time, until he slumped forward over the mule's neck. Henry led, stepping gently to test the uncertain ground. Delta stayed beside the mule, silently praying every protection spell she knew to keep them from breaking through and falling into the cave.

One of Ole Sal's hooves caught in the roots and she sank into the ground. Henry tugged the lead line, trying to break free. The frightened mule hawed and whined, wanting to bolt. "Delta!" he hollered. "I got to yank the hoof or she'll break a leg. Come pull the lead line."

Quickly Delta tied Lafette's hands to the saddle with the reins then touched his shoulder, wishing she didn't have to leave his side. She took Henry's place in front of Ole Sal and gently pulled her ear to calm her.

Henry disappeared beneath the mule. She could barely see him sawing at the roots with a pocketknife, and her memory flashed back to him showing her that same blade when he cut Lafette out of the Elisha Tree. Soon Henry stood up and pressed the mule's nose into his neck. He stroked her jaws, calming Ole Sal enough to help her struggle. The hoof came loose from the earth along with a sickening sound of ripping earth. They jumped onto hard ground just as the hole opened into a darkness that fell farther than any of them wanted to see.

Delta trudged on without a backward glance, thinking only of home. By the time they came into sight of the mountaintop, the sky was dark blue and patchy with rain clouds. How Henry got them up the hillside was a feat that amazed her. She stumbled on rocks, scratched her legs on vines, and slipped on moss-covered roots. All she could think was getting Lafette into bed and tending his wound. He remained conscious—a good sign—but did not speak or give any indication of feeling pain. That worried her.

At Cat's Crossroads, Henry put his arm around Delta's shoulders, warming her against the chill that gripped her muscles. Touching her chin, he raised her face to his. "You know whose bones those were, don't you?"

She nodded, biting her lower lip and hoping that the darkness hid her face. Strain showed in the deep wrinkles around Henry's eyes. Dark half circles bruised the skin under the bloodshot whites. She would not have made it without him. Lafette would have died. She might have fallen through to the cave and died as well. How could she let Henry go? She needed him here. She needed him as she'd never needed another human being in her life. She wrapped her arms around his neck, trying to bite back words she could not keep from passing through her lips. "Henry," she said, unable to stop the quivering in her voice. "Don't leave. Please don't leave."

He pulled her close and held her gently, then drew back and looked down into her eyes. His serious expression seemed to indicate a danger he wanted to hide from her. "There's torch light up ahead. Somebody's waiting for us at the house." He reached down and took her hand. "You stay here. I'll go see if it's safe."

He started to walk away, but she called out after him. "We'll go together. All three of us. Come what may." That was the least she could do: pledge their lives beside his. She owed him that much.

Four horsemen, two holding torches, waited. Blue stood at attention on the porch ready to attack should the men come any closer. He jumped up and howled as Delta and Henry approached, racing toward them, tail wagging in excitement that they were home.

One of the horsemen pulled out ahead. Delta put her face close to Lafette's. He opened his eyes and focused on her. "Don't you say nothing," she whispered and placed his hand on a rifle strapped to the saddle. Carefully she angled Ole Sal sideways so no one could see it.

The man stepping out was Jedidiah Tolliver. Valentine straddled the end horse, hunched up like a beaten puppy. He leaned sideways and anchored his torch into the fork of a dogwood tree. Jedidiah's black handlebar mustache emphasized the frown on his face. As they approached, he pointed to a lanky, blond man holding the other torch, and a heavyset woman, her hair cut short as his and wearing a man's pants and shirt. She sat high in the saddle, proud as a vindictive queen.

Delta whispered to Henry. "You know Nadine McKinsey and Archie Devery?"

Henry nodded and Delta stepped up beside him. "Jedidiah bought most of the Kingsley land," Henry said, "paid a fair price even though he might've got it for less. He's a good friend."

Nadine and Archie cast glances at one another, and she slipped one hand under a coat draped over her lap.

Delta was relieved that Henry was comfortable with Jedidiah Tolliver. She'd only heard Lafette's stories about a fierce man who tolerated no nonsense and often wondered if it was only Lafette's imagination or Valentine exaggerating his father's menace. But Nadine and Archie, this brother and sister who passed secretive looks, worried her. She knew them the way she knew the lay of her land. They were the kind of back mountain people who lived by the law of revenge, as cunning as foxes, fiercely loyal to kin, and always ready for a fight. She could smell the sweat on them and memories of her childhood flooded up within her like sour boiling soup.

"Remember that land down by Frog Creek?" Jedidiah asked, then continued before Henry could answer. "I gave it to Nadine and Archie."

"I see," Henry said.

"Seems our boys got into a ruckus with their boys, Frank Devery and Arlis McKinsey. Both dead." His lower lip pushed into his mustache and he spat some chewing tobacco to one side. "I don't have the son to waste." He looked past Henry at Delta. "Figure you probably don't either."

She stepped forward. "Lafette's near dead hisself! You can see that." She pointed at him, still slumped over the horse.

"That's right, Daddy," Valentine ventured. "They started it! They caused it all!"

"Shut up!" Jedidiah's booming voice brought stillness to the air like the pause that occurred after thunder. Valentine stared at his horse, not risking a glance at his father as if afraid he'd be struck.

Delta recognized the posture—one she'd assumed many times with her own father and all at once she knew all Lafette had said about Jedidiah was true. A cricket dared to make a sound, then a bullfrog. The evening air chilled and she decided to bring this business to a close so she could get Lafette inside. She touched Henry's arm and whispered, "They want us to buy Lafette's life?"

"Would ye expect any less?" Archie leaned forward. "We could've come after him and finished him off." He pointed to Lafette as if he were a dying animal.

"Equal terms is equal terms," she said. "If it was a fair fight, and the Deverys lost, then there's no quarrel." She didn't like their looks. They were too much her father's people, too ready for a fight, always owed and never owing. There would be an easy justification for the way they'd been wronged by an innocent bystander, then a demand for settlement or else—all before they even bothered to mourn their dead.

Nadine pulled on her brother's arm. "Let me handle the bitch."

Delta snapped at her, "Mess with me, woman, and you'll have more trouble than you *can* handle!"

Nadine leaned back, one finger curling her brown hair behind her ear. As she spoke, her missing side teeth made her face look lopsided. "Think I don't recognize ye? You figure you've bettered yourself, living way up here like a Jesus on a cross, 'spectin' people to pay ye homage like in the old days." She cocked her head to one side and gave a hen-like cackle. "Part Devery, ain't ye? Yer one of our brood."

Henry touched Delta's cheek as if to say, trust me. "All I got left is the house," he told Archie. "If that ain't to your liking, I can sell it and give you the cash."

"No, wait!" Delta rushed into the house and ran her hands along the top kitchen shelf. She knocked over a jar, spilling strawberry leaves onto the floor before finding the box with King Kingsley's bad luck coin. She'd sealed it in magically protected tobacco and kept it in the farthest corner to isolate its power. Gripping the box, she stared out the window at the three Tyme plants growing among Arn's rocks. Their silvery leaves reflected the torchlight's orange haze. "Arn, am I doing the right thing?" she whispered. She'd never purposely visited evil on another being. Every fight with Kate had been to protect herself. King Kingsley had hated her because she wouldn't bend to his will. If she passed this coin to the Deverys, they'd be wiped out.

Outside, she opened the box and the silver coin glinted in the dark tobacco leaves. "This," she asked hesitantly, "will this do?"

Delta offered the coin to Archie, and he passed the torch to Nadine so he could inspect the coin. As he held it between them, their eyes grew wide. Nadine nodded to Archie, turned the horse's reins as he dropped the coin in his shirt pocket and followed her. She glanced back with a smile on her toothless side. "Me and you will meet again," she told Delta. "Count on it." Then holding out a torch, she and her brother disappeared over the mountainside.

The instant they were gone Valentine jumped off his horse and ran to Lafette, asking frantically, "Buddy, ye all right? Ye all right?"

Lafette managed to lift his head and nod. Valentine saw the rifle, blinked and looked over at Delta with the respect he might have shown another man. She stared hard at him, a warning to say nothing about the gun. He absorbed her meaning, then said in a pleading tone, "Daddy, I want to stay with Lafette. Gotta make sure he's all right."

Jedidiah inhaled a deep breath then took a roll of bills from his pocket and handed them down to Valentine. "One week," he said. "Then get yourself over to Quinntown." He looked at Henry. "I don't trust the Deverys. You might think on sending the boy away soon as he can travel."

"We'll think on it," Henry said, and shook his hand.

Jedidiah focused on Delta and paused as if about to speak. His eyes flitting over her face in a confused but respectful regard. Finally, taking the torch, he started down the mountain. "One week," he called back to Valentine. "No longer."

ᐯ 42 ᐯ

VALENTINE CARRIED LAFETTE inside and stood back with Henry as Delta dressed the shoulder wound. The bone meal packing held down the swelling, and Delta had Henry bring willow bark, tobacco, and boiling water for a new poultice. Valentine went out, returned with the rifle and whispered to her, "I'll stand guard on the porch."

Delta saw the little boy in him, scared to the bone, wishing he could take back all that he'd done. His eyes were wide as a catfish's and his bottom lip trembled. "If he gets through tonight," she said, "he'll live. I know you're wondering."

Tears spilled down Valentine's cheeks. He grunted, holding in his emotions, then turned away to stand guard.

Henry returned with fresh cloth and herbs, and together, they mixed the poultice. The room filled with a tobacco scent mixed with metallic blood. Even the breeze from the open window did not freshen the odors. Delta packed the herbal mixture around the bullet hole, and Lafette tossed in pain until the sheeting dripped with his sweat. She asked Henry to bring crushed honeysuckle root then dipped a cloth into hot water.

"I'm gonna change the poultice again," she said, pulling off a layer of saturated cloth. "The strength's gone out of this'n." Lafette wrenched away from her but Henry held his head against the pillow. She stripped away the cloth, then gasped, "Oh Lord!"

Henry struggled with Lafette and gave her a questioning stare.

"The entrance wound's infected," she said. "I got to cut out around it." The shoulder skin was red-streaked and crusty with yellowish pus. "If the infection gets in his blood, he won't make it." Her throat filled with anguish and her head spun with a dizzying heat stronger than staring into a midsummer sun.

"Do what you have to, Delta." Henry crawled onto the bed, dragged one leg over Lafette's and pressed him into the mattress by lying partially on top of him. "I'm ready."

She burned her sharpest fish knife in the bedside lantern's flame. When she looked at Henry, he nodded. Her hand trembled. Henry's gaze was strong and steady, and gave her courage. She sat on Lafette's left arm and cut his shoulder.

His piercing scream shook the house. Henry held Lafette's convulsing body as she cut away the infected skin. Outside, Valentine sobbed.

Within minutes, Lafette passed out and a chill spread through his body. Delta poured Aunt Verdie's distilled herbs over the wound, redressed it with a fresh poultice, and pressed more medicine between his lips. "Have to wait now." Her muscles ached with weariness and she wanted to cry, but each time Henry looked at her, she drew on his strength. They took turns wiping sweat from Lafette's brow, and each held his hand and spoke to him in gentle words of things they would do when he was better.

The night stretched on. They clasped their hands over the young man as he fought with death, watching each breath. The intimacy the three shared was thick as fog, as dense as hope itself. They were beyond prayer and in the hands of a greater power.

In the early morning hours, Henry broke the silence, "Deverys might come back."

"They won't be back," Delta said. Haltingly she admitted, "They got... Polly Huston's bad luck coin." She glanced over to see if he would challenge her. He did not.

The crickets hushed, night birds ceased their calling to one another, frogs stopped croaking. Blue curled himself at Delta's feet, staying in the room as if he were a blood relative. Several hours later dawn broke, coloring the sky in a pinkish glow. A redbird lit on the window and sang its song. Henry and Delta held still, feeling blessed, a smile their only movement. The bird flew to a nearby tree when Blue rose up to stretch. Lafette was still breathing—deep and regular.

"My grandmother's a Devery," she said. "Me and Lafette... we are better than them. We made ourselves so. No matter what the means, we made ourselves better than them."

"No need to explain to me," Henry said.

"Do I need to explain how I come by your Daddy's silver coin?"

"Silver ain't gold. It's moonlight and deception. Best it be on its way." He came around to her, wrapping his arms around her shoulder while they stared down at Lafette. "Eight years ago, I adopted this boy. He's our son, Delta. And he's alive by whatever means we have. He's our son. That's all I need to know."

Part III

∞ Nine Months Later ∞

♆ 43 ♆

SLUMBERING UNDER THE backyard willow tree, Lafette swatted a bumblebee buzzing around his nose. Raising his head, he looked around. Henry gathered corn in the garden. Delta's white cat balanced on a fence post spying on the chickens, and a gentle honeybee hum made the afternoon seem tender. He closed his eyes, savoring the soft blueness behind his lids. The scar on his shoulder itched but he ignored it, letting the irritation fade on its own.

Lithesome willow limbs swayed above him, yet no breeze blew. He cracked open one eye. The sickle-shaped leaves swished back and forth. The ground beneath him trembled. He bolted upright as the earth continued to quake. Clutching fistfuls of grass, he steadied himself against the tree trunk until he could stand.

The branch movement slowed to a gentle quiver. Moist July air hung heavy as the shaking ceased. The forest grew as silent as when a tenderfoot hunter alerted wildlife. Lafette's heart raced to keep pace with a shallow pant. He stilled himself to sense what was about him. Nothing. Up the hill Henry still pulled corn. His stooped body faced the sun and he worked steadily as if he'd not noticed the earth shaking.

Lafette thought he'd suffered one of the dizzy spells that had plagued him in the weeks after he'd started to recover. The world around him danced in a sparkling purple and blue tornado, and he would remember nothing until he came to himself, usually with a worried Delta and Henry pressing him against the cold ground, wiping spittle from his mouth and steadying his flailing arms and legs. He hadn't had a bout in two months and held out his hand to see if his body was trembling.

His hand held firm, feet solid on the ground. The dirt and rocks had shaken as if thunder were bubbling from the soil. *Earthquake.* He couldn't form the word and put a hand against his chest to measure the pace of his heart. Momma! he thought but still could not speak.

Taking long strides toward the house, he was careful not to jar his shoulder. The back door hung open, gently tapping against its frame. *Momma?* Again, unable to speak. He leaped onto the porch and rushed through the kitchen.

Delta rested in the blue velvet chair, hands tenderly massaging her swollen stomach over a yellow shift that she probably hadn't worn since she'd carried him in her womb. Beside her, drawings lay scattered. She filled all the paper she could get her hands on. The last few portraits were of Lafette as a little boy. She called to him when he turned away. "You're not bothering us." She twirled her hand for him to sit. "You've been such a help around here," she added, rubbing his hand. "Don't know what we'd've done without you."

Lafette knelt beside the chair, balancing on his knees. He could barely look at his mother, her arms and legs grotesquely swollen, face blotchy, lips so pale he could hardly distinguish them from her face. She concentrated all her energy on the unborn infant. Resentment surged each time he recalled seeing her by the Elisha Tree with Henry, and now, she was pregnant with his child.

Lafette bunched his fists and shook them, indicating the quaking earth. Delta's eyes narrowed questioningly. He pointed at a walnut basket overturned on the hearth, nuts tumbled out across the floor.

Delta sighed a lilting laugh, arched her back and rubbed her hands together as if warming them. "Wampus footsteps, honey. His comings and goings jar the earth. You needn't worry, he's practicing closing his door. Not much room for him in this world anymore." She bit her lip, then looked up into his eyes. "Time's come for some energies to journey on. Others will be born. I'm only sad that I won't live to see how they make themselves known."

Lafette picked up the basket and avoided looking at her. *Wampus footsteps*. Pregnancy was making her crazy. He'd seen it when he opened his eyes from his sickness. Her face had been fuzzy, although he'd made out Henry standing behind her as distinct as a portrait. It was as if she faded in and out of the world and it took several minutes before he could see her clearly. She'd insisted he stay in bed even though his shoulder had healed and only pained him when he lifted beyond his strength.

She and Henry took turns sitting beside him, bringing his food, changing bandages that didn't need changing, and talking about how happy they were that he was better. They'd fortify the mountaintop, making entry impossible for the uninvited. They'd build him a cabin where he could live undisturbed, where one day he might bring a wife. Finally, Delta asked him if Henry's talk interested him. He'd discovered that he couldn't answer, but for many months told himself that he had no interest in speaking.

A swirl of confusion had prevented his feelings from gelling. As he watched Henry and Delta, they changed, and sometimes he had to look at them for several seconds before recognizing them. She grew big with her child and moved like a cow in too small a stall. Her angled face rounded. Henry was the opposite. His hair had faded to white and had thinned until his scalp showed. His hooded eyes hid the brilliant brown irises, and his skin took on a yellowish cast. Lafette was unsure if he imagined these changes or not.

Finally, he tried to speak, but when he opened his mouth no words formed. He tried again when he was alone, unsuccessfully pressing his lips into vowels. His throat would not release sound.

He stepped from bed a month later, head inches from the ceiling. His muscles were hard and had not atrophied. Except for his eyesight that still focused better on the distant, he felt accustomed to his body. Hearing his movements, Delta and Henry had hurried into the room. They'd looked upon him, shocked by his stature. Her face had brightened with pride and she placed his hand on her stomach, beginning to swell with Henry's child. Lafette realized then it was good that he couldn't speak, for all he felt toward this baby was resentment.

"It's your Daddy's doin'," she had whispered to him when they were alone. "Arn helped me conceive this child."

Lafette had barely been able to look at her when she spoke Arn's name. His father was dead. Didn't she know that? She believed a dead man could come back and affect the living.

Arn's name evoked fury in him that made him hate the baby and wish it would never take a breath on this earth, then afterward, consumed with guilt, he hid from sight.

Now, within days of the birth, he worried endlessly that his mother's legs would give out and she'd fall. If her food went uneaten, he'd sit with her until every morsel was swallowed. He rarely ventured beyond hollering distance. Every waking hour revolved around Delta. But he could not place an importance on the child she carried.

"Wampus footsteps, honey," Delta told him. Lafette turned to her. "Must mean your daddy's passing over this way. Remember how he used to say the Wampus had to be called to stop the thundering storm." She smiled almost as if she wanted to provoke a reaction from him. "He and the beast had a... complicated relationship." The skin under her eyes showed its purplish tint when she looked into the sunlight pouring through the open front door. "Still don't remember what happened to you on the dark side of the mountain?"

Better not to upset her, he thought. She'll only put a foolish magic meaning to it. He hadn't been to the dark side of the mountain in years. She continued to ask him the same question: Did he remember? Did he remember? The more she asked, the more he told himself not to speak. He couldn't fathom what she wanted from him.

"Lafette," she called to him softly. "Kate Huston once told me that she gave Arn the silver he needed." She hesitated, watching him without looking directly at him. "Only thing I can figure for Arn to go on a fool's journey looking for silver is he must have had reason." She blew out a controlled breath. "You were that reason, baby."

Lafette took hard steps toward the door but he couldn't leave. His limbs felt tied to the walls.

"Your daddy's greatest strength was his greatest weakness."

Lafette turned toward her as if to ask what she meant.

"He loved his family. He would do anything for them." She bit her bottom lip. "Kate's dead. Your daddy's dead. I can only imagine it now. She held it over him. That silver. He had the power. She had the silver. Only way to get his freedom was to find the treasure himself. Only reason to hunt it out was for us. Don't you see, son. He loved us that much. He wanted to be free of Kate and maybe even this mountain. But always remember, 'Fate. Sliver ain't gold. It's moonlight and deception."

Lafette exhaled a shivery breath. His mind spun with her words, images he didn't understand. On one hand the past was about greed; on the other she proclaimed magic. The two reasons disjointed his mind. All he could do to hold to his sanity was store the thoughts in a deep, dark place of himself where he vowed never to venture again.

"Your father knew what I didn't, what Kate refused to acknowledge. It's time for the Watcher to go out into the world. Living in the world requires different skills, a different currency. He thought it was silver. I think it's, well, a kind of knowing, knowledge, something no man can ever take away." Her wrist bone cracked as she repositioned herself. "Come over here, Lafette."

He knelt beside the chair and rested one hand above her knee. His fingers sank into her swollen, watery muscles and he jerked back as if stung by a bee.

The lines on her forehead curved down around her temples and deepened as she spoke, "I don't feel bad, honey." She reached out and caressed his cheek as if to reassure him. "I got you. I got Henry. I got the baby. I even got ole Blue, there." She pointed at the dog spread across the front doorway, tongue hanging out as he panted to cool himself. The fur around his eyes had turned white and his skin hung loosely on his bones. "Maybe we should get a woman to stay up here. Rosy or Nancy would come if I asked. Ain't seen Rosy since I made her that love potion. Reckon she's all right?"

Lafette bit his tongue and nodded his head, but knew he couldn't bring Rosy up here. If Delta ever found out she sold herself, it might affect his mother's health.

"Nancy'll want some time away from her young'un. You could go down," Delta paused, then shook her head. "No, no need to set them at hazard." She closed her eyes, and softly rubbed her stomach. Humming that same childhood tune she'd begun to hum nine months ago, then she softly sang, "Who looks like the devil? He looks just like me."

Again Lafette pushed away the feeling that she was provoking him in some way. *Set them at hazard*, he repeated her words to himself. He went into the kitchen. There was some danger, he decided, a danger she hid from him. Pinto beans simmered on the stove and the salty aroma made his mouth water. Sifted meal dusted the counter with a yellowish film. *What did she mean, hazard? The Devery clan?* He exhaled a breath that tasted sour in his mouth. Had to be the Deverys. He'd brought this trouble upon them.

He dipped a drink from the water bucket. It was lukewarm and he thought about going out to the newly formed streams that meandered through the black rocks. It made the water especially cool to the taste, but each time he'd drunk from it, his dreams were troubled with images of the living and the dead. He chuckled to himself, wondering: Was this the famous magic of the mountain? Clearly, the rocks infused the water with some substance that evoked wildness of the mind. Was this how people saw the dragon? Another trick, he thought. All trickery.

At times he longed to escape the stuffy house and the sight of his mother. He'd rarely paid any mind to pregnant women. Delta's pregnancy worried him endlessly. He monitored her every symptom, afraid any moment the baby might arrive. She seemed unable to drink enough water even though he hauled bucket after bucket up from the creek. She ate without end for weeks, only to fast afterwards. At night, she went out alone to the rocks of Arn's Volcano. He didn't know what she did there and didn't want to know. Most of all, he'd be relieved when this was over.

Henry bounced a basket of corn on the porch. He layered the top ears so the yellow corn silk was smooth as combed hair. "Your Momma's hair used to be this color," he said to Lafette. "You remember that far back?"

Lafette nodded that he did, annoyed all the same by the question. Henry watched him as if wanting something. Lafette stared at the ground, smoothing his boot over pebbled dirt and crushing it into a fine dust. He caught Henry's eye, pointed to the cornfield then patted his chest.

"Naw," Henry said, "it's easy enough work. Better you to do the heavy chores." He motioned Lafette to follow him into the corn patch. "Good job on the winter wood. No need to plow that far field. I ain't got many pumpkin seeds this year."

Lafette figured Henry didn't want Delta to hear whatever he was about to say; his nervous rambling was like a child's stammer. He followed Henry, whose limp was worse than usual and he had to work his hip upward, almost swinging his leg to be able to walk.

"Arm ain't troublin' you, is it?"

Lafette shook his head no.

"Can't get down the mountain this month." Henry rubbed his hip joint and stared at the blue-green mountain range. "Need you to get coffee, sugar, some flour, and your Momma's gonna need material. Get white sheeting and flannel if they have it." His heavy breathing matched the sweat on his brow. "Reckon you can do that?"

Lafette nodded yes, resenting the question even though he knew it wasn't meant to humble him.

Henry took bills from his pocket. "Go to Kentucky. Next month to Tennessee, and after that Virginia." His eyes, dimmed with a yellowish film, darted as he spoke, trying to gauge the extent of Lafette's understanding. "If you see a Devery or even a McKinsey head the other way. Understand, Son?"

Lafette nodded that he understood, hating it when Henry addressed him like a child.

"Your momma thinks a hard time is coming. Something about testing worthiness, a new cycle opening and closing of an old. I'm a mite more practical. Deverys saw what they could get and they'll be back for more."

He played back the fight with Frank and Arlis. Could as easy been me and Valentine layin' dead, he thought. Deverys had no claim to his life and he'd kill anybody declaring otherwise.

Henry nudged his cane in the dirt, unearthing a burlap sack. He tapped what was inside and it made a sharp metallic sound. "My Winchester," he said. "A shotgun's buried in the rear barn stall, a pistol is under the porch steps, another Winchester's tied to a fake wall in the outhouse." Using his boot, he smoothed the planting soil over the rifle. "All armed, ready to go." His lips pressed into a thin line. "Just in case," he added.

Lafette looked away, unable to acknowledge that this

pathetic old man had done all this for his sake. His eyes threatened to water and his nose burned. Garden dust floated in the air and tiny flies soared through the stalks. He swiped at the dust, pretending that it irritated his eyes.

"Deverys lost half their young'uns to pneumonia over the winter," Henry said. "Two families moved North after smallpox hit 'em, but there's still enough around here that'll remember and might come looking for vengeance." He placed a hand on Lafette's shoulder. "Sure wish ye'd say something, Son."

Still unable to look at him, Lafette patted Henry's hand, pressing it until the cold flesh warmed, then stepped away. He wished he could speak to him, but at the same time an aching emptiness swept through him and thoughts would not manifest.

Out near the cliff, a river of grass and dandelions was overtaking Arn's rocks. Lafette perched close to the edge. Blue had followed him and he knelt to pet the old dog's belly. *What are we gonna do, Blue? What are we gonna do?*

Down the slope, acreage flourished with ferns and mountain laurel. Pine trees dotted the area where once had been broken trunks and blasted dirt. Tulip, maple, ash, oak, and black locust sprouted in the old Tyme tree groves. The land sprang to life. Less a towering fortress than in past years, Shadow Mountain had blended with the landscape. Lafette didn't object. The place of his youth had changed, just as clearly as he was different.

He pointed, *Blue, stay here,* then pointed at the house. The dog licked his jowls and seemed to understand. The sun dipped into mid-sky and reflected on a lake, making it look like a mirror dropped into the Kentucky hills. He anticipated the cool night air that would accompany his journey home, and the darkness that would hide him.

He made his way down the cliff, following Tyme Creek to the Elisha Tree. He looked around anyway to ensure he was alone, then reached into the hollow trunk and pulled out a moonshine jar. Valentine met him on nights of full moon, told him outside news and tried to talk him into coming to the Quinntown mine soon as he was able. What was left of the Devery and McKinsey clans never ventured far as Quinntown, Valentine had said. Lafette listened, but some part of his mind kept him from deciding, as if a missing link in his life story kept him from moving forward.

Lafette swallowed a drink, exhaling the burn with a hiss. He cleared his throat. Today, he would say his name. He parted his lips and pushed his tongue against his teeth. His throat strained in a grunt. *Lafette, he thought. Lafette. Say it!* One single word, his name. Then he'd be all right. He repositioned his lips. A sound gurgled, startling him, a sound he couldn't control. "Arn, Arn." He grimaced. If that was the only word he could manage, he'd rather not speak.

My voice, he thought, my voice. He had his mother. He had his mountain. He had Blue. The thought blossomed: *Guess I even have Henry... and that baby.* Perhaps his voice was not such a huge loss. Perhaps being unable to say his name might mean he no longer had to be Lafette. Except for Henry's vigilance about the Deverys, a benevolent tranquility rested on the mountain, a peace he accepted. Tonight, he would sit under the stars, Blue at his side, his mother and Henry in their rocking chairs. He didn't need a voice for this. He was happy. He was simply and truly happy.

♆ 44 ♆

DELTA PEEKED OUT the front door, made sure Lafette and Henry were nowhere in sight, then walked into the yard, waddling from side to side to lessen the strain in her lower back. Chickens scratched in the dirt beside the barn, leaving half-exposed red worms squirming on the ground. Her hogs thrashed in the mud inside a trough. A half dozen fireflies blinked in the wisteria vines dangling from a trellis boxing in the side porch. A soft scratching came from the barn and she realized Henry was cleaning out the stalls. Only the bees hummed, unusually quietly for so warm an evening.

Blue patrolled the mountain edge like a lone sentinel. He twisted his neck upward and howled at the darkening sky. The frantic trills of crickets and katydids continued as she passed. “Odd,” she thought, “like they don’t know I’m here.” A green snake slid through the grass, ignoring her and the dangerous chickens nearby. *Something was coming... but what?*

A gibbous moon hung low, and stars peeked through the blue-gray sky. Venus and Jupiter shone like bright pinpoints and Delta focused on a slender cloud dissipating between them.

The clear night tinged with the heavy moistness of a summer storm. She shivered, unable to shake the worrisome feeling. "Lafette," she called out. No answer. Good, she thought. Henry would be busy in the barn until after nightfall, giving her time to tend to her body without interruption.

Back in the house, she stretched out in her blue velvet chair. From underneath it, she pulled a stalk of Tyme plant. Brown and dry as tobacco, its fragrance gone until she crushed two of the last four leaves between her fingers. The cinnamon aroma rose like fresh flowers. Delta spread the crushed leaves over her stomach, rubbing them into oil. The baby moved, responding to the Tyme leaves. She picked off shreds that hadn't been absorbed into her skin and ate them. The bitter taste numbed her mouth, and for some time after, she experienced the sensation of floating as pinpoints of light flashed wherever she focused.

The cramps began as she swallowed the last bit of leaf. Delta dug her nails into the velvet armrests, gritting her teeth. "Rest, little baby. It'll pass. Tyme leaves'll make you strong. I promise. Little bit at a time. Stronger than all the Watchers before you." The baby calmed and her stomach stilled except for a steady pulse around her belly button.

She lowered her dress and hid the other Tyme leaves under the chair to use just before the birth. The last plant, still growing in the protective rocks of Arn's Volcano, would be saved for the baby. She'd pour the last of the magic into her infant.

Blue howled and Delta went out onto the porch into a purplish dusk. A movement in the trees caught her eye, and she stared steadily until her sight adjusted. Across the yard, Polly Huston crouched down in the ferns, still as an old owl.

A rush of fear spread through Delta, tightening the muscles of her abdomen. The old woman had something in her hands: a round, coarse-looking ball. She tossed it back and forth from her left hand to her right, held it up to the stars, then threw it at the moon. The ball arched and fell to the ground with a thud. A deep contraction spread through Delta's stomach. She puffed out little breaths, afraid to take her eyes off the old woman.

Polly turned in a circle, stamping her feet lightly against the ground. She traced the outline of Delta's body with a forefinger, but did not acknowledge her. Delta rested both hands on her stomach, squeezing them so tight her knuckles ached. Another contraction. She felt about to fall but forced herself to hold together long enough to handle Polly in case she'd led evil this way. She made her way into the yard. Polly's rhythmic dance pulsed like a drumbeat as she gyrated around a small fire. Her gray hair hung in her face, making her look like an ancient, primordial conjurer. "Won't let her hurt you," she told the baby.

Delta realized she'd have to fight her on magical ground and dipped her hands into water pooled in a hollow of Arn's black rock. Bringing the fluid to her lips she sipped. The moisture flowed down her throat in a burning surge.

The ball Polly had thrown glowed like foxfire. The old woman clapped her hands three times. The sound penetrated Delta, making her thoughts a confused mass of violent images as Armageddon played out before her. The inner earth was carpeted in bloody bodies, broken beyond identification. Stones as black as Arn's Volcano gleamed like diamonds and men filled their pockets only to be pulled into the earth by the weight of the rocks they refused to give up. Delta watched a portentous vision of the future, a world her blood-kin would know. Smoky air suffocated her, and she might have fallen dead except for a golden beam penetrating as the sun making its way toward her. A brown-eyed boy offered her his hand and when she clasped it, she could breathe.

Polly cupped both hands around her mouth. "The way is open," she announced. Her voice shivered in the rising wind, blowing hair from her face.

Delta moved forward, ready to shove Polly away and crush a bad omen. The old woman eyed her. The glowing globe on the ground between them dimmed as Delta approached. Polly matched Delta's steps in reverse, both women tense as warriors in a death dance. When Delta reached the ball, Polly disappeared over the mountainside.

Delta stooped down, holding one hand on her back, and picked up the orb. It was string, thicker than sewing thread, too thin to use for tying a package, but it vibrated in her hand.

Chickens fled to their coops and hogs hid in their covered pens. No neighs from the horses or moos from the cow. Henry was nowhere in sight. She was alone. The night sparked with tense electricity and it snapped against her skin. Polly Huston had opened a portal and Delta didn't know if it was for good or evil. Polly still blames me for Kate's death, she decided, that's why she gave me the spell that destroyed the Tyme trees. *This ball has to be destroyed.*

Delta flung the ball into the fire. The end of the string stuck to her hand and the ball exploded into colorful sparks. She pulled the cord off her palm, but it stuck to her other hand. "Stop it!" She wiped her hand on her dress and the string stuck above her stomach. When she wiped it with her arm, it stuck to her again and again, winding around her fingers more tightly as she tried to tear it away. No matter what she did the string clung to her like a tie line meant to lead the lost home.

An indigo flame shot up the cord and struck her skin. Vibrations shocked her body and she scuttled to the creek, plunging into the icy water. As if waking from a dream, her senses cleared. The string had dissolved. Delta returned to the house. Blue shivered on the back porch. He whimpered and flattened his ears. "Come here," she crooned, "Polly's gone. Nobody's left to hurt us." She petted his head, soothing him. He licked her hands. "Good dog," she said, scratching his jowls, then he sat at attention and growled. What had Polly done? What power had she unleashed? A clap of thunder startled her.

"Get inside, Delta," Henry said from behind her. He stood flat against the side of the house, holding a rifle across his chest.

She struggled with the weight of her stomach. Wind rustled the trees and cast shadows in all direction. Henry must've seen Polly, she thought. He knows something's wrong. Fearfully, the baby dragged her down and her water broke. The slippery wetness covered her thighs and her body pulsed with the wild beating of her heart as a panicky reason took hold of her.

Pulling Blue inside the house, she went into the farthest bedroom corner where he'd told her to stay if danger threatened. She wrapped her arms around Blue and prayed that Polly and whatever she'd brought with her had left. A frightening, queasy vibration filled the air. Polly Huston's doing! She'd opened a vortex of magic stronger than Delta had ever known.

As a contraction crescendoed through her body, she breathed through it. What was happening outside the house? Blue licked her leg and remained protectively beside her. She closed her eyes and tried to see into the spirit world. Aligning herself with the vibration, she focused on controlling it. Another contraction made her blood surge and her muscles twang. Her body pressed for attention.

There was movement outside the window, then the vibrant calls of night birds and screech owls. Blue's fur was soft over his loose skin but she felt him tremble, and his fear scared her more than her own imagination. She pressed both hands to her face. Her teeth chattered and she held a hand to her mouth. She gripped her stomach, determined to inhale slow breaths. No harm could come to this baby. This Watcher. How could the mountain allow it? Yet doubt spoke to her as if the ghosts of every Watcher that had ever been stood in the room. *You thought Lafette was the Watcher, and he wasn't! What makes you think this child is the Watcher? What makes you think you're worthy of birthing a Watcher? Why should the mountain protect you?*

Sweat drenched her face and her hair matted against her scalp. She panted through a harsher contraction. "Arn told me," she whispered to her accusers. "I made love to Arn nine months ago. This child's as much his as Henry's." She pictured herself at the Elisha Tree, looking up into Henry's face, but it was Arn staring down at her with as much conviction in his eyes as the final time she'd made love to him. *"You will birth the Watcher," he said, "You will bear his child and be his child."*

Cramps clutched her body, her eyes rolled back and she bit down until her jaw locked. She panted, wishing the darkness would take away her pain. Thunder rumbled outside and a storm threatened to break. Wind whipped around the house so fast the walls creaked. No harm could befall this baby. She had to believe that. But now, all she really had was her faith. "If you're here, Arn," she whispered, "if you're really here, help me. Help me now!"

Blue howled. Webbed lightning flashed, striking the ground just outside the window. White sparks shot off all directions. The mountain lit up as if the moon were bursting from the earth. The baby dropped lower and she couldn't keep from crying out. The window became a flurry of blue sparkling light. The spirits of Elisha Thunderheart, and Kate, and Arn, flew past, the oldest with a white beard that reached his chest, deep-set black eyes underneath bushy eyebrows, a wave of white hair at the crest of his forehead, his skin a warm brown, lined with wrinkles.

Kate stood behind him, young and beautiful, her face as pale as narcissus and with blue eyes that rivaled the color of distant lake water. This Kate had been Delta's teacher and her friend with none of the later bitterness. She radiated a clear pink light as if the sun rose behind her. Arn passed by, familiar and strong, at peace with himself.

Behind them were spirits of other Watchers who had lived before Arn, Kate, and Elisha Thunderheart. An old Indian woman danced a dance of life. A young white girl crossed her hands in front of her like a saint. A Melungeon woman bared her chest, showing a deep scar across her heart, wearing it like a badge of honor, proud that her life had been sacrificed for the mountain and its magic. Delta longed to hear the stories that the character in their faces suggested.

This ancient chain of protectors circled around her, ready to bear witness to the birth of the new Watcher. Their combined radiance moved toward her, blinded her—enveloped her—consumed her flesh like fire burning through her body. She screamed as the last contraction brought the baby through her legs. The child was lifted up into the light, and rested in Arn's arms. He looked down at her with an unfamiliar expression. As her consciousness faded, she realized it was the first time she had ever seen him smile.

∀ 45 ∀

LIGHTNING STREAKED THE sky, breaking up dusk in a haze of blue light. Lafette raced along steep paths like a soldier in battle. Sparks shot up from the mountaintop and he imagined fiery blazes destroying his house. Each thunderclap seared his heart.

Near Cat's Crossroads he dumped the supplies under a pine tree, then listened for Henry's owl call to judge where he was hiding. Nothing. He cut into a briar thicket, making his way to the cabin, tensely alert for whatever danger lay ahead.

The thunder lessened to a low roar. He cupped his hands, barked and moved east so Henry would know his position. From a point directly north, Henry answered with the piercing panther cry. Recognition. Meet in the cornfield. He moved silently, worrying about his mother. Wind pelted him with twigs and rain. He grabbed onto vines and pulled himself uphill. Dark knots on trees resembled the hollow eye sockets in the face of a skull, a terrifying image that followed him.

The smell of wet corn hung in the air. He sensed a presence and tensed with anticipation, praying, *Let it be Henry*. All he had with him was a hunting knife; not enough against an armed enemy. He crawled between the cornrows toward the buried Winchester. Despite the lightning and thunder, rain fell sparsely. The moist earth mashed through his fingers and soaked his pants at the knees. Three rows away, the corn stalks parted. A tall, shadowy form stepped toward him.

He pressed himself to the ground, face against a dusty corn root, lips brushing the earth. The figure stood taller than Henry. Lafette tightened his grip on his knife and slowly turned his head upward. His muscles hardened and his chest filled with the fury of a panther defending territory.

The circular wind patterns filled the air with dust so thick he could barely see. It sucked out his breath, leaving him dizzy and fighting for consciousness. The tall, lean figure stepped over him and disappeared into the swirling wind, moving toward the house. Lafette raised his head and saw a footprint. But it was the sole of no man. Part pads, part claws, part hoof. Exactly like the Wampus tracks he'd seen at the Elisha Tree the first time he saw his father. *Arn, his father. The only man known to be able to call the Wampus. Only the Wampus can scare away the thunder.* Lafette fought through the cornstalks to the buried rifle and dug into the dirt until he grasped the barrel.

Wind-blown grit and corn leaves pelted his face. He held up a hand to shield his eyes. Almost like the smothering June bugs that had swarmed around him last year on the dark side of the mountain, he thought, and memories erupted in him. *Arn shook the June bugs from the tunnel branches. Couldn't see my hand in front of me, and he knew it. The ole codger shoved a skeleton in my arms just when I reached for him. He tricked me.* Sudden realization broke the paralyzing embrace of the past nine months: *He's here. Arn Marlon's on this mountain! He's called the Wampus, but why?* What had his mother said? *The Wampus was closing the door. The Wampus wasn't of this world anymore.*

Lafette lunged out of the garden, kicking a spray of pebbles. He jumped boulders at the cabin's edge, scraping a hand on the rough rock, and rolled into the yard. Lightning cracked again, striking the house, a blazing blue zigzag so stark he clenched his eyes shut. A howl ripped the night, deafening and stalwart. Lafette covered his ears. The howl invaded every part of him until he collapsed.

Then, silence. No lightning ripped the night sky. No thunder rumbled like cannon fire. It had ceased the instant he reached Arn's rocks. The cabin's side wall, sprinkled with burning cinders, gave off a scorched smell. The moon lit a white path across the yard and a million stars floated like snowflakes. It could have been any other night. Nothing looked unusual now, but something was different. He could sense a difference. The night rang hollow.

Where was Henry? Where was his mother? No human presence. In frustration he slapped his hands against his head. Nothing was out of place, yet Shadow Mountain had changed. He stumbled over a dark lump, looked down but could barely make out a form. As he lifted it with his boot toe, a weak squawk broke the silence.

The dark lump was a dying chicken. Probably ran out in the storm, he figured, got too close to the lightnin'. He stepped on another one, and another. Dead chickens lay all over the yard. Cautiously, he stepped to the barn, flattening himself against the wall. Blue, he thought. Why hadn't he come out? Why wasn't Blue howlin' up a storm?

Lafette cracked open the barn door. His legs trembled. The

mule, the horse, and cow had dropped as if lightning had struck them where they stood. Their stiff legs were splayed like animals dead a long time. The barn was an odorless shell. Even owls nesting in the rafters had fallen to the ground in rigid lumps as if something had sucked the life from them. Lightning must've hit the barn and killed 'em all, he decided. He passed the pigpen, not bothering to inspect the dead hogs.

Outside, he stared at the house and the flickering flame in Delta's bedroom. He crawled along. The back door, torn from its hinges, lay several feet away. He leaned into the kitchen and slid across the floor on his stomach. The stove fire had burned out and he could smell cold pinto beans. He crouched in a ball, then peered around the corner. Someone sat in the blue velvet chair. It wasn't Delta. A tinny ringing in his ears marred the silence.

He risked standing, slowly and with extreme caution. Stones had fallen inward into the fireplace; the chimney had collapsed. Walnuts spread across the floor. Blue lay asleep just inside Delta's bedroom door. Lafette felt a flash of annoyance. *Somebody or something kills all our livestock, and that dumb dog's sleeping.*

He cocked the rifle, pressing the cold metal against his chest, then slipped into the room and pointed at the person in the chair. The figure was still. As Lafette stepped closer, the bedroom lantern lit up the side of Henry's face. His head resembled a skull thinly covered with skin. Lafette staggered as if he'd been punched in the face. His blood drained to his feet, and his limbs weighed heavy as iron.

With effort, Henry raised his eyes and smiled wearily, almost unrecognizable. His swollen gums left gaps between his teeth, and raised blue veins bulged under his yellowish-white skin. His hair was gone. Lafette choked up. He held out a hand, offering to help Henry stand.

Henry reached out, but his trembling frame could not sustain the effort of rising. "Take me in there," he whispered, pointing at the bedroom.

A floorboard squeaked as Lafette bent beside the chair. Henry's arm, fragile as a dried corn stalk, fell onto his shoulder. The squeak continued, then stopped; not a floorboard. The sound came from Delta's bedroom. He chanced a whisper, "Momma?" It emerged from his throat like an ax scraping wood. No answer. The golden glow from her room meant the lantern was up high, so he could easily see anyone trying to hide.

Lafette placed Henry's hand gently on the armrest and lifted his chin to see if he was conscious. Henry stared at Delta's room, mouthing words Lafette couldn't make out. He squeezed Henry's shoulder to indicate that he'd protect him. He helped the frail man as they stepped past Blue, into the bedroom. Delta lay under the sheets, face turned away from them. The lantern burned steadily. Blue's paws were spread like stiff sticks. *Same as the cow and mules.* Lafette knelt down and touched a corpse, cold as creek water. "Oh, Blue," he moaned. "Nooooo."

He turned the dog over. The glassy eyes looked peaceful, mouth curved open in a smile, like a hound that had run his last hunt. Lafette squeezed his paw, brushing the fur under his chin as he'd done when Blue was a puppy. Lafette was ready to kill whoever had done this.

Hesitantly, he looked across the floor toward the bed. Delta lay still, her knees drawn up under the sheet. If she was the same, he'd not be able to stand the sight. He stood, afraid of moving closer. The sheet over her hung off the end of the bed, and corn shucking had scattered to the floor. The edge of the covering dripped blood. He gagged. The room spun. As he struggled to get his breath, hard, stiff fingers touched his palm.

Henry intertwined his hand with Lafette's. Stooped and trembling, he was no bigger than a child, his cold flesh like stone against Lafette's skin. They stepped forward together. The sheet bunched around Delta's neck so only her face showed, pale pink cheeks against moon-white skin. Lafette's hand trembled as he reached to pull back the sheet, hesitating as he touched the cloth. His head felt heavy and congested, eyes fighting the swell of grief. "No, Momma," he said in a choked, raspy voice. "Don't let it be."

Her eyes opened. Lafette jumped. Henry collapsed on the bed. She was not dead. Thank God. Her lips moved, trying to form words. Lafette dropped to his knees. "Who did this, Momma?"

"Lafette, thought you might be the Wampus." Her voice was hoarse, yet the corners of her mouth curled upward in a slight smile, the way they always did when she'd kidded him about the monster. She raised a finger and touched his lips, acknowledging his returned voice. She blinked several times, as if many thoughts were passing through her mind, and licked her parched lips. "Nobody did this, honey. Tornado hit."

In an instant, she'd become the mother who had raised him, not the dreamy-eyed stranger of the past nine months. She stared directly at him as if about to give instructions on planting a garden, then lifted her head with a look of wanting to rise. At the sight of clothes strewn everywhere, and overturned furniture, she lay back again. Her features melted into a weary mask. Henry crawled beside her and stroked her forehead. She pressed her lips to his fingers.

Lafette turned away, more from desire to give them privacy than displeasure over their affection. He dug his hands into his pockets and stared out the window where the tattered shutters clung to the frame. Scorched cinders shot through the air with each breeze. He figured she'd said tornado to keep him from seeking vengeance. When he looked over at Blue's body, he could not let this pass. "Momma, don't you know Blue's dead?" He wondered if he dared tell her about the rest of the livestock.

A pained look came over her face, and she pressed her lips together and squeezed her eyes shut. A tender cry came from beneath the blanket. She struggled to raise one arm and pull back the sheet. A tiny baby kicked its hands and feet against her chest. "Reckon this boy's the only family you've got now," she said guardedly.

The infant, soaked with birth fluids, was veiny and purplish. Though he'd seen plenty of animal litters, Lafette had never seen anything like this miniature being, and embarrassment filled him as he watched it suckle her breast. He managed to stutter, "I'll clean him up, Momma." He reached out and noticed that his hand was as large as the baby.

"No," Delta said, wrapping her fingers around its back. "Let me hold him a little bit longer." Her face swelled and tears slid down her cheeks. Her lips shivered as she tried to hold back her feelings. "I'm sorry, Lafette." The words flowed out like a song sung high and full of grief. "It took all the life I had to birth this child." She looked up, her irises large and brown, with only a hint of green at the outer rims. "I don't have nothin' left." One hand reached out to him, touched his arm then dropped to the bed.

Tears continued streaming down her cheeks. Her moan trailed off into a whisper as if she couldn't clear her throat, and then stopped. A gentle breeze blew through the room, leaving behind the soft scent of wisteria. Lafette wanted to cry but told himself to hold back, to not upset his mother. He reached to pick up the baby so she could rest.

Henry's bony hand clasped Lafette's like the spiny legs of a wood spider. "Son, what's left of my life can be measured in minutes." He lifted the baby with all the strength he could muster and cradled him against his chest. "Surely you can see that."

Lafette stared at the floor. The room's sour smell was suffocating. He felt nauseated, as if he'd eaten bad meat. The baby whined and Henry rocked it.

"I'll get a doctor, or Nancy."

Henry smiled as if he understood Lafette better than he understood himself. "Look at this little baby, 'Fate." He laid the child into the crook of Delta's arm and stretched out beside her. The infant's pinkish skin made it look delicate as a newborn opossum. It had a smattering of blond hair and its tiny fists roamed around its face as if exploring. "It's of Delta's body. Can't you see Delta in this child's face?" The baby began to whine. "Would you do one thing for me?"

Lafette avoided looking at Henry. He clenched his hands deeply in his pockets, stared at the ceiling, yet always coming back to the squalling infant.

"Would you let me name this boy?" Henry adjusted his legs and pulled the sheet over himself and Delta. "Elisha Kingsley." He paused and looked up at Lafette. "I want you to know you're as much my son as he is. You be Lafette Kingsley if it suits you." Then he kissed the child's forehead and held him out. Lafette's hands trembled as he accepted the baby. Henry sank into the bed. Weariness lined his face, his jaw muscles sagged and his eyes lost their luster. He looked over at Delta and smiled once again that beautiful smile that Lafette could never resist or forget, then wrapped his arms around her. His eyes fluttered and closed. His lips parted slightly and he whispered, "You'll never be far from my thoughts."

Lafette couldn't tell if Henry spoke to him or to Delta.

The baby paddled its hands and feet as if swimming. At the side of its mouth was a brown speck, and Lafette pulled it off. It was the texture of tobacco but rubbery. He rolled it between his fingers, and it emitted a faint cinnamon smell. Tyme leaf, he realized. "Momma, did you feed this to the baby?"

She didn't answer. He knelt by the bed, resting the infant on his knees and enclosed Delta's hand in his own. Her flesh was stiff and turning blue. "Momma?" He squeezed her fingers, waiting for a response. Something else felt icy against his palm. He opened his hand. On her middle finger was a silver ring, a large band, starburst design cut in the center. He compared it to the smaller woman's ring he wore on his little finger. They matched. She was wearing Arn's ring.

Delta's lips parted slightly, and her white teeth gleamed in the lantern light. Her hair was brushed back as for a night's sleep. Lafette touched her eyelids and closed them.

He walked outside toward Arn's black rocks, wrapping the infant in his own shirt and resting it between two rocks. A trillion stars spread across the sky like a spider's web. Now he knew what the hollow emptiness had been. It was just what she'd always said: magic. There was no longer any magic here. If Shadow Mountain had been magic, it was the magic of her. But now it was gone. Even her spirit did not stay to bless this earth with an essence.

Lafette picked up a black rock and pressed it between his hands. Delta had told him that the magic of Arn's Volcano lived on in the rocks. The stone was cold and rough and had sharp edges. It was just a rock. There was nothing left. With all his might he threw it up, toward the stars. Fury erupted in his body and he groaned in rage. "I know you did this, Daddy!"

He jumped up and down, his feet beating the earth. He ran from one side of the mountain to the other, picking up the black rocks and throwing them in whatever direction he faced. "I know you did this, Arn Marlon!" As exhaustion consumed him, his anger gave way to sobbing. Even in his anguish, accusations burst from him. "You did this, Daddy! I know you did this."

His body shook and seized. Sobs transformed into howls. Wild dogs and wolves joined in all around him. When he had no voice left, he stretched open his mouth and tore his vocal cords muscles with whatever sound he could make. How much time passed? It didn't matter. He might prostrate himself here for the rest of his life.

At the house, the lantern burned out. He lay on his back in total darkness. The moist ground soaked his clothes. Wisteria sweetened the air just as the smell of birth and blood soured it. If crickets, frogs and other creatures of the night also ruled the mountain, he denied their presence, preferring the empty darkness left to him. Only the musical crying of a hungry infant broke through and wrapped the silence like a ribbon around a package. Finally, he rose and walked toward the baby.

♆ 46 ♆

BY TORCHLIGHT LAFETTE tore down a barn door and wired it to a plow harness. He tied a corn shuck mattress to it, then used the sheets he'd bought in town to wrap Delta's and Henry's bodies. He placed them next to each other on the mattress. Blue lay at their feet, wrapped similarly and seeming small as a puppy. Lafette boxed a cradle at the head and swaddled the baby in flannel before gently laying him inside. He'd fed the child by soaking a rag in milk and dripping it into the infant's mouth and the babe had been quiet since. Other than Delta's drawings, he took nothing else.

A wisteria vine blew from the porch and landed across the crib. Lafette left it after making sure it didn't obscure his view of the child. Elisha wiggled like a newborn pup. Lafette petted his head. The baby's swollen eyes cracked open, revealing dark orbs that reminded Lafette of blackberries. The lantern light reflected in the infant's eyes made a frightening starburst pattern, the same pattern he'd seen in Arn's eyes. *This is Henry's child,* he told himself, but the thought that Arn was looking out through this baby's eyes did not leave him. He sucked in a deep breath, then fit himself into the harness as he might a mule.

The heavy leather straps cut into his skin as he pulled. He ignored the pain, ignored the newborn's occasional whine, ignored any other feeling that might distract him and focused only on stepping forward. He inched along, careful to avoid too steep a grade, and held the lantern in front of him as if guiding himself through a cavern. A golden circle of light became his world.

As he approached Cat's Crossroads, sweat dripped over the leather harness and stung the raw flesh on his shoulders. He bit his tongue, huffing as he pulled until he tripped and dropped to his knees. He rested on out stretched hands. The baby gurgled from time to time but mostly remained quiet.

He felt the ground between his legs to see what he'd fallen on. A root. He held it up. A Tyme root. Light from a gibbous moon filtered so brightly through the trees they looked solid enough to touch. He held the root in a moonbeam. The last of Delta's Tyme plants. Blown down from the mountaintop by the storm.

The root curled around his wrist like a snake. He untangled it but the vine coiled up his other arm. Confused and shaken, he left it, letting it hang on him. What did he care where it dropped? In his exhaustion he counted each step to twenty-five, then started over again. His focal point was the stripped leather on his boots, and he listened to neither the baby's whine nor the voices in his mind calling out to him to stop... to think... to understand what had happened. He focused only on his boots... the numbers he knew... and kept trudging ahead.

∞

Several hours later, Lafette bent over Tyme Creek and splashed water in his face. Two mounds of earth behind him, the baby rested in the cradle wrapped in its flannel blanket. The infant boy gave off a whimpering moan that suggested he knew his mother and father were buried nearby. Lafette tried ignoring the cries but they had a pattern and a pitch that pierced him. "Shhh!" he said as if the newborn could understand. The annoying, continuous crying reminded him of when Blue was a puppy and would howl at any sound for the pleasure of it. "An untrained puppy is what you are," he said, and snuggled the blanket more securely around the child. "Think I'll call you Elisha Blue."

He squinted to see through a soupy fog filling the air with wetness and clouding the murky sky. He dipped his hands in the creek to wash the dirt then cupped water enough to drink.

The baby whined again. Lafette soaked his handkerchief and carried it to the bundle. As he pulled back the flannel covering, a pink face bobbed out like a turtle's head emerging from a shell. He held the handkerchief just above the child's lips and squeezed it gently, letting the water drip down his hand into the little mouth. The bow-shaped lips puckered around fingertip and sucked. He couldn't help but laugh.

Lafette turned up the lantern wick. The baby's eyelids were shut and Lafette was glad not to see the mysterious glint in this child's eyes. Elisha's lips smacked together as if he wanted to suck on Lafette's finger again. Lafette wanted very much to hate this baby, but his heart would not let him.

A shovel stuck upright in a dirt mound where he'd buried Blue. He pulled it out, patted the loose dirt, then threw the shovel into the creek. In his pocket the curved Tyme cane handle pressed against his leg. He'd buried Delta and Henry at the exact place where he'd found the handle, on the soft grassy mound where they'd conceived this child.

Lafette moved the lantern and the baby, then jumped to the opposite side of the Elisha Tree where his father's and Elisha Thunderheart's names were carved in the inner bark. Anchoring his hands on the rim of the wood, he broke off a four-foot section. The sour rotting smell wafted up and dissipated.

He carried the wood to the grave and placed it over the loose dirt where Delta and Henry rested ten feet down on the corn shuck mattress that cushioned them. Both silver rings were on Delta's left hand and Henry was holding his cane. Lafette took the handle of the remaining Tyme cane, wound the wisteria vine around it, and mashed it into the dirt. In a few years, the mulch would spread the roots and this place would flower with her favorite scent.

Lafette held the baby in one arm and the lantern, dangled from his other hand, tapping his knee in a rhythm that seemed to say, *Shadow Mountain. Shadow Mountain.* "Elisha Blue," he murmured, "it's a story you'll never know and troubles you'll never have a part in. Promise you." The baby gurgled as Lafette's voice soothed him.

Frogs and crickets, comfortable with his presence, blurted their nightly calls. "Doubt I'll be back this way, Momma." He spoke toward the grave as if it were a bed she was simply sleeping in. Just as he was about to step down the hill, he turned to look again at the mound. No one else would be able to tell that Delta and Henry were buried here. Part of him hoped that in time he'd forget as well. His eyes swelled and he wiped his nose on his shoulder.

Another step would move him far enough away that he'd not be able to see the grave, the creek, or the Elisha Tree. It was his last look at where he'd grown up: the tree that had been his secret hiding place, the spot where Henry had found him and asked to be taken to Delta, the creek where he'd have drowned except for her and Henry and Kate. It was his last look at his mother, and he filled with such an ache he was determined that it also be his last thought of his father.

Part of him did not want to take that step. He wanted to sit there by the grave and talk to Delta. He wanted to hear Henry's stories, ask him questions about training horses, practice bird calls with him. He wanted to pet Blue's head and scratch him behind the ear. But time wouldn't stand still for him. As he looked up at the fog-shrouded mountain, the sun crested the top.

In the first glimmer of sunrise, Lafette saw that the Tyme plant had fallen from his arm and rooted itself on Delta's grave. "Well," he said, staring at it in wonder, "what about that?" He watched as the Tyme bud opened, flowered, and stretched out its petals as if they were muscles. *This one, he realized, this one will live.*

The angle of the sun caused it to cast a shadow as long and wide as the Elisha Tree had once been. It was Delta's magic, and Lafette saw in his mind the huge, mighty tree this little plant would become. He hugged the baby to him. Tears brimmed his eyelashes and skipped down his cheeks. For the first time, he understood the magic.

In the distance a dog gave a high, yodeling bark, pursuing prey. It was a happy sound. A rooster crowed. Night was over. Lafette inhaled a breath that refreshed his lungs like the tingling of mint. He raised his hand and called out, “Bye, Momma. Bye, Henry. Bye, Ole Blue.”

The baby wiggled against him. Its tiny eyes rolled under the lids and it smacked its lips. “You’re hungry,” Lafette said. “Better tend to getting you some food.”

THE END

Author's Note

Sometimes a story is a nail, sometimes a bird, sometimes a door, sometimes a prayer. The world of Shadow Mountain has been my obsession since I was a wee-acolyte in James Baker Hall's, Gurney Norman's, and Ed McClanahan's classes at University of Kentucky.

It started as a short story about a boy named Elisha Blue based loosely on my paternal grandfather. I fiddled with it throughout my college years, putting it away, revising, and bringing it to class the next semester with a slightly different twist. Harry Caudill's Appalachian history class woke up a sense of lineage in me, a need to understand where I came from and use that knowledge to make my future better than the past.

The story waxed and waned, lying dormant for months and making its way to California with me in a sack of writing, some typed, some hand-written, in a time before computers. But Elisha Blue was never far from my imagination.

Years passed, and I forged a new life far from home like a shapeshifting Jack out to seek my fortune. And fortune found me in the way of James N. Frey's writing classes. Where college classes were explorations into the cauldron of imagination, Frey's tutelage grounded me in craft. Elisha Blue grew into a novel.

Not unlike genealogy, one character led to another that led to another and another with all of them wanting their side told.

Elisha Blue held my hand through the din, calmly teaching me the complexities of the human psyche. As I wrote what was to become his novel, another character watched in the shadows. I forged forward on the story of Elisha Blue, but kept looking over at someone I couldn't quite understand, a character with a kind, gentle spirit that rarely let me see that side of him. Lafette Marlon whispered in my creative ear, and before long I'd fallen in love with him as strongly as I could have any corporeal man. There was nothing to do but go back and write his story that also became Delta and Henry's story, and subsequently, put a new spin on Elisha Blue and all of Midnight Valley.

Though completed, and in time stored on my computer, *Shadow Mountain* and *Elisha Blue* remained in a buried to-do file. Other projects took precedence, life meandered, flourished, knocked me down a few times, then like a slap in the face, Shadow Mountain took hold in the final Alma Bashear novel. What the frack? Could this really be, I wondered? What did these modern characters have to do with this old stuff? How was I going to pull this off and make sense of any of it? Shadow Mountain didn't care. Shadow Mountain just said, "Do it."

The lore of old ways seeped into my story knowledge, and even though I knew protagonists from the Appalachian Trilogy and the Crimson County Quartet, Alma Bashears and Connor Herne, were the *Watchers* of their age, I didn't know how to convey that to the reader, especially since the characters themselves didn't know. So the information stayed with me like a tic that couldn't stop pulsing. It was a voice from the past that jarred me from my complacency, a letter from a man I had been head over heels in love with as a young woman, written to a mutual friend. The letter fell into my possession after his death, and I read that the reason he held me at a distance but at the same time couldn't let go of me was because I had this "witchy Appalachian thing going on." Stunned, I read the sentence over and over. A 38-year-old letter telling me something I'd never considered. A lost love naming what I'd never known. A message: *Be what you are*.

I had to go back to the beginning. I had to come out of the closet and name these stories for what they are: a living, breathing mythology that grows to this day and continually surprises me. It will likely take me the rest of my life to hear those stories and write them down. There is a grimoire and book of legends passed orally from one *Guardian of the Gate* to another, and in recent years, parts of it have been put to paper. In time, it will be a free download from my website, so keep checking at TessCollins.com.

Significant conflicts tore apart a society transitioning from the agrarian age into the industrial, not unlike today as we transform out of the industrial and into the technological age. The characters in the Shadow Mountain Saga forge forward carrying the seed of the past inside of them. They can't escape it any more than I can be something other than "witchy Appalachian." These stories have nailed me to a mission; taken my imagination to flights of wisdom that give me new perspective; opened doors to my thinking outside the paradigm; and left me in prayer that these tales are of service to all who read them. Our ancestors once saw magic in the darkness that today we call unexplained phenomena. If you don't understand it, sit alone in the forest, close your eyes; it is there you will find Shadow Mountain.

Coming soon from BearCat Press

Book Two in the *SHADOW MOUNTAIN SAGA*

ELISHA BLUE

by Tess Collins

THE FALL OF 1920 commenced a Wampus Winter. The first sign Lafette Kingsley and his brother, Elisha Blue, saw was the bark on a hundred-year-old hickory tree. Usually shaggy and curling at the ends in feather-like layers, the bark this year was smooth and held to the tree like a warrior's armor. Lafette knew the cold would take hold early and death would haunt the hills with a vengeance.

artistic rendering by Paula Hayes

About the Author

A coal miner's granddaughter, Tess Collins was born and raised in a crater. Yes, really, a crater formed by the impact of an asteroid millions of years ago where her hometown, Middlesboro, Kentucky, was eventually built. Tess spent her younger years in a one room Carnegie Library reading around the room. She started at *BLUEBERRIES FOR SAL* and ended with *WAR AND PEACE*, at which time she thought, "I want to do this."

Tess is the author of six novels and a non-fiction book on theater management. She attended the University of Kentucky and has a Ph.D. from The Union Institute and University.

Visit her website at TessCollins.com

CPSIA information can be obtained
at www.ICGtesting.com
Printed in the USA
LVOW12*0238061017
551386LV00002B/16/P